THE ~~GIRL~~ ON THE
MOUNTAIN

Carol Ervin

CHAPTER 1

This is the forest primeval

— HENRY WADSWORTH LONGFELLOW:
EVANGELINE

When Jamie was home, May Rose felt safe. Saturday afternoons he jumped from the log train as it slowed down the grade in front of their cabin. Sunday evenings he caught the train back to Logging Camp Number Six, where he lived through the week.

This Saturday he walked from the train as if dragged down. His eyelids drooped at the outside corners, bits of dust in his thick brown lashes. His sun-dark face bore new scratches, like his hands, scarred by twigs and briars. In the week since she'd seen him, he'd grown a thin, rust-colored moustache.

He pulled his suspenders from his shoulders as he came through the door, stepped out of his trousers and kicked them to a dusty heap. His bath was ready, the washtub partly filled beside the table, crowding their one-room cabin. Kettles of water steamed on the cook stove in the corner. She handed him his drink and added water to the tub.

At the stove, she poked a fork into the rooster that simmered with noodles in yellow broth. Its flesh fell away from the bones. In camp, Jamie ate meat three times a day, had fruit pies and light bread with butter instead of lard.

She did not speak of her week or her new suspicion until he slid down into the water and his face relaxed. She scrubbed his back with a soapy cloth. "I think someone has been stealing the eggs." She did not mean to complain, but he needed to know. He sold and traded eggs for tobacco and moonshine.

"Harder," he said.

She dug her fingers into the cloth and rubbed up, down, and sideways, leaving red marks in his skin, along his wide shoulders, wetting hair that curled on his neck. He drained the jar and pushed it into her hand. "Keep the chicken coop shut up and snakes won't get the eggs."

The thief was no snake. She barred the chicken coop door every night, and even in the day, after she turned the chickens out.

She refilled his jar, letting him see how much liquor she added. Later she might get away with mixing in more water, then somewhere between his first and last jars he'd forget his disgust, and he'd sing to her and maybe ask her to read to him, like she used to do, *Evangeline*, or *The Song of Solomon*.

Dirt lay in a scum on his bathwater. He hated being dirty, complained of his dirty job, but he loved to talk about it, and he was gifted with words. In his stories she saw the muscled arms and quick hands of swampers, sawyers, and grab-drivers. She heard the thunder of trees falling to earth and logs skidding down to the railroad landings, the snorting of horses, sixteen hooves stomping the ground, chains rattling, undergrowth crackling. He made her laugh at the peculiarities and failings of the seventy men in Camp Number Six. Wood hicks, the loggers called themselves, proud to take the strains of such work, proud to be young and tough.

He had opinions and ambitions—as soon as he saved up, they'd go to California, maybe Texas. Anywhere, if she could have him home at the end of every day. Away from brutal work, surely he'd be more himself.

"I saw somebody last night," she said. "And this morning, the eggs were gone."

"You saw somebody? Did they come to the door?"

"I saw someone at the edge of the woods, near dark."

He set his jar on the floor and rubbed his hands through his hair. Bits of leaves and bark fell into the water. "Who'd come all the way up here? And at night?"

Nobody up to anything good. They had no road, just the railroad track and the trail, a tortuous walk through the woods. The Winkler Company had covered up the old road with the railroad to the camp and log landing. When they'd moved here, Jamie had brought their goods up on the train that supplied the camps.

"Give me that cloth," he said.

She soaped the cloth and set it in his hand. Deep in her belly she felt the start of cramps. Again, no child. Soon the century would turn over to nineteen hundred, and she'd be twenty-one. Jamie said he'd lost track of his age.

No matter what he said, last night someone had run along the trail, a shadow in the trees, not deer, not a bear, a thin, swift-moving shadow with arms. She'd come inside and barred the door, blown out the lamp, and watched from the cabin's one window. From there she had a view of the western sky and the railroad track, but everything else was behind the cabin—the head of the trail, the chicken coop and other sheds. She'd kept her shotgun near, ready to run outside and shoot if she heard a pig squeal or chicken cackle. They'd not been alarmed, yet someone had stolen the eggs.

Jamie rubbed the cloth over his face and scrubbed his armpits. She longed to see him smile. He didn't have to sing, only smile and say he was glad to be home.

When they were newly married, he'd come home every third evening, riding down with the logs and rising from bed in the middle of the night to walk back, because work began at dawn, well before the morning train. He'd chosen this place because it was closer to his camp. She wouldn't like the town, he said, a dirty, noisy place. This was better. With his arms wrapped around her, of course it was.

Today she'd carried water from the springhouse, first for her bath, later for his. She'd brushed and scrubbed her stained hands and freshened them in dried wildflowers, sat cross-legged in sunshine and frowned into her hand mirror at hair that seemed less golden, lips and cheeks less full, the rest of her shrunk to knobs and angles.

She found no resemblance to herself two years ago, when she'd been courted by men as old as her uncle and boys not long out of short pants. From this confusion of suitors, Jamie had stood out as most handsome and most happy, and he'd won her with stories and songs and the lightness of his hand at her waist when they danced. Last winter, snow had kept him in camp weeks at a time. Shut up in the little cabin, she'd brought to mind those happy days and danced again under a starlit sky and laughed in the bosom of her family. For company, she'd brought Nellie, the sow, inside.

Nellie and passing trains kept her steady. Every work day two trains chugged through the clearing, one in the morning hauling supplies to the camps, and the one in the afternoon pulling logs down from the mountain. She always waved, and had come to know the faces of the engineers, firemen, and brakemen who waved back. The company doctor waved when he passed by on the speeder, a little gas-powered railroad cart. She knew his name, Dr. Hennig.

Yesterday, she'd worried because there were too many trains.

She spread Jamie's clean clothes on the bed. "Did something happen yesterday? I saw a special train, and the speeder, twice.

He grunted. "Man got himself killed. Potts, a teamster. His logs got to running down the skid, pushing him and the horses." Jamie dropped the cloth into the water. "What a sight. Dumb old shit didn't hook his logs proper. He pulled his team off the skid into a J-hole, but the logs didn't uncouple like they do when they're fastened right. The logs swung around and busted into him, horses too. Fine horses, two dead, and the other two had to be shot on the spot."

He gagged, coughed, cupped water in his hand and rinsed his face. "Guess who got to clean all that up?"

"Let's sell out," she said. "Go somewhere else."

He tilted his head, squinted. "There'll be a place for a new teamster. I plan to be that man." As a swamper, Jamie made a dollar fifty a day, half as much as the highest paid men in camp, though it was not the low pay but the low regard for the job that irked him. Swampers cleared logs, stumps, and brush to make roads for skidding timber. They also made the escape ramps, the J-holes. He said any idiot could do it.

She scooped a cup through the water and rinsed his back. It wasn't something he'd believe, and nothing she would say, but the very thing she loved most about him—his high spirit—made him a poor man with horses. When he wasn't worn down like this, he craved excitement, and he had no patience. She'd seen it in St. Louis, how he confused and agitated her uncle's team.

"Enough," Jamie said. "This water's cold."

She wrapped a potholder around the handle of the iron kettle and lifted it with both hands. "Are you ready for me to pour?"

"Just do it."

She held the pot at arms' length. "Can you move your knees to the left?"

He moved his legs to the right edge of the tub. She carried the kettle to the other side, paused to make sure he was watching, then trickled the steaming water into a spot where his skin would not catch it first. She swished her hand through it to mix hot with cold. "Are you ready for me to wash your hair?"

"Make it quick."

She touched his chin and tipped his head back, flexed her hands through his hair and pushed the suds up his neck, resisting the desire to pull his wet head to her breast and run her hands over him in the water, never certain he'd like it.

As she poured the first scoop of rinse, he leaned forward to lift his jar, and soapy water ran over his face. He jolted upright, grabbed the bed sheet set out for him to dry, and dabbed at his eyes. "You stupid farmer. I didn't give you leave to blind me with lye soap." He threw the sheet on the floor and splashed down in the tub. "Rinse, and be quick."

She steadied herself with a hand on a chair. Good times seemed easier to remember when he wasn't there.

When she bent and picked up the sheet, he said, "Look at yourself. You're pitiful."

Nauseous now with cramps, she did not need his words to know her heavy bleeding had soaked through. While he ate, she dipped a bucket of bathwater for her soiled dress and set his work clothes to soak in the washtub. He ate and drank without talking, his eyes growing dull.

After supper, she rubbed soap into his underclothes and set them to boil on the stove. He dozed, tipped back in his chair with legs stretched under the table, one hand on his jar, his mouth open. With her laundry stick she lifted the scalding cloth into rinse water, humming softly, as she did most days, to keep herself going. On the porch, she wrapped the legs of his pants around a roof post, stood back, and twisted each piece till no more water dripped out. Then she hung them on a line near the stove. Jamie sprawled across their bed, face down. She knelt beside it, touched his arm with her forehead, and inhaled his scent, like new-sawn wood.

Sunday, Jamie slept, got up to eat and drink, and slept again. On happier Sundays, she'd led him around to show all she'd done while he was gone—spring greens found—corn sprouted, hoed, harvested—cabbage planted, cut, salted. The pigs, how they'd grown.

Sunday evening when they heard the train coming, he bent and pecked her lips. He stopped her on the porch as the train came into view, flat cars with wood hicks sitting on crates and barrels, supplies for the camp. "Get back inside," he said. "There's no need to be showing yourself to this bunch."

The next Saturday Jamie did not come home. She watched the log train from the cabin window. From a distance, any of the young men astride the logs of the flatcars might have been him. They all wore hobnail boots, loose gray pants, broad suspenders, and had shaggy hair under every sort of hat, a few with shapely brims, like his. She held the edge of the curtain until the caboose passed, the rumble faded, and the black smoke dissolved in the air, because sometimes he jumped off on the other side of the track. Then she sat at the table beside the tub of water and pulled petals from the jar of purple asters while the cabin filled with the aroma of beans baked with molasses.

She pushed through her evening tasks, humming to hold herself together, mumbling a verse of scripture: *whatsoever things are lovely...and of good report...think on these things.* But that night she lay on the mattress tick stuffed with fresh corn husks and remembered a long-ago neighbor whose man had gone west without her, and another whose husband had left with no warning. Anything could happen.

Sunday evening when the train carried men back to camp, she waited behind the scarecrow in tall garden weeds where the wood hicks would not see her. Weary-looking young men sprawled on wooden cartons and bales of hay or sat with legs hanging over the edges, some looking toward the cabin, none of them Jamie. There was a familiar hat on one who faced the other way, though Jamie didn't own a red shirt.

At dusk she dragged the porch stool and the shotgun to the middle of the clearing and watched the dark spaces between the trees to prove she had nothing to fear. A tract of thick virgin timber, saved from the logging company by a surveyor's mistake, surrounded the clearing on all but the west side. There the railroad track passed at the edge of the sky. Her ears tuned to sounds of leaf whisper and high cricket drone. Hawks drifted in circles above and below her line of sight. This, like dawn, was the clean time, when the earth did not tremble with far-off crash of trees, and passing trains did not smother the air.

The better parts of two years with Jamie begged to be remembered. They might be as much as anyone had. They might be more. She closed her eyes and saw how his face transformed when he smiled, how the edge of his lip turned up. She remembered the rhythm of his work songs, how she shivered when his hands stopped her in the garden or at the stove. She felt his lips on her neck and the length of him against her those Saturday nights, when he took her breath—those Sundays, when they knew what mattered.

Maybe because she'd grown up among Ohio's flat fields, the clearing felt like a perch on the side of the mountain. Just beyond the railroad, the land dropped down in a rockslide, and as far as she could see, mountains sloped toward each other like laced fingers. Soon color would break out like a last, fervent wish. Then snow. He claimed there was twelve years of work here. She prayed they would not see it. The man who'd built their cabin had moved on, an old settler who said rich men were destroying creation for toothpicks and clothespins.

The clearing grew bright as the lowering sun lit the gap in the leafy wall. Just beyond the light, a shadow passed from tree to tree and blended with the night. Her breath stopped between excitement and fear. She picked up the shotgun, moved her stool to the edge of the cabin porch, braced the stock of the gun between arm and hip, and pulled back the hammers with soft clicks.

Her heart drummed. She searched the night sounds for something different—a footstep, the squawk of a kidnapped chicken, a whisper in the dark. Bats swished in and out of moonlight.

The shotgun was heavy as a stack of iron skillets, but she held it until her neck and arms stiffened and her eyelids ached. The silhouette of a fox streaked past, head lifted, a rabbit in its jaws. Able to watch no more, she carried the gun to her bed.

CHAPTER 2

He was a valiant youth, and his face, like the face of the morning,
Gladdened the earth with its light...

— HENRY WADSWORTH LONGFELLOW:
EVANGELINE

When roosters crowed and dawn birds called, May Rose opened
her eyes and laid her hand on the shotgun beside her, glad for
morning and the peaceful rise and fall of her breath. Last night
someone had snuck along the trail, a dark path by day, said to
have been laid down in ancient times by animals and Indians. The
stranger might have good reason to travel at night, and good
reason to hide himself. He might intend her no harm. He might
have seen her gun and been afraid.

She lit the lamp and poked the coals in the stove. From the
woodbox she chose a piece of pine for heat and a chunk of walnut
for a lasting fire. Then she unbarred the door and carried the
shotgun into the morning.

The scarecrow's blue shirt waved in the breeze, and Nellie and
her pigs sprawled behind their fence. She counted the chickens as
they hopped over the threshold. All present, twelve brown hens

and three roosters. She picked three eggs from the nests and left two, in case whoever she'd seen might only be someone hungry.

For breakfast she soaked Saturday's cornbread in coffee with a pinch of sugar. A whistle blew, the morning train, flatcars and a boxcar with horses for a new teamster. Not Jamie, she prayed.

He worried her more than any stranger wandering near. She shoveled globs of chicken dirt from the chicken house floor, thinking how his ideas crowded out her own, like weeds taking over the garden. He'd chosen this place, and she'd tried to love it. In nearly two years, he'd taken her to town four times. He wanted her to go nowhere alone, but he no longer seemed to worry that she lived alone here.

Glancing frequently toward the trees, she scythed the weeds from the potato patch and dug into the first hill. Potatoes rolled from the overturned clods, not many and not big, but only a few cut by the shovel. She rubbed off caked dirt and spread the potatoes to dry in the shade. The cut ones she took to the cabin. In all she had about two bushels, not bad for a rocky, shady patch, and enough for the year, as long as Jamie ate in camp.

She kept the shotgun near. The pigs needed to forage in the woods, but she hesitated to turn them out, afraid they would not come back. Her poor corn had made enough ears to feed only half the chickens through the winter. With an odd sense of doing things for the last time, she tugged cabbage roots from the baked earth and scattered them in the bare hog lot so each pig might have a chance at something. Into their slop trough she poured dishwater with pumpkin peels. Like wild things, like humans, they squealed and shoved for advantage. Then she took her shotgun, bucket, and shovel and ventured among the trees.

Jamie had taken her over a portion of the forest trail to town and back, and twice they'd followed a branch to his brother's house on the other side of the mountain. The first time at his brother's she'd traded a knotted quilt for Nellie, just three months old. They'd come home the next day, tugging the young pig along on a rope. By the time Nellie came in season, May Rose had taught her to trot along with an occasional prod of a stick, and they'd walked her back there to be bred. Jamie's brother, Russell, had offered no food, but had let them sleep both times in the corn crib. Jealous, Jamie said, because he was an ugly man with no beautiful wife. Mean, May Rose thought, though later he came to their place and helped Jamie castrate the little boar pigs. She'd made him a nice supper, and he'd slept on the porch, perhaps at Jamie's direction. He was older, a man used to being alone, and he always looked displeased. Maybe he saw how he made her nervous.

Not far into the trees she found acorns. Watchful as a bird, she shoveled them into the bucket and hurried back to open sky. One bucket of acorns was not enough. Living in a shadow of fear was not enough.

Near evening, she hung over the hog lot fence and scratched Nellie's bristly ears. The pigs, weaned and growing fast, pushed against the boards. She'd not named or petted them, and she'd never told Jamie about Nellie sleeping in the house. Nellie might come in again this winter, when her pigs were sold off, if she and May Rose were again alone.

"Jamie doesn't like it here," she said. The words slipped out, not sadly, for she'd dissolve if she allowed herself a moment of sympathy. She could not say the other thought—that Jamie didn't love her anymore. "We need to be together, that's all."

Nellie snorted.

That night May Rose kept no vigil in the dark, but barred the door and slept with the shotgun.

The next morning she walked up the track toward his camp, seven steep miles. He'd told her not to go there, just as he'd said she shouldn't go to town alone, but she needed to go somewhere. The work area changed every day, so she had no idea where he'd be or if she'd get close enough to see him. She did not intend to let him see her.

High on the mountain the air vibrated with shouts of men, and the earth shook with falling trees. Flinching at every warning shout and crack, she got no farther than the landing where men unhooked huge logs from skidders, and steam engines swung them through the air to flatcars. Even the railroad track did not feel safe. She hurried home, thinking how right he was, telling her to stay away. She wanted him away, too.

That afternoon she laid her last sheet of writing paper on the table and dipped the nib of her pen into ink.

Winkler, West Virginia
September 19, 1899
To Albert V. Jonson
Fargo, North Dakota

Dear Uncle Bert and Cousins Margaret, Leola, and Mary Agnes,

We are well and hope you are the same.

I wonder if my first letter found you. If you have addressed a letter to me at Jennie Town, it has not found me. We are not living there, as Jamie planned. When we arrived from St. Louis, we found all the nearby timber cut and other stands ruined by fire. Men were tearing down the saw mill to rebuild it somewhere else. The only work was at the tannery, which Jamie did not like to do, so we came on to Winkler, higher in the mountains. He has family here.

Your wedding gift went a long way toward the purchase of our home, which Jamie bought for less than the cost of a good horse team. Right away he built a hog shed and put new boards on the spring-house. Jamie is a powerful worker.

Dear girls, every day I tell stories to my friend Nellie about our adventures in Ohio. We wonder about your new life in the Dakota Territory. I hope we may come soon for a visit.

Uncle Bert, your advice is always in my ear, as well as the teaching and cautions of Aunt Sweet, our dearly departed. They are my guide in all things.

SHE WIPED the nib with an inky cloth and laid the pen aside. Uncle Bert's advice and Aunt Sweet's cautions had not dimmed the appeal of Jamie. They'd met at a square dance in St. Louis where Uncle Bert had laid over while he bought wagons and supplies for the last part of their journey from Ohio to Fargo. Her marriage had torn another hole in the fabric of the family, for since Aunt Sweet's death, May Rose had been mother to her young cousins. They had no one else. When she married Jamie, none of them expected she'd be far away, because like them, he'd been bound for a new life in the territories.

She blotted the letter and laid it aside to finish when she could say something they would like to hear. She did not know how to encourage Jamie, or why now, when he was home, she turned deft as a stump, burning herself on the oven, boiling over the coffee, tripping on the hem of her dress. She floundered in a fog of his hatreds and desires, his contempt and envy of absentee owners who got rich on the backs of men like himself. He belittled wood hicks like himself who looked ahead only to the next meal, the next pay, their next day off, and who were proud because the work hadn't killed them. He called wood hicks fools and owners crooks. He'd not sung in a long time.

Aunt Sweet had said a man might be head of the household, but he needed a woman to keep him strong, to lift him up in sickness and encourage him when he didn't know what to do next. If he wasn't a believer, his wife should lead him to the Lord. Aunt Sweet did not live to meet Jamie, who would not be led, at least not by May Rose. After two years, she knew her husband was a powerful worker only when something caught his interest.

She dipped her pen in the ink bottle and held it over the lip while the excess dripped off. Had they traveled on with Uncle Bert, Jamie might now be his own master. If she wrote how she longed to be with the family, surely Uncle Bert would send for them. She imagined herself telling Jamie, offering him a new life. If he wouldn't take it, she might be the one who left.

Late in the day, she buried the potatoes in the winter pit between layers of dry grass. The pigs waited for her to throw or pour something. When she slid the bar to open the gate, Nellie trotted through and the eight pigs shoved behind her. They raced to the weedy garden and rooted up the ground like plows. Soon they were venturing in and out of the forest, and then they disappeared from view. Her concern for them faded as she thought about going to town tomorrow to post her letter.

She washed the worst dirt from her arms in the stream from the spring house. In the cabin, she heated water for a half bath and scrubbed the thick, darkened soles of her feet. Excited now by thoughts of her adventure, she took her shoes from the clothes box and rubbed her thumbs over thin places in the soles. In her family, Uncle Bert mended everyone's shoes. She'd thought Jamie would do that, too.

At the bottom of the clothes box lay three hairless rag dolls, fashioned and named for her cousins, Margaret, Leola, and Mary Agnes. They'd helped her through the winter, first as she assembled them from scraps, and later when she arranged them on the bed and read aloud chapters of *Evangeline* or Bible stories about Rachel, Rebekah, and Ruth.

She went outside when the log train ground down the grade.

Jamie said the logs were too heavy and the grades and curves too sharp for ordinary engines. These trains were pulled and pushed by Shays, powerful geared locomotives that ran on a narrow track.

The trainmen waved, and she waved back.

Before dark, the pigs ran out of the forest and slurped up the swill she'd poured in their trough. She closed their gate, chased the chickens into the coop, and barred her own door against the night.

CHAPTER 3

Now faith is the substance of things hoped for,
the evidence of things not seen.

— HEBREWS 11:1

From habit, May Rose glanced toward distant ridges and sniffed the air. Sometimes breezes carried a scent of coffee or bacon from an unseen homestead. Today everything seemed ordinary, except her pigs were running loose in the woods, and she was going to town. She needed to post her letter while its appeal seemed a good idea.

By way of the winding railroad track, the company town was four miles down. Taking the forest trail was quicker, but she chose the track for its open sky. When she and Jamie had walked the trail, he'd taken the shotgun.

She started down the track carrying her shoes, a burlap sack of feathers, and a basket of eggs. A flat straw hat hung by a ribbon around her neck, and she'd braided and pinned up her hair. The letter to her uncle lay in a deep pocket of her dress. She had to believe her letter had gone astray and not that Uncle Bert was too angry to write, or worse, that something bad had happened.

The track went downhill most of the way, crossing wet places and ravines on wooden trestles, some no more than a few feet high, others braced by tall posts buried in tangles of mountain laurel. At the first trestle, she placed her bare feet on the rails to check for vibration. A train this time of day would be unusual, but these bridges had no separate walkways—if a train surprised her, she'd have to jump off. At the second trestle, long and high with spaces in the deck, she focused on the other side so she wouldn't get dizzy. Midway across she heard a clack and whine on the rails, the speeder, gearing down.

She waved the bag of feathers and the driver pumped his foot on the brake. The speeder's wheels squealed.

The speeder was a platform on wheels with four posts and a roof. Once she'd seen it carry two standing men who held onto the corner posts. Today it had one, Dr. Hennig, and his medicine bags. He stopped close to the hem of her dress.

"Mrs. Long?"

She welcomed his voice, the first she'd heard in days. Because they'd never spoken, she was surprised he knew her name. He reminded her a little of her uncle, maybe his black suit and narrow dark beard.

"Dr. Hennig, I'm sorry to be in your way."

He stepped to the front of the platform and offered his hand. "Let me carry you across."

She set the eggs and feathers on the platform and let him help her up. From childhood she'd been warned about men offering favors, but everyone trusted a doctor.

He motioned to the bench in the middle. "Sit there, it's safer." She'd seen the speeder rock when it hit a juncture of track, and Jamie said it wrecked easily, jumping the tracks on curves, or anytime, going too fast. She settled on the left side of the bench and pulled the bag of feathers to hide her bare feet. He pulled a rope and sparked the engine. She gripped the handrail.

Sunshine broke through gray-edged clouds as the speeder

reached the end of the trestle. She got a firm hold on her bundles and sat forward, preparing to stand. "Thank you, I'll get off here."

The doctor did not brake, but shifted an iron lever down for the long grade ahead. "Aren't you going to town?"

"I am."

"Then why not ride with me?"

Why not? It might be bad for her if Jamie found out, but she'd tell him herself, bring their differences into the open. She smiled. "Thank you, a ride will be helpful."

Dr. Hennig inched the speeder down the grade, then shifted to a higher gear. They picked up speed. The basket of eggs slid toward the front of the platform and she reached out, lost her balance and fell onto the feathers. The doctor's bony arm scooped her up. Clacking wheels drowned out the engine's put-put.

The seat was hard and the ride bumpy, and she watched as though her vigilance would keep them on the rails. For a while the doctor concentrated on guiding the speeder, and she worried about what might happen if they wrecked, how long before they'd be found.

Sunbeams flashed on a succession of leaves—green, a few turning red and gold. Slender tree shadows tumbled in stripes across the track, and wind dusted her face and bounced the hat on her back. They crossed over a shallow, rocky stream and traveled for a while beside it. In places, the slope was like a wall she might reach out and touch. They did not try to talk over the speeder's racket, but the doctor glanced at her more often than seemed safe or proper. She fixed her eyes ahead.

By the time they reached gentle hills, her rear was numb and her hands damp. They passed along slopes where tree tops lay jumbled and rotting across a base of stumps. She set her hat on her braids and struggled into her shoes.

The sounds of Winkler came first—blasts of steam, thuds and reverberations, muffled shouts. Then she saw the valley, first the woods on the opposite hillside, then three terraces of unpainted, tin-roofed houses. The valley floor had one main street, many railroad tracks, the sprawling sawmill, and the river. Plumes of black smoke slid over an arriving coal train. Downstream, the tannery squatted on the riverbank, staining the river black and wafting putrid odors away from town.

The speeder rattled across the river bridge onto a side rail not far from men offloading logs into the mill pond. Nudged by pikes, the logs splashed into the water and whacked against each other with a thunderous force that made her wince. Other men jabbed at the floating logs to direct them to the jack-slip at the entrance to the mill. Chains clattered, pulleys whined, and spikes in the chain caught the logs and pulled them one at a time up the slip and into the building. On another track, an Italian section crew stood shoulder to shoulder along a section of rail, prying iron bars under it and lifting in unison to a sing-song chant.

The doctor jumped down and extended his hand.

She stepped down into grit, swaying a little on feet narrowed and pinched by leather, and shouted over the noise. "Thank you, I'm steady now."

Still holding her hand, he removed his hat and leaned close. "You and your husband are doing well?"

"Very well, thank you."

"I see him, occasionally, at the camp."

She nodded.

"It must be lonely for you on the mountain."

"Not at all."

"Good, good." He squeezed her hand and peered at her face.

She drew back and pulled her hand away. "Do I look ill?"

"You hide your feelings." He smiled. "But no, you don't look ill. You look perfect."

She never could think of a response, polite or otherwise, to something inappropriate.

A man approached, looking out of place in a close-fitting suit and shining shoes. By the surprise on his face, she supposed a woman in the mill yard was unusual. He acknowledged her with a nod and beckoned the doctor.

"Until we meet again," Dr. Hennig said. The two men walked across the tracks toward the street, the doctor tall and round-shouldered, the man beside him short and trim.

She stood by the track and breathed the smoky air, relieved the doctor had gone, and ready to learn something about Winkler for herself. From Jamie she knew the Winkler Company owned almost everything, houses for the workers, church, school, store, and of course the sawmill in the middle of the valley.

Jamie had once told a joke about Winkler whores, and she'd asked, "Where do they live?" He'd said, "How would I know?" But he knew everything else—that the company made its own electric, had a slaughterhouse and employed a policeman, and that the railroad company brought Italian immigrants right off the boat to build and repair the roadbeds, tracks and trestles.

Her ride with Dr. Hennig meant she'd have more time to linger in town and explore other possibilities, maybe work for herself and a house to rent. She checked the position of the sun and calculated where it should be when she started up the track so she'd reach home before the log trains came down. The whine of saws made her eyes water, but the sight of women on the street lifted her spirit.

Imagining conversations, she hurried toward the boardwalk on the upper side of the street. For now, it would be enough to hear them say "good day". Ahead, a young woman with a child turned a corner, and another went into a house. One in a green dress stood on the store steps.

May Rose stopped at the store and smiled up at this woman, who gazed along the street as though looking for someone. She wore her brown hair in two large coils on each side of her face, and her dress looked plush, like velvet.

Because the steps were long and steep, May Rose shifted both bundles to one hand and used the other for the center railing. The woman stood at the rail's other side. May Rose smiled again. "Good day."

The woman had a sallow face and a crooked nose, and she did

not show that she heard or saw. Two others came from the store and stepped around her.

"Good morning," May Rose said. They turned their heads like they mistrusted the look of her. She touched her hat to see if it sat straight and checked her dress for dirt. Jamie might have been right about not living here, though surely there were good people everywhere.

Inside, she forgot about the slights, uplifted by the store's abundance, rows of labeled cans, a rainbow of cloth, shining tools, overflowing barrels, baskets, and crocks, a strong smell of leather. Light fell from six windows set high along both sides, and electric bulbs hung on long cords from a stamped metal ceiling.

Two men by a stack of deer hides peered from under their hat brims. She acknowledged them with a nod.

A shelf the length of the store was devoted to footwear, mostly hobnailed boots called corkers, but also children's and ladies' low-heeled slippers and high-tops with buttons and laces. One pair sat apart, creased and scuffed but with stout soles. She turned to the storekeeper, Mr. Ramey, the only other town resident she knew. His small features seemed to peer from the valleys of his plump face.

When she had his attention, she lifted the feathers and basket of eggs. "I've these to trade."

He glanced at her in a bored way, then slapped his hand on the counter and cursed as metal crashed behind her and something thumped to the floor. Startled, May Rose turned to see the woman in the green dress lying amid soot and sections of a fallen stove pipe, her skirt drawn up over bruised legs. The men who'd leaned against the deer hides stuck their cigarettes in their mouths and lifted her by the arms. When they let her go, she sank to the floor, and her eyes rolled back in her head. Her mouth hung open, showing pale gums and an edge of blackened teeth.

May Rose knelt beside her and looked to Mr. Ramey. "Can I help? Get the doctor, or call her family?"

One of the men laughed. Mr. Ramey cursed again and nudged the woman with his boot. "She's drunk."

May Rose took the woman's dry, hot hand. "She's sick, don't you see? Does she have family here?"

"That's a good one," Mr. Ramey said. "Boys, this here's Jamie Long's woman." They laughed again. "You can be her family. Help me, boys."

They dragged the woman out of the store. May Rose followed, hoping for more compassionate help on the street. Saws split the air in a steady scream.

"Not in front of the store," Mr. Ramey said. He motioned. "Take her on across the alley, there, to the church—it might do her good." The men lowered the woman to the church's stone step and went back to the store. She sprawled in noisy sleep, hair loosened, brown strands falling over her face. Closely viewed, her velvet dress showed ragged lace and patches of moth damage.

Mr. Ramey called from the store steps. "You gonna trade or not?" He held up her bundles.

May Rose glanced along the empty boardwalk. Across the tracks, a few workmen went about their business. She bent over the woman, smelled alcohol, and heard regular breathing. "I'll be back," she whispered. "I'll get the doctor."

Inside, Mr. Ramey set the bag on the counter and stuck his arm into the feathers, brought out a fistful and frowned.

May Rose lifted her chin. "They're clean."

He closed the bag. "We've a lot of feathers on hand. Ten cents?"

She had no other place to sell them.

"Fifteen for the eggs."

Jamie never said what he got for them. Mr. Ramey thumbed through a fat account book and stopped on a page headed by Jamie's name. "Twenty-five cents, for everything. Put it on account?"

The page had several lines of purchases. Was he trying to cheat her? "When did we buy those things?"

"Saturday."

"A recent Saturday?"

"Last Saturday." He turned the book for her to see. Shoe laces, tobacco, cigarette papers. The last item was a man's shirt, red wool.

Her sight blurred. Jamie loved pretty things and lively times. Likely he would not bring the shirt home to be washed until it was old enough to pass as something won at cards, what he'd said about his sheepskin coat.

She straightened. "Yes, on account, please."

He penciled twenty five cents on a line and glanced up. "You needing anything today?"

She set her letter and a penny on the counter. "Is there mail for me?"

He slid the penny into a drawer, tossed her letter into a basket, and glanced at a wall of wooden pigeonholes. "Nothing today." One by one he moved the eggs to a box, his sighs suggesting she'd disturbed his day. *No mail.* She'd lost her family, and Jamie was slipping away.

She forced a smile. Manners, her aunt said, were useful in any situation, but a little sweetness, even false, helped many a predicament. "Might you know of anyone needing a woman to work?"

He slid her basket across the counter. "You might say everybody. None with money to pay."

"I see." She took the basket and said, like she'd only just thought of it, "What do you give for pigs, going on five months old?"

"Nothing. Two-to-three dollars a head, if you grow them out, say through November. 'Course, someone might give you half a dollar right now, but you'd be a fool to sell when you can fatten them in the woods." He came from behind the counter and picked up the sections of blackened stove pipe.

She started to the door, and turned back. "I forgot to say, I know how to take care of sick people."

He fit the pipe to the stove. "You might ask at the preacher's house, Preacher Gowder's, right there beyond the church. He knows people's needs."

Outside, she looked across the alley to the church and the preacher's house beside it. The woman was no longer on the church step nor anywhere in view. She hoped someone had helped the poor thing home.

She knocked on the preacher's door. Jamie had spent at least one weekend in town. It must not seem so bad to him.

CHAPTER 4

Talk not of wasted affection, affection never was wasted;

— HENRY WADSWORTH LONGFELLOW:
EVANGELINE

The preacher's house had no welcoming porch nor sheltering roof above the door. May Rose stood on a step of chiseled rock and rapped the knocker. A window curtain moved and the door swung wide.

With a shriek, an old woman pulled her over the threshold. "Angel, my angel!"

Caught in the woman's bony embrace, May Rose stumbled into a room that smelled of camphor and cooking grease. She shifted to keep her balance and turned her head from the woman's rancid curls.

Light from the open door fell across bare floor boards, up a wall of painted lath, down onto a pot-bellied stove, a rocking chair, and a straight chair with wide wooden arms. On the floor, a stack of books.

"I've come to see the preacher. Is this the right place?"

The woman pulled her farther into the room and collapsed

25

into the rocker, sending May Rose to her knees so forcefully that she struck her chin on the rocker arm. She rubbed her chin and blinked away tears.

"Please. My name is May Rose, and I've come to see the preacher."

The woman had gray ringlets, a child's plump cheeks, and a tiny bow mouth. She seized May Rose's skirt with knobby fingers and touched her coiled braids. "I said you'd never burn in hell!" Her lips trembled. "You've seen Jesus—right there is heaven's crown of gold."

"Hello?" A man appeared in the doorway to a back room, holding a chamber pot. "Mother, who do you have there?"

The old woman moved her hand to May Rose's flat stomach. "Poor cherub, all gone."

May Rose flinched, drew herself up and looked from the strange woman to her son. He did not look old, yet he had waves of white hair, black eyebrows, and a short white beard trimmed to a point. She tried not to stare.

He shook his head. "Please excuse Mother. And excuse me. I'll return in a moment." He carried the pot into the room beyond.

The old woman closed her eyes and rocked. The house filled with sounds of pumping water, brisk footsteps, doors opening, closing, and clinks of dishware.

The preacher came back, crossed the room and closed the front door. "How do you do? I'm Humphrey Gowder, Preacher of Free Grace Church. This is my mother, Mrs. Ruie Gowder."

"He can recite scripture all day long, but he's a hypocrite," the old woman mumbled. "His father was a great preacher."

The house warmed with the scent of biscuits. "Mrs. Gowder, Preacher, how do you do? My name is May Rose Long, Mrs. Jamie Long."

He shook her hand. "Mrs. Long, we're happy to meet you. Can I help you in some way?"

"Humphrey, don't be like that. This is our Angelina." Ruie

turned to May Rose. "Humphrey needs a wife, don't you think? You and me will have to help, for he'll never get one on his own."

He sighed with a tone of long-suffering. "My sister died tragically, and Mother sees a resemblance in every young woman she meets."

"I understand. Mr. Ramey said you might know of someone needing a woman to work. I can care for the sick."

He shook his head. "I need help, as you can see, but presently cannot afford it, not even one of the Italian women. I haven't seen you in church. Are you recently arrived?"

"My husband works for Winkler. I'd like...we'd like to move to town."

Ruie's eyes snapped. "I know my girl. She forgives you, and look how pretty." She reached toward May Rose. "You knew more scripture than him. Now fix us lunch."

May Rose patted her hand. "Mrs. Gowder, I'll come at a better time."

The preacher looked hopeful. "Mother will be happy to have you visit. Perhaps you could stay here while I go out for a short time? I need to check on one of my flock."

Ruie's head wobbled. "He loves the Lord with all his heart and all his soul and mind. I say charity begins at home."

The odor of fresh biscuits encouraged her, but log trains might rumble across the trestles before she reached home. "I'm sorry, I can't today."

"Silly girl, come along." Ruie got up and toddled to the other room.

The preacher motioned for her to follow. "A few minutes will be fine. Please sit and eat. Mother does better with company."

Ruie shook her head. "I just pick."

"A few minutes then," May Rose said. She sat with Ruie at a table, and the preacher ladled two bowls of brown gravy and set them down with a platter of biscuits. Ruie dipped a biscuit in gravy and brought it, dripping, to her mouth.

He tied a cloth around his mother's neck, avoiding her swats. "Did you give thanks?"

Ruie sopped up the gravy with sideways glances as though they might steal her food. "I always do."

"I have to leave soon," May Rose said. "I meant to tell you, a few minutes ago a woman lay unconscious on your church step."

"Do you know her?"

"I don't. She fell in the store, and men carried her outside. When I came out, she was gone."

"She must have recovered."

"She was unable to stand, unconscious. She wore a green dress. I thought she might have crawled into the church."

He stroked his beard. "A green dress. I may know who you mean, not one of my flock, no. I doubt she went into the church, but I'll look." He snatched a biscuit and left.

May Rose dipped a biscuit in gravy and let it drip over the bowl before bringing it to her lips. The gravy tasted of strong, salty ham. She could not remember the last time she had eaten someone else's cooking.

While Ruie slurped and chewed, May Rose admired the wooden ice box and the water pump bolted to a counter beside a tin sink. The kitchen was very clean, pans spaced evenly on a wall, no smears of coal dust on the floor, yet Ruie did not appear capable of caring for it, and the preacher said he had no help. He must have made the biscuits. She had not known a man could do women's work so well.

After eating everything but May Rose's portion, Ruie licked her fingers and the edges of her bowl, then took May Rose by the hand and led her into the front room to the straight-backed chair.

Ruie dropped into her rocker. "Now, isn't this nice?" She began to sing. "*Safe in the arms of Jesus, Safe on His gentle breast.*" Her song trailed off in a snore.

Anxious to leave, May Rose listened for the door latch and watched for the preacher to return. She judged an hour to have passed, then two, and spread her anger from him to her husband, who also took advantage. She wondered what excuse Jamie would give for his weekend in town. From the beginning, he'd kept her isolated, and she'd excused too much.

Winkler wasn't as bad as he'd said—already she took less notice of the saws. People here did not have to carry water to their houses. They had electric lights and neighbors. Not everyone seemed friendly, but maybe they were shy. Some weekend soon, Jamie might jump from the log train and find her gone, maybe no farther than Winkler, but maybe all the way to Fargo.

Children's voices rose outside, groups walking home from school. With a last look at Ruie, she set her hat on her head and lifted her basket.

The preacher rushed through the door. "One of my flock took me to her mother's sickbed, and another waylaid me about a disturbance at one of the camps. Could you possibly stay longer? I should make another call."

"I can't. I have to reach home before dark."

"The woman you saw wasn't in the church."

Nodding, she backed out the door and turned toward the lower end of town. The sun dipped too near the horizon to go back the way she'd come. The old trail would take her home in half the time.

She hurried across the tracks and through the mill toward mounds of sawdust and lumber docks where men loaded thick yellow boards onto flat cars. The rhythmic slap of wood on wood slowed as she neared. A worker whistled and called an unfamiliar word, and others hooted. Rude men. She could imagine Jamie among them. She bent her head and stepped carefully around half-buried wood scraps. A voice barked an order, whistles trailed off in laughter, and the slap of boards resumed.

Near the docks, a footbridge held by cables crossed the river to a few sheds and the start of the trail up the mountain. The bridge swung with her first step. Loose boards shifted, showing the river below, shallow, rocky, and fast-flowing. She squeezed the rusty handrail.

On the other side she leaned against a tree and pulled the shoes from her swollen feet, an effort like husking a tight ear of corn. She tied the shoelaces to each other and hung them and the basket to the sash at her waist, then found two stout walking sticks, extra legs for the climb. Ahead lay a brushy slope of rotting stumps and fallen crowns of ancient trees. She was not certain how to find the opening to the trail, but when she came out of the brush, she saw it, a dark space between two giant trunks.

Entering the forest was like pulling a blanket over her head. Ahead was a faint corridor with a blanket of pine needles and leaves, fresh and brittle on top, loamy underneath. Her toes spread into the leaves and gripped the soil, lifting musky scents. She pushed the sticks hard against the ground to release her anger and to chase away anything hidden that might bite.

Her thoughts reduced to essential truths. She would not come through another winter alone without turning crazy as the preacher's mother or drunk as the woman in the green dress. And she would no longer be like a poor hen pecked by the flock, the one she wished would peck back.

The trail twisted upward, skirting rock outcrops, damp ravines, and dense mountain laurel that grew tall with shining leaves and white flowers. Here and there a ray of sunlight fell through the canopy, brightening an orange leaf or a spot of lichen-crusted rock. She might say nothing to Jamie, fatten the pigs another month and somehow sell them on her own. One thing she knew—if he sold the pigs, she would never see the money.

Going home, always bear left, he'd said. But the path was sometimes hard to distinguish. According to the old tales, men and deer alike had lost their way and starved to death in the miles of laurel. When she'd followed Jamie, she'd given no attention to landmarks.

An hour or more might have passed—with tree-tops covering the sky, she had only fatigue to judge the time. Where the trail crossed a tiny stream, she refreshed her feet in cold water, sat on a rock and wiggled them dry. Behind her, foliage crunched, and she held her breath and clutched her walking sticks like clubs, remembering stories of panthers trailing prey. Something moved at the edge of her vision, and she straightened and felt her flesh expand like a rooster puffing up to look fierce. In the silence, water dripped. Wolves, Jamie said, had left these mountains long ago, and only a few wild things did not fear humans. Skunks, for one. A human's greatest threat was another human. She listened until she felt foolish. If someone wanted to do her harm, he could have done it already.

Trudging on, watching the ground, certain she'd gone too far on the wrong path, she came around a tree and was struck by a furious beating of the air. She ducked and shielded her head as leaves and feathers fell. Above her, a turkey gobbler beat his wings in a struggle to lift away. She'd thought she was dead.

She'd barely caught her breath when the ground rumbled underfoot, and Nellie and all eight pigs burst through the trees and bumped around her legs. They wheeled and raced on, but came back to crisscross her path as though leading the way. Ahead she saw a column of daylight. The pigs ran through it and she stepped out under the sky. Home.

Grateful, she paused at the edge of the clearing. Directly ahead, chickens pecked at dirt near the stream. Nellie and the pigs slowed and trailed toward the hog lot. Catching a sudden strong odor of smoke, she whirled to see her cabin. All seemed fine. Then she turned the other way.

In her garden plot, the scarecrow was afire.

CHAPTER 5

Silent a moment they stood in speechless wonder, and then rose
Louder and ever louder a wail of sorrow and anger...

— HENRY WADSWORTH LONGFELLOW: EVANGELINE

On the scarecrow, fire spread from the flapping arms of Jamie's old blue shirt to his shapeless hat. May Rose trembled as the scarecrow dissolved to a blackened cross, a reminder of saints and sinners burned at the stake. She ran after sparks where they flew, tramped them out, whirled to see what next, what else?

The fire might be a prank or the beginning of worse to come. Someone had set the fire just as she neared home, had meant her to see it. From the garden she could not see the cabin porch. She imagined drifters waiting there, maybe with her shotgun.

She ran along the edge of the clearing to the railroad track where she could see the front of the cabin from a safer distance. Her bowels contracted when she saw the door hanging open. A gust of wind whipped at her skirt. Thick black and gray clouds bunched up in the west, and wind blew in her face. She turned and ran along the back of the cabin toward the lean-to and its stacks of wood.

The ax was lodged in the chopping stump. She wrenched it free and hurried on to the outhouse. Inside, she barred the door, lifted her skirt and sat over the hole in the wooden bench. Rain fell like stones on the tin roof. Under cover of the noise, she cried and screamed, angry to be afraid of home. When she'd exhausted her body, she placed the cover over the hole, dropped her shoes in a corner and huddled on the bench, one hand on the ax. Wind blew through cracks in the wood siding.

She woke in cold dark silence, sprang up, crashed into the door, and groped for the bar that held it closed. Outside, the moon ran in and out of clouds. No smoke rose from her chimney. If someone was in the cabin, he'd let the fire go out. He might be asleep; he might be gone. She hugged the ax. She'd chopped the heads from living chickens, killed a rattlesnake with a hoe, chopped wood chunks into kindling with this ax. Laying it into a man, if necessary, seemed a thing she could do. She'd have to be close, with the advantage of surprise.

She crept along the porch to the open door and inched her fingers along the edge of the jamb to the wall inside where she'd left the shotgun. Gone.

A raucous snore shocked her to motion. Raising the ax overhead, she burst through the door and tripped. The ax flew from her hands and landed with a muffled thump. She fell onto something solid as a sack of flour, but warm. Grunts erupted around her, the breath of snorting pigs.

She stretched up and stumbled over them, found the stove, groped for the match tin and found a single match on the shelf. A pig stepped on her bare foot. She patted her hands along the wall, unhooked a string of dried apples and tossed it out the door. The pigs jammed through and fought over the apples. Her hands shook as she struck the match along the stove's rough surface and lit the lamp. In its glow, she saw the bed.

The ax lay in her split pillow. Feathers covered the bed, her blue dress, mourning dress, bloomers, shawls, her long coat, and the overturned clothes box.

A rooster crowed and a pig wandered back across the threshold. Sucking in a sob, she turned the pig out, barred the door, lifted a dress, crushed it against her, let it drop. Someone had dumped her clothes on the bed, had set a fire for her to see. Someone had waited, watched at least part of her progress up the trail, could have hurt her, but had not. Everything seemed less than an attack, but more than mischief. Someone had her shotgun.

She set the globe on the lamp base and searched for the match tin. It was gone too. Dawn brightened the window.

The stove was cold and no coals smoldered among the ashes. She shoveled out the firebox, laid a small base of kindling, and shaved wood curls on top. Every match she had was in the tin, but the tin was not in its place on the shelf and it wasn't on the floor or behind the stove. She lit a sliver of wood from the lamp and held the fire against the shavings until they caught.

For a while she went from task to task without finishing any, scooped feathers into a flour sack, swept pig hair out the door, repacked the clothes box. Only when she'd folded all the clothes and set them in the box did she notice what else was missing: Jamie's long-johns and sheepskin coat. They weren't under the bed, nor hanging on a nail, nor tucked over the rafters. He might have taken these things while she was gone, but more likely he would come home on Saturday and blame her for their loss. Only when she lay on the bed and reached to cover herself with the woolen blanket did she see that it, too, had disappeared. She turned to her side, drew up her knees and wrapped her arms around herself.

A racket at the door startled her awake. Thumps shook the door and shouts echoed in the clearing. "Mrs. Long? Mrs. Long!"

From the edge of the window curtain she saw Dr. Hennig and men with rifles. Beyond them, two speeders sat on the rails. She slid the bar and the door gave way. Men crowded past the doctor into the room, fouling the air with their unwashed clothes and scarring the floor with their hobnail boots. One looked under the bed, and another poked at the rafters. She backed to the stove.

A burly man in a red checkered shirt shoved toward her, a man she recognized from Jamie's stories, rotten front teeth beneath a moustache like boar's hair. "Where's your husband?" He was Bright, the swamper boss, in Jamie's words, a self-righteous snake.

The doctor touched her arm as though to waken her. "Mrs. Long, where is your husband?"

"In camp. Winkler Number Six. He's at work." She saw by their faces that he was not.

Bright waved the others outside. "Did Jamie Long come here yesterday?"

"I don't know. Yesterday…"

"Yesterday, I gave Mrs. Long a ride to town," the doctor said.

Bright glanced from him to May Rose. His garlicky breath soured the air. "You say you don't know, but I think you do. Where'd he go?"

"I'll deal with this," the doctor said. "Mrs. Long, might your husband have come here while you were in town?"

She looked at the bed. "His clothes…someone stole his clothes. I haven't seen my husband in nearly two weeks."

A pitiful squeal pulled her to the porch. One of the loggers held a pig by its hind legs while another wrapped a rope around them.

"Stop that!" Her voice was shrill and weak.

"Blood gift," the first man shouted. "For the dead man's wife."

Blood gift? May Rose clung to a porch post. A man was dead, and Jamie was missing.

The doctor stepped down from the porch. "We'll settle that later. Untie the animal."

The second man shoved a pole between the rope and the pig's legs, and together they lifted it, upside down, into the air.

"You ain't the boss," the first one said.

"I'll speak to Mr. Townsend," the doctor said.

The clearing quieted as the doctor and the men with the pig

glared at each other. After a few moments, Bright called, "Stimmel! Let it go."

Stimmel glanced at Bright and cocked his head toward the doctor. "Have it your way. But it's only right." He untied the ropes and the pig scrambled to its feet and ran into the woods. "There'll be payment to Donnelly's widow, one way or other."

Bright ran his tongue over his teeth. "Mrs. Long, your man's done murder. Plenty of us seen it, enough to hang him. He knifed a man, yesterday, lunchtime, and that man died this morning. So go ahead, run to wherever he's went. There'll be no help for you here."

Her knees hit the porch floor. Jamie—joyful, reckless, bitter—had killed a man. She suffocated under the weight of it.

Bright left the porch. The doctor tried to help her up. She brushed his hand away, hating them equally, the doctor, the wood hicks, and Jamie, who always knew better than anyone. He'd come here, taken his things, left her to these men.

"Mrs. Long," Dr. Hennig said, "I'm afraid your home is no longer a safe place. Things have been said. You may be blamed, unfairly, I'm sure, but you also may be sought by some who know you to be alone, and assume you are now...available."

How unkind of her body to weaken when she needed to be strong, how wrong for her mind to shatter, when she needed its direction. How unreasonable of her heart to freeze, when she needed its comfort. She struggled for words. "Let me be."

"The men have gone, searching the woods, I think. But some may come back. And after them, others."

A ray of sunshine struck the porch and warmed her back. She stared at the weathered floorboards and the broken-down leather of the doctor's boots, the thin soles. Nobody who worked for the company had anything. The strip of sunlight on the porch narrowed, clouds closing like a curtain.

She shivered. "Does Jamie have wages coming?"

"I'd say he does, for days he worked this week. These men

may want the paymaster to give it to Donnelly's widow and children. It's not proper, but many will think it's right."

He'd left her without a single coin. She had to get his wages, sell the pigs, everything. "I'll need a ride down the mountain. Tomorrow."

"Come with me, now. Do you have a place to stay? Friends?"

Friends? She stared at her mud-caked feet. "I have to clean up."

He pulled a watch from his coat pocket. "I must get the speeder off the rails ahead of the train."

"A few minutes."

The stream from the springhouse ran full from the night's torrents. She dampened her face, soaked her feet and scrubbed her soles with grit from the sandy bottom. When she came from the cabin, wearing shoes and her blue flowered dress, hair hastily braided and pinned, the doctor's expression sparked to life. "You look very pretty."

His opinion did not matter. She needed only to look respectable.

Wind dusted grit in her eyes as the speeder rocked and swayed down the mountain. She blinked, washing her eyes with tears.

Dr. Hennig seemed as cheerful as if he'd solved her problems. "Tomorrow we'll come back for your clothes and anything else you want."

Clothing was not on her mind. Today she needed to reach the paymaster before Donnelly's friends.

When they reached town, the doctor walked her to the main road and pointed downriver toward a section not owned by the company. "Down there you'll find Hester's Boardinghouse. I'll call for you in the morning after the service trains leave. There's a whistle at the mill at five, another at six, and the trains go up not long after that. Watch for me." He pressed her hand between his and bent so his face was close. "Goodbye, until tomorrow."

She lowered her eyes from the expectation in his face. Let him think as he wished.

They went in opposite directions. The empty street stretched like a black divide between mill and town. Her shoe's thin sole caught on a pebble, and she stumbled a step, and glanced to see if anyone had noticed. She cautioned herself not to fall, and never again to submit, like a pecked hen. No matter how desperate, she must appear strong and whole, and if necessary, peck back.

Locomotive smoke darkened the sky. She followed the board-walk past the sooty walls of the preacher's house and church, stepped down to the alley and up to the boardwalk again. In front of the company store, women in dark skirts clustered near a Copenhagen Chewing Tobacco sign. They lowered their voices and passed cautious looks as she neared. She needed her uncle's letter more than ever. The store smelled of newly-oiled floors. She asked for her mail.

Mr. Ramey didn't bother to look. "Nothing today. Anything else?"

"I'd like to advertise the sale of my place. Can I do that here?"

"I expect your husband has to do it."

"He's gone."

"So I hear."

Outside, the women pulled aside limp skirts to let her pass. Across the street, a train with a passenger car sat at the depot. A man loaded gray sacks stamped U.S. MAIL.

She found the paymaster in the office building beside the depot. There, clerks in white shirts and black vests wrote on slanted tables.

"Mrs. Jamie Long," she said. "For Jamie Long's pay."

The clerks glanced toward her. The paymaster didn't blink or smile. "Payday's Saturday."

"He's left your employ," she said.

"Saturday noon." The paymaster motioned with a paper. "The window outside. Line up with everybody else."

The room was quiet as she left. Saturday. Two more days.

She walked in the street downriver toward the part of town not owned by the company. Broad signs topped two-story, unpainted buildings, none with a look of permanence, all on the uphill side of the road. *Pizzy's Bar and Restaurant, Roy's Pool and Billiards, Woodman's Retreat.* A walkway of smooth river rock knapped into the earth led to a white-painted house with a picket fence. A sign on an iron gate said, *Room And Board. Rates by Day, Week, or Month. Hester Townsend, Proprietor.* Dr. Hennig expected her to stay here.

She could not speak to another person and be turned away. If she had to say her name, say she wanted a room with an indefinite promise to pay, she'd break. Saturday would be soon enough. Saturday she'd come with Jamie's pay in her pocket, maybe money from selling the stock and her home goods. Saturday there might be a letter.

Again she walked through the mill yard, now deaf to the workmen's taunts. On the other side of the footbridge she tied her shawl around her waist and her shoe laces around her neck. She found new walking sticks and punched the ground, left and right, pulling herself up the slope. If any chickens had survived the wood hicks, she'd close them up. Bar her own door, sleep with the ax, drive Jamie from her thoughts, expend all effort to finding her family. Maybe Saturday, instead of going to the boardinghouse, she'd take a train to Jennie Town, where a letter might have been waiting all this time.

She plodded upward, bending her head against dust and chaff, wanting food, but even more, water for her dry mouth. Wind whined in the trees. Then, a piercing tone, a shriek. She stopped, and heard it again, a sound carried and sharpened on the wind. Whirling around to find the source, she saw a flash of red.

She hurried over and around mossy rocks and uprooted trees into a patch of fern where two boys held a girl to the ground. A boy in a red cap knelt at her head and pinned her arms. The other knelt over her, his bare bottom working back and forth like a saw. The hem of the girl's dress was pulled up and stuffed in her mouth, but she grunted through the cloth and flailed her legs.

May Rose screamed, startling herself and the boys. She rushed forward and whacked her stoutest stick against the fat white butt of the one on top. He yelped, leaped to his feet, stumbled backwards, ankles bound by his dropped trousers, then fell and stumbled up again. Snarling, she swung her stick in threatening circles. The boys ran away downhill. Tree tops battered the wind.

The girl rolled to a defensive crouch and drew upright, her wide eyes on May Rose. Dirt clung to her straggly brown hair and loose dress, a girl who looked twelve or thirteen. She ran toward a brake of laurel, then turned and cupped her hands around her mouth. "Don't tell! Don't tell!"

The girl disappeared in the brush. May Rose stood confused, then dropped to her knees, laid her face in her arms, and cried. Leaves fell on her like a blanket.

THIN SMOKE TRAILED from the chimney when she reached the clearing. She drove the hens into the coop and paused at the empty hog lot. Had the wood hicks captured the pigs after all?

Jamie had taken the shotgun, but she had the ax. She set the walking sticks against the porch wall. Two more nights.

Stuffy air overwhelmed her when she opened the door, making her first thought *pigs*, then immediately, *Jamie?* A man sat in Jamie's chair, drinking from his jar, but with greasy hair, scraggly beard, bigger than Jamie, smelling of manure. His brother, *Russell.*

In a movement that seemed too swift and light for a man of his bulk, Russell put himself between her and the door. "My turn," he said.

CHAPTER 6

Lay not up for yourselves treasures upon earth,
where moth and rust doth corrupt,
and where thieves break through and steal…

— MATTHEW 6:19-21

Russell, a long-limbed, hairy man, loomed above her. He wore a ratty knitted cap the color of grime, and his graying hair reached his shoulders. "No need to wrinkle your nose at me," he said.

Her first hope did not live long enough to breathe. Russell had not come to help. She lifted her shoes from around her neck and gripped them by the laces. "I'm sorry my nose is wrinkled. It's the smell in here."

He slid the bar to latch the door. "I don't smell nothing." His eyes darted back and forth, a restless habit Jamie had warned her to ignore. He'd said Russell punched when he could not explain, was too stupid to do anything but cut tanning bark and raise pigs, too lazy to wash, and too different to mix with other humans. Russell had lived with their mother until she died, but now he went for months without seeing anyone. Already he'd said more to May Rose than in all their previous meetings.

He dragged a chair to the door and sat there, blocking it. "Ain'cha gonna ask why I'm here?"

She matched his surly speech. "It's kind of you to visit. Do make yourself at home. Jamie will be glad to see you." She hung her shoes on a peg and shoved wood into the stove, enough to smother the coals, or smoke the cabin, or catch the chimney afire. The ax lay in shadow beside the bed.

Russell's laugh was short and bitter. "Your precious Jamie's a fool and a whining boy. He'll not be back."

She wanted to know what Jamie had said and where he'd gone without sounding like she cared. "So you saw him."

"So I did. Ain't it something? What's bad for him might be good for me." He jerked a string of dried pumpkin from the rafters. "I believe we'll start with a pie. Then we'll see."

Beads of moisture cooled her forehead. "The pumpkin has to soak. Come again tomorrow, I'll have the pie ready."

He dropped the pumpkin and kicked it toward her. "I'll be staying over. Bake some light bread while you're at it. I ain't ate light bread since Ma died." He tossed a string of dried apples onto a hot eye of the stove. "Apple pie don't take no time, bake one o'them."

She grabbed the apples and dropped them into a crock, then sorted through pans and utensils, making noise, soaking up time, gathering her wits. Russell seemed nervous. If food would distract and settle him, she'd cook all night. Maybe he'd drink himself to a stupor. She chopped pumpkin into a pan of water, put the pan at the back of the stove, and set about scrubbing utensils that were already clean and assembling ingredients she did not need, conscious of him moving to the table, watching her.

When she'd collected herself, she faced him. "Jamie means me to go to him. He said he'd send word. Did he tell you where?"

"Nope."

"Do you know where he is?"

"Gone, and he ain't sending for you."

She'd known he wouldn't, had soberly considered what to do, yet Russell's words stabbed her heart.

He spat on the floor.

"Don't spit in here."

He wiped his hand across his mouth and beard. "I spit where I please. This is my place. Gave cash for it, yesterday, so your boy could give 'em the shake." He rocked back in his chair.

Gave cash? She threw back the trap door in the floor, sank to her knees, bent over the cold hole. Her eyes and nose dripped.

He scraped the chair. "What're you doing there?"

"You want bread, I'm getting the yeast." With a shaking hand she probed the screened box under the floor. *Gone, and worse, sold out to Russell. No word for her, no sign he'd given her a thought.* She had to believe Russell. Jamie liked to say his brother never cheated if he didn't have to and never lied on purpose.

She brought up one of Jamie's jugs, set it on the table and took the lamp.

"Hey," Russell said.

"I need light to find the yeast."

He grabbed the lamp base. "No."

She held onto the handle. "Then you take the light and find the yeast. It's in a small crock."

"Sit there on the bed where I can see you."

While he reached his arm into the hole she nudged the ax under the bed with her heel. He came up with the crock.

"That's it," she said.

Thumps shook the cabin door. Russell kicked the cellar lid shut, took three strides to the door, and threw back the bar. Someone pushed from the other side, and cold air blew into the cabin.

Bright leaned in with his hands braced each side of the doorframe. "We're collecting for Donnelly's widow. Livestock, home goods, paper money, what'er you got." Behind him, a man held a torch and another held a squirming burlap bag.

Russell wrenched the bag away and threw it to the cabin floor.

Three hens flopped out and shook their feathers. He pulled a hunting knife from the sheath at his belt and pointed it at Bright. "Collect somewheres else. This here's mine. I got a paper to prove it."

The men murmured. Bright looked from the knife in Russell's hand to May Rose. "Her too?"

"That's my business. Woman, shut the door." Russell looked rougher than Bright and less predictable. Bright stepped back from the blade.

Russell gripped her arm while she pushed on the door. As soon as he closed the bar, he seized her dress by the collar. "This is all your doing, whore." He slipped the knife in the cloth near her waist and sliced it upward. She gasped and twisted away but he pulled her back, grabbed the gathered skirt at the waist and slit to the hem, flipped her around and pulled the dress off her shoulders.

He peered at her chemise and knee-length bloomers like they were unexpected. "Take that there off."

"Jamie will kill you," she said. "Or I will."

Russell laughed. "Jamie's gone and you're a whore."

"You're crazy."

"Take it off." His eyes darted side to side. He pulled her braids, sheathed the knife and shoved her toward the bed. A hen flew onto the table, and he swatted it across the room. The hen squawked and fluffed her feathers. "You went naked for them!"

"For *them*? For who?"

For a moment, his eyes stopped their wild movement.

"Say who!"

"You stood naked and waved to them men on the train, morning, noon, and night. Jamie fought and killed a man 'cause of you."

"I did not. What liar said I did?" One rushed to her mind, Donnelly, the man Jamie had killed.

"No more talk. Get naked."

She slipped to the stove and broke a chunk of yeast into

another crock. "Behave yourself, and be patient. Let me start your bread. I make good bread, like your ma did." Jamie had said Russell wouldn't know what to do with a woman. She wondered if he'd sent Russell to punish her, and if Jamie believed the lies.

"Naked." Russell's eyes shifted side to side.

"I won't. If you treat me bad, I'll poison anything I cook."

"You'll taste of it first."

He lifted the jug and threw back his head to drink, and she grabbed the iron poker and stirred up the firebox. Sparks flew. The end of the poker glowed red.

"Put that over here," he said.

"What?"

"Don't 'what' me. That poker. Set that poker on the table by me. *Easy.*"

He could reach her in a single step. She dropped the poker on the table, and he grabbed it and pulled her cleaver and carving knife from nails on the wall. Heart thumping, she back-stepped and looked around the stove for another weapon. The cabin seemed unbearably hot, and when he opened the door, cool air rushed in with fresh hope. The bucket of pig slop sat by the stove, half full of greasy water. One sidestep put it in reach. When he threw the implements into the yard, she lifted the bucket and held it behind her skirt. He came back in and kicked the chickens to the porch. She raised the bucket to toss, but he saw and prepared to dodge, so she threw the slop on the coals and shut the damper. Black smoke poured from the firebox.

She slipped around him when he rushed to the stove, but he caught her on the porch and dragged her back into the smoke. With one hand he grabbed her arm, and with the other he opened the draft and shut the firebox, cursing all the while. Then he pulled her back to the porch while the air cleared.

"You're a devil and a whore. Jamie should never of fought for you."

"You're hurting me. Let loose—I can't go anywhere. I've nowhere to go."

"I ain't hurt you yet. We're going back inside and you're gonna scoop out them wet coals. Then build up the fire and make my bread." He pulled a coil of rope from a rafter, tied one end around her waist and the other to his wrist.

While she cleaned out the stove and rebuilt the fire, he uncorked the new jug and sat at the table, jug on his left and the hunting knife in his right hand.

She mixed bread dough and pie crust, taking her time, thinking. He sipped from Jamie's jug of unmixed liquor. He'd said no more about her getting naked, but he wasn't going to let her go. After a while she noticed him squinting. His head and shoulders drooped.

By the time apple juice bubbled through the piecrust, his head had dropped to the table and he appeared to sleep. He didn't wake to the yeasty bread smells nor the scrape of the clothes box sliding from under the bed. He slept on, undisturbed by the loud beat of her heart as she sawed the rope with the ax blade and put on her old dress. She took the pies from the oven so their burning wouldn't wake him, lifted her shoes and shawl, and unbarred the door.

Frost sparkled on the ground and a full moon shone in the dome of a clear midnight. She ran barefoot toward the trail, renewed by cold air. With the aid of moonlight, she might get far away before he woke. She paused at the hog lot where snoring pigs sprawled. "Nellie," she whispered. "Nellie."

A jerk on her braids wrenched her backwards.

"Whore."

CHAPTER 7

Daily injustice is done, and might is the right of the strongest!

— HENRY WADSWORTH LONGFELLOW:
EVANGELINE

With one hand Russell pulled her hair at the crown and with the other he pushed her toward the cabin. She stumbled with each push, but each time regained her balance, planted her feet in the icy weeds and braced for him to shove again. His breath panted on her neck; his body crowded her back. When her feet slipped, he pulled her up by her hair. Halfway to the cabin, he yelled and released his hold, and she fell headlong, scraping her palms and elbows along the ground.

She looked back at a great commotion, Russell hopping on one foot, grunting, cursing, and kicking. Nellie had the ankle of his boot in her jaws, and snorting pigs surged against him.

As May Rose scooted away, Russell raised his arm and smashed his fist into Nellie's snout. Nellie released his ankle but chomped down on his hand. Bellowing, he fell to his knees. For a few moments only his head and shoulders showed above the circling pigs. Then he thrust his wounded hand in the air. By moonlight, the blood running into his cuff looked black. Nellie dropped his fingers, and the pigs shoved and snarled over them.

He staggered to his feet, breathing in gasps. May Rose sprinted toward the trail with Nellie galloping by her side and hooves of the pigs rumbling behind them. Near the dark wall of trees, Nellie whirled and circled toward the cabin, and May Rose followed her toward light, a stout door and an ax under the bed, all better known than a dim trail.

Nellie scraped her belly up the stone step and trotted through the open door. Once inside, May Rose pushed the door against the pigs, but Russell slammed into it and knocked her backward into the table. The lamp tottered. She steadied it with both hands, then picked it up and backed to the bed as Russell kicked the pigs out and closed the door with the flat of his boot.

Slobbering into his beard, he pulled the knife from its sheath and held out his mutilated hand, all bone, blood, and ragged red flesh. "Forget what you're thinking to do with that lamp. You fix this here or I'll slit the sow's throat." He dragged a chair against the door and dropped onto it.

She held tight to the lamp. Russell had the knife in his left hand. If she tossed the lamp against the wall and let oil and fire spread over the bed, would he fight the fire or kill them first? Nellie sat beside her, mouth open, her little eyes on Russell.

Tears streamed into his beard but his voice was hard. "Pour that likker into something."

She gripped the lamp and considered his dripping fingers. Except for his bulk against the door, she had the advantage. Maybe he'd faint. She brought a bowl and filled it from the jug. He set the bowl on his lap and slid the knife part way underneath, then plunged the stubs of his fingers into the liquor. He groaned. The liquor in the bowl turned red.

After minutes of soaking, he lifted whitened stubs. "Wrap these up." Nellie had chomped off three fingers past the big knuckles, plus the tip of his little finger.

Because he sat against the door, because he had the knife,

maybe because his eyes showed suffering, May Rose wound his fingers with strips of a clean kitchen rag. His hand quivered, and hers trembled at the ugliness of the wound and the effort of being close, smelling and touching him. He had tobacco stains and grit in his beard.

"You should see the doctor."

He spat on the floor. "I'll get by—tomorry I'll be butchering that sow."

"Turn her out—unless you care to give her another taste."

He stood and motioned with the knife. "Do it, then."

Ready to run, she prodded Nellie to the door, but Russell shoved between them and shouldered the door shut as soon as Nellie ran out. Blood dripped through the rags on his fingers. Even in dim light, his face looked pale. He fell into the chair. "Pull that table back over here." His voice shook.

She might have escaped him in the woods after all. He might have fainted after three steps. She braced a hand on the table. "I won't. I'll stay here and watch you bleed to death. You can chase me in a circle till you drop. *Or.* I'll help you if you help me. My wedding money bought this place—pay me for it."

His lip trembled. "You're a whore. Been paid enough."

"Then I'll sit over here and watch you die."

Russell filled his cheeks with air and puffed through his mouth. His eyes closed in pain. "All right. You kin have the place."

"I don't want it. I'll take half of what you paid Jamie."

"Woman, I got nothing. I paid him fair. When he left, he stole my stash."

Jamie had stolen Russell's money? She liked that. She shoved the table across the floor until his feet were under it. He laid out his injured hand, gripped the wrist, spoke through clenched teeth. "Fix these up again."

He took swigs from Jamie's jug while she brought more rags and packed the stubs in flour to staunch the bleeding.

"Bring the pie."

She set a pie and fork close to him. The bread dough had risen to the top of the bowl. She punched it down and put it in pans to rise. Russell's head lay on the table between his outstretched arms, the pie untouched, the new bandage dark with blood. His breath was hoarse and deep, and he didn't stir when she slid the ax from under the bed.

Imagining a blow to his head, a slice into his neck, she raised the ax overhead, then gagged and sat down. In the heat of struggle, she'd have done it without thought. With this advantage, she could not. Better to let him think she'd given in. She slid the ax under the bed and curled in a ball. The window was too small to crawl through, but he couldn't guard the door forever.

She woke with a scrape to her neck and Russell standing over her. A strip of light showed through the space in the window curtain, and the smell of baking bread filled the room. She didn't remember putting the pans in the oven. With a jerk, a coil of coarse rope closed around her neck. She seized the rope and tried to slip her fingers under it but it tightened like a snare.

"Get up."

When her feet hit the floor, she dropped to her knees and swept her arms under the bed for the ax. A tug on the rope pulled her upright. She grabbed the rope with both hands to ease the pressure on her neck and stumbled after him into a dawn stilled and silvered by frost. He dragged her toward the outhouse.

The door wouldn't open. Russell rattled the handle and looked at May Rose like it was her fault. "What's wrong with this here?"

She shivered and stamped her feet. "The closer's fallen down inside. Put something in the door crack and lift it."

He dragged her around the yard and found a stick. "Jiggle it loose, then."

She pried the stick through the crack and lifted the bar, but it fell back. Prying upward again, she felt a downward pressure on the stick, someone on the other side. She flashed a look to Russell. *Jamie?*

He pounded on the door. "Open up or I'll burn you out!"

The door sprang open and a girl flashed by, brown ragged hair, brown dress. Russell looked surprised. "You! What the hell."

The girl raced barefoot toward the railroad track.

Mumbling curses, Russell stepped into the outhouse, yanking May Rose to her knees. He snarled, "You stay out here." He closed the door over the rope.

What did he think, she wanted to go with him? She stretched to the end of her tether, eyes on the girl, who sneaked back and sawed at the rope with a rock.

May Rose whispered, "There's a cleaver and a knife on the ground near the porch."

The girl disappeared around the front of the cabin.

He stayed in the outhouse for several minutes. When he came out, May Rose whined, "I have to go, too."

The rope under the door allowed just enough room to sit down inside. She held her breath against the odor he'd left and sat longer than necessary to give the girl time. When she opened the outhouse door he pulled her toward the cabin. She trotted after, holding the rope to ease its pull on her neck, watching her steps. In the white grass, smaller footprints mingled with her own.

He pushed her ahead to open the door. As she crossed the threshold she saw the girl standing on a chair by the wall, an iron skillet lifted above her head. At the same time the boiler of a Shay engine released shrill bursts of steam. Russell looked toward the track, and the girl smashed the skillet onto his skull. His eyes rolled back, then closed, and he crumpled in the doorway.

The girl jumped down. "Help me turn him over." When they had him on his back, the girl took his knife from its sheath, sawed the rope and loosened the noose to free May Rose. "Let's get."

Somewhere down the track, the Shay screamed again. Blood seeped through Russell's hair and dripped onto the threshold.

"Have you killed him?"

The girl shrugged her thin shoulders. "He's too dumb to die."

A cloud of black smoke drifted up through treetops. May Rose grabbed one of Russell's thick arms. "He'll be seen. Help me pull him inside."

They dragged him over a smear of his blood, pulled his feet out of the way, and closed the door just as the engine came into view.

The girl licked her lips. "Bread's baking, and I'm hungry."

May Rose stepped over Russell, leaned against the door, and squinted at the girl she'd rescued on the trail. "Who are you?"

The girl smiled. "Let's tie him to the bed and eat."

They heaved him into the bed, and the girl tied his ankle to a post with a snare knot. May Rose washed blood from his hair and probed the gash in his scalp with the kind of care she'd give a caged snake.

"Why you bothering with that?"

"I don't know. He's bleeding on my bed." It only seemed the next thing to do.

Each step May Rose took, to find more rags, to throw out bloody water, to fetch more water from the spring, the girl was in her way. A thin figure with thick wild hair, a sapling with a crown of dead leaves.

Russell woke when she changed the bandage on his hand and moaned as she cleaned the fingers. His hand was swollen. She wrapped his arm and hand around a cloth-covered piece of board. He passed out, or slept. She hoped he'd die.

The girl flitted around the cabin, touching things, jumpy. "How'd he lose them fingers?" She jabbed the air with Russell's knife, ran her thumb along the sharp edge to the nick near the handle.

"He kicked my pet sow."

The girl giggled. "He should know better, him a pig-man."

"You know him?"

They stood side by side and looked at Russell, who lay with closed eyes. His breathing sounded regular. His bulk filled the bed.

The girl took the sheath from his belt. "Know him to see him.

He's my uncle. Hates me and Ma, though. Might be he hates everybody. Can we eat that bread now?"

"Uncle?" May Rose opened the oven door and tapped the browned bread. Done. Russell must have put it to bake while she slept. The girl sat at the table, her dirty fingers picking up crumbs left from Russell's pie. Under the grime, she had nice features—a tip-tilted nose, large brown eyes, thick lashes.

May Rose slid the bread pans from the oven. "You're related to Russell, and to Jamie Long?"

The girl nodded, brown eyes fixed on the bread.

Jamie had said little about family, only that he and Russell had grown up helping their father clear their land, ringing trees, stripping hemlock bark to sell to a tannery downriver, later shaping ties for the railroad. From the look of her, the girl's parents were no more civilized than Russell.

"The bread will cut better when it's cool. How about pie for now?" She took the other pie from the shelf above the oven, cut a fourth, and gave her a fork. "My name is May Rose. I'd like to know yours."

"I know your name. Mine's Wanda. Jamie's my pa."

May Rose's breath slowed until her chest felt heavy as stone. She could not deny the girl's resemblance. Jamie had a daughter, perhaps an entire family, abandoned, never mentioned. Blind trust had made May Rose his fool, but from the look of this girl, others had suffered more.

Russell snored. Wanda chewed, her foot jiggling against the floor. Jamie's daughter. May Rose lifted his jug, swished a mouthful of liquid fire, and spat into the woodbox. She bent over the box and waited for her stomach to settle or turn inside out. It settled.

Wanda watched, wary as a wild thing. "This here's good pie." Her eyes and long lashes were the light brown of her hair, like Jamie's. "We ain't seen him for quite a while, not since he brung you here." She had a lopsided grin, like his. "There's talk of him since yesterday. You, too."

He'd not put her name on his work papers, had kept her on the mountainside, perhaps for good reason. But his daughter looked like she'd had neither mother nor father for a long time.

"Jamie's...run off."

The girl lifted her plate. "He does that. You got more?"

May Rose set another quarter slice on the table and glanced toward Russell. Maybe she was what he'd said, Jamie's whore. At the moment she did not care. She sawed into the warm bread with a table knife, crushing it.

"I seen you lots of times," Wanda said. "Never saw you show yourself naked, like they say."

"You've been here?"

"Sometimes I hop the train, go all the way up to number six. When there's nobody to see, the cook gives me stuff to eat. He likes me to sit on his lap." Wanda looked up like she'd been corrected. "I don't let him do nothing."

"Wanda. Do you have a mother?"

She nodded.

"Does she know you're here? Does she know about the cook, or those boys?"

Wanda talked around the pie in her mouth. "I wouldn't like to worry her. Besides, she's busy where she stays now, at Suzie's."

"Suzie's?"

"You know, the whoring place."

Russell laughed. May Rose turned her back and pressed her fingers to her breastbone.

Wanda danced around the room, striking Russell's knife against objects, playing a tune. *Jamie's daughter.* Once upon a time, Jamie had walked and talked with elegance. Been joyful, loving.

Russell grunted to a sitting position and put his legs over the edge of the bed. He braced his wounded hand against the good one. "Cut me loose or I'll drag this cot over there and do it myself."

Her advantage over Russell would not last. "Do what you like. I'm leaving."

"I'll just go along with you," Wanda said.

May Rose shook her head.

Wanda stilled. "I'll be good. I can help. I helped already, didn't I?"

"You did. Do you have brothers and sisters?"

"No. Do you?"

"Cousins, I'm not sure where."

"Girl, cut me loose," Russell said, his growl weak. "I gotta go home and tend my stock." He fell back on the mattress.

While Wanda gathered eggs and turned out the chickens, May Rose sewed together the ripped edges of the blue dress. When she came back, Wanda went around the room, saying, "Can I have this? And this?" She put spoons into a bucket, a string of dried apples and one of fodder beans, bread, eggs, a tin of sugar, the cleaver, a jar of lard, and Russell's knife. Russell lay still as death.

May Rose poured water in a basin, and screening Wanda with her own body, pulled off the girl's filthy shift and instructed her to wash.

Wanda whined. "Why we doing this?"

May Rose didn't know, except that attending to Wanda took her mind off everything else. "When we look good, folks think better of us." *But none who thought she was a whore, and Wanda a whore's daughter. Was that what the doctor thought?*

She tossed a loaf of warm bread onto Russell's chest. He opened his eyes.

"If I think of it," she said, "I'll ask the doctor to stop and see about you. There's a piss pot under the bed. Sorry, I forgot to empty it."

She left with her old carpetbag stuffed with clothing. Wanda carried her bucket of plunder and wore the blue dress bunched up at the waist and tied with a rope from which she'd hung spoons and a spatula. By the hog pen, May Rose pulled a brush from her bag and worked it through Wanda's tangled hair.

Wanda whined and bobbed, jangling the utensils on the rope, noisy as a gypsy wagon.

CHAPTER 8

Behold, I will do a new thing; now it shall spring forth; shall ye not know it?

I will even make a way in the wilderness...

— ISAIAH 43:19

Wanda leaped down the forest trail, nimble and noisy as a colt in a harness of bells. Nellie and the pigs raced around her, snapping and whuffing. May Rose came last, run-walking, unbalanced in shoes. She stopped and worked them off. Nellie came back and trotted near while Wanda and the pigs, who never stumbled, ran on. When they reached the valley, the pigs ambled over the footbridge. Wanda scooted close to May Rose. "How far we going?"

"Not far, today. Soon, I'm going a long way." She put on her shoes. She wanted to stay in motion, continue the delicious sensation of leaving, leap ahead to a time of forgetting. But her body needed rest, and she needed money and a sure destination.

The pigs followed through the lumber yard, where men whistled and called "soo-ey." Wanda laughed but May Rose stared ahead. "Do you live in town?"

"Mostly."

"Mostly? You and your mother have a house?"

"I said already, she stays at Suzie's."

"But what about you? Where do you stay?"

Wanda skipped ahead, turned and walked backwards. "Nowhere special. I sleep out." She swung her bucket. "I like it. Sometimes. We ain't been here long, just since our house burned." She seemed to blame nobody, but May Rose's steps faltered.

At the tracks, Wanda turned around and walked so their arms touched.

"Wanda, I never knew about you. What about Jamie? Did he know you had nowhere special to stay?"

"Maybe. Where we taking these pigs?"

"I need to sell them." She took Wanda's hand. It was hot and hardened, with ragged, dirty nails. "Maybe you can help me."

"Slaughterhouse."

"These pigs are young for slaughter. Who might buy them to fatten?"

"Miss Hester has a pig pen. Nothing in it but weeds."

"Who is Miss Hester?"

"The lady at the boardinghouse. You can stay there, and I'll stay with you. Times is getting cold."

Cold times were indeed ahead, but rest was costly. She could imagine herself getting used to Winkler, staying because it was familiar, no matter how far from what she wanted.

The boardinghouse had a wide porch with tall-backed rocking chairs and a yard enclosed by a fence of iron pickets. When she opened the gate, the pigs crowded through and raced toward the back lot. Wanda started to chase after them, but May Rose took her hand. At the rear door, she smiled at a short, round woman and asked for the proprietor.

Hester Townsend came to the steps, a tiny person with a large bosom, brown hair in a bun, almost no chin, and pop-eyes. She frowned at Wanda, but her eyes brightened at Nellie and the pigs, now rooting in an overgrown garden. "Are you selling these?"

"I am. And I need a room. For two, maybe only one night, a few nights at most." Wanda pressed to her side.

Hester looked at Wanda's dusty feet. "I know this one, a little hellion, comes and goes at Suzie's and who-knows where else."

"She's with me now," May Rose said. Beside her, Wanda was still as a post.

"I have a room for you," Hester said. "Just you."

May Rose held Wanda's hand. "My name is May Rose Long, and this is Wanda. Make me an offer for the pigs. If you cannot accommodate both of us, we'll find another place to stay."

"Long?" With her head thrust forward, Hester had the look of a sharp-eyed bird. "You're the girl on the mountain."

May Rose blinked. Wanda squeezed her hand.

"You had a visitor," Hester said. "Dr. Hennig stopped early this morning, seemed to think you were here."

She'd forgotten his suggestion as easily as she'd dismissed it. To give herself a moment to think, she looked at Wanda, who shrugged and looked perplexed.

"I don't know why," May Rose said.

Hester switched her attention to the pigs. "Did you close the gate?"

"I did."

"How many pigs?"

"Eight. It's the sow's first litter, and she's very tame. After they get used to this place, you can turn them into the woods to fatten."

"Folks don't like pigs running about town," Hester said. "Let's see if there's room in the hog lot." She marched off through straggly grass toward sheds at the back fence.

Weeds had gone to seed in the hog lot. Wanda called, "sooey," and when Nellie lifted her head, May Rose waved her on. Hester tugged the gate open and Nellie trotted into the weeds and began to snap them off. The pigs came running.

Hester counted as they ran through the gate.

Wanda pulled open the door to the shed and peered inside.

"Spidery in there, but it's roomy. Got a place to pour slop and such."

"Twenty dollars and fifty cents," Hester said.

"Very well." May Rose turned so she did not have to see Nellie.

"Wait here, please."

Hester came back from the house and counted a silver half dollar and two ten-dollar greenbacks into May Rose's hand. May Rose frowned. Her uncle had never trusted paper money.

"It's legal tender," Hester said. "United States notes, you see? Not bank notes, I never take them myself. I can also pay in company scrip you can use at the store."

"No. This will be fine." May Rose wrapped a kerchief around the greenbacks and pushed them deep into her pocket. Then she handed the silver coin to Wanda. "For a rainy day."

Wanda's mouth gaped.

May Rose did not look back. "Let's go."

Wanda swung her bucket. "Where now?"

"To the store, and then to the depot to see about a passenger train."

Beside her, Wanda unclenched her fist and looked at the silver coin. "You leaving now?"

"I have something to do tomorrow, and I'd like a night's sleep before the trip. Then I'll go to Stillwater, Ohio, where I used to live." Where no one knew Jamie.

"Is your ma and pa there?"

"She died a long time ago, and he left."

Wanda nodded like she knew this story. "Here's the hotel."

Woodman's Retreat sat in the middle of a wide lawn between the boardinghouse and Pizzy's Bar. As they climbed the steps, a man pushed himself up from a deep wooden armchair. "Something I can do for you ladies?"

May Rose slid her hand into her pocket and touched the wrapped greenbacks. "How much for a room for two?"

He shook his head. "We don't take women. We got bachelors

living here permanent and wood hicks on the weekend—they stay in our dormitories, big rooms with lots of beds."

"You have no rooms for travelers?"

"Men travelers. This place wasn't built with ladies in mind."

"I'll come back when I know how long I'll need to stay." She put her arm through Wanda's and turned her toward the steps.

"You can't stay here," he said.

"We'll be back."

When they reached the bar building, Wanda pulled her arm away. "That was real good. But you're passing me the shakes." She pointed to May Rose's trembling hand.

"I was awake most of the night, and I didn't sleep much the night before. I'm about to fall asleep on the street."

"Wood hicks do that. I've slept in a boxcar, and one time in a caboose. It was nice, but the second time they rooted me out."

"Where else can we rent a room?"

"Not in a company house, I bet'cha. People ain't too friendly to me, and most of their houses is crowded with kids and grandmas. We can ask at Italian Town, upriver. Have you been there?"

"No. Do the Italians speak our language?"

"Kids do."

"Let's go to the store and depot first."

At the company store, Mr. Ramey's eyes opened with interest as he looked from her to Wanda. "There's no mail for you."

She stared at the pigeonholes on the wall behind him. "My family thinks I'm at Jennie Town. Could letters be waiting there?"

"Doubtful. There's been no post office at Jennie Town for a year or more."

"No post office? Is the town gone too?"

He sighed in a bored way. "Just about."

She held her hand over her pocket. "What happens to mail sent there?"

"Returned to sender, I guess, or put in a dead letter box somewhere."

She imagined her letters to Fargo in a dead-letter box.

At the depot she learned the next passenger train would leave on Tuesday. "Four nights," she said to Wanda. "I need a place to sleep for four nights."

They found Preacher Gowder at the church. He confirmed Wanda's belief that none of the company houses had an extra room to rent.

He pointed downriver. "The only place for you is Hester's boardinghouse."

When they left him, Wanda pointed upriver. "Italian Town."

Where the main street ended, they crossed the river on the footbridge to Italian Town and walked along a lane of one-story cottages with flower boxes and benches against the outside walls. The air was rich with the odor of fermenting fruit.

Wanda stopped at a cottage with an open door. "This is their store. We can ask here."

Two women came out with brown paper packages, speaking rapidly together in a tongue no more sensible to May Rose than the chatter of birds. The women smiled and bobbed their heads, and she did the same, trying not to stare at their dark eyes and heavy eyebrows, their head scarves and gathered skirts.

Inside, sausage links and strings of dried peppers hung from the ceiling, and soup simmered on a stovetop. Behind the counter, a black-haired girl bounced an infant on her lap, and a man cut thick slices of ham.

The man extended his arm with a flourish and gestured from one side of the small room to the other. "Welcome, welcome. Everything fresh, everything good. We got baked ham and fresh ham today, we got pickles, salami, olives in a jar, pasta, spices, semolina, corn meal. Ask what you need."

"We need a place to stay," Wanda said. "Four nights, her and me."

"Ah, my wife washes for Hester's boardinghouse. There you stay."

The girl set the infant on the counter. "Hi, Wanda. This is my sister."

Wanda held out a finger and the infant pulled it toward her mouth.

May Rose shifted her carpetbag to the other hand. "Is there no one here with an extra room?"

The store man looked thoughtful. "Doctor has-a house, only thing empty here."

"Does he let it out?"

"He keeps a lady there," the girl said. "No one now."

The man stopped slicing. "Go the boardinghouse. Nice for you there."

"I'll ask Dr. Hennig," May Rose said, after they left the store.

Wanda chewed on a dried apple from her bucket. "I'll be all right—you go on to Hester's."

"It would be nice to stay in Italian Town, don't you think?"

"Anywhere suits me."

"Then take me to the doctor. We'll tell him about Russell and ask about the house."

As they crossed the footbridge, Wanda pointed uphill to a house on a knoll with its own lane. "That's his place."

May Rose had hoped never to see him again.

Shouts from the hillside above stopped them in the street. Wanda perked up. "Something happening, let's go see."

"Wait."

Wanda ran uphill, her bucket jangling. May Rose hurried after her toward a commotion of running feet, galloping hooves, and shouts of women and children. She caught up with her at the highest street, where Nellie and eight pigs raced through back yards chased by Hester Townsend and the round woman from the boardinghouse.

"Loose already," Wanda said.

When they ran to head them off, Nellie stopped and trotted to May Rose, and the rest of the pigs veered from their course and circled back.

With Wanda dangling her string of dried apples and May Rose

talking to Nellie, they lured the pigs back to their pen. May Rose pointed to holes under the board fence.

"I should have known better," Hester said. "I'll have to put rings in their noses to keep them from digging out."

"Fill in them holes with rocks and give them lots to eat," Wanda said. "Then they won't want to go no place."

Hester nodded to May Rose. "I owe you a reward. A free night's lodging."

She felt close to collapse. "I need a room for two until Tuesday. Nothing has to be free."

Wanda's eyes sparkled. "I'll close up them holes. And I know where acorns is. Gimme a sack and I'll haul 'em in."

May Rose touched Wanda's shoulder. "She's a helpful girl."

Hester leaned back and gave Wanda the same look she'd had when appraising the pigs. "Looks like you've cleaned her up, so we'll see how she behaves. Four nights with board. You, Miss, will not be seen nor heard."

May Rose sat on the back step, half-asleep, her arms and legs heavy as tree trunks, while Wanda ran back and forth from the hillside to the pig pen, carrying rocks and plugging holes.

The boardinghouse smelled of roasting meat and furniture wax. At Hester's prompting, she left her carpetbag in the kitchen and made Wanda set her bucket beside it. A toilet flushed somewhere near the long center hall, and a man in a suit emerged from a door under the stairs.

Wanda tugged her sleeve. "This is grander than Suzie's!"

May Rose wondered if Jamie had ever stayed here or at the hotel and if he knew the place Wanda's mother worked.

Hester's heels clicked on varnished boards as she led them through the hall. "A reservoir on the hillside feeds water to the kitchen pump, commode, and tub room. Baths cost extra. I've two women who wash the bedclothes on Mondays and guests' laundry on Thursdays. You can do your own laundry or pay for it if you stay that long." She paused under an arch near the front entry. "This is the parlor."

The room had lace curtains, woven rugs on shining floors, chairs with tapestry backs and seats. An upright piano stood against the front wall, and in the center of the room there was a mahogany table with books and a newspaper. May Rose could not take her eyes from it.

"The paper comes a day late," Hester said.

Wanda rushed to the piano and lifted the lid over the keys. Hester pulled her hands away, closed the lid, and turned her by the shoulders.

"Hello."

May Rose startled at the deep, cautious voice. A man stood under the arch, tall, slightly bent, with arms that looked no more substantial than branches of a willow tree. His rumpled suit seemed too large, and his collar was loose on his long neck.

Wanda wrested herself from Hester's grip. "Good morning, teacher."

His lips stretched nearly the width of his face. "Good *afternoon*, Wanda."

"Mr. Cooper, Mrs. Long," Hester said. "Mr. Cooper stays with us during the school year."

"Mrs. Long." He shook her hand. His was unsteady. "Wanda, it would be good to see you in school again." Wanda shifted from one bare foot to the other. He inclined slightly to Hester. "Will we have singing this evening?"

"Not tonight. Sunday evening, Preacher Gowder and Miss Ruie will join us."

"I like singing," Wanda said.

Mr. Cooper looked at Wanda like she was as important as anybody. "Then we hope to see you Sunday night."

Wanda's mouth twisted in her lopsided smile.

Hester frowned. "Mrs. Long may attend." She directed them into the hall, where Wanda stooped to watch the pendulum of a grandfather clock. "My brother and I have rooms down here. Barlow Townsend, I suppose you know of him? General Manager of Winkler Logging and Lumber Company? I run the boardinghouse, but Barlow built it. He has great responsibility, and he's particular. I try to keep his home quiet and comfortable."

Wanda ran her fingers along the wood paneling. Hester clicked her tongue. "Our boarders also appreciate a quiet atmosphere, so the girl must not to roam about the house, or sit in the parlor. She'll take her meals in the kitchen and use the back stairs."

May Rose nodded. "Then I will too."

As they followed Hester up the staircase, a flourish of piano music rose from the parlor, then a man's voice. *"O promise me that someday you and I..."* Wanda bolted down the stairs, spoons and spatulas jingling.

May Rose reached her at the archway and turned her toward the stairs. Hester shook her head.

When they were finally alone, Wanda said, "Ain't Mr. Cooper funny-looking, and don't he sing beautiful?"

May Rose sat on the bed and emptied her bundle. Mr. Cooper did seem strangely put together, but she didn't like to ridicule, even silently. "Your teacher likes you, I think. And he does sing beautifully."

Wanda danced from door to window, waving her arms and swinging her skirt. "He ain't my teacher—he teaches the big kids. But he's nice to everybody. I never knew he sung so good."

As May Rose had feared, the room lured her with comfort and a sense of security, threatening her resolve. The iron bed had a stitched crazy quilt over a mattress on coiled springs. A single window with a curtain and window shade gave a view of the back yard, where the pigs now appeared to be testing the board fence for weakness. There was a skeleton key in the door, and a hook-and-eye lock. She laid the dolls on a pillow.

Wanda sat on the bed and bounced the springs. "It's awful high. What if I fall out?" She grabbed the largest doll. Its dress had tiny blue ruffles in the same material as the dress now worn by Wanda, and eyes embroidered with thread pulled from scraps of blue cotton. Wanda ran her hands over the doll's bald head. "Where's her hair?"

"I need to buy yarn for it."

"Get brown." Wanda set the doll aside. "Like mine."

She'd planned yellow, for her fair-haired cousins. She untied the rope at Wanda's waist and dropped the implements into the bucket. "We need to talk a bit about what comes next. What do you want to do with these things?"

Wanda hugged the doll. "Keep 'em. There's more things up at your place I'd like to get. Them rabbit-fur boots hanging under the eaves, be nice for snow. Wisht I'd brung 'em. I'll go now, won't take long."

"Not now."

Wanda laid the doll beside the others. "I believe I'll just run up there."

May Rose pulled her back. "Wanda, if you want to sleep in this nice place for a few days, and eat food like we smell right now, you must mind Miss Hester and me. And you have to keep clean, and wear underwear and shoes."

"I got none of them things."

May Rose sorted through her older and newer set of undergarments, black dress, long apron, her jaws clenched in disgust for the father and mother who'd abandoned this child.

"We'll make do. Starting tomorrow, we'll gather nuts every day to keep the pigs satisfied, and maybe Hester will pay you to do that after I leave. If they make new holes, fill them in. The pigs will need water, soon, and you better find the doctor and tell him about Russell."

"You said a heap of things. Which you want first?"

"Water the pigs, then tell the doctor about Russell." May Rose retied the rope belt and bunched the dress over it so Wanda would not trip. "Tomorrow, I'll alter this dress to fit you better, and we'll give it a wash."

"When can I go for them boots?"

"When we've given Russell time to go home. When it's safe."

Wanda laughed. "A feller can't never wait for that. Every critter's got something waiting to get it. Big things eat the little ones, even big trees choke out the shoots. And guess what? Them trees ain't safe neither—wood hicks cut 'em down." She smoothed the dress and threw open the door. "I'll be good to this here dress—it's the best I ever wore."

May Rose put a finger to her lips. "Remember, back stairs, quietly."

The door slammed shut. May Rose sighed. Her cousins had been such docile little girls. Like herself.

CHAPTER 9

Friend clasped friend in his arms, and they who before were as strangers,
Meeting in exile, became straightway as friends to each other.

— HENRY WADSWORTH LONGFELLOW:
EVANGELINE

Drowsing in and out of sleep, aware of the muffled vibrations in a house of strangers, May Rose did not at first distinguish the knocking at her door. It was still light. Wanda had not returned, but the business-like raps did not sound like her. She opened the door wide enough to see Hester's pinched lips.

"Mrs. Long, Dr. Hennig is here to see you." Her tone disapproved.

May Rose leaned her forehead against the door. "I sent word that my brother-in-law needed medical attention."

"It's your business, but just so you know, Dr. Hennig has a wife."

Heat flowed to her scalp. "He's the only doctor."

"I can tell him you're indisposed."

"You're very kind, but I should hear what he has to say."

When Hester left, May Rose smoothed the quilt over the bed

and changed to her black dress. Her hands shook, working little buttons into loops up the back. Food would help, and a full night's sleep, and knowing Wanda was not somewhere at the mercy of those boys. The high-necked dress suited her mood.

She hesitated downstairs under the parlor arch. In the parlor, Dr. Hennig paced back and forth, looking like everything was wrong and he was too weary to fix anything. The front of his dark suit coat had a blotch of rusty brown, maybe blood. In a blur of compassion she saw him as one who knew too much of suffering.

He hurried toward her. "I worried, yesterday, when I came and you weren't here."

As recently as two days ago, the thought of anyone worrying about her would have lifted her spirits. Two days ago, when she'd only been lonely. Before Jamie left her to Bright and Russell, before she knew Jamie had a daughter and another woman she could not bear to think about.

"Please don't worry. Did you get word that my husband's brother needs doctoring?"

"The girl said his injury wasn't urgent. I'll check on him in the morning."

She smiled. If he hadn't already cut himself loose, Russell would have a bad night. He might give gossips a new story, but by then, she'd be where no one had ever heard of this place.

"When you see him...he treated us badly...you'll see, his fingers..." She turned her palm over and studied it. "I didn't do that. I tried to stop the bleeding."

If Dr. Hennig heard, he didn't show that he cared what she had or hadn't done. He narrowed the space between them, putting her in shadow. Wiry hair outlined his chin, his cheekbones, and the ridges of his brow. She wanted to step back, but straightened her back and held her place.

"The men looking for Jamie have been called back to work," he said. "The company will expend no more man hours for the search."

His tone felt intimate.

She made hers hard. "So, Jamie is safe?"

"Our police sent notices statewide, offering a reward, but some think he's not gone far. They believe he'll come back for you."

She shrugged. Discovering the true, deceiving Jamie Long had not erased all feeling for the false, loving one. She wanted him to return so she could accuse him and hear him lie. Then she'd be done.

Dr. Hennig said, "I hope you won't go. I hope you'll stay here in Winkler."

"My plans are uncertain." She liked the power of these words, as though she might stay or go on a whim.

A woman's heels clicked and Hester entered from the hall. The room had filled with waning afternoon light, but Hester lifted a pink-flowered globe and struck a match to the wick. Neither May Rose nor the doctor spoke while Hester tugged on the window curtains, pushed a glass-footed stool close to the piano, and stacked sheet music on top. Chaperoning or eavesdropping, May Rose didn't care.

Dr. Hennig twisted his hat in his long fingers. "I'll let you know about your brother-in-law."

"His name is Russell Long. Thank you for seeing him, but please, there's no need to tell me anything further. I don't want to hear of him again."

Hester opened sliding doors at the rear of the parlor, revealing a dining room and the round woman setting plates on a linen-covered table.

"Tomorrow night," the doctor said, "the wood hicks will blow in and take over this part of town. You should stay inside. I hope their carrying on won't disturb your sleep." He lowered his voice. "I'd like to see you again."

Hester hovered nearby, perhaps supervising the table setting. May Rose imitated her hard smile. "Naturally, if we need a doctor, we'll send for you."

He backed toward the door, smiling as though she'd promised something entirely different, then wavered as the door burst open, barely missing him. Caught in its draft, he collided with Wanda. The door slammed against the wall.

Laughing, Wanda untangled herself from the doctor and ran up the stairs she wasn't supposed to use.

SATURDAY MORNING after they fed the pigs, Wanda ran off with no explanation, perhaps to the place where her mother worked. May Rose cautioned herself against worrying too much about her. Jamie should have done that. Her mother should do that.

Wanda had not returned by noon, when the saws stopped and May Rose left the house to stand in the cold line at the paymaster's window. Mill workers shifted flat-footed behind her, older than the wood hicks, smoking pipes and mumbling greetings, only one other woman among them. A roof overhanging the paymaster's window trapped odors of tobacco and sweat.

When she gave her name, the paymaster spoke with another man in the office before coming back to the window. "You say you're Mrs. Long, but I guess I need some proof to hand over a man's wages. His papers don't show a next-of-kin."

She gripped the window ledge. She'd been Jamie's wife for two years—her name was written on the *Holy Matrimony* page of the Jonson family Bible. "The store manager knows who I am," she said.

The paymaster flicked his fingers, her signal to move away.

"Mr. Ramey," she said. "The store manager."

"I know who Mr. Ramey is. I'll need some proof of who you are."

"I'll be back," she hissed, angry to be denied and ashamed that three dollars meant so much. She touched her pocket to make sure its treasure was secure.

She waited impatiently to cross to the store. In Winkler, everyone walked or rode the train, but today there were wagons and a few riders on horseback.

A wagon passed with a father, mother, and an old woman on the seat, and four little ones in the wagon bed who leaned out and stared at town children. She understood their wide eyes. Winkler was as uniform as a crazy quilt, everyone recently arrived, with different, specialized jobs. Even their talk sounded different. She smiled at the women in the wagon. Their faces looked surprised, then grateful. She felt better.

"Mr. Ramey," she said in the store. "Please write a note to the company paymaster that I am Jamie Long's wife."

He shook his head. "Ma'am, I don't know Jamie Long's business."

"We were married in St. Louis."

"Then give the paymaster that paper."

She didn't know what Jamie had done with it.

Mr. Ramey looked toward a disturbance in the store, a game of tag around burlap sacks of flour and corn meal. "Hey, you kids!"

They ran from the store, Wanda in the lead. May Rose hurried out but stopped on the steps. On the boardwalk below, Wanda faced two boys. *Those* boys. She held a knife in thrusting position, Russell's broad-bladed hunting knife.

"No!" May Rose ran down the steps.

Wanda looked startled. The boys jumped into the street and ran a few steps, then slowed to a jaunty walk, jabbing each other, looking back and leering.

Wanda evaded May Rose and pointed the knife toward a row of younger boys hunched at the store wall. "This is mine." They grinned, except for a dark-haired boy who soberly pushed a wad of tobacco into his jaw.

"Let's go home," May Rose said.

Wanda sheathed the knife in the folds of her skirt.

They walked unevenly together, her heels rapping the board-walk, Wanda's bare feet padding half a step behind.

"You can't carry the knife," May Rose said. "Those boys could snatch it away, and then what?"

Wanda looked grim. "You bet'cha they'll stay away from me now."

"Maybe the next time you see them they'll have knives too."

"More's the reason," Wanda said.

"You should go nowhere alone."

Wanda shrugged.

At her corner of the scarred kitchen worktable, Wanda bolted down a second helping of potatoes and warm bread pudding while May Rose watched and wondered. Wanda needed a place to live and work, but who would hire an untrained girl who insisted on doing everything her own way?

The round cook, Dessie, lifted May Rose's plate. "You done?"

"Yes, thank you. It was wonderful."

Dessie grunted. She handled their plates roughly and spoke only in short replies. Her round face made her dark eyes seem small and close-set, and her mouth seldom smiled or opened wide enough to show if she had teeth or not.

May Rose felt guilty sitting idle while Dessie rushed back and forth through the swinging door, refilling serving bowls and dropping empty pots into the tin sink. Clearly, Dessie needed a helper, and here was Wanda, who in two days would need a way to provide for herself.

Wanda's fork clattered on the plate. "Hear the wood hicks hollering out there? By and by Suzie's will get busy, and the bar and pool room, and young fellers from the mill and the tannery will come this way to play cards and they'll all get into it, you bet'cha. Midnight, they'll be out in the street, bruising and busting up their pretty faces. I seen it lots of times."

"Dessie," May Rose said, "if we heat and carry our water, may we have a bath tonight?"

Dessie leaned over the sink, scrubbing a pot. "Water for dishes comes first. After I've got the kitchen cleaned up, you can do what suits you."

"We'll help," May Rose said.

Dessie's voice echoed from deep in the pot. "No, you won't."

"I'm just gonna go out for a while," Wanda said.

May Rose reached across the table and touched her hand. "We have to stay in. We'll have baths, and tomorrow we'll go to church."

Wanda whined.

"There'll be singing."

Wanda shifted her eyes but looked interested.

It was hard to know whether to leave their dishes for Dessie to clean up, or to stack their plates near her wash water.

"We'll get out of your way," May Rose said.

Dessie nodded. "Good."

Later that evening, May Rose went downstairs for her bath, leaving Wanda asleep, wet hair spread over her pillow and a doll in the crook of her arm. The tub room adjoined the kitchen, a spacious room with a bathtub, a wooden ringer-washer, rinse tubs, ironing board, and shelves of folded sheets and tablecloths. She'd begun heating water for their baths as soon as Dessie left the kitchen. Now she emptied the pots into the bathtub, added cold water from the pump, and returned the pots to their hooks.

She bathed quickly, conscious of occasional gunfire and shouts of wood hicks, feeling like someone might break in at any time. When she returned to the kitchen, Hester sat at the worktable, her hands wrapped around a cup.

"I've been hearing gunshots," May Rose said.

"Wood hicks shooting rats over to the dump," Hester said. "Better than aiming at each other. It's getting close to electric shut-down time. I don't know if you were awake for it last night, but the electric goes off at ten-fifteen. The mill whistle blows a little before, gives us time to light the lamps. There's matches on your dresser."

"Thank you." She was damp and chilled under her dress, but

she pulled out a chair and sat across from Hester. "Miss Townsend, I'm reconsidering my departure time. To be frank, I don't want to leave Wanda with no home and no means of support. I'd like to stay until she's well situated."

Hester straightened herself. "I doubt there's enough days in a year for that, not for her, and not here. Mrs. Long, I grew up in my mother's boardinghouse. You can believe I saw more than a child should know, but it was good training. There's times now I have to look a boarder in the eyes and tell him to pay up. Or pay up and get out. It might be he brought liquor to his room, or women, or he's rude in the dining room."

"Have Wanda and I upset anyone?"

"Not yet. I believe in giving guests their privacy, you included. I want each one to feel this is his home—indeed, for two of our boarders, it is their only home. But you can imagine. I have to pay attention to certain things."

May Rose grew colder.

Hester peered as if to make sure she was paying attention. "My brother has told me this business about your husband. You have to understand, nothing truly interesting happens here, so a whisper echoes all over the mountains, and people can't tell or don't care if it's true or not. If you stay longer, I'm afraid your presence will bring unwanted attention to the house."

For Wanda's sake, May Rose held her tongue.

Shouts roared up from the street. Hester shook her head. "Tonight the wood hicks are busy with their usual entertainments. I doubt they know you're here. But if you're here next Saturday they'll know about it, and after a few rounds, some will decide to call on you. Because of what's been said, you know."

"None of what's been said of me is true."

"It doesn't matter—the result will be the same. There's been talk of you for quite a while. These men have built you up in their minds, knowing you were alone on the mountain, young, and pretty, so many of them young and single. You see what I mean?"

"Surely I'm safe here."

"Oh, we won't let them in. But we need to preserve the peace and respectability of this house, surrounded as we are by establishments where men are free to misbehave." Hester brushed a hand across the table and caught at the edge what might have been crumbs. She crossed the floor and dropped them into the coal bucket.

May Rose stood. "Then I'll leave on Tuesday as I planned, if you will please have a care for Wanda. She'd be fine help for Dessie, and she wouldn't need pay—just food and a cot somewhere."

"Well, that's the other thing. My brother doesn't like Wanda in the house. She's earned her bad name."

Cold water dripped from her hair and rolled to the base of her spine. "Maybe I'll take Wanda with me." The idea seemed less practical than taking Nellie.

Hester clicked her tongue, a sound of exasperation. "The girl has a mother here."

"No one takes care of her."

"I can see how it might be good to get her away, but it wouldn't be right."

"Where will she sleep? What will become of her?"

"She'll work at Suzie's, I suppose. There's little you and I can do to prevent that."

"At Suzie's? She's my husband's child!"

"If you say so. Her mother lived off several men. Anyway, she might not care to go, even if Evalena gives permission."

"Evalena?"

"Her mother."

"I see." May Rose walked to the stairs and steadied herself against the railing. "Dr. Hennig wants to help. I may have to accept his offer."

"That's your decision. But anything you do with that man will make people talk."

"I won't be here long enough to care."

Hester pushed a chair under the table. "Even so, watch yourself."

Watching herself, watching Wanda—she was doing nothing else. "We're going to church tomorrow. Will that be a problem, with wood hicks in town?"

"Not in the morning. They'll sleep it off till about noon. But in the afternoon they'll bury Andrew Donnelly, so get right back here after service. And don't be surprised if you get a real cold shoulder in church."

Uncle Bert had regularly accused churches of being full of hypocrites, but Aunt Sweet always said what did he expect, when ordinary humans tried to be as good as God? "We all fall short," she'd said. "I want to be where I'm encouraged to do better."

May Rose had survived worse than cold shoulders. She went to bed slightly encouraged by Hester's warning, which made her seem like a mother who slapped then kissed the spot to make it better.

Beside her, Wanda slept with a doll in her arms and a knife under her pillow.

CHAPTER 10

*Come unto me, all ye that labour and are heavy laden, and I will give
you rest*

— MATTHEW 11:28

Even if Wanda agreed to leave Winkler, May Rose needed her
mother's permission. Wakeful through the night, she faced
Sunday's dawn with one conclusion: if neither was willing, she
must help the girl find work. Her arguments were like prayers
and her prayers like arguments. The church service, she hoped,
would introduce Wanda to the town's more charitable people.

Wanda's delight in dressing for church brought May Rose a
flush of happiness. She gave silent thanks for two more nights to
sleep securely in a room with plastered walls and for the friend-
ship of this child.

Wanda smiled at her image in the mirror—a fresh-scrubbed
girl in a blue dress hemmed evenly mid-calf. An insert of white
eyelet covered the ragged seam where Russell had slit the bodice.

After puzzling what to do about Wanda's bare feet, May Rose
opened a muslin bag with white satin slippers and white stockings, unworn since the barn dance in St. Louis where she'd met

Jamie. Wanda was more affected by the shining shoes than by the dolls. She stuffed crumpled paper in the toes and twirled before the dresser's long oval mirror, admiring the squash heels and her legs in white stockings.

A tip of brown leather slipped out from her sleeve—the knife's sheath.

"The knife must stay here," May Rose said.

Wanda cupped her hand over it.

May Rose nodded. "As long as we're together, we're safe."

Wanda jabbed the knife toward the mirror in a threatening pose, then hid it in the doll's skirt.

Aunt Sweet always said a person should go to church expecting a blessing. May Rose left the boardinghouse full of dread, wondering if her aunt would have welcomed the daughter of a whore and a woman rumored to display herself naked—the wife, or worse, of a murderer. Jesus had dined with sinners, but ordinary people protected themselves and their churches from people who broke the rules.

She and Wanda crossed to the river side of the road to avoid walking close to the bar and pool room where a few wood hicks sprawled in noisy sleep. Then they crossed back and walked the empty boardwalk, side by side in the Sunday morning hush.

"You may say hello if someone speaks, but otherwise, no talking in church," May Rose said.

Wanda danced along beside her. "How about them songs?"

"What about them?"

"I've listened from outside but I can't hardly catch the words."

"There may be hymnbooks. Are you a good reader?"

"I plan to be. I plan to love reading."

May Rose squeezed her hand.

The church was a whitewashed building, larger than the company houses, with a steeple Jamie said looked like a pointy hat on an outhouse. May Rose stopped at the step where she'd last seen the woman in the green dress. "People may stare," she whispered. "Just smile and don't show you notice."

Wanda skipped up and down the steps, watching the flash of stockings and slippers below the hem of her dress. "They're gonna look at us 'cause we're fancy."

May Rose girded herself with hope, the most necessary state of mind. Wanda had not sat still for braids, and only a few moments for hair brushing. Her face seemed to peer from a brown bush.

"They'll look because we're new. Some may act surprised to see us. Watch me, don't talk, and don't stare." Her aunt's lectures echoed weakly in the here and now. She opened one of the double doors and led Wanda inside.

"Here's the church," Wanda said, "and here's the steeple. Open the doors. Where's the people?"

Rows of dark varnished pews stood empty. The center aisle led past a pot-bellied stove to a low railed platform with a tall piano on one side, a red plush chair on the other, and a pulpit in the middle.

"I guess we're early," May Rose said. Though she hoped for better than cold shoulders, she preferred to be the last to arrive and first to leave. "Shall we go out and walk a while?"

The door opened and a voice cracked, "My angel!" Ruie, the preacher's mother. May Rose braced for attack, but the old woman passed her by and seized Wanda.

May Rose stepped close to help. "Miss Ruie, how are you today?" Ruie wore a black dress and an old-fashioned black bonnet with ribbons tied under her chin.

Preacher Gowder followed his mother. "Good morning, good morning, how do you do? Mother, release that child."

Ruie purred. "My Angelina!"

Wanda slid down through Ruie's arms to the floor and came up laughing. May Rose urged her into a nearby pew, and Preacher Gowder set his mother across the aisle. The double doors opened again and people flowed between them. The preacher greeted Dr. Hennig and a woman on his arm. Hot-faced children chased into the pews.

Everyone's eyes swept past May Rose, and not even the doctor paused to say hello. Clearly his offer to help did not include being introduced to the bony-faced woman who must be his wife. May Rose thought wickedly of forcing someone to speak, perhaps Mrs. Hennig, or of slipping into the circle of broad-backed matrons gossiping in the aisle. She wondered if they avoided her because she was a stranger, or because they thought they knew her too well.

From the front, a single tone vibrated, then another and another. Wanda stood at the piano and struck keys one at a time, low to high. She reached the highest key and started over.

Conversations hushed as May Rose walked to the platform. She whispered, "Come and sit down, or we'll be turned out."

Wanda marched her finger across the ivories like she knew there was no truth to her threat.

"If we're turned out, you won't learn the songs."

When she reached the topmost ivory for the second time, Wanda left the platform and sat in the first row close to the piano.

"We'll sit in back," May Rose said.

Wanda slid her hands under her legs and stared ahead.

At a rickety trot, Ruie Gowder came down the aisle and dropped beside Wanda. "Sweet Angel!" She kissed Wanda's hand.

"Not my name," Wanda mumbled.

May Rose gave up and sat on her right.

Preacher Gowder strode toward them, his white hair bouncing and his face expectant. "Ah, I see Mother has found you. She's more at ease when she's with someone she fancies. She'll be all right when the service begins—you'll not know she's there."

"We'll be fine," May Rose said.

Wanda stared at him so intently that May Rose touched her arm, afraid she'd ask how he got that white hair or if he knew his black eyebrows and pointy beard gave him the look of a devil.

Wanda tapped her foot. "When do we get to the music?"

"Right away." With a display of elegance, he set a bench out from the keyboard and adjusted himself on it. Then he stretched his feet to the pedals and raised his hands over the keys. When he struck the first chord, Wanda scooted to the edge of her seat. He waltzed his arms side to side, embellishing introductory notes with frills and flourishes. After a minute, he signaled the congregation to stand, and they roared forth, led by his voice, "To God be the glory, great things He has done!"

May Rose had never heard a hymn sung with such extravagant accompaniment and vigorous harmony. Wanda sang too, her voice chasing the music, repeating words a moment after she heard them, adding beats of irregularity to the rhythm. But by the second repetition of the chorus, she knew both words and tune, and her voice raised above the others: "Praise the Lord! Praise the Lord! Let the earth hear His voice!" The preacher glanced away from the keys to see whose voice praised louder than his own.

Submerged in sound, May Rose sang without fear of being heard. Joining so many voices made anything seem possible. She would find a way, a word would be spoken that would lead to another, and another. God would provide.

At the end of the hymn the preacher stepped to the podium, clasped his hands, and closed his eyes. "The word of the Lord." His voice turned solemn. "Given in Psalm 84."

It was a psalm her aunt had loved, full of feminine sentiments —the sparrow finding her nest to lay her young, the heart and flesh crying out for the living God. May Rose could not imagine it spoken by a man—she'd never known a man to cry tears, and had not thought they might cry out in their hearts. Yet the preacher's recitation hushed everyone.

"For the Lord God is a sun and shield: the Lord will give grace and glory: no good thing will he withhold from them that walk uprightly."

She supposed the strongest man and woman needed a sun and a shield. And promises. If she walked uprightly, no good thing would be withheld.

Her assurance lasted only a short time.

The preacher opened his eyes. "Today we need to remember

the Donnelly family, not only in prayer, but with any assistance you can give."

The congregation murmured sympathies. May Rose stared at the whitewashed wall behind his head. Jamie had left Wanda and her mother destitute, and now the Donnellys. She felt burdened by his sin, and by her own, repented long ago, but maybe not soon enough.

"Let's have more singing," Wanda said.

"Shush." Ruie spoke as loudly as Wanda.

May Rose heard little of the sermon and did not come from her daze until the preacher sat down. Immediately an old man stood and boomed forth a prayer that seemed to enumerate all the sins of mankind. When at last he sat down, another old man devoted a prayer for undisciplined men to be converted to pathways of peace, and another begged for mercy and blessing on Donnelly's widow and fatherless boys. Finally, a younger man prayed for the prosperity of the company and safety for the workers. Throughout, the congregation interspersed "uhums."

She had nothing to put in the collection basket. At the end of the service, the preacher strode up the aisle without a glance or word for his mother or her keepers.

When Wanda stood, Ruie hugged her from behind. Wanda wrapped her arms around May Rose. "This old woman's gonna pull me down."

May Rose patted Ruie's shoulder. "Miss Ruie, it's time to leave. Let loose now."

A stronger hand grasped May Rose's arm. "Would'ja look who's here." The hand whirled her around. Bright, the swamper boss. "Making yourself to home?"

With Wanda clinging to her waist and Ruie holding onto Wanda, May Rose struggled to stay on her feet. "Remove your hand," she said to Bright.

He pushed his bristly moustache close to her face. "Will you be showing your business any time soon? Shall I tell the boys?"

She flushed. "Mr. Bright, you forget where you are."

"Likewise. Get to the altar and repent." His twist on her arm might have knocked her to the floor had Wanda and Ruie not bolstered her from behind. Letting go, he backed into the approach of a smaller man. Bright snarled. "Watch where you're going."

"I beg your pardon?" The man spoke quietly, separating his words. In contrast to the loose jackets of other men in the church, his was well-fitted, with a vest. He carried a spotless bowler hat.

"Mr. Townsend, I'm sorry…"

Mr. Townsend frowned. "Make your apologies to the lady."

"I don't guess you know who she is."

"Apologies," Mr. Townsend said.

Bright glared.

"Look at her when you say it."

Bright turned an angry face to May Rose. "I apologize." He shoved away past spectators in the aisle.

Mr. Townsend watched him for a moment.

"Thank you," May Rose said.

"You're very welcome. Are you well acquainted with Samuel Bright?"

"He was my husband's boss."

"I see. We haven't been introduced, but I know you're a guest at our house. I'm Barlow Townsend. Hester is my sister."

May Rose unlocked Wanda's arms. "I'm May Rose. This is Wanda."

"Wanda." He bowed slightly. "And Miss Ruie, good morning."

He glanced toward the men and women watching from the aisle. "May I escort you back to the house?"

His offer meant a safe return along unkind paths. Her breath steadied.

"Mr. Townsend, we would appreciate that very much."

He stood aside so they could precede him up the aisle. She walked through a gauntlet of disapproving faces that turned bland when he stepped forward and slid his hand under her elbow. Still trembling from Bright's assault, she startled at his touch.

Ruie hung onto Wanda until they reached the door, where they were struck by the noon sun and a hot wind. Mr. Townsend shook Preacher Gowder's hand.

Wanda skipped down the steps and away from the crowd.

"Thank you, sir, for attending," the preacher said. "And of course, Mrs. Long. Oh, where's mother?" He hurried to the boardwalk, where Ruie had attached herself to a group of girls.

Mr. Townsend paused in front of the store and struck a match against his shoe. Cupping his hand to shield the flame, he lit a thin cigar.

He waved the cigar toward the barrels on mill roofs. "I don't care for this weather, too warm for fall, and too dry. You see our fire protection, hardly better than a bucket line. We constantly caution the men about smoking." He puffed his cigar. "And these houses—ten feet apart. When they were built, I wanted more distance. A fire in one could ruin everything, especially with wind like this."

"It's terrible to imagine." She'd seen the crews following trains in dry weather to stamp out cinders that flew from the engine's firebox. And everyone knew the lumberyard was pure tinder. She hoped he would continue to speak on matters unrelated to her, no more about Bright, nothing about Jamie or Donnelly.

An empty funeral wagon went by in the street, pulled by two glossy black horses. The driver tipped his hat and Mr. Townsend nodded.

He glanced at her again. "We've a situation at the mill." He did not speak for a few steps, as though thinking about the situation. "Am I walking too fast?"

"Not at all." The bottom of her shoe had finally worn through and the uneven sole scraped with every step.

"We've an employee whose work is vital, but in recent weeks he's been absent many days."

She walked with her toes bunched and her foot arched away

from the scrape. Mr. Townsend kept looking at her. He dropped the little cigar and wiggled it flat under a shining brown boot.

"His name is Morris Herff—he files the saws. His wife died several weeks ago and left him with three children."

"I'm sorry to hear it."

Wanda turned and walked backwards, watchful.

The boardwalk ended and they crossed to the sawmill side of the road.

"Various women have tried to help, but Herff is an obstinate sort, and he can't keep anyone steady. I think he's ready to move on. I've been patient, given him leeway, because he's highly skilled. If he leaves, the mill is in a bind."

"Unfortunate," she said, thinking of the children.

Men lounged on the pool room steps, one with his head between his knees, others drinking from dark bottles. Another lay in the street. On the hotel porch, wood hicks moved in a slow line to the door. Jamie might have waited for dinner in that line, wearing his new red shirt, handsome as the first time she'd seen him.

Wanda walked through the boardinghouse gate, pulled an apple from a tree and glanced back, listening in a sidelong way.

Mr. Townsend held the gate open. "Hester tells me she's allowed you a room for only a few days."

"It's all right. I'm leaving Tuesday on the train."

"Oh, very good." He cleared his throat. "However, if you're not quite ready to leave Winkler, perhaps you'd like to work for Morris, take care of his children, so he can get back to his job. I'm sure the boardinghouse can accommodate you for a longer stay."

Stay. Just as she'd resolved to go. "That's very considerate, but may I suggest someone else?"

Wanda kicked her toes in the grass.

"Certainly you may suggest."

"I've grown attached to Wanda, my husband's daughter. She's a brave and helpful girl, and she needs a way to support herself.

In just a few days I could train her to take care of Mr. Herff's house and children."

"I'm afraid it wouldn't do. Even if she were...well, she's a child herself."

"She's not too young. I took care of my cousins when I was her age, and their sick mother too."

He kept a pleasant tone. "I'm sure you did, but I couldn't recommend her to Morris. I'm sorry." He motioned to the front door. "Shall we go in for dinner?"

"I'm having dinner with Wanda."

"I see. You know you're welcome in the dining room."

"I do. Thank you." It seemed both too late to help Wanda and too soon to leave her.

In the kitchen, Dessie ladled chicken and dumplings into serving dishes for the dining room. She frowned at May Rose. "I'm not dirtying no extra bowls. I'd appreciate you dipping yours outa the pots."

"Gladly," May Rose said.

Grim-faced, Wanda wiped up a spot of gravy with her finger and stuck it in her mouth.

May Rose started to correct her, but stopped at a worried glance from Wanda. Instead, she laid her napkin on her lap and smiled across the table. "I'm glad we're eating together, away from the others. It feels more like home."

"I can eat anywheres," Wanda said. "But I get nervous, you watching me."

Dessie carried a tray to the dining room.

May Rose attended to her dinner. "I've never thanked you for helping me get away from Russell."

"It's all right. Was me burnt the scarecrow. Busted the eggs, too, and stole some."

"You came at night? Watched me?"

Wanda shrugged. "He left us for you."

Pain passed between them. May Rose whispered, "He left me, too."

"He kinda had to."

"I think he would have left, anyway." She felt better, saying it, and ready to brave something else. "When I leave Winkler, will your mother let you come with me?"

Wanda bristled. "I couldn't go far from Ma."

May Rose got up and spooned another dumpling onto Wanda's plate. Evalena did not deserve such a daughter. But since she did not appear to take care of her, she might have no problem entrusting Wanda to the woman who'd taken Jamie. Possibly May Rose could do something in return. She couldn't think what Evalena might want, but in her place, she'd want to escape her present life.

"She could go with us," May Rose said.

Worry flashed across Wanda's eyes. "No, she couldn't. Ma don't go nowhere. Drinks and sleeps, and…you know. Gets no money either, just a place to roost."

"I should meet her."

"That'd be nice."

CHAPTER 11

How good and thoughtful he is
  The world seems full of good men, even if there are monsters in it.

— BRAM STOKER: DRACULA

The springs squeaked each time Wanda sat down, got up, or fell across the bed.

"Most people rest on Sunday afternoon," May Rose said. Since dinner, the boardinghouse had seemed empty beyond their room, not so much as a creaking floorboard or clink of pot lid.

Wanda arranged and rearranged the dolls on the pillows, now the big one in the middle, arms spread as though holding the hands of the others.

"When can I go out?"

"The funeral will be over soon, and the wood hicks will go back to their camps. Then we'll go to the woods for acorns." The funeral for Donnelly. She could not say his name.

Wanda paced. "Read me something."

May Rose turned pages of her Bible, looking for something that might appeal to Wanda and didn't suggest that God rewarded deceit and violence. Not Eve giving in to the temptation of the serpent, not Cain killing Abel, nor Abraham preparing to sacrifice his son. Not Rebekah and Jacob deceiving his father to steal from Esau, not Rachel stealing from her father. No stories of harlots. She settled on Noah's ark, a story of obedience.

Wanda listened quietly to the end. "Was there dogs on the ark?"

"There must have been, for we have dogs now."

"I had a pup but Jamie killed it," Wanda said. "He said it would bring the hydrophobia."

May Rose winced. Jamie hadn't let her have a dog, either.

Wanda bounced on the bed. "I learned a Bible verse in school. 'For I know the thoughts that I think toward you, saith the LORD, thoughts of peace, and not of evil, to give you an expected end.' Jeremiah 29:11. I never did know what it means."

"I think the verse means God has good things planned for us."

"When we gonna get them?"

"I don't know."

"Well, it'd help if I knew when to look and maybe what to look for. Can I go out now?"

"I have an idea." May Rose wrapped a rag around her foot to protect the sore, then pulled a stocking over it. The rag made the shoe tight.

Wanda rushed to the door. "Where we going?"

"You wait here and I'll bring something from the parlor. You'll like it." She eased the door shut and tip-toed down the front stairs.

Three books were arranged fan-like on the parlor table. As she reached for the first, she heard a page turn and saw Mr. Townsend in a wing chair. He'd shed his jacket, but not his vest and tie. His shirt cuffs had gold studs.

"Mrs. Long, good afternoon." He stood and motioned to the chair beside him. "You're welcome to sit."

His stiff manner made her nervous. "I've come to borrow a

book, something to read to Wanda." She lifted a brown cloth-covered book. *Wealth of Nations.*

He strolled to the table, bringing cigar-scent. "Perhaps not that one."

She set it in its place and opened the next book to a woodcut of a craggy mountain with an ancient castle at its peak. Mr. Townsend looked over her shoulder. "Ah, *Dracula.* It's meant to frighten. You should read it yourself before deciding its suitability for a child. Even…"

She nodded. Even for Wanda.

The third volume was *The War of the Worlds.* "I was hoping to find something like *Evangeline.*"

"Longfellow," he said, "one of my favorites. I should order a copy. I'll ask Mr. Cooper if he has anything appropriate for your girl."

"It's all right, we won't be here long."

"Tuesday, you said?"

She nodded.

"You don't think your husband will return?"

"I haven't included him in my plans."

He rubbed a finger against his cheek. "I'm sorry for your circumstances. I had a word with Samuel Bright."

"You've been kind. Thank you."

Behind them, Hester said, "Mrs. Long, is there something I can do for you?"

"She's looking for a book to read to the girl."

"We have nothing suitable for a child," Hester said.

"We were discussing that."

May Rose stepped away. "Good afternoon, then."

From the stairs she got a sense of their conversation, though not the words, the sister's whispered bursts, the brother's tone careful but persistent.

Wanda frowned when she entered the room empty-handed.

"Let's tell a story about the dolls," May Rose said. She

propped them against a pillow. "Once upon a time there were three sisters, Margaret, Leola, and Mary Agnes." With each name she saw them, Margaret's pale eyebrows and anxious look, Leola's overbite, Mary Agnes trying not to lisp as she said her own name, *Mary Agneth. May Rothe.*

Wanda shook her head.

"You don't like those names? We can call them something different. What do you think?"

Wanda lifted the largest doll. "This 'un is Ma's little helper. This 'un..." she pointed to the middle doll, "...does bad things. And the baby one runs away."

May Rose set the other two in Wanda's lap. "But we love them, even so. We take care of them."

At the end of each doll's stuffed arm, May Rose had tied a string to make a pouch, a clumsy hand. Wanda pinched each one. "I suppose."

"Shall we call one Wanda?"

"It don't matter. I'm too big for dolls."

The toilet flushed. From the tracks came a long whoosh of steam, and on the street, men's voices.

Wanda shoved the dolls aside. "Can I go now?"

May Rose put an arm around her waist. "I don't want anything bad to happen to you."

"I can't stay in all the time."

"You mustn't let boys get you alone. Or men."

"I'm a good runner."

"There's a policeman. We could tell him."

"Big Frank?" Wanda clucked like an old woman. "He don't care what a bad girl does."

"But you're not a bad girl. You'll be good, here, in school, everywhere."

"I'm too big for school."

"You're not. Children go to school until they're big as I am."

"Not me. I'm too big to sit with the little 'uns." She pressed her forehead to the window glass. "Folks don't like me, but I don't care a bit."

"Oh, Wanda. Some people enjoy saying mean things. I like you and I admire you. You have a gift of happiness. My cousins are nice little girls, but they're not brave like you, or good runners."

Wanda opened the door. "I'm gonna go." She stepped back as Hester appeared with a stack of clothes.

"I thought you might make something of these for the girl." Frowning, she laid out faded black skirts with worn hems, stained shirtwaists, a nightgown, and patched bloomers.

May Rose laid a hand on Wanda's shoulder. "This is very kind."

"Them's ugly things," Wanda said.

Hester's eyes widened.

May Rose shook her head. "She doesn't know how much this means."

"Indeed she doesn't," Hester said.

Because Hester was nearly as short as Wanda, only her shirtwaists were too large. While May Rose ripped seams, fitted, and sewed, she made up stories about a doll who spoke in haste, a doll who was ungrateful, and a doll who remembered to be polite in every circumstance.

Wanda didn't miss the point. "She didn't want me to have 'em."

Neither questioned where Wanda was supposed to keep the clothes when May Rose left.

That evening Wanda sat cross-legged in their open door as they listened to songs May Rose had learned in school. When the parlor music ended, May Rose helped Wanda learn the words to "Beautiful Dreamer," but when she sang to show how the words fit the tune, Wanda stopped her and sang it herself. Jamie had never let her sing, either.

Before bed, May Rose looked up from her prayers to find Wanda watching. She'd prayed that Hester or Mr. Townsend might relent and help this girl.

"God don't save us from trouble," Wanda said.

May Rose put the wrapped greenbacks under her pillow. "No, not all trouble." She turned off the electric bulb and waited while her eyes adjusted to the dark. "Maybe just the kind we're tempted to make ourselves."

EARLY MONDAY, May Rose followed Wanda uphill, both carrying burlap sacks. She shouted to be heard over the grinding saws in the valley and the wind in the trees.

"What if your mother wants you to go away with me? Will you come?"

Wanda trudged ahead without looking back. "I told you, I can't leave Ma. I don't get why you have to go."

"I have nothing here. No family, no work."

"Well I got Ma."

"But do you have a home? Someplace to sleep this winter?"

"I might sleep under Winifred's table. I did that once."

"Who's Winifred?"

"Suzie's cook."

May Rose had to ask, though she did not want to know. "Where is Suzie's place?"

"Over-top Pizzy's."

"The bar? So close?"

"Close to what?"

"I don't know. I didn't know, that's all." Close to decent people, she'd meant.

Wanda threw her bag down under an oak tree.

They scraped away leaves with their hands and scooped acorns into the bags. May Rose admired Wanda's assurance. Maybe the girl trusted herself because she'd not been hampered by discipline, while she herself had been corrected so often she never felt certain of anything.

What was wrong with staying here a few days or weeks? No one was expecting her. Townspeople might treat her with suspicion, but Mr. Townsend had offered a job. She could help Wanda.

"E-yow!" Wanda stumbled backwards, shaking her hand.

"What? Are you bit?"

"Jaggers—they caught me and wouldn't let go."

A mass of low-growing briars lay under the leaves.

"I'm ripped to pieces."

Blood seeped slowly through gashes in Wanda's dirty fingers and palm, but pumped from a nick at her wrist. May Rose grabbed her kerchief and pressed it to the wound. The white cloth turned red. Blood dripped to the ground.

"Press hard on that," she said. "I need something else."

While Wanda pressed fingers on her wrist, May Rose shook out another kerchief. She wrapped it tightly over the sodden cloth. "Now, let's get to the doctor."

The new bandage reddened, but not as fast.

"Ma and Winifred can doctor me," Wanda said. "You take care of them acorns."

"I'll go with you and come back for them later."

"I'll go faster by myself." Wanda ran off.

May Rose finished filling the sacks and dragged them in two trips to the boardinghouse. She worried when Wanda didn't come running into the yard. The morning passed. May Rose paced in her room. In two more days, she'd leave Wanda behind, still without a proper home. And once she left, she'd never know.

At lunch time, Wanda ran into the kitchen, her hand and wrist wrapped firmly in strips of white cloth.

"It took a while to stop the blood. And I fell asleep, after Winifred burned the place with a knife. E-yow, I yelled for that, you bet'cha. And I forgot your kerchiefs."

"My kerchief!" May Rose felt one pocket and then the other, both empty. "What have I done?" She ran upstairs and lifted her pillow, searched the covers, looked under the bed. Each morning she'd moved the greenbacks to her pocket. Had she done that today?

In the doorway, Wanda chewed a piece of buttered bread.

"I've lost my money. Oh, Lord, I've lost my money." She ran down the stairs and out toward the slopes. She remembered ripping the kerchief from her pocket, remembered wrapping it around Wanda's hand. In imagination she saw the greenbacks float to the ground, saw them lying among acorns.

They found the place where they'd raked the ground. May Rose held her arms out from her sides. "Stand still and just look."

"I don't see anything," Wanda said. "Maybe they blew away."

"Or maybe their color hides them. Step slowly. They're brown on one side, green on the other, with a bit of red. The red might stand out—look for that first."

They walked back and forth under the trees, first without disturbing the ground clutter. Later, May Rose kicked through it.

Wanda sat on a rock. "Maybe you scooped them with the acorns."

May Rose choked on a sob. "I was thinking too much, not paying attention."

"I figger pigs would eat greenbacks good as anything."

May Rose dropped to the ground and bent her head to her knees, wondering if good things ever happened as quickly as bad.

"Come on," Wanda said. "They might of just blew somewhere."

They circled the area, ranging farther and farther.

"We'll find 'em," Wanda said, when May Rose sat again.

"No, I don't think so."

Wanda pulled her half dollar from the pocket of Hester's hand-me-down skirt. "We got this. You can have it back."

"I can't take it."

"Sure you can. It's my dumb fault for getting in them jaggers."

"I was careless. Now I don't know what to do."

"You got stuff up to your place. I'll help you sell it."

"Even if I could get it to town, I doubt it would bring much."

Wanda mumbled.

May Rose wiped her eyes. "What did you say?"

"I said, why do you say 'no' all the time?"

"I'm sorry. So much has changed—I'm not myself."

With her good hand, Wanda pulled May Rose to her feet. "A girl is always herself, whether she likes it or not."

CHAPTER 12

We are all drifting reefwards now, and faith is our only anchor

— BRAM STOKER: DRACULA

May Rose backed into a corner of the kitchen while Hester and Dessie bustled around each other, washing, wiping and stacking china plates and cups.

"Go on," Hester said.

"We searched, but either the wind blew my money away or the pigs ate it. I'm sorry…I can't pay my bill, and I have no money for tomorrow's train."

Dessie sent her a look of sympathy.

Hester laid her towel aside and picked up a pan of rolls. "I guess you don't need my lecture, and I'm too busy at present to give it. Mr. Townsend has a special dinner tonight." She slid the pan into the oven.

"He spoke to me about working for Mr. Herff," May Rose said. "I'll ask if the job is still available. I'll pay you somehow."

"Don't bother him today. The owners are here, Mr. Winkler himself, and Mr. Winkler Junior."

"So when…?"

Hester lifted the stack of china plates. "I'll ask later. Can you help us tonight in the dining room? I guess you can carry a bowl without slopping it?"

"I'll start now, do whatever you need."

"Clean up, first. You look like you've wallowed in dirt. If you wear that black dress and my organdy apron, the Winklers will think we've got a high-class serving girl." With both hands holding the plates, Hester backed against the dining room door. "On second thought, wear a plain apron. We don't want them thinking we're rich."

Dessie smiled.

After the boarders left the dining room, May Rose and Hester set the best china, silverware, and wine glasses on the table for Mr. Townsend, the two Winklers, and three managers from the mill.

Hester stopped her as she carried cups and saucers to the sideboard. "Get that frown off your face."

"I'm sorry, I'm concentrating." She lifted her eyebrows and smiled.

"Oh, my, not like that—what will the men think? Just be calm and assured. Pay attention to everything, but don't look directly at anyone unless they speak to you. Never mind, I'll do the serving. You carry in and out, and keep your eyes on me."

Fortunately, the men at first seemed more interested in their food than in how smoothly it was being served or by whom. But after they satisfied their hunger she caught glances directed her way by the guests as well as their host. She kept her face immobile, watched Hester, and carried in and out.

When dessert conversation turned to the issue of keeping quality workers, she set cups on saucers without a clink and listened for a mention of Morris Herff, the skilled man who filed the saws and had three motherless children.

"News spreads through the camps," one of the managers said. "Men hear there's better pay somewhere, and soon as you know it, they've snuck their families away in the night. Most of the time leaving a store bill."

"Italians would be less likely to leave," Mr. Winkler said.

"True," the manager said, "but they just about have to work with their own kind 'cause nobody else knows what they're saying. That's why the railroad puts them together on section crews."

"We should hire Negroes," Mr. Winkler Junior said. "They work cheap, they work good, and there's no trouble understanding them."

Mr. Townsend frowned. "If we hired Negroes, we'd have to build a separate town, and I don't know where we'd put it."

Junior looked around the table. "From what I've seen, men work fine with Negroes."

"I know. But they won't live side by side."

"Some of your men can't seem to live with their own kind," Mr. Winkler Senior said. "Recently you had a man killed in a fight. What are you doing about that?"

May Rose studied the flowered carpet and listened to the silence in the room.

"Hester," Mr. Townsend said. "We'll adjourn to the parlor, with coffee."

Hester slid open the parlor doors and the men followed her through.

Mr. Townsend stopped near the sideboard. "May Rose, thank you for helping."

"I'm glad to do it."

He tilted his head and smiled to her downturned face. "Everything works for the best."

"Of course."

Only for some people, Jamie would say.

WEDNESDAY MORNING MAY Rose shook off the remnants of an odd, unpleasant dream. She and Wanda were attempting to board the train, but Mr. Townsend kept pulling her back, saying Wanda was his child.

The dream seemed even odder because she'd gone to bed happy. She wasn't completely destitute. Mr. Townsend had arranged her job.

She left the room without waking Wanda and came down the back stairs. She found Hester flipping patties of corn meal mush.

"May Rose," Hester said, "will you carry a lunch today?"

"I suppose I'll eat with the Herff children."

Hester and Dessie exchanged a look. Hester pointed to a pan of mush on a side table. "Take that along. Neighbors send over food now and again, but you don't know what you'll find."

"There's two boys, school age," Dessie said. "And the baby, a girl."

Hester slid cakes of mush onto a plate for May Rose. "Maple syrup's there in front of you, and stewed apples. Would you help yourself to coffee? The baby might be two or three. Dessie, what's her name?"

"Glory," Dessie said. "Lillian Herff got sick after she was born. She never had no help, just them boys. The neighbors were good to them for her sake, not his."

May Rose was relieved to hear of good neighbors. Dessie carried two lunch boxes into the dining room and returned before the door stopped swinging. "Where's the girl? She eats when meals are set, or not at all."

Hester filled a platter with mush cakes. "She can't stay here while you're at work."

"She'll come to me today, but I'm encouraging her to go back to school."

Mr. Townsend entered from the dining room and set his bowler on the pie safe. "Good morning, Sister, Ladies. I'll sit here for a bite this morning."

Dessie stared. Hester frowned.

He pulled a stool from the worktable with a deliberation that might have been the result of studying the best method.

With greater haste but equal care, Hester poured his coffee. Dessie brought his place setting and one of the lunch boxes from the dining room. He studied the plate, smiled at all of them, and lifted his fork.

A song rang through the house, "Beautiful Dreamer," a woman's voice.

Hester looked toward the ceiling. "Could that be your girl? She'll wake the house!" Thunder rattled the windows.

May Rose stood. "I'm sorry. I'll correct her."

Mr. Townsend stood when she did, catching his napkin. "Surely there's no one left to wake."

"Miss Hester is correct," she said. "Wanda can't sing out whenever she feels like it."

"We must invite her to sing in the parlor," he said.

She paused at the bottom step. "You're kind to suggest it, but she's…"

"Undisciplined," Hester said.

He resumed his seat. "Perhaps unready to perform for company."

"She sings nice," Dessie said.

As she climbed the stairs, May Rose rehearsed how she'd correct Wanda, first by telling her how much Dessie and Mr. Townsend admired her singing.

THUNDER ROLLED and lightning streaked the dark morning. Mr. Townsend carried a lantern. May Rose carried the pan of mush and watched her feet in the circle of light.

"Careful, there," he said. He offered his arm and guided her around a puddle. Water splashed on his waxed shoes and soaked the rag inside hers. She walked in awe of him, a man so different.

The silence between them grew uncomfortable, but she could think of nothing to ease it except words that seemed frivolous or personal. He gestured toward the lumber docks. "We aim to saw

130,000 board feet a day. Is that a familiar term to you? A board foot is one inch thick, twelve inches wide, twelve inches long."

Jamie had said the mill sawed eighteen acres of timber each day, a description she understood.

Mr. Townsend pointed to dark towers of lumber on wooden spacers. "We plane and dry our lumber and ship it all over the world. Over there's our dry kiln. We've six boilers, all fired by our own sawdust." He kept glancing at her, as though to judge or engage her interest. "Think of the men who provide for their families because of the Winkler Company, nearly four hundred here and in the camps, and all those down the line, shippers, builders, furniture makers and the like. And our town serves other people in these hills."

"I see." Her estimation of the company was based more on employees she'd met—Bright, Dr. Hennig, Mr. Ramey, the paymaster. Jamie.

"Morris Herff is our filer, a saw-sharpener, highly skilled. We have another filer, but he's a poor substitute. When Morris stays at home, our production suffers. A dull saw, you see, slows the work."

They crossed to the boardwalk. She tightened the cheesecloth Hester had wrapped around the pan. The boys would go to school, so she'd have only the baby through the day, a girl of two or three. "What will Mr. Herff pay?"

Mr. Townsend was quiet, like he hadn't considered this, or it was not polite to ask. After a few steps he said, "The company will pay the first month."

"And then?"

"Morris will have to hire you, or hire someone else, or leave. We'll be looking for a replacement, but we hope he'll stay."

So her job might be temporary. They turned uphill at the alley between the company store and the church.

"And the company? What will the company pay?"

"Fifty cents a day. You'll collect Saturday noon at the pay window, like all our employees. I hope that will be satisfactory."

"Until I find something better, it will have to be."

When they turned into the first terraced street, he lowered his voice to a near-whisper. "I'd like you to keep me informed about Morris's intentions, and anything else you think I should know. When his wife died, he talked of leaving. I don't want to wake up tomorrow and find myself short a filer. If there's anything you need to do your job, speak with me."

The houses sat on the uphill side of the street, identically built and all unpainted, with two stone steps from the road to a slope of packed dirt and coal dust, and two wooden steps to a door. Straggly weeds grew around the Herff house.

Mr. Townsend knocked and held up the lantern when a man wrenched open the door. He had high cheekbones, a sharp chin, and skin that looked scraped and irritated. Wood chips and sawdust clung to his frayed work clothing, and he held a carving knife. The mill whistle blew.

"Morris, this is Mrs. Long. You can tell her what she needs to know. I'll wait and walk along to the mill with you."

Morris Herff opened his mouth, closed it, and frowned. "I forgot you were coming. What's her name you say?"

She spoke for herself. "Mrs. Long. May Rose Long."

He looked from her to Mr. Townsend and swiped the knife on his sleeve. "This is what you got to look after my kids? The girl from the mountain?"

May Rose stiffened her hold on the pan of mush.

"Morris," Mr. Townsend said, "I don't like to speak ill of the dead, but you know and I know Donnelly was a liar and a troublemaker. What he said about Mrs. Long sounds to me like his regular kind of mischief, only Jamie Long took the bait. Others will vouch for her character."

"I'll bet they will."

"Samson, one of our engineers. Oliverio, boss of a section crew. They say Mrs. Long never did anything but wave…" He lowered his voice. "And was always decently clothed."

She bit the inside of her cheek.

Herff ran a hand over his face, spilling fine dust. "I'll give her a day's try."

Mr. Townsend backed down from the step. "Do you want to show her anything in the house?"

"If she don't know what to do, she won't last. I'll come at noon to see for myself." He jumped to the ground and strode away.

Mr. Townsend lowered the lantern past his clenched jaw, leaving his face in darkness.

"Good bye, then," he said. "I trust all will go well."

"I'll do my best."

Alone on the step, she hummed a tuneless melody. In the yard below, someone tended a fire under a kettle. May Rose stepped through the Herff doorway, prepared, she thought, for anything.

The house smelled of ammonia—somewhere, a bucket of soiled diapers. To her left, a stairway led upstairs, where the children might be sleeping, for she saw no one and heard no sounds. To her right, a dim bulb hung over a workbench with wood shavings, a bottle of linseed oil, and rags. An unfinished carving lay on the bench, three deer emerging from a background of pines. Tools with smooth wooden handles hung from nails.

A bulb in the kitchen lit wooden floors crusty with spills, ash, and other loose dirt. There were dark smudges around the doorknob, a wash pan of foul water, a table littered with empty food cans, and a cold cook stove. The only place to sit appeared to be the stool by the front room bench.

If the children did not appear soon, she'd have to wake the boys for school, but not until she warmed the house. She set the mush on the table, cleared cans into the coal bucket, and carried ashes to a heap at the back edge of the yard. In the washhouse she found a short stack of wood, along with a wooden tub of smelly sheets and clothing, an iron tripod and kettle for boiling, a weathered bench, a rub board, and a sliver of soap.

Back in the kitchen, she built a fire and pumped water for the stove's heating well, then set a pot on a burner. That done, she went to the front room and pulled the cord on the overhead light.

A flock of wooden birds seemed to fly over the corner walls, and squirrels with curvy tails fairly wiggled along carved tree branches. Below them on the floor, something she'd not noticed on entering, a fence-like enclosure with dark eyes watching through the slats. A child, still as a stone, thumb in her mouth.

"Hello," May Rose said. "Are you Glory?"

The child had a tiny face and large eyes, and she sat in a puddle of her own making. Her long undershirt was visibly wet to the chest.

May Rose cooed to hide her horror. "Just a moment—we'll have you dry in a moment." In the front room upstairs she found a bed with rumpled covers and a few garments hanging on hooks. The adjoining room had no bed or clothespress, only a heap of clothing and bedding in the middle of the floor and a chamber pot in a corner. Its lid was not enough to contain the stink.

A small foot pushed out of the bedding. One of the boys, or both, slept in that heap. She hurried downstairs with a ragged flannel shirt, not too grimy.

"Can you stand?" She moved the child's fingers to the tooth-marked top rail and stripped off her wet shirt. Two years at most, and small for that. A three-cornered diaper, heavy with urine, hung from her little hip bones. Since the floor already had a puddle, May Rose unpinned the diaper and let it fall. The child did not flinch, though her skin was wet and cold. May Rose wrapped her in the shirt and carried her to the kitchen, where the stove gave off a faint heat.

"Glory? Is your name Glory?" The child's eyes followed her. What first? Warm water to wash, something for drying, a clean diaper. Breakfast. The mother had been dead for a month, sick before then. The neighbors' help was not enough.

She set her on the table with her back against the wall. "Can you sit there and not fall off?" Glory stuck both hands in the mush and began to shove it into her mouth.

May Rose pulled the pan away. "Oh, sweet thing, let me warm it and find a spoon."

Glory wailed and threw herself toward the edge of the table. When May Rose caught her, she strained toward the mush. A boy of eight or nine came into the kitchen and snatched the pan, then a bigger boy ran in and took it away from him. May Rose seized the edge of the pan, but he held fast.

"Let go," she said. "Everyone will eat."

The boy shifted his eyes to his brother and sister, and May Rose raised the pan overhead. "Find a knife." Both boys ran to the front room. Each came back with a carving tool. "One will do," she said. With Glory in one arm, she cut squares of mush, then watched the children push them into their mouths with dirty fingers.

"I'm May Rose. Do you have dishes, spoons and forks?"

The younger pointed to a shelf with a wooden box that looked like trash but held dishes and pots caked with food and mold.

"Are there chairs somewhere? Other furniture?"

The bigger boy stuffed another square of mush into his mouth. "Pa sold most o'that."

The boys had dark hair and eyes and sharp chins like their father. The younger was nearly as tall as his brother. "Pa don't work," he said.

"Well, he's working now, and I'm here to take care of you."

The taller boy shook his head. "Won't last. He don't want to work, he just carves. Them critters on the wall? He sold our bed, but never a one of them."

Glory kicked the empty pan to the floor, and the boys raced from the room. May Rose called upstairs after them. "I've water heating so you can wash for school." With a sticky hand, Glory pulled May Rose's braids.

She waited at the bottom of the stairs. "Your wash water is ready," she said, when they came back down. They dodged her and ran outside. She watched them sprint barefoot down the alley. To school, she hoped.

With Glory on her hip, she upended the infant pen and dragged it outside.

The Herff laundry was stained, mildewed, and rank. She rolled her shirtwaist cuffs above the elbows, carried bucket after bucket of water, added wood to the fire, rubbed the sliver of soap into dark smears, pushed thin diapers and underwear against the ridges of the board, soaked, boiled, and wrung until her arms ached. The day turned sunny, with a wind, and the fire wrapped her in smoke. Quiet, Glory peered at the sky and picked at grass.

Neighbors pinned up their wash and talked in pairs and groups, but none came her way. Long before she was ready to put diapers on the clothesline, their sheets and bloomers had dried and their shirts and work pants flapped in the breeze.

Before she reached the pile of his work clothes, Morris Herff came back, gripping his sons' arms. "You're about useless. They're to be in school, not running the streets." He shoved the boys through the back door.

May Rose grabbed up Glory and followed, aware of the sudden stillness in yards along the hill. Inside, the boys backed to the wall of wooden birds and squirrels.

She stopped in the doorway. "I'm useless? How long has it been since your children ate?"

He took a board from his workbench and moved toward the boys. His face looked pained. "Bend over and hold your ankles."

She stepped between them and their father. "How long since this one had dry clothing? Yesterday? The day before?" She lifted the shirt and showed him Glory's red pimpled bottom. "Your sons ran off, I thought, to school."

He frowned at Glory like he didn't know her. "They'll see to her. Step aside. We don't need you no more." He raised the board.

May Rose stepped back until she felt the heat of the boys behind her. "You leave her by herself?"

"Set her down and get."

May Rose locked her hands over her wrists and tightened Glory to her chest. "Mr. Townsend hired me."

"I don't need him to do my hiring. If you need work, go to Suzie's."

"Mr. Herff, go back to the mill. I'll take care of your family."

He dropped the wood and slapped her face.

She staggered against the boys and ran with Glory out the back door. If he wanted to abuse her, let the neighbors see. Face stinging, she pried the child's arms loose and set her in the infant pen. Then she dumped his clothes into hot water, stirred the paddle, and watched the door. Her head boiled. Sweat ran into her eyes. A man would not have taken the slap. She kept a firm grip on the paddle, hoping he'd try to slap her again, but he did not come out. Her head ached.

In nearby yards, women moved quietly along their clotheslines.

Wanda ran into the yard, swinging her bucket and tugging at the collar of her shirtwaist. "These clothes is hot. Old Herff is gone. He gave Will and Charlie a beating and chased them off to school."

"He beat them? I didn't hear them cry."

"They don't cry. I could see their clothes was painful." Wanda set down the bucket, took a shirt from May Rose and pinned it to the line. "I could eat something."

"You saw him go to the mill?"

"Followed him a ways."

He might have had second thoughts about firing her. As far as she knew, he hadn't even looked to see if she and Glory were in the yard. She inspected Wanda's bucket. Dried beans, apples, and eggs from the cabin. No knife.

She re-pinned her braids. The sliver of soap was long gone, and the last and worst pile of laundry smelled like vomit. "Stay here with the baby while I go to the store for soap."

"You got soap up to your place. If you let me run up there for it, I can fetch back my old dress and them rabbit-fur boots."

"Sunday," May Rose said. "We'll go then."

At the store, Mr. Ramey pulled out Jamie's bill. "You come to settle?"

"My husband has wages due."

"I hear the company paid that to Donnelly's widow."

"Then the company is a fool. It might have put that money on Jamie's bill." She stared until he dropped his gaze. "I need two bars of soap, and a sack of oatmeal, dry beans, and a ham hock. Shoes for a girl."

He shook his head. "Better settle up."

"It's for Morris Herff. Except the shoes. They go on my account."

Mr. Ramey sighed. "You don't have an account, and he's been cut off."

"He's working again."

"Nope."

"I'm on the company payroll, and I need an account for myself."

He walked away from the counter.

She raised her voice. "Mr. Townsend said I should speak to him if I needed anything."

Mr. Ramey smirked throughout her transactions, but she left with shoes for herself and Wanda, and satisfaction that Glory and the boys would eat for a few more days.

She was paid by Wanda's delight in lace-up shoes of her own, brand new. Wanda pulled one over a dirt-crusted foot.

"I forgot to buy stockings," May Rose said.

"It fits pretty good."

May Rose pinched the toe. "A little space to grow. You need stockings, or the leather will chafe and rub sores. And you should wash your feet."

Wanda laced the shoes and stood. "My feet's tough, and I washed 'em Saturday night."

"Wash them again, so the shoes will stay clean on the inside," May Rose said.

Wanda pulled off the shoes and rubbed them against her skirt. "I'll get me some stockings." She ran from the yard.

While she was gone, May Rose swept the upstairs rooms and stacked clean diapers and clothes in the corners. She was taking work clothes from the line when Wanda reappeared with a pair of black stockings.

May Rose did not ask where they'd come from. "Help me hang these last pieces, then we'll bathe Glory and mop the kitchen floor."

"Cook those beans," Wanda said.

The sun-dried laundry freshened the house. Wanda sang "Beautiful Dreamer" and walked Glory, who preferred holding on to walking alone.

"She's penned up too much," Wanda said.

"I haven't heard her say a word."

"Nobody talks to her."

They sat on the stairs and watched Glory teach herself to walk up and down, one little hand against the wall.

"Does anyone else know the state of this family?"

"Guess so. People know most everything about everybody, whether it's right or not. Ask me something. Want to know what they call you?"

She did not. "What are the boys' names?"

"Charlie's the little 'un. The other's Will. Ask me something harder." Glory let herself fall against Wanda, who hugged her and kissed her hair.

"Here's a hard one. Where are the good neighbors?"

Wanda laughed. "They're minding their business. That's what Granny always said, 'be good and mind your business.' Folks has all got their own troubles." She wiggled her new shoes. "Ma's good. And you. You done good today."

"What about those big boys? Do people know they're bad?"

"I reckon."

"So Frank, the policeman, knows too?"

"He watches 'em, watches me too." Wanda picked up her bucket. "I'm gonna go."

May Rose thought about what she should say. Surely it was normal to tell a child to be good and to be careful, even if the child knew more about the world. Yet cautioning Wanda seemed disrespectful.

"When you're ready, let's talk about those boys. Don't gather acorns without me. We'll take Glory with us."

Wanda stopped in the doorway. "They don't all think you was naked."

CHAPTER 13

Patience; accomplish thy labor;
accomplish thy work of affection!

— HENRY WADSWORTH LONGFELLOW:
EVANGELINE

When the saws stopped, the air felt lighter. Crickets droned, and
mothers called to children playing kick-the-can in the street. May
Rose waited in the Herff doorway and watched for Will and
Charlie as the sky moved toward night and workmen paraded
home. Glory slept on her shoulder, but she had not seen the boys
since noon. It was dark when Morris Herff turned from the street
toward his house. She laid Glory on a clean blanket in the infant
pen and passed him at the door.

"Your sons didn't come home. There's food on the stove.
Expect me tomorrow."

He closed the door behind her. With no lantern, she eased her
way down the dirt slope of his yard and into the street.

She carried her old shoes and wore the new ones, which
chafed. At the church step she pulled them off and touched the
blisters on her heels. No one would notice if she wore shoes or

not. As she straightened, she bumped into someone coming out of the dark.

A hand steadied her, and a shadowed face dipped close. Dr. Hennig. "Mrs. Long? Are you all right?"

"Yes, thank you. Good evening." Uneasy, she let her shoes swing by the laces.

The doctor released her arm but walked beside her. "I understand you're working for Morris Herff."

News spread, she supposed, along laundry lines. "This was the first day." The store's lights went off, leaving the street in deeper darkness.

"How do you find the children?"

"In need of a mother."

"Yes. My wife has been concerned. Did you get on well?"

"I did what I could." She stopped. "Thank you for your interest. Good night, Dr. Hennig."

"Tell me about it." He lowered his voice. "I like to hear you talk."

"I'll be late for dinner."

He took her shoes and fitted her arm through his. "Then we'll walk faster."

She pulled loose.

He chuckled. "I didn't find your husband's brother. The one you said was in the cabin? It was in strange disarray."

In a terrifying memory, she saw Russell against the door and felt his knife rip her dress. How soon might that story echo through the mountains?

At the end of the boardwalk, she reached for her shoes. "I'll take myself home now."

"Let me bring down what you need from your place. We can meet early on Sunday. Perhaps by the mill pond, where we parted the other day?"

She considered for a moment. Wanda would like riding on the speeder, and they could bring heavy things, like potatoes, to sell. But his suggestion was improper, and she disliked his pretense.

"There's nothing I need at this time."

He followed her into the street. "Nothing? I'd like to be your friend. You can do better than Morris Herff."

She walked ahead with her shoes swinging at her side, ready to hurl them if he touched her again.

He caught up with her. "I think about you all the time."

At the mill gate, Mr. Townsend stepped from the shadows.

Dr. Hennig stopped. "Mr. Townsend. Good evening."

"Good evening. May Rose, shall we go on together? Doctor, are you walking our way?"

A door opened at Pizzy's Bar, letting out a wedge of light and a flourish of piano music. The rooms above glowed red, like they were on fire. *Suzie's place.*

"I'm going to the bar," the doctor said.

Mr. Townsend took her arm as they crossed to the stone path. "Watch your step, there. I'm sorry I can't light the way—out of fuel. Tell me, did you get on well with the children?"

She did not know how to begin. "They're in great need."

He paused at the boardinghouse gate and lit a cigar. "I see."

She doubted he did. "I opened an account at the store."

"Oh, very good. How did Morris seem?"

"Odd." It was the best she could say.

"I suppose he is. But the job suits you?"

"It does and it doesn't. My wages will not be enough to pay room and board. I'll have to find other work or a room I can afford. I'll be sorry to leave the children."

"Ah." He puffed the cigar. "What must be, must be. But Dessie and my sister frequently need help. You and the girl might earn your way here."

She liked that he'd included Wanda. "I'll do any kind of work."

He opened the gate. "Should I broach this subject with Hester?"

His help seemed necessary, for Hester would easily turn her down. Yet she felt sure Hester would resent her if he interfered again.

"I'll do it," she said.

They said goodnight and she hurried on through damp grass, followed by the scent of his cigar. In their room, Wanda sat against the pillows, singing to herself and smiling at her legs in black stockings.

"I'm so glad to see you," May Rose said. She wondered if Will and Charlie had come home, and if anyone would hold Glory that night.

IN THE MORNING, emboldened by her first sip of coffee, she watched for a good time to ask Hester about work.

Hester looked up from stirring a pot of grits. "How are those children?"

May Rose took a deep breath. "I didn't see much of the boys, but the girl is a sweet child."

Dessie and Hester waited, as though eager to hear the awful truth. "I'm sure things was in a mess," Dessie said.

"It was...surprising."

Hester spooned grits into a bowl. "I can imagine. I'm relieved you're there to help."

May Rose blinked and shook her head. "Not for long, I'm sad to say. Fifty cents a day is not enough to pay our way here."

Mr. Townsend entered from the hall and set his hat on the ice box.

"Fifty cents?" Hester rapped a spoon against the pot's rim. "That old skinflint."

"Good morning, Ladies." He cleared his throat. "Skinflint?"

May Rose kept her eyes on Hester.

"Morris Herff. He's paying May Rose fifty cents a day."

Mr. Townsend sat at the table. "So far, Morris hasn't agreed to pay anything. The company is paying. I consider it a temporary increase in his wages."

Red-faced, Hester set a bowl of grits at his place. "The company? Well, that explains it. Good heavens, I pay our wash-women seventy-five."

Dessie set a lunch box on the table. "There's few paid jobs for women in this town. Mrs. Hennig has a hired girl. There's me and the washwomen here, and Winifred, the cook at Suzie's. One of Suzie's girls cleans their place."

"I've been hoping to hear from my family," May Rose said, "but I fear we've lost each other."

Hester poured Mr. Townsend's coffee. "Somebody needs to help those children."

"I'm doing as much as I can," he said. "I can't interfere in a man's family."

"His hired help could be paid a living wage," Hester said. May Rose did not know if the contempt in Hester's voice was for her brother or for the company.

Dessie winked at May Rose.

Mr. Townsend shrugged. "Fifty cents is not unusual for women."

"And maybe they're glad to get it, if they've got husbands who work," Hester said. "May Rose, if you'll continue to help that man's children, you can have extra work here, evenings and Saturday afternoons."

"You're very kind."

With a clatter, Hester dropped a lid on the grits. "Nonsense. I'm tired of doing everything for no pay at all."

Mr. Townsend smiled at his biscuit.

WHEN NO ONE answered her knock, May Rose eased the door open. Will and Charlie sat against the wall by the stairs. On the other side of the room, their father scratched abrasive paper on the rounded top of a new chair. Glory's eyes peered from the slats of the infant pen and drew her forward. May Rose lifted her. The room was cold and the child's clothes were sodden.

The boys stared at the opposite wall.

"Mr. Herff, somebody needs to keep your daughter dry, or she's going to be sick."

He tossed the paper to the bench and shoved the chair across the floor. "They're to sit against that wall until school time. Make sure they get there."

After he left, Will and Charlie squirmed but did not get up.

"Today will be better," May Rose whispered, changing Glory. "Tomorrow too." She sneaked glances at the boys, Will the older, Charlie, the younger.

"I'm sure your father meant you to wash and eat. Did you have supper last night?"

They frowned.

She set Glory between them. "You need to take care of your sister when I'm not here."

"Women's work," Will said.

"Nonsense. You children have no Mama. You must look out for each other."

Charlie's eyes shifted to his brother. "Will spits 'bacca juice at me."

"Charlie lies," Will said.

THE SCHOOL SAT on a knoll upriver near the footbridge to Italian Town. Carrying Glory, she followed Will and Charlie and waited to make sure they didn't run back out. In the schoolyard, a girl pulled a rope to sound the bell, and a group of dark-haired children on the footbridge began to run. Two stout boys waited on this side of the bridge, the shorter one in a red cap. They let the little children pass, then blocked the bridge so the big girls had to press against them to get by. After a tussle, the boys stepped aside and the girls hurried on to the school.

May Rose walked toward the boys so they'd know she'd seen them, not just today, but on the trail with Wanda. Their faces were round and childish, their shoulders wide, their feet large. They gave her a look and ran along the river, laughing.

In the afternoon, Wanda sat in Morris Herff's new chair and wrote her numbers.

"I saw those boys today," May Rose said.

Wanda shrugged.

"You know the ones?"

"Think so."

"Will you tell me their names?"

Wanda lifted her eyes. "That'd do nobody good."

AFTER A WEEK of regular meals and clean clothes, May Rose got Will and Charlie to wash without prompting and to set Glory on a little pot. The house smelled better, but none of them spoke a word about anything she did. Herff's only instructions were, "Don't touch my workbench."

Saturday she applied twenty-five cents to her store bill.

"I heard something about a telegram," Mr. Ramey said.

"A telegram for me?"

He penciled the payment on her account page. "Maybe. I thought they said Jamie Long."

For Jamie—unlikely. For her, from Uncle Bert.

She hurried across the street and waited in the telegraph office for her turn. "Mr. Ramey said there was a telegram for me. May Rose Long?"

"Nope."

"For Jamie Long, my husband?"

"Nothing like that has come through here."

"It's important."

"They all are."

Her feet felt nailed to the floor. "Why would Mr. Ramey say

there was a telegram?"

"Ma'am, I don't know, ask him." The agent looked past her to the next customer.

Again she waited in line at the store. "Mr. Ramey, how did you hear of the telegram?"

He waved his hand. "I heard it here. There's a reward out, and men was talking about a telegram come for him. They thought it might lead to where he went."

Either the telegraph agent had forgotten, she thought, or someone was lying.

~

SUNDAY, when thunder and lightning cancelled their plans to go to the cabin, Wanda protested. "Things will be all stole when we get there. And what about them chickens? I was gonna bring one for Suzie's cook. She's fed me a lot."

May Rose didn't like to disappoint her, but Sunday afternoon was now the only time she didn't work, and she was happy to rest with her shoes off. "The chickens are probably long gone."

Wanda paced. "Singing school starts tomorrow night. The preacher and Mr. Cooper runs it. It costs fifty cents. Lots'a people goes, but I never been."

"I've paid out every penny I've earned."

"It's every night, all week, then Friday night they sing for everybody."

"Do you have your half dollar piece?"

"I bought Ma a shawl like yours. I could run up to the cabin tomorrow and get some stuff to sell."

May Rose shook her head. "Not alone."

"Then I'll get fifty cents from Suzie."

"Please, not from her."

"You think I like that old woman, but I don't. What she hands over don't change me a bit."

May Rose pulled on her shoes. "It's not honest to take gifts when you never intend to give in return."

"Puhhh! You want me to give Suzie something?"

THAT EVENING when May Rose carried slop to the pigs, Russell stepped from behind the shed. Greasy liquid splashed from the bucket onto her shoes. She gripped the bucket rim and bail, ready to toss slop into his face.

He raised his left hand. "I didn't come to hurt nobody." His face was roughly shaved, and he wore a leather glove on his right hand. Three fingers of the glove had been cut off and crudely stitched.

He nodded toward the pigs. "I heard they was here."

May Rose strode past him and tipped the bucket over the chute. "If a single one goes missing, I'm going to send the law for you. They belong to the boardinghouse now."

Without his wild beard, Russell's face looked pale and weak. He took a step back. "I don't want pigs, I'm after Jamie. Thought you might know where he's hid out."

She closed the shed door. "I haven't seen him and I don't know anything."

"That's all right. I've thought of some likely places. If I find him, I can give him a message."

"You should have offered to do that earlier."

"I'm sorry for that there. I thought you'd wronged him."

"So now you've a change of heart?"

"You didn't let me bleed to death. You took in his girl."

She breathed easier. "Tell him there's a reward. But maybe that's what you're after?"

"I don't want no more than what he stole from me. When I get it, I don't care where he goes. You want me to come back and take you to where he is?"

"He doesn't want me."

Russell's eyes shifted. "If he don't, it's 'cause you're better'n him."

CHAPTER 14

Beautiful dreamer, awake unto me

— STEPHEN COLLINS FOSTER: BEAUTIFUL
DREAMER

Someone in the boardinghouse might have lent May Rose fifty cents for singing school, possibly the teacher, Mr. Cooper, who'd seemed sympathetic to Wanda. May Rose could not bring herself to ask.

Monday when they washed for dinner, Wanda let May Rose brush her hair and tie it with a yellow ribbon.

"You don't want me to go," Wanda said.

"That's not true. I want you to have everything you want."

"But not now."

"Now is not the time for everything."

Downstairs, Wanda helped her clear the dining room while Dessie set the dishes in hot suds water. Then they sat at the work-table for their dinner. Loud talk came from the hall, the voice of their new boarder.

"It's that Mr. Tackett," Dessie said. "Some o'these men is more trouble than they're worth. Did you get on all right today?"

May Rose covered a yawn. "Glory made everything harder. She cried to be held all day, even outside while I washed clothes. The neighbors kept looking at us."

Dessie shook her head. "Still not friendly?"

"There's one who smiles. Nobody speaks."

"It's probably 'cause you're so pretty," Dessie said. "Some women is afraid of ones who are real good looking, same way they're scared of rich people. I was a little scared of you myself."

May Rose rested her forehead in her hand. "I think you're trying to make me feel good."

"I need to go to that singing school," Wanda mumbled.

Kitchen sounds faded. When May Rose lifted her eyes, she was alone. Possibly she had dozed. The toilet flushed, and Dessie entered from the hall.

May Rose looked up. "I think I fell asleep. When did Wanda leave?"

"I didn't see her go. Take your time, eat. We're behind already."

May Rose ate quickly, hoping Wanda had gone to their room.

Dessie handed her an apron. "You wash. I've done enough scrubbing today. If Hester hadn't hired you, I'd of had it all to do by myself this week, since she'll be off every night to the singing school."

"Work suits me," May Rose said. Her red hands stung in the hot water.

Dessie dried dishes faster than May Rose could wash. "It's as much a curse to be pretty as homely, don't you think?"

"I don't think about such things," May Rose said.

Dessie leaned on the counter. "Maybe not. But it's good Hester cares about them little kids, or she'd worry how Mr. Townsend favors you."

Heat crept up her neck. "Mr. Townsend wants to keep Morris Herff in his job."

"Oh, he favors you," Dessie said. "They all do—I see how they look. Probably something you're used to, men's looks."

"Oh, Dessie." May Rose laughed until her eyes watered. "I don't notice what men look at." But she knew what an interested man looked like. Jamie. Dr. Hennig. Not Russell, or Bright, or Mr. Townsend. She wiped her eyes with her apron.

"Believe me, Mr. Townsend favors you. Taking his breakfast in the kitchen? Never done that, ever. I'm real surprised Hester hired you, but it's not only 'cause of those kids. Right now she's smitten with the preacher and excited about the singing school."

May Rose set a dripping pot on the drain board. "You work morning to night. When do you have time to notice men's looks?"

"You're right about the work part, I get no rest a'tall. But noticing takes no time. By and by Hester will see how her brother looks at you."

"Maybe I should wear a bag over my head."

Dessie laughed. "Well honey, that wouldn't hide everything. You got that little sway."

"I don't sway."

"You do. I don't think you do it a'purpose. It's your natural gait, not a sway, exactly, but a sweet glide. Swings your skirt. Nothing wrong with that. Men like a little sway."

Dessie carried plates to the cupboard. "I'm only saying a girl like you's got lots of choices. Maybe even the preacher, if the town ever gets over that gossip about you going naked. Miss Hester won't marry him 'cause of his mother, and he sure needs somebody. There's Morris Herff too, he needs a mother for those children. Though I don't know if anybody short of a saint could tolerate Morris."

May Rose splashed the last pot into the water. "This is silly talk. I'm married to Jamie Long. It was done by a Methodist preacher in St. Louis, April 1st of 1898."

"Now, now," Dessie said. "I'm sure you was. But you see, Evalena always let on like they was married. And you know Jamie ain't coming back, don't you? A woman has to look out for herself. Let's just say if you want Morris, he won't be particular about Jamie one way or the other. And look, already you've stood a week with those kids. There's also our Mr. Cooper—the teacher, I expect you've seen him, the one the kids call 'Scarecrow.' He looks at you too, but he's too poor to take a wife, and he's a long ways from tidy. Mr. Townsend's the best catch, but he'll probably want to know for sure about Jamie. You might ask Evalena. If him and her was legal married, I mean."

"You're enjoying this," May Rose said.

Dessie giggled. "I am. What else do I got but work? Wait and see. If you give Mr. Townsend the littlest sign, Hester will try to sweep you out. Then we'll see who's boss. I'd enjoy that. Not you getting the boot, I mean Mr. Townsend standing up to her."

Wanda wasn't in their room. May Rose imagined her sneaking along dark streets, listening outside the school building.

"May Rose?" Dessie's voice at her door. "Someone downstairs to see you."

Likely Dr. Hennig. "I don't want to see him."

"It's a woman. You might be interested."

Near the kitchen door, an old woman in a crisp black dress hovered as though hesitant to step farther into the house. She had a short, round body, gray hair skinned back in a bun, and small dark eyes. She held a lantern in a spotted, palsied hand.

"This here's Suzie," Dessie said.

"How do," Suzie said. The way she lifted her nose, like she was sniffing the air, reminded May Rose of a groundhog. "I've come on an errand, it's about the girl." Her jaw worked around loose dentures.

"Where is she?"

Suzie shrugged. "Ain't seen her today. It's her ma, Evalena, wants to see you. Could you step over a minute?"

Dessie's eyes warned against it, but May Rose followed Suzie and her lantern into the yard. Without a word or a backward look, the old woman opened the gate and tramped along a dirt path behind the lots. May Rose hurried to stay within the lantern light.

At the rear of the bar building, Suzie opened a door to a stair dimly lit by a red bulb. May Rose followed her up stairs and along a narrow hallway. Suzie opened a door and stepped aside. The room smelled of sweat and alcohol, and it barely had space for the iron bed pushed against the wall. A woman lying there raised herself to her elbows.

"Evalena," Suzie said.

May Rose recognized the moth-eaten velvet dress, then the brown hair and sallow face of the woman she'd left unconscious on the church step.

She clasped her hands and pushed them to her middle. "I'm May Rose."

"They said you was pretty," Evalena said. "And Wanda says you're good." Evalena lay back against the pillow, closed her eyes for a moment and tried to smile. "Take Wanda. Soon as you can." Her voice was no more than a whisper.

May Rose shared Evalena's sadness. "She won't go without you."

Evalena glanced at Suzie in the doorway. "Could we talk alone?"

"It's business hours," Suzie said. "Don't be lingering." She closed the door.

"Suzie wants her," Evalena said. "She'll use her, make money, you see."

May Rose clasped her hand. "I can't afford to leave now unless my uncle finds me. When the time comes, please tell her to go with me."

"I tell her every day."

"I'll keep her safe. We'll send word when we're far away."

"That would be nice. But mail's an undependable thing." Carefully, as though her limbs hurt, Evalena adjusted herself on the narrow bed. "Suzie might give a letter to me and she might not, and if she's crossways she might make up one with bad news. Don't write. I'll know she's safe somewhere."

"We might be here for quite a while. I have to save up."

"Russell can help."

"I doubt it."

"Wanda likes you. That makes me feel good."

Suzie opened the door.

"I hope you're better soon," May Rose said.

Evalena smiled. "We'll all be better by and by."

In the hall, Suzie said, "It's so sad, how she's turned out. And she's got no real customers anymore, just a few old fellas that pay to drink with her an hour or two each night. So she says."

A door opened, blocking the exit. Suzie stretched her thin lips in a smile. "Now here's a surprise I've fixed."

A man came into the dim corridor, his face hidden by his hat and stubby beard. A wide-shouldered, long-armed man in a sheepskin coat, full lips in a lopsided smile. She knew every part of him. Jamie. He wrapped over her like a blanket. Her limbs weakened as if her blood had drained out.

At first the shock was Jamie's appearance in this unexpected place. She had a moment of forgetfulness and joy, the surprise of someone loved and lost, now found. Then a spike of angry questions.

"Good luck," Suzie said, "and get going."

Dizzy, May Rose let him lead her down the red-shadowed stairs.

The mill whistle warned of the power shutdown.

He breathed in her ear. "You knew I'd be back for you. Tell me you knew."

She hadn't hoped. He moved her along too fast through slippery grass. They stopped in the shadow behind the hog shed and listened to distant voices. Nellie snorted for attention.

Jamie kissed her fingers. "What a girl, getting the sow and her pigs down here, getting a job, taking care of Russell like that, tying him like a dog. Yeah, Suzie hears everything. Don't worry, she's careful who she tells."

Dry leaves blew around them, and Jamie opened his coat and wrapped her to his chest. "Get your coat, and bring something to eat. I'll wait right here by old Nellie, and when the town's all dark, we'll cut out."

"Tonight?"

"On the Tannery Road. By morning we'll be in Jennie Town. Board the train there, it's safer."

Walking all night to Jennie Town. He never liked her to suggest a better way.

"You sold our place. What did you think would happen to me?"

"Honey, I came back for you." He ran light fingers along her neck. "If I hadn't gone then, I'd be dead. It still ain't safe where Donnelly's got friends."

She warmed in his hug. He'd come back, risked capture for no other reason than he wanted her and a new start. Together, they'd take Wanda away from Suzie. That alone might make her forget the rest.

"If we disappear in the night, will anyone come after us?"

"People disappear all the time, nobody looks. They'll think you went back up the mountain. But for sure if I'm found here, they'll hang me from a tree."

Might Hester raise an alarm about her disappearance? Dr. Hennig? She could imagine the doctor setting someone like Bright on their trail. "If you'll give me some money, I'll settle our bills tomorrow. After that, we'll board here and meet you at Jennie Town. Don't worry, I won't give you away—I'll let Hester think my uncle sent the money."

"Wait now." He stepped back. "*We'll* board? Who's we?"

"Wanda—your daughter—and me."

"May Rose. You can't believe every little thing folks say. I never claimed that kid was mine."

"It doesn't matter. I want her, and Evalena wants her to go with me."

"There's another liar. The kid's not coming. I told Suzie she'd be staying."

"You told Suzie?"

"Look, she's been hiding me since Russell grabbed my getaway cash. If I don't live up to my part of the deal, she'll give me up."

"So you made a deal? I go away with you and Wanda goes to work for Suzie?" She choked. "Doing that?"

"It won't be forever. Suzie's old, did you notice?" He reached into his pocket and brought out a pistol and a wad of bills. "This'll let us start over."

She knocked the bills to the ground. "You traded Wanda."

He bent and picked them up. "I didn't know you'd want her." He put his hands each side of her neck, ran them down her shoulders, down her arms. She stiffened.

"Rosie, I provided for you. I killed a man, defending you! I'm here where men want to kill me. For you."

"No." She'd come through the worst part of losing him. She pressed her face into his bristly cheek and breathed his scent. When he moved his lips over hers, she turned her face away.

"You won't go? Because of a whore's kid?"

She did not speak.

"All right. All right. We'll take her. Get her and be quick."

A light appeared in the back upstairs window, their room.

She lifted her eyes to his. "Jamie, go your way. You don't want me, and I don't love you." It was mostly true.

WANDA BOUNCED THE BEDSPRINGS, singing. "Do-ti-do-sol…me…re-ri-ra-la. How 'bout that?"

May Rose poured water into the basin and submerged her cold, shaking hands. "It sounds like 'Beautiful Dreamer.'" She loosened her braids and jerked a comb through the kinks in her hair, bringing tears to her eyes. She blinked them away and picked long strands from the comb. "Do-ti-do, is this what you learned from singing school?"

"It's how you learn music! Do-re-mi-re-do-do-do!" Wanda sang up and down again. "Like that."

Jamie would be well past the tannery, walking in the dark of the moon toward Jennie Town. It would be better when she could no longer imagine him anywhere. Wanda looked so happy.

May Rose stretched her tight cheeks in a smile. "Is that a song?"

"Singing practice. Right at the end, the preacher taught 'em Beautiful Dreamer, but I could sing it already. I couldn't go inside and I couldn't never see 'cause people crowded the door. I liked it anyways."

May Rose blew out the lamp. Tomorrow she'd ask Mr. Cooper if Wanda could walk back and forth to singing school with him.

"I like the Beautiful Dreamer words," Wanda said, "but some are funny. "*Beautiful dreamer, wake unto me.* Is that a fancy way to say wake up?"

"Yes," May Rose said. Wake unto me, see who I am, love me.

She lay a long time without sleep, aware of Jamie on the road to Jennie Town, stretching the final distance between them. When she slept at last, it was not rest, but frequent wakening from an endless dream, Jamie singing to her in moonlight, Wanda singing louder, Jamie telling Wanda she had no voice, Wanda downing him with a skillet, and Jamie tearing May Rose's dress right before she chopped off his fingers with the ax.

CHAPTER 15

Feeling is deep and still; and the word that floats on the surface
Is as the tossing buoy, that betrays where the anchor is hidden.

— HENRY WADSWORTH LONGFELLOW:
EVANGELINE

May Rose slipped from bed near the end of night when snores had ceased and Wanda lay so quiet she seemed almost not to breathe. In a few hours, Suzie would discover that Jamie had left with her money, alone.

In the kitchen Dessie poured coffee. "Well, there you are, early-bird. Sit. I'm about to have my morning cup."

May Rose sat and closed her eyes.

Dessie set another thick mug on the table. "Not awake yet? I get like that. Can't sleep, can't get awake. So, how was it, last night?"

Coffee scalded her tongue. "Last night?"

"At Suzie's."

Best not to think, and never to tell.

"What did you think of Evalena? And Suzie's place?"

"Evalena. She was very kind."

"She always was. Me and her went to school together for a time, Russell, too. I guess you know Jamie's brother, Russell?"

"I know him."

Dessie had a habit of angling her head to pay particular attention, like she could see better that way. "He's a strange one, ain't he? I always liked Evalena."

"You lived here before the mill? You knew Jamie?"

"Nobody lived here before the mill—this was just a trading post. I'm talking about the other side of the mountain, in the big valley over there, past Russell's. Jamie was younger, so I didn't know him so much. Odd, ain't it, me knowing all of them, and now you and Wanda. When you go way back with a person, like when you was kids, you feel closer. Not that I see Evalena anymore, Hester wouldn't like it, and I ain't told her none of this. But Evalena was a sweet girl, just not able to help herself. I always felt bad how things turned out."

"Evalena's sick," May Rose said.

"So they say."

"She wants me to take Wanda away where Suzie can't get her."

Dessie nodded. "It'd be for the best."

Shortly, a train would take Jamie far away. Each time she twinged with envy or regret, she thought of his deal with Suzie.

WANDA BURST into the Herff house mid-morning as May Rose patted out dough for apple dumplings and Glory played with pans and spoons on the floor. She'd charged sugar, apples, lard, and flour to Morris Herff's account. Let him complain. Maybe if his family ate sweet things, they'd be kinder to each other.

Wanda looked wilder than usual. "Suzie said you lit out with Jamie. Why'd she say a thing like that?"

She handed Wanda an apple slice. "Suzie's not a good person."

"But Ma said it, too. Said you'd gone. She cried when I come, said I was supposed to go with you. I told 'em Dessie said you was there for breakfast. Suzie's mad enough to spit."

May Rose sliced the dough into six portions, wondering what to tell. She sprinkled sugar on the apples and brushed her hands over the bowl. "I hope to leave when I have money saved. Your ma wants you to go with me. Suzie doesn't." She paused and looked up. "Do you understand?"

Wanda chewed the apple. "Whew, sour. I know what old Suzie wants."

"Maybe your ma will get better and go with us."

"Suzie says Jamie stole from her, says she's gonna call out the police. And guess what—them pigs is gone. Me and Dessie looked for 'em all over town."

AT NOON, Morris Herff brought home a poke of eggs and canned milk.

"I see you're charging to my bill."

She lifted Glory and set her in his arms. "Do you think supper drops from the sky?"

He looked confused. "Neighbors…"

"Hold her while I dish up your lunch."

He sat stiffly with the child on his lap then dug into the warm apple dumpling like a starved man.

"Feed some of that to the baby," May Rose said. "She likes it."

Will and Charlie tramped into the house, but backed against the kitchen wall when they saw their father. They carried their dumplings outside.

Morris Herff lifted the edge of his plate and scraped the spoon across it. "Directly you should go to the store and get supplies for a week or more, whatever Ramey will let you have. There's been a wreck, there below Jennie Town, so we'll not be supplied till the trains run again. That means no cattle for the slaughterhouse, no hay for the camp horses, no coal, nothing. In a couple of days, food will run short."

Wobbling, she braced her hand on the table. "A train wreck? Was anyone hurt?"

He rubbed his mouth and wiped his hand on his trousers. "One of them big trestles gave way, took down the engine and coal tender, maybe another car. There's different reports."

"Oh, my." She held on to the edge of the sink.

He stayed with Glory while she went to the store and joined a line stretching down the steps to the boardwalk. Women speculated about the wreck and what might be left to buy when they reached the counter. They neither ignored nor included her. Some said the trestle was newly repaired but the maintenance crew had left out critical bolts. Others were certain logs had escaped from a timber landing, plunged down the slope like an avalanche and crashed into the trestle. She chewed her lip until she tasted blood, imagining Jamie crushed and dead.

The line moved slowly toward Mr. Ramey's counter. Customers left with as much as they could carry, increasing worried comments among those who waited.

Mr. Ramey's voice rose over the chatter. "Mrs. Donnelly, you'll have to cut back. Less you strike gold, you'll never pay down your bill."

May Rose winced. Another woman in her predicament, with a name and cause too familiar.

Mrs. Donnelly stood her ground, a woman with rusty, straggly hair, as tall as a man with shoulders broader than most, dressed like everyone else in a dark skirt and shawl. "Me and my boys is stuck here. Do you mean to let us starve?"

"Basics, ma'am. Beans and cornmeal and potatoes. Plenty get by on less."

"Sugar?"

"I'm running low. See me when the train comes again."

With a whip of her skirt, Mrs. Donnelly stopped beside May Rose. "Don't think I don't know who you are. No less than the cause of my trouble." Around them, women stopped talking and stepped out of the way.

May Rose opened her mouth to speak, but Mrs. Donnelly thrust a broad palm against her chest, and she wobbled back over the pickle barrel and fell hard on her rear. A young woman helped her up and retrieved her basket. Gasping, May Rose thanked her and brushed grit from her hands.

Mrs. Donnelly turned to Mr. Ramey. "Now she thinks she's respectable. You better not give her no sugar."

Mrs. Hennig stepped forward, a tall woman in brown taffeta and a brown feathered hat. "Irene, violence killed your husband. You must set a better example for your boys." She walked Mrs. Donnelly away.

Mr. Ramey scowled. "Next?"

He brought May Rose's requests to the counter and jotted them on the Herff account.

"No mail," he said. "Not till trains run again." She hadn't asked.

~

Late afternoon, May Rose set Glory on her hip and walked Will and Charlie through town to the boardinghouse.

"I'd like to see that wreck," Charlie said. "Do you suppose a feller could walk down there?"

Will kicked a pebble. "My teacher said if you started in the morning it'd be dark when you got there."

Charlie raced ahead and kicked Will's pebble farther down the road. "I could sleep out, see it in the morning."

"You don't want to do that," May Rose said. "It's cold at night."

Will jostled Charlie with his hip. "And there's dead people."

"Let's not talk about it," May Rose said. "Did you hear anything at school today about pigs running loose?"

"Just the wreck," Charlie said.

In the boardinghouse yard, Hester asked the boys' names and held out her arms for Glory.

"I'm sorry about the pigs," May Rose said.

"It's a terrible time to lose them."

May Rose expected to see holes under the hog lot fence, but found an unlatched gate. "Someone let them out. If they've gone to the woods, I can coax them back."

"Thievery," Hester said. "They'll be splayed and roasted by now."

"I'd say it was mischief." Last night, she and Jamie had stood at that gate. "The pigs would give thieves a merry chase and raise a ruckus. You can't hardly catch a pig."

"It's too near dark to search now," Hester said, "but maybe you and Wanda could look for them tomorrow. Mr. Townsend can get someone else to mind these children."

As May Rose and the children walked home, two big boys cut through a nearby yard. She knew them well.

She bent to Charlie. "Who are those boys?"

"Them that just run through?"

"Yes."

"Donnellys. We hate 'em."

"Walk on, not too fast." She patted Glory's back as though the child was the one who needed comfort.

When they turned the corner onto their street, Will and Charlie ran ahead. Will shouted back, "There goes Miss Ruie. She ain't supposed to be out by herself."

The old woman tottered along toward the far end of the street. May Rose walked faster.

Will reached her first and dodged as she slapped the air around him. Charlie stepped in front of her, and May Rose came up behind, holding Glory.

"Miss Ruie," May Rose said.

Ruie turned and stared.

"I'm May Rose, remember me? Let's walk together, back this way."

Ruie reached for Glory. "That's my girl's baby."

May Rose tightened her hold. "She's heavy. I'll carry her for you. We'll go along to your house."

Ruie pried her knobby fingers around Glory, but May Rose stepped away and handed Glory to Will. He put her on his hip and walked off toward their house.

Charlie slipped his hand into Ruie's. "Miss Ruie? Would you take me home?"

Ruie blinked. "You poor little boy. Where do you live?"

He pointed to the church steeple. "Down there."

"I'll take care of you," she said. "I had a little boy your age."

When they reached the church, Preacher Gowder ran down the steps and threw his hands in the air. "What now?"

"There's been a wreck," Ruie said. "I rescued these people."

He looked at May Rose. "She was sleeping when I left. I can't stay with her all the time."

"Just holler for me," Charlie said. "I'll take care of her."

The preacher gripped his mother's hand. "You're good to offer, but even I'm not strong enough when she gets contrary."

Charlie shied away when May Rose attempted to hug him.

When she left that evening, she had to peel Glory's hands from her dress. Sobbing, Glory clung to the doorframe.

From the street she heard Morris Herff shout, "Boys, mind the baby."

She went back inside and found him at his workbench. "Mr. Herff, comfort your daughter. She misses her mama."

His face puckered like he might cry. She stood at the door until he walked across the room and reached down for his daughter.

The image of Glory in her father's arms soothed May Rose for a few homeward steps before she wilted under her own troubles —Jamie, Jamie and Suzie, Suzie and Wanda, Wanda and the Donnelly boys—all more terrifying than the prospect of a town cut off by a wreck.

At the store, men clogged the steps, going up one side and coming down the other with cans of snuff and cigarette tobacco.

"May Rose." Mr. Townsend fell in step beside her.

She hadn't seen him since Dessie's talk about men's looks, and she'd had no leisure to wonder if Dessie might be right.

He seemed to be thinking aloud. "You've heard of our wreck?"

She felt like she'd been in it.

He didn't wait for an answer. "If it stops work in the camps for more than a few days, our wood hicks will hike over the mountain to other jobs." He stopped and gazed along the tracks from the mill pond to the lumber docks.

She waited a short distance away, wondering if she should walk on.

He resumed walking, now at a faster pace. "Soon after the logs stop coming, we'll lay off mill hands, too. Things could get grim."

She doubted he knew the meaning of the word.

"We'll pay in scrip as long as there's work, but after a few days money won't matter—there'll be nothing left to buy."

Finally he slowed and looked at her. "I need to tell you something. Someone here has reported that Jamie Long boarded the train at Jennie Town. And you know, the wreck…"

"I see. Thank you." If he watched to see how she felt, he'd find no clues in her face. She'd had a night and a day to wall herself off from Jamie. Humming silently, she brought to mind an image of Wanda in white stockings and satin slippers.

AT DINNER THAT EVENING, May Rose dished up in the kitchen and washed pots and pans while Dessie served the dining room and relayed news about the wreck.

"They all want to see it," Dessie said. "Mr. Tackett, that's the salesman, says if the railroad can't get him out of here, it can give him a free ride down there to see the wreck."

Wanda jumped up from her seat at the worktable. "Can I go?"

"There'll be no sight-seeing. Mr. Townsend said the railroad don't want rubberneckers down there. Did you hear about the passenger car? They say it's on its side, top o' the engine. Some think the trestle may have to be fixed before the car and engine can be lifted. A work train went down to bring out the passengers, dead or alive."

May Rose pressed her fist to her lips.

Dessie patted her shoulder. "Oh, dear, it is upsetting, ain't it. But I doubt any on the train was known to us."

CHAPTER 16

Fair was she and young;

— HENRY WADSWORTH LONGFELLOW:
EVANGELINE

May Rose waited under the parlor arch with Wanda, who looked ready to spring. Dessie had paid for Wanda's singing school, and Mr. Cooper had agreed to see her safely along. He came from the parlor as Hester descended the stairs.

"Walk like a lady," May Rose whispered.

Wanda followed Hester and Mr. Cooper through the door with an added wiggle in her stride.

Behind May Rose, Dessie laughed. "She's a spark, ain't she?"

May Rose followed her to the kitchen. "Suzie wants her."

"Suzie wants..." Dessie dropped to a chair. "Ahh, we've worried of something like that. It's good Wanda's got you."

"Jamie was supposed..." she choked... "to take me away. Last night. Suzie paid him, so Wanda would have nobody."

Dessie snorted. "Jamie and Suzie, what a pair of snakes."

"I think he boarded the train from Jennie Town this morning."

"No. That train?" Dessie stood and hugged her. "You all right?"

"I've had better days. Can we wait dishes a minute? I need to talk with Evalena."

"Suzie won't be cheered to see you. She might not let you in, but you could sneak through the kitchen down below." She tied her shawl. "Let's go."

Dessie guided her to a tin-plated door at the rear of Pizzy's Bar and into a kitchen with a sticky concrete floor. Boisterous piano music roared in from the bar.

"They got one a'them pianos plays itself," Dessie said. "It'd drive me crazy, but Winifred's near deaf. That's her over there."

A stout woman with her back turned plunged a potato masher into a bowl. The door to the bar swung open and a man in a butcher's apron came through with a tray of mugs. He dipped his face toward the cook, shouted, "Company," and turned her toward Dessie and May Rose.

The cook held her hand behind her ear.

"Hello, Winifred," Dessie shouted. "We've come for a word with Evalena."

Winifred pointed to a flight of steps.

"You go along," Dessie said. "I'll holler at Winifred a second and get back to the dishes."

The stairs brought May Rose to the end of the hall opposite the main entry. Below, the piano music changed to a sad ballad with fancy trills, and a male voice sang along. With no one to stop her, she walked quickly and rapped on Evalena's door. She thought she heard a voice telling her to come in, but when she opened the door, her face grew hot. Evalena sat on her bed, smoothing thin hair from the forehead of a man who lay with his head in her lap.

"Oh, pardon me."

Evalena looked up and smiled. "It's all right."

"I'll come another time."

"I'm glad to see you."

In the hall, Suzie blocked her way.

"Ain't this interesting," Suzie said. "I'll bet you're here to crow 'cause you skipped that train."

"No thanks to you." May Rose tried to walk around her.

Suzie stepped into her path. "You and me's got no quarrel."

"We do. Wanda."

"I love that girl like a daughter," Suzie said.

"I'm not going to let anything bad happen to her."

Suzie's puckered lips broke in a laugh. "What a fool thing to say."

"You know what I mean. She'll not do your work."

"You think you and her are better'n me? Sooner or later you'll see we're all the same. We grow up thinking men will take care of us, then we learn they're weak and faithless. If they mean to keep us on our backs, we're fools not to take advantage."

"You take advantage of poor women."

"What do you know? You can't judge by Evalena—she was done for when she came here. I took her in."

"So generous."

"Listen here, I was brought up to this, never knowed anything else. I got seven mouths to feed, not just these girls but the cook and our bouncer and handyman. Some of them's got families."

"Feeding people doesn't make any of this right. You won't get Wanda." May Rose stepped around her and walked toward the stairs.

"You may be surprised what she chooses."

May Rose stumbled home through the grass. In the kitchen, she snatched a dishtowel with one hand and plucked a handful of forks from the rinse water with the other. Half the forks clattered to the floor.

Dessie picked them up and dropped them back into the rinse. "Trouble over there?"

"Suzie thinks Wanda will choose to work for her."

"She's got nerve, don't she? Miss Hester and the doctor's wife would like to run her off, but Mr. Townsend says he can't do nothing 'cause the place ain't on company property." Dessie shook her head. "Most act like Suzie's business is a necessary evil."

"Even the police?"

Dessie laughed. "Frank's a friend of the business. Not many here know or give a hoot if she works girls too young, no more'n they care if she chucks them out when they're too old to do anything but wander off and die. But the same will happen to me, 'cause I got nobody and nothing." Dessie stacked clean pots on a low shelf. "Honey, you look to yourself while you're young, catch a man of means and get kids to take care of you in your old age. If you go somewheres else you don't need to say you was ever married. Or thought you was."

That night May Rose burned the lamp while Wanda sang every note and repeated every word she'd learned at singing school.

Finally exhausted, Wanda threw herself back on the bed. "I'm the best."

May Rose tucked her under the covers. "I know you are."

WEDNESDAY MORNING, Hester said her brother had arranged a substitute at the Herff house, so after breakfast, May Rose and Wanda trudged up the trail, calling for Nellie and the pigs.

"If we get as far as the cabin, you can bring back whatever you can carry," May Rose said. "But if we find the pigs first, we have to coax them back to Hester's."

Wanda hopped along with extra steps. "Last night, folks at the singing school said Jamie was dead in the wreck. Did he go off on the train?"

"I'm not sure."

"Do you miss him? Ma got sad when he left us. She missed him awful."

May Rose stabbed her walking stick ahead. "I don't think of him."

Wanda stopped and sniffed. "I think I smell them pigs. I do, I smell 'em."

The tall oaks and hickories cast long shadows across the forest floor. From somewhere came a scent of rotting apples.

Wanda cupped her hands around her mouth. "Soo-ey, soo-ey."

"Here." May Rose poked her stick at pig droppings. "This is what you smell. Not dry, so not old. They've been this way."

They reached the clearing with no other sign. The place looked almost as they'd left it, but without smoke from the chimney or chickens pecking at the stream.

Wanda ran heedlessly into the cabin, while May Rose walked as though one of Bright's men might ambush her. The bed had been pulled from the wall, its length of rope cut. Russell—or mice —had left no crumb of bread or pie. She had no desire to stay long enough to put anything in place.

"I like this little house," Wanda said.

May Rose stared at the smear of blood in the doorway. She couldn't say she did or didn't. She had changed what she could and endured everything else.

She found her copy of *Evangeline*, took her coat from the clothes box and closed the door behind them. A gust of wind blew across the tracks from the west, whipping the trees with such noise that she did not know the speeder was coming until she saw it and heard its brakes. Dr. Hennig.

"We should take corn," she said, watching him. "I doubt Russell's carried it away. If we run across the pigs, corn will help get them back to Hester."

Wanda pulled the rabbit fur moccasins and Jamie's stiff hunting jacket from pegs on the outside wall. "Like a trail?"

The doctor jumped down from the speeder.

"We won't lay a trail unless we find them. Run to the corncrib and see what you can find."

Wanda glanced from the doctor to May Rose, then twirled across the grass.

May Rose put on her coat and watched him draw near.

He shaded his eyes. "You don't know how I miss seeing you." His voice broke. "There in the doorway, in your blue dress, or out in the yard throwing grain, chickens at your feet. I still watch for you each time I pass—I can't help myself. Seeing you now lifts my heart." He laid his hand on his chest. "My cornflower girl!"

In the corncrib door, Wanda held up two rusty buckets. "These be good?"

May Rose nodded but watched the doctor. "Dr. Hennig, you have a wife, and I'm not who you think I am. I don't like this sort of talk."

Harsh sunlight shadowed his sunken cheeks and caught the silver in his untrimmed beard. He squinted in the glare. "I dream of a day when nobody is hurt or sick. I dream of going away and living on the side of a mountain with you. I pray to God to be delivered from evil desires." He took her hand, but loosely. "Pray for me."

She pulled away.

"Let me take you down on the speeder."

"Not today."

"You have other admirers now."

"We should not speak again." She walked toward the corncrib.

He called after her. "If your husband isn't dead already, he'll be found and hanged."

She watched the speeder disappear down the track.

Wanda stood in the open door of the shed, looking solemn. "He used to like Ma."

They ripped dry kernels from the cobs until they had two heavy buckets. "Too full," Wanda said. May Rose poured what they couldn't carry into a crock and covered the top with a board.

Near town, the pigs found them. From that moment, she and Wanda ran among hooves that tramped too close and snouts that snapped at their fingers. They swung the buckets overhead from hand to hand and tossed corn to the side. Laughing, shrieking, they ran like this through the mill and into Hester's yard.

A man leaned on the back fence.

Wanda sucked in her breath. "Russell."

He looked at May Rose. "I found Jamie and took my money back. So the place is yours again."

"Thank you, but it makes no difference." She shut the gate after the pigs. Her wedding gift had bought it, but without proof that she was his wife, she'd have no claim even if he was found dead.

Wanda went to the fence. "Lemme see them fingers."

He put the gloved hand behind his back. "I heard of the wreck."

"You've cleaned up," Wanda said.

"Same to you." He looked at May Rose. "They're saying Jamie was on that train. I might go down there, find out for sure."

"If they find him alive, they'll hang him," she said.

He turned away, raising his gloved hand in farewell. "Let me know."

Wanda called, "What'cha mean by that?"

He looked back at May Rose. "Let me know, happens you need something."

They stood at the gate as he shuffled away.

"He's sorry." Grinning, Wanda shifted her eyes side to side.

"Please don't do that," May Rose whispered.

CHAPTER 17

Even if she be not harmed, her heart may fail her
in so much and so many horrors
and hereafter she may suffer, both in waking, from her nerves,
and in sleep, from her dreams.

— BRAM STOKER: DRACULA

Glory's exhausted wails reached May Rose on the street below the house and hurried her up the dark slope to the door. The front room bulb was off, but light from the kitchen showed the legs of two boys who sat on the floor.

"Will, Charlie," she said. "Good morning." Their father had not punished them like this for the past week.

From the infant pen, Glory stretched up her arms. May Rose bent, and the child wrapped chilled arms around her neck.

A broad shadow came between them and the light, a woman, her features unclear.

"Here, now, what're you doing with that child?"

"Hello? I'm May Rose. I take care of her."

"No more you don't." The woman snatched Glory and set her behind the bars. Glory wailed. "She's been spoiled," the woman said, "but I've got her now." She pulled the string that lit the bulb. *Mrs. Donnelly.*

May Rose whirled to the boys. "Will, where's your father?"

"Gone to work, soon as she come through the door."

"Morris don't need a fancy troublemaker like you," Mrs. Donnelly said.

May Rose lifted Glory again and backed toward the kitchen. Wetness soaked into her shawl and dress. "Mr. Townsend hired me, so I'll be here until he tells me different." She breathed faster. "Boys, have you had breakfast?"

Mrs. Donnelly pointed a finger. "They're to sit until school time. No need to bother yourself with my business."

"How is this your business? I've been here more than a week, and the children know me. The job isn't yours because you came early today."

Mrs. Donnelly marched to the door and opened it. "Time for you to get out."

May Rose bent her face to Glory's wet cheek. "Mrs. Donnelly, I wish you well, but this is my position."

"You're a dumb cluck, and this door is letting in the cold."

"I'm going to start oats so the boys won't go to school hungry. Go ask Mr. Townsend if you're supposed to be here."

Mrs. Donnelly rushed from the door and pulled Glory from her arms, and in another swift movement seized her wrist. The boys sucked in their cheeks and watched with wide eyes.

May Rose reached for Glory with her free hand, but Mrs. Donnelly leaned toward the infant pen and dropped her into it.

"Please," May Rose said. "Let's talk with Mr. Townsend."

Like she weighed nothing at all, Mrs. Donnelly dragged her to the front door and pushed her outside.

May Rose stumbled down the steps. The light in the front room went off. She faced the door, humiliated and hot enough to force herself inside and let Mrs. Donnelly throw her down and push her out again, more violence for the children to see.

Glory sobbed.

May Rose raised her voice to be heard inside. "Will, Charlie, be good today, and take care of your sister. I'll be back tomorrow."

Glory's cries held her until they fell to whimpers, then she pulled her shawl close and walked toward the main street. She could excuse Mrs. Donnelly for fighting for this job, but not for letting Glory cry, nor for putting new terror in Will and Charlie. Even if tomorrow she reached the house first, at some point Mrs. Donnelly would engage her in a scratching, clubbing fight that would end badly, whoever won.

Though it had been only two days since the wreck, the valley looked and sounded different. The saws still whined and logs rolled off into the mill pond and clattered up the slip jack, but she heard no bawling from cattle cars and no whistles of arriving trains. Townspeople walked on the street as though on holiday, and a few mountain people stood on corners, offering game and fish, corn meal and potatoes at high prices.

On the brick platform by the railroad she shuffled with others toward the company office, feeling like a child on her way to tattle.

Around her, men talked of the wreck and women jostled babies and worried aloud. "We've got nothing saved up," a young woman said. "Nothing. And we've already ate most of what I raised this summer." The woman adjusted the child on her hip. "Even if we knew where to go, we'd have to walk and carry everything. We got no horse, not even a hand-cart."

An older woman coughed into her handkerchief. "The company wants us to stay right here. 'Course it will go on charging rent, even while there's no work. We'll be in a hole so deep we'll never climb out."

Wind blew along the track. May Rose hugged her arms to her body and listened to echoes of her own fears.

"We was fools to come to this dead-end place."

"It makes no sense to stay."

"But how will we leave?"

"The only roads out is hell," a man said, "cause the company don't never use 'em. Washed out and rocky as a creek bed. And there's no towns for a long ways."

"The company's got to help us."

A door opened, and the crowd rushed forward. Mr. Townsend came out and worked his way slowly toward the tracks, speaking to this person and that, shaking one's hand, waving another off. He looked surprised to see May Rose, but took her by the arm and walked her toward an engine coupled to a short red caboose.

He did not speak until they'd moved past the others. "Does Hester need something?"

She shook her head. "I went to work today, but Mrs. Donnelly…" A burst of steam covered her words.

He cupped his ear and leaned close. Smoke swirled around them.

"Mrs. Donnelly believes she has replaced me. At Morris Herff's."

"Mrs. Donnelly? Yes, from yesterday. I haven't thanked you for finding the pigs. We're very grateful." He pulled a watch from his pocket. "Is there something else?"

A trainman at the back of the caboose watched their approach. May Rose tried to speak calmly. "Did you hire Mrs. Donnelly in my place?"

"For yesterday, yes."

"Not permanently?"

"I don't think I gave that impression."

"She's there now, and won't leave. I thought Mr. Herff was pleased with my work. I know the children like me."

Mr. Townsend stopped at the caboose. "I'll see what Morris has to say. I'm sorry, I'm in a bit of a hurry, going down to the wreck." He climbed the steel steps.

She clutched the rail. "Mrs. Donnelly will not be good for the children."

He waved from the platform, so polite, but perhaps too busy to care.

She turned around in time to see the few people left on the

depot platform step out of the way of a trio weaving among them. She caught her breath, recognizing a wild bush of hair, the flash of a red cap. Wanda ran along the track toward the caboose, chased by the Donnelly boys. The shorter boy caught her and tried to push her to the ground. When she swung loose, the taller slammed into her.

May Rose ran forward, calling "help." A blast of steam smothered the sound.

Wanda punched the shorter boy's chest and jabbed at his head, but the taller caught her from behind. He squeezed his arms around her waist while his brother dodged her jabs and pulled at her clothes. The boy holding her was nearly as big as his mother. May Rose flung herself onto his back. When he wiggled to throw her off, she dug her fingernails near his eyes. He yelped, released Wanda, and twisted May Rose from his back.

She grabbed Wanda's hand and ran toward the caboose with the boys thumping close behind. The engine puffed black smoke, and wheels turned. May Rose jumped onto the first step, pulled herself up the next and reached back to seize Wanda's hand. The caboose jerked and swayed down the track with May Rose and Wanda on the steps, clinging to the railing.

"Whoosh," Wanda said, her face red and wild. She pointed to steps on the other side of the caboose platform.

Charlie Herff held on there, laughing.

The Donnellys ran alongside, losing ground and shouting, "Whores!"

A man in a striped trainman's cap opened the caboose door. "What the hell?"

Mr. Townsend appeared behind him. "May Rose. Perhaps I should have invited you." His expression made her think she must look as wild as Wanda.

The caboose rocked. She stepped up to the platform, and the trainman pulled Charlie and then Wanda up beside her. "Inside, all of you," he shouted. "It's not safe to ride out here, and we're not stopping now."

Inside, Mr. Townsend pointed to a leather bench along one wall. "It would have been better to ask if you could come along." He raised his voice above the engine noise.

"I'm sorry to disrupt your trip," May Rose said.

Charlie stopped at the ladder to the cupola and climbed to the second rung. "I jumped on," he shouted, "and they followed to fetch me back."

"And who are you?"

"Charlie Herff."

"I see." The caboose swayed. Smoke rolled past the windows. Mr. Townsend leaned toward May Rose. "Keep them close until we return."

She sat on the bench with Wanda and motioned to Charlie, but he hung on the ladder and peered up into the cupola.

The caboose had front and back doors, a window on each side, a built-in desk, and a pot-belly stove. Mr. Townsend took the desk chair and drew a folded paper from an inside coat pocket. "I hope they'll be quiet. I have to make use of my time."

The trainman built a fire in the stove, then both he and Charlie climbed to the cupola and watched forward.

Wanda scooted close on the bench and spoke in her ear. "They got my knife."

May Rose took her hand. They did not try to talk, quieted by events, by engine roar and clack of wheels, and by the example of Mr. Townsend, absorbed at his desk.

Her worries rocked with the caboose while she gazed at everything from the domed wooden ceiling to the brass spittoon. From time to time she glanced at Mr. Townsend, bewildered by Dessie's ideas. To make him less intimidating, she tried to imagine him as a boy, but he remained stiff and standoffish, a sober child who kept his young thoughts to himself. Maybe shy.

Wanda stared at trees flashing by, but revived when the engine stopped and Charlie jumped down the ladder.

Mr. Townsend stopped them at the door. "You'll have to stay here until I see if there's a safe place to view the work."

When he and the trainman left the caboose, Wanda climbed to the cupola. "Can't see much 'cause of that train ahead."

"Work train," Charlie said. "It's where they stay at night."

Wanda climbed down. "Do you think they got Jamie laid out on the ground somewhere?"

May Rose felt faint. "We don't know he's dead, or that he was on this train." Even so, at unexpected times she saw him cold and flattened by tons of steel.

Mr. Townsend returned, pulling on gloves. "I've found a place where you may watch safely." He looked from Charlie to Wanda. "Stay close to Mrs. Long. No running around."

They emerged under a gray sky and walked along the track toward the bridge. She'd hoped to avoid it, but now the scene drew her with shouts and thumps. Mr. Townsend led them to an area of trampled weeds. From there they could see to the other side of the break and down into the ravine where a passenger car lay on its side, the engine below it.

Charlie inched toward the edge.

"Charlie," May Rose said. "Hold my hand."

He grimaced.

"If you won't, we'll go back to the caboose."

He slid his dirty hand into hers and frowned toward Wanda. "What about her?"

"She's a big girl, and she wasn't sneaking off."

In the middle of the bridge, a section of ties and rails hung precariously over a gap, and workmen crossed on boards laid down in the decking. On the far side, a steam engine and crane waited on the rails.

Steep paths cut through laurel on both sides of the ravine. At the lowest point, men with crosscut saws worked to clear a jam of logs.

The trainman stopped beside them and pointed to the shattered trestle framework. "The logs run downhill and slammed into the trestle, and the weight of the train took it down."

Mr. Townsend blew cigar smoke. May Rose wondered if he felt responsible.

Two men on the trestle's middle tier hung like monkeys and sawed at a brace. Someone called, "Look out below!" Men scrambled away from the logjam. The sawyers made the final cut and leaned back as the brace tumbled, crashed, and bounced.

Mr. Townsend ground his cigar under his boot and motioned to the far side. "I need to speak with the superintendent over there. Please keep the children here." He crossed the temporary deck with cautious steps.

The trainman stared solemnly into the ravine and shook his head. "Nasty business."

She had to ask. "Were there survivors?"

"Not sure," the trainman said. "The engineer and fireman's dead, and still under there. I knew 'em both, good men. Six passengers was pulled out yesterday, all dead. One of the work trains took them back to Jennie Town, and their bodies was claimed. The stationmaster said he ticketed seven passengers, but nobody's come forward about the seventh except Frank, who thinks he has an idea who it was. The feller might be somewhere they can't get to him. If he fell into the laurel, they'll smell him before they find him."

Her stomach heaved. Wanda latched on to her other hand.

In the ravine, men stumbled over and around the passenger car, slipping on the steep ground and fastening cables while the bridge crew sawed and bolted supports in place. From the other side, a hoist lowered new timbers. Snow began to fall in fat wet flakes. Curses echoed through the ravine.

They were back in their seats when Mr. Townsend returned with his hat and shoulders covered with snow. He brushed himself off, shook his gloves and laid them on the stove top, where they sizzled. He turned them over, waited a minute, and put them on again. He smiled at May Rose. "I suffer of cold hands."

He took off his hat and sat at the desk. "There's one good thing about today." He took a newspaper from under his arm, opened it and gave it a shake. "A gift from the superintendent."

The engine backed steadily to Jennie Town, where it reversed itself on a siding and pulled them on toward Winkler. Charlie again climbed to the cupola. Wanda chewed her nails.

Mr. Townsend turned pages and folded the newspaper to read particular sections. May Rose studied the backs of his pages, but could not escape bad feelings. A quarter-page box ad listing Campbell and Smith's sale of house furnishings led her to think of the bare Herff house, Mrs. Donnelly, and her sons' attacks on Wanda. When she tried to read a news story headlined "Woman in Trousers," she became nauseous from the motion of the caboose, and thereafter focused on controlling the urge to throw up.

By the time they reached Winkler, snow was melting under the noon sun. Charlie ran off across the tracks, and Wanda jumped down and waited a short distance away. Mr. Townsend stepped from the caboose, placed his newspaper under his arm, and extended his hand to help May Rose.

"Thank you for putting up with us," she said.

He held her hand a moment. "I know you were doing your duty. It worked out better than I thought."

"Will you speak with Mr. Herff about my job?"

"If I have opportunity." He started to turn away, then held out the newspaper. "Would you carry this to the house? The boarders will be happy to see it."

She took the paper, *The Pittsburg Press*. "I hope I can return to the children tomorrow."

He stared down the track. "I wonder if Morris's home is a good situation for you—they say he was mean to his wife. There might be another possibility. Humphrey Gowder will need someone to stay with his mother—he's going to work for our purchasing office. You should inquire there." He tipped his hat and strode away.

She caught up and walked beside him. "I think Mr. Herff has

started to trust me. Perhaps Mrs. Donnelly can care for Preacher Gowder's mother."

"Perhaps," he said.

"You'll ask Mr. Herff?"

"I will, but Mrs. Donnelly may be better suited. We'll leave it to him."

She bit her tongue.

He stopped in front of the company office. "You'll see, everything will be fine."

She watched the door close after him. Dessie was wrong. Perhaps the heart of a man who carried the burden of the mill and the livelihood of hundreds of families had no room to care for one. Or he suffered from more than cold hands.

"OH, SHIT," Dessie said. "Pardon my French." A bowl of mashed potatoes lay upended on the kitchen floor.

May Rose stooped and touched the bowl. "It's cracked to pieces."

"Slipped right out of my hands," Dessie said. "Now what to put on the table to go with gravy?"

"I'll mix up biscuits," May Rose said.

Dessie slid the coal shovel under the mess. "The mill's gonna let out in a few minutes. You take the lantern and see Morris about your job."

The saws stopped as May Rose reached the mill. She stood in the middle of the street and lifted the lantern. Men plodded through the gate and flowed around her. One with no teeth grinned and tipped his hat. "Looking for me, sweetheart?" There was a little laughter as the steady march of men moved him along.

In the mass of shadowed faces she might have missed Morris Herff except that he showed himself by glancing away and slipping back in the crowd.

She waited and fell into step beside him. "I want to go on taking care of your children."

"It's been settled another way," he said.

"Did I do something wrong? Your children were happy with me."

"Leave us be."

"This isn't just a job to me. Do you think Mrs. Donnelly cares for your children?"

"She'll do." He lengthened his stride.

She did not try to keep up. Mr. Townsend was right—Mrs. Donnelly suited him better. But not the children. Surely not.

MAY ROSE FROWNED AT WANDA. "You don't want to go to singing school? It's the last night."

Wanda stared at the remains of her dinner.

Hester bustled into the kitchen. "Wanda. We're leaving."

"I don't feel good."

"I'm sorry," May Rose said. "I guess she's not going."

Hester arched her brows. "I suppose seeing the wreck upset her. I hope she's learned her lesson."

"She's just sick," May Rose said.

Wanda did not look up.

"You know, if you don't attend tonight, you can't be in the concert," Hester said.

Wanda shrugged.

Hester turned to May Rose. "Such a waste. She did well."

When Hester left, Dessie patted Wanda's shoulder. "Don't mind her—I'm glad you could go when you did." She touched Wanda's forehead. "Cool as a cucumber. Maybe you just need to turn in early."

Nodding, Wanda walked quietly up the stairs.

Dessie shook her head. "What's got into her?"

May Rose scraped Wanda's dinner into the slop bucket. "She had a knife, and now it's gone. I think it made her feel safe."

Dessie sighed. "Little girls shouldn't carry knives."

"They shouldn't have to. She got in a scrap with the Donnelly boys, and they took the knife. I helped her get away."

"Oh, my. I don't know why them Donnellys hasn't left town. I suppose kids pick on Wanda because of what Evalena does."

"And what Jamie did," May Rose said.

That night, she woke with the creak of their door. Wanda stood in her nightgown, a silhouette against the hall's dim light. When she turned toward the front stairs, May Rose slipped out of bed and followed her along the hall. "Wanda," she whispered. "Where are you going?"

Wanda did not speak, but let herself be turned back to the room. Her eyes flicked side to side.

CHAPTER 18

Many already have fled to the forest, and lurk on its outskirts,
Waiting with anxious hearts the dubious fate of tomorrow.

— HENRY WADSWORTH LONGFELLOW:
EVANGELINE

May Rose dipped a spoon in her oatmeal, pretending she could not hear the argument at the table. She'd begun to wonder about Mr. Townsend's help, and Hester's, too. Maybe they'd only kept her close as a lure for Jamie. But now Jamie seemed beyond their reach, and they were deep in other worries. Trusting Jamie had left her wary. Their motives would be clear if they turned her out.

"You have a responsibility to our business as well," Hester said. "I merely think, for the purposes of rationing, the boarding-house should be counted as more than one household. We've nine mouths to feed, and if the meals aren't up to standard, the boarders will want their rates reduced. While I pay more for less."

Mr. Townsend stroked butter on half a biscuit. "Some families here are nine or more in size. You've a full pantry and those pigs, more than most households."

"Nine mouths," Hester said, "will reduce everything quickly. When the mill stops sawing..."

"Sister. This kind of talk does no good."

"When the mill shuts down and there's no more sawdust for electric, we'll have to fall back on our lamps, and where's the kerosene to come from? Or coal, for that matter?"

"If it comes to rationing, everyone will have to be resourceful."

"I'd like to hear your plans for bringing in supplies," Hester said.

"And I— since I have to hear talk like this all day—would like to have my breakfast in peace."

Hester pushed back her chair. "I'll say one more thing. If this goes on and on, we'll have thievery. The pigs won't be safe."

"Then butcher them."

Hester stomped out, and Mr. Townsend finished his breakfast in silence.

"It ain't lack of food that bothers Hester," Dessie said after he left. "It's the idea that her pantry will thin down, and she'll pay more for cream and eggs the hill people bring in. But she's got money to buy, where most don't."

May Rose carried her bowl and spoon to the sink. "I need to ask the preacher about taking care of Miss Ruie. He's going to work for Mr. Townsend when the trains run again."

"That's Hester's doing," Dessie said. "The preacher don't get hardly enough in the collections to feed himself. She wants him to have an office job, but Mr. Townsend says he'll have to work outside first. She's afraid the preacher's health will suffer if he has to unload freight in all kinds of weather, but I think manly work might build him up."

May Rose found Humphrey Gowder in the church, sweeping the floor, and Ruie at the piano, playing three notes over and over.

"Mr. Townsend said you might need someone to stay with your mother," she said.

"Oh." He leaned on his broom handle. "I've hired Mrs. Donnelly. I'm truly sorry—Mother would get on much better with you."

"So Mrs. Donnelly isn't going to take care of the Herff children?"

"She'll help both of us, get the boys off to school and bring the little one here. Mother will like having a child in the house, so that part is good." He blinked. "Mrs. Long, is something wrong? Is there news of your husband?"

She swiped at tears. "No. I'm sorry to bother you."

For the rest of the morning, she polished door knobs, washed lamp globes, and dug her nails into dirt waxed in the corners of the upstairs hall, eager for Hester to decide her labor was worth the price of room and board.

"We might have to go to the cabin," she said to Wanda. They'd have a roof and a fire, potatoes for a few months. She shivered at the thought.

Tempered since the skirmish with the Donnellys and the loss of her knife, Wanda lay on the bed and studied the engravings in *Evangeline*. "I'd like to tell this story to Ma, but I don't want to make her cry."

May Rose sat beside her. "Crying can be good. Sometimes I feel stronger when I'm cried out."

Wanda traced a finger over the picture of Evangeline and other Acadians forced from their homes. "I don't never cry."

UNCERTAINTY about her welcome in the house drove May Rose to energetic scrubbing and polishing and prompted her to eat sparingly at lunch. In the afternoon, she sat with Dessie at the work-table, peeling potatoes.

"There's only one good thing about the new boarder, Mr. Tackett," Dessie said. "Being a salesman, he talks to everybody, gets about town and gathers the news. Mr. Townsend probably knows more about the wreck but he don't tell us anything. Mr. Tackett's jealous 'cause you and Wanda got to ride down to see it. I told him Wanda snuck on the train and you had to follow her."

May Rose laughed. "Charlie Herff told nearly the same thing to Mr. Townsend. In truth, Wanda and I were running away from the Donnelly boys. I didn't see Charlie until he climbed on from the other side of the tracks."

"Did Mr. Townsend see the fight?"

"He didn't say." She hated to think he'd seen her scratching like a wildcat on the Donnelly boy's back.

Dessie pumped water into the teakettle. "Your Jamie's still causing talk. If he's found dead, will you bury him?"

May Rose's paring knife slid into her finger, and the potato reddened with blood. She pressed her tongue against the cut.

"They wouldn't let me claim his pay or his property. If the railroad killed him, the railroad can bury him."

"Smart girl." Dessie carried the teakettle to the stove. "Maybe Russell will do it. Course it's not unheard of to take a man's property to settle the burial and his other debts. I don't mean to say that's how it's gonna go. Just supposing."

"I know." Her finger smeared everything she touched.

Dessie ripped two small pieces of cloth from a clean rag, pressed one over the cut, twisted the other to a string and tied it around the bandage. "Mr. Tackett thinks the railroad will sue the Winkler Company for them loose logs that busted the trestle."

May Rose poured peelings into the slop bucket. "Maybe the families of the dead should sue somebody."

"Maybe they will," Dessie said. "More worry for Mr. Townsend."

Hester entered from the hall. "Dessie, have you counted what we've got in the cellar?"

"All but the berries."

Hester lit a lamp and handed it to her. "Until further notice,

Mr. Townsend will take all his meals in his parlor. I know he's worried about this shutdown, but he could at least acknowledge my problems."

Dessie took the lamp to the cellar steps.

Hester sat at the table with her account book. "Now, May Rose, let's talk about you."

The cabin, May Rose thought.

Hester's mouth turned down. "I can't tell you how upset I am that my brother let Mrs. Donnelly take your job. If her own boys are any sample, imagine what she'll do to those poor children."

"I hope I did nothing wrong."

"Of course you didn't. There must be something else going on, a problem, I'd say, between Morris and my brother. Don't worry, I'm not going to turn you out. When this wreck business is over, I'll try to help you find work in a city, say Pittsburg. I'm sure you see there's no future here."

"I do." She felt better to be secure for a while longer with no need to suspect Mr. Townsend and Hester of helping for the wrong reasons.

Dessie returned and read from a scrap of paper. "Two crocks of kraut, one of salt pork, ninety quarts of beans, sixty-two pints of piccalilli, thirty quarts of blackberries."

Hester wrote in her book. "Is the teakettle hot? We should sit and make plans."

Dessie brought cups and May Rose poured hot water over the leaves in Hester's china pot.

After her first sip, Hester set the cup aside and laced her fingers. "Tomorrow's logs will make one more day's work at the mill. The men will be happy not to work for a day or two. Then, trouble."

May Rose tried to imagine it. "Has anything like this happened before?"

"Not to us," Hester said. "The camps will close for the duration. Mr. Townsend says many of the younger men have no home nearby. I don't know what they'll do."

"I look for them to camp near town," Dessie said. "They can hunt, long as there's bullets. And they'll have other entertainments."

Hester closed her eyes. "I'm afraid we'll get very tired of them, and maybe of each other, too. Already my brother is barely speaking to me. Well, I suppose we'll survive. Now, about rationing. I've been thinking of a way to stop second and third helpings at dinner."

~

THAT EVENING instead of taking serving bowls to the table, Dessie filled plates at the stove.

"These two are for our old fellers," she said, handing the plates to May Rose. "Smaller portions—they don't eat so much."

May Rose set the plates in front of Hester's distant cousins, the elderly Hershman brothers. Dessie said they'd come to Winkler to live out their old age, and that Hester worried they'd outlive their money and their ability to care for themselves. "I'm no nursemaid," Dessie said, "nor Hester neither. But the old gentlemen helped Mr. Townsend get his start in the company, and they got nobody else, so I'd say we're stuck."

Slight and stooped, the Hershman brothers wore vested suits that seemed too large, and their faces were shaved in patches.

Dessie heaped Mr. Cooper's plate higher, but gave a moderate portion to the salesman.

"Watch out for that Mr. Tackett," she said. "He's got loose hands."

After setting a plate in front of each guest, May Rose stood at the sideboard, ready to refill water glasses and pour coffee. Mr. Tackett's glances made her self-conscious. He probably had heard stories of her standing naked to the view of loggers and trainmen. She wished he and everyone else knew the true and more scandalous story, how the man she'd married in good faith had tried to trade his daughter to the whorehouse. She pressed her lips to hold back a smile as she imagined how she might lead them to speculate about Jamie's grisly death or daring escape, or tell about Dr. Hennig, who wanted to live with her on the mountain. Such gossip might flourish at Suzie's, perhaps even be whispered at church. Though getting revenge on gossips like Mr. Tackett might bring some satisfaction, she would never do it, and never in Hester's dining room.

Mr. Tackett dominated the dinner conversation with stories of excess, the most horrible accident on record, the most daring and unimaginable rescues. He kept swiveling his head to May Rose, who watched Hester for a signal to remove the dinner plates.

"May Rose," Mr. Tackett said, "since you're the only one of us who has seen the wreck, you might give us your impressions."

Surely they had imagined and re-imagined everything. "I believe it's all as you've heard," she said.

"But my dear, give us the personal side of things. How did you feel? Did you see the bodies?"

Even Mr. Cooper paused in his eating, though he did not look up.

"The repair seems dangerous work," she said, noticing that Mr. Cooper's sleeve had dipped into his food.

Mr. Wilbur Hershman put his hand to his ear. "What's that?"

Hester repeated in a louder voice. "The trestle repair is dangerous work."

"It'll be unsafe," he shouted. "They should reset the bents."

Mr. Tackett leaned forward. "Reset the what?"

Mr. Cooper dampened a napkin in his water glass and wiped gravy from his sleeve. "Mr. Hershman is speaking of the vertical and diagonal supports of the trestle frame. The bents. He means they should rebuild everything."

Everyone fell to silent eating, perhaps to contemplation of trestle parts, or thoughts of the town stranded beyond endurance. A plate clattered in the kitchen, then the doorknocker rattled, and Dessie's steps echoed through the hall.

At a signal from Hester, May Rose took away plates and began serving bowls of rice pudding.

An angry voice rumbled from the front entry.

Dessie entered and bent to Hester. "Mr. Herff wishes to speak with Mr. Townsend. Should I bother him?"

"I'll speak with Mr. Herff."

As Hester left the room, Mr. Tackett said, "Herff. There's an odd name. I heard something about a Herff today."

Mr. Hobart Hershman put a hand behind his ear. "Speak up!"

"Shh." The salesman put a finger to his lips. Voices in the hall grew louder, one blurting, one controlled, both angry.

A few moments later, Hester closed the sliding doors to the parlor. "An employee has come on a personal matter. Please go on with your dinner. Is the rice pudding satisfactory?"

Mr. Tackett wagged his spoon. "Herff. I remember. There's talk of him marrying that woman whose husband was knifed to death last week."

May Rose stiffened. Mr. Cooper coughed as though his pudding had gone down the wrong way.

Hester's face turned red. "Well. I hadn't heard."

The salesman sounded pleased. "Folks think it's hasty, for the woman. I mean, she's been widowed barely two weeks."

"If you're speaking of Mrs. Donnelly, we know she's much in need, and she has a family," Hester said. "For his part, Mr. Herff has motherless children. I suppose it's an arrangement of convenience."

The front door slammed.

Hester stood. "Everyone should leave early for the concert, because seating will be hard to come by. Mr. Tackett, in case you haven't heard, the concert is in the church. I'm sure you know where that is."

~

Because they were performing, Hester and Mr. Cooper left the boardinghouse ahead of the others.

"We all better go around on tiptoe," Dessie whispered, as they cleared the table. "Mr. Townsend's already in a stormy way, and Mr. Herff didn't make him no better."

May Rose realized the wedding might have made her happy for the Donnellys had she known nothing about them, and if she hadn't known Glory, Charlie, and Will.

As though reading her mind, Dessie said, "The Lord protects helpless children."

"I hope so," May Rose said. They'd seemed little protected thus far.

CHAPTER 19

Weep no more, my lady...

— STEPHEN COLLINS FOSTER: MY OLD
KENTUCKY HOME

Men, women and children sat shoulder to shoulder in church pews, side aisles, and along the back. May Rose and Wanda squeezed into a gap in the middle of a back pew, while Dessie found a single spot near the front. The room was bright with electric light and hot with bodies, but cold air blew in every time the door opened.

For the opening number, Mr. Cooper went to the piano and Preacher Gowder brought the children's ensemble to the platform. The audience hushed as the preacher raised his arms and high young voices sang "O! Susannah!" Swept along in merry sound, May Rose forgot her worries. Wanda tapped her foot. When a young boy and girl sang the final chorus of "My Old Kentucky Home," the purity of their voices and the sadness of "Weep no more, my lady" caused even men in the audience to sniff and swipe the dampness from their cheeks.

Next, Preacher Gowder accompanied and directed the adult

ensemble in a program of sacred and secular music. May Rose watched Hester and Mr. Cooper and felt her chest swell with love for every singer.

All singing school students came to the platform for the finale. In a hearty voice unmatched to his thin frame, Mr. Cooper sang "De camptown ladies sing dis song" and the students sang "Doo-dah, doo-dah."

The audience had been quiet and attentive, but now boys standing in back began to shove each other around and echo "Doo-dah, doo-dah!"

Some in the audience turned to look and shush or give disapproving looks. Mr. Cooper sang on, but having been noticed, the boys chanted louder.

Beside May Rose, Wanda mumbled and squirmed, then turned in her seat. The boys leaned between them and shouted. "Doo-dah, doo-dah!" *Donnellys.* May Rose touched Wanda's arm to restrain her, but when the boys leaned forward again, she stood and jabbed her fist into the chin of the nearest.

He lurched away, and two others grabbed Wanda's hair. She screamed and chopped at their arms. On the platform, voices faltered, and people in the audience stood. May Rose flung her arms around Wanda's waist to keep the boys from pulling her out of the pew, and two men collared the boys and made them release Wanda's hair, now wilder than ever. The Donnelly boy jumped around, yelling. "She punched me first! She punched me first!"

May Rose urged Wanda outside.

"We better run," Wanda said. "They'll be after us for sure."

"Not that way. That's how they'll go, and I can't outrun a baby in these shoes." Pulling Wanda into the shadows, May Rose pointed to the hillside.

"There's mushy ground up there," Wanda whispered. "Roots and stumps to trip us."

Three boys burst from the church, jumped down from the boardwalk, and ran side-by-side down the street toward the boardinghouse.

Wanda pulled her hand. "All right, uphill, I better go first."

"Wait," May Rose said. The concert audience was singing "Camptown Races" again.

She glanced down the street toward the boys, dark blobs in the distance. "Follow me, and say nothing, no matter what you hear." They hurried along the boardwalk and crossed to the depot where Frank, the company policeman, sat in his cubbyhole.

Breathless, May Rose said, "I heard some boys say they were going to steal Mr. Townsend's pigs. Donnelly boys, I think they are. They ran toward his house."

Frank blinked and yawned like he might have been sleeping.

"Mr.Townsend's pigs," she said. "The Donnelly boys."

He stretched. "I know them boys." May Rose and Wanda backed outside to give him room to come through the door. "Reckon you're right."

Big-eyed, Wanda said, "Ain'cha gonna take a gun?"

He picked up a lantern. "Nah. These boys is skeered o'me." Frank looked to be twice the size of most men in town. "They know I'm looking for one more reason to send them off to reform school. You coming along?"

"We have to go back to the concert," May Rose said. She and Wanda crossed again to the boardwalk.

"Now you may lead the way along the hill. No need to hurry, just so we get there before Dessie locks the doors."

They reached the hillside above the boardinghouse in time to see Mr. Townsend in the light of the back door. A lantern bobbed through the yard. Wanda giggled and pointed to three running shadows, visible for a moment as they passed behind the hotel.

"It's not funny," May Rose said, "and it's not over." They waited in the dark until the lantern left the yard and the kitchen light went out, then they opened the gate and stepped through the grass. The door was locked.

"Do we go to the front?" Wanda asked.

"Not yet." May Rose listened to voices in the street, Mr. Tackett and one of the Hershman brothers.

When the kitchen light came on, they knocked, and Dessie let them in. She scolded Wanda with a look and tossed each of them a rag. "How'd you get them shoes so dirty? And the bottom of your dress!"

"Puddles," May Rose said, wiping her shoes.

"You must of splashed like a kid. And you, Miss Wanda. What was that at the concert?"

May Rose turned Wanda toward the stairs. "We'll tell you everything tomorrow." Safe in their room, she turned the key in the lock. "I don't want to see Hester tonight. Tomorrow, she might not be so angry."

Wanda dropped a shoe to the floor. "Angry for what? I helped."

"In a bad way. You'll be blamed for upsetting the concert, and no one will remember the boys started it. I'm sure Hester feels we've disgraced her."

"That's silly," Wanda said.

May Rose turned out the light.

"I can't see," Wanda said.

"Shh. If there's a knock, we're sleeping. We'll go out early for acorns, avoid Hester a bit longer."

WANDA WHINED and curled in a ball when May Rose woke her Saturday morning. "I got a nice warm spot here."

May Rose pulled her covers to the foot of the bed. "I don't want to see those boys again, do you? We'll gather nuts while it's safe to be out."

Wanda pulled the covers back to her chin. "We'll miss breakfast. Dessie won't hold nothing back."

"We'll eat extra at lunch. From now on, be on your best behavior. Wait until the hall is silent then tip-toe down the stairs. Don't say anything unless someone speaks to you, and don't go anywhere alone."

Wanda's mouth grinned in its lopsided way. "You mean be sneaky. I'm good at that. But I can't hide out forever. Anyway, them boys will be laying low too. Frank's right, they're scared of him."

"If you let me tell Frank what they did to you, maybe he'll send them to reform school."

Wanda got out of bed and buttoned her shoes. "People think bad of me already. I don't want them knowing that."

Every day they went farther to scrape up enough acorns for the sow and her eight growing pigs. This morning they crossed the slick footbridge in search of new sources, Wanda carrying a broken-handled shovel. They tramped along the slope from tree to tree and filled two sacks.

As they dragged the sacks downhill, a boy appeared from behind a knoll and crossed the river, leaping from rock to rock.

Wanda pointed. "Lookit that—it's Charlie, up to something, you bet. See that smoke?" She dropped her sack and ran toward the knoll.

May Rose found her on the other side with the remains of a fire.

"Bet'cha he slept out, last night. The fire's still warm." She toed a partly burned piece of wood, a smoothed and detailed panel of deer cut from a forest of pine trees.

"Poor Charlie," May Rose said.

"He's burned his pa's stuff. Why'd he go and do that, with heaps of kindling all around?"

"Maybe it's not Charlie's fire. Maybe he found it, like us." She followed Wanda back to their bulging sacks. "We should not say anything about this."

"I never tattle on nobody I like," Wanda said.

After they fed the pigs, May Rose hurried Wanda through the empty kitchen and up the stairs. They stopped short at the top, finding Hester in their open doorway and Dessie in their room. Their mattress was off the bed, and May Rose's carpet bag sat open on a chair.

May Rose looked from Hester to Dessie. "What is this about?"

Dessie shook her head. "I'm just following orders." She pulled the mattress back to the bed and picked up a sheet.

May Rose jerked the sheet from her hands. "Hester? Am I not entitled to privacy?"

Dessie retreated from the room and Wanda came in and tucked the sheet over the mattress.

Hester sighed. "Mr. Herff said Wanda stole some wood carvings from his home."

Wanda snorted. "I wouldn't bother with them old things."

May Rose took Wanda's hand, wondering if they should mention the fire. "Why would Mr. Herff think she took them?"

"Mrs. Donnelly's boys say they saw her."

"Oh, Donnellys." May Rose gave Wanda a look meant to be encouraging. Maybe now she'd tell everything. Hester and Dessie would be sympathetic.

"I been helping May Rose at the house," Wanda said. "I went in thinking she was there, and them boys chased me out. I didn't take nothing."

Hester looked contrite. "Yes, Donnellys, the boys who were after our pigs. Morris didn't notice anything missing until last night. It's why he came here, just before the concert. Mr. Townsend told Morris he'd search, just to get rid of him, you know."

May Rose closed the carpetbag. "You should have waited until I got here."

Dessie shrugged. "She's the boss."

"I apologize," Hester said. "This wreck's got everybody crazy. I can't sleep. I'm afraid the wood hicks will stay and cause trouble, and my brother's afraid they'll leave. He worries about losing mill hands, says some will hike out and never come back."

"Them Donnellys," Dessie said. "With them in his house, Morris Herff had best look for his thief close to home."

Poor Charlie, May Rose thought. And Glory, and Will.

Downstairs, Dessie motioned to the worktable where she'd saved their breakfast.

"Now, Miss Wanda," Hester said. "You need to apologize to Preacher Gowder and Mr. Cooper for upsetting their concert."

Wanda chewed a biscuit. "Them's mean boys. People couldn't hear the singing."

Hester looked weary. "I know. One good thing came out of last evening. My brother is getting us a night watchman."

Wanda brushed a hand across her eyes. "I'm gonna go see Ma."

"I'll walk you over," May Rose said.

Hester pulled her shawl from a wall peg. "No need for you to go. I've a word to share with Suzie. Wanda, you may walk along with me."

"Hester's hard to read," Dessie said, watching them go toward the back fence. "But if you get her in your corner, you've got somebody."

CHAPTER 20

There is a reason that all things are as they are...

— BRAM STOKER: DRACULA

At the back door, May Rose watched the path behind the lots for Wanda to return.

"For the life of me," Dessie said, "I can't see why Morris would pick the Donnelly woman with you in the house every day."

May Rose continued to watch out the window. "The first day he yelled and slapped me."

"He didn't!"

"He improved after that. I thought we were getting along."

"You're well out of there. But even if he likes that witch, I don't know why he'd add those boys of hers to his troubles."

May Rose had a recurring desire to steal his children away. "I told Will and Charlie I'd be back, and now I don't know if I'll see them to explain. And poor Glory, what will she think?" She put on her coat. "I can't wait for Wanda any longer. I have to collect my pay before the window closes."

"Hour or two, wood hicks'll be blowing in," Dessie said. "All o'them, this time, not just a few looking for a good time."

"Hester was afraid they'd storm the house because of what was said about me."

"Oh, she frets too much. Most of the wood hicks is decent men, and she knows you better now. She'll keep you on, like she said, and help you find a place after all this is said and done." Dessie paused with a grim smile. "Unless something worse happens."

Something worse seemed likely.

At the company office, May Rose got in line, claimed her dollar and took it to the telegraph agent. He was nearly as busy as the company paymaster.

He tapped a stack of paper against the counter, giving the stack a straight edge. "A telegram to Fargo might cost two to seven dollars, depending on the number of words. You ready to send it?"

"Not today."

"Then come back when you're ready, and please, not on payday."

Outside, a solemn group of wood hicks trudged in the street, packs strapped to their backs. Some carried a rifle or shotgun.

Mr. Cooper stopped beside her. "Mrs. Long, good afternoon."

"Good afternoon," she said, glad for his familiar face.

He nodded at the passing men. "The mountain camps are clearing out." They watched together.

"Are they leaving for good, do you think?"

"They'll go on to family someplace or make camp here. A few will lodge in the hotel." He turned and smiled. "I have to send a telegram. Would you care to wait and walk back with me?"

"Indeed, I would."

She followed him inside and waited near the wall while he moved up in line. When it was his turn he set a pouch of coins on the desk and the agent spilled them out in controlled fashion. Mr. Cooper wrote on a form with a shaky hand, and the agent read his directions aloud, six dollars and fifty cents to Mrs. Anna Cooper in Uniontown, Pennsylvania.

Mr. Cooper's lips stretched in a rueful smile as he held open the door for her to pass outside. "There's no such thing as privacy in these places, is there? Not that I have any secrets. I teach the high school, and at night I ruin my eyes, scribbling stories in bad light, and I support my mother, and go home to her in summer. That's everything there is to know, and everyone knows it."

"You also sing beautifully, and Wanda likes you, so you must be a good teacher."

"Thank you. I enjoy finding traces of genius in my pupils as well as helping the dullest strive for something better. Wanda is a quick learner. For a child, her voice has extraordinary depth and range. With opportunity, she might have a career."

They passed tracks where railroad cars and engines sat idle, and open ground along the river where wood hicks were setting down their packs. Mr. Cooper's gentle manner made her want to tell everything.

"I don't know how to guide her," she said, "except by rules my aunt imposed on me. But Wanda is stronger and more determined than I ever was. And I don't want her to turn out like me."

"Well now, you seem quite strong and capable. But I know what you mean. Wanda should not be made to conform too much. It takes nerve, you see, to break away, and rise...above ordinary life."

She did not answer for several steps, wondering if he spoke his own desires. "I admire her courage when it doesn't frighten me, but I'm afraid she's in danger here, from the place where her mother works and from those boys." May Rose felt better, sharing her worries. "Do you understand what I mean? And who?"

"I'm afraid I do."

"She won't let me report the boys."

"Yes. I've heard what they call her, likening her to her mother, you see. The town has also judged her."

"I try to keep her close. Her mother wants me to take her away."

They crossed to the hotel, his arms swinging awkwardly. "I was assaulted, my first year here, beaten by some drunken men who found me easy prey."

"I'm sorry."

"Mr. Townsend didn't want to fire those men, but Hester insisted, and they left town, because there's really no other employer here but the company. About Wanda's troublemakers, I can't say what to do, especially if they become Morris Herff's stepsons. Morris is not likely to be fired, no matter what Miss Hester might want."

"Wanda doesn't want people to know she's been hurt that way."

"I understand. It's humiliating. I'll watch out for her when I can. If you don't mind, I'll ask other teachers to do the same, no particulars mentioned, of course."

He held open the boardinghouse gate. "Tonight we're having music in the parlor. Do you think Wanda would sing for us?"

"She might, but she's banned from the parlor and dining room."

"I'll speak with Hester. Music draws us together, don't you think?"

WHEN MAY Rose came into the kitchen, Wanda bounced up as though sprung from her seat. She pulled May Rose to the stairs. "Come up, come up, you gotta see."

A blue flowered dress lay on the bed, wrinkled where it had been folded. Wanda held it against herself, then whipped it around, held it to May Rose's shoulders, and turned her to the mirror. "Ain't it beautiful? Blue like mine, blue like your eyes."

The dress had a gored skirt, fitted bodice, puffed sleeves, and a high neck edged in lace. "Where did you get this?"

"Suzie's!"

May Rose let the dress fall to the floor. "Take it back."

Wanda picked up the dress. "It ain't mine, it's for you. Don'cha think it'll fit?"

"I don't want anything from Suzie, not for me, not for you."

"It's from Sears-Roebuck, the catalog. Suzie's had it awhile, said a man left it, she won't say who. But why'd he leave it there?"

May Rose shook her head, afraid she knew.

"Today Suzie passed it to Miss Hester. I think Miss Hester's dying to know what it is. Think it was Jamie? Put it on. I'm sick of that black thing."

"I can't wear it."

"Never?"

"Did Suzie open the package?"

Wanda held the dress to her shoulders and swayed in front of the mirror. "I did. I couldn't wait. I guess that was bad, but I held off till I got here."

"Have Dessie burn it in the stove."

"I won't! I'll grow into it."

"Then hide it away." Jamie had never given her anything. She didn't want to think who else admired her in blue.

That afternoon, wood hicks made fires along the river and on the slopes behind the boardinghouse and built shacks of wood, tin, and blankets.

Wanda pressed her face to the kitchen window. "We're surrounded. Hey, there—some of the wood hicks is looking at our pigs."

"Hester's pigs," May Rose said.

She found Hester roaming the house, lifting the edge of curtains, watching the slopes and riverbank fill up with shacks and tents.

"Wood hicks are watching the pigs," May Rose said.

Hester echoed Wanda with a more desperate tone. "We're surrounded. And we're going to need more than one watchman."

Late in the day, sounds of an army on the march took them all to the porch. First thumping, the rattle of tackle and shouts of men, then horse teams paraded by, a few hitched to wagons covered in canvas, but most with men walking behind handling the reins. The massive horses looked eager, heads up, ears forward. Their handlers looked grim. Wanda ran to the gate and waved.

Mr. Townsend stood on the step beside May Rose. "Teams from the mountain camps," he said. "Their handlers are taking them out till this is over."

Mr. Tackett spoke behind them. "It's near night. Why set off now?"

"Locals tell of an abandoned farm two hours down the road where there'll be forage and water for the night. Some may stay there. Others will have to look farther."

Hester stepped down between him and May Rose. "I wish you'd told me they were going. Can they bring back supplies?"

"They may not go as far as a town, and they'll not return until they hear the trestle is repaired and we have fodder for the horses. By that time, we'll all be supplied."

"But why not send the wagons farther for food?"

"Why not? Because the company will authorize no transport of food or coal while we're shut down. We're on our own."

"We've depended too much on that store," Hester said.

And on the company, May Rose thought. She vowed to tell Charlie or Will about her potatoes.

Dessie pointed. "There go some wood hicks." A group of men at the hotel fell in behind the last team. They looked as though they might have padded themselves with two or three sets of faded clothes.

Mr. Townsend hurried into the road and waved his hands. "You can't stay with the teamsters. They have nothing to share."

The men moved around him, mostly silent, with slow steps for a long trek. Some cursed both the company and Mr. Townsend. A few paused to listen.

"Stay here," he urged. "We'll make do."

They touched their hats and trudged on.

May Rose gasped. Women and children walked among the men.

"And the mill's not yet shut down," Hester said.

Dessie nodded. "They'll have a bad time of it. The ones who stay will likely be better off, but they won't believe it."

CHAPTER 21

...Even as pilgrims, who journey afar from their country,
  Sing as they go,
  and in singing forget they are weary and wayworn.

— HENRY WADSWORTH LONGFELLOW:

EVANGELINE

May Rose noticed how Dessie grumped at the prospect of Hester's new watchmen eating in her kitchen until she met Tom. His regular job was assistant cook at Camp Four, and he smiled at everything Dessie said. Dessie smiled back.

Saturday evening, May Rose piled wet dishes on the drain board while Dessie leaned against the counter, towel in hand, listening to Tom chatter about the wreck.

"They brought out the engineer and fireman," he said, "but didn't find nobody else. There's talk the seventh passenger never got on the train."

Dessie puckered her little mouth. "I suppose it'll all come out in the end."

May Rose took the towel from Dessie's hand and swiped it over a plate. Surely it was best that everything not come out, not

Jamie's deal with Suzie, nor that she and Wanda might have been on that train. She also did not want Wanda to know of her talk with Mr. Cooper, for it felt like a betrayal of trust. Then there was Charlie Herff and his father's burned carvings. Even between them, Wanda and May Rose had said no more.

Dinner had gone smoothly, with Mr. Townsend still absent, and no complaints from the boarders about the lack of second helpings. Hester, still apologetic about searching their room, had invited Wanda to sing in the parlor that evening. Hester had laughed at her change of schedule. "We'll sing every night and keep the dark away."

Tom pushed out his chair. "I'm sad to leave you ladies, but it's time for me to get to work."

Dessie smiled him away, then turned to May Rose like she'd forgotten her. "Why, May Rose, you've cleaned up everything. Now what was in that package Hester brought from Suzie's?"

May Rose stared at spots of light that glittered on the kitchen's windowpane, reflections of wood hicks' campfires. She'd planned what to tell about the gift, something else she didn't want to come out.

"It was a dress for Wanda, from Evalena. We've put it away until she grows."

"Well, that's real nice."

"No." May Rose sighed. "I've not told you right. We put the dress away for Wanda, but it was not for her." She lifted her apron hem and blotted her forehead. "A man left it for me. Suzie would not say who."

Dessie gaped. "Can I guess?"

"You may guess all you please, just don't tell me. And please don't tell Hester anything unless she asks."

IN THE PARLOR, Preacher Gowder's right foot pumped the piano pedal and his hands pounded the keys with military pomp. Brave songs, May Rose believed, to encourage men marching to war, good choices for anxious times. After the marches, he played light waltzes. From her seat between Dessie and Wanda, she saw fingers tap and faces relax. Ruie and the Hershman brothers closed their eyes and might have been sleeping. Mr. Cooper bobbed his head. Hester sat beside the piano with a look of pride, and maybe love.

"And now, Miss Hester," the preacher said, swiveling the piano stool, "let's give them a duet. Ladies and gentlemen, from Victor Herbert's new operetta 'The Fortune Teller,' we present 'Gypsy Love Song!'"

Hester moved to the hallway arch where she had a view of the preacher as well as the circle of listeners. She clasped her hands and gazed upward as he began a mournful, rolling accompaniment.

He sang first.

"The birds of the forest are calling for thee,
And the shades and the glades are lonely.
Summer is there with her blossoms fair,
And you are absent only."

He signaled Hester to sing the next verse, which started on a higher note and moved faster.

"No bird that nests in the greenwood tree,
But sighs to greet you and kiss you.
All the violets yearn, yearn for your safe return,
But most of all I miss you!"

May Rose felt a nudge from Dessie's elbow. Hester's eyes had closed with emotion, perhaps theatrical, but maybe true. The accompaniment changed to a gentle rocking rhythm, and the preacher and Hester sang together, watching the music, but lifting their eyes to each other for the final words, *"All my heart's true love."*

Everyone in the circle of listeners looked sad and teary, as if the music had touched wounded, aching parts, perhaps unspoken longing. Ruie slumbered on.

Hester seemed flustered. The preacher stood and raised her hand, then together they bowed, first to the audience, then to each other. As everyone clapped heartily, Hester moved from the arch to her chair, revealing Mr. Townsend behind her in the hall.

He might have been staring in reverie, but to May Rose, his intense gaze seemed directed to her. When she smiled, he looked to the window, and she dropped her head. Dessie was right. Mr. Townsend, the man with the cold heart, had a spark of feeling, and he didn't want her to know.

Fortunately, Preacher Gowder beckoned to Wanda, and May Rose stopped considering Mr. Townsend's heart. Wanda clasped her hands like Hester's and looked at each person in the circle. Stick-thin, she showed no sign of maturity other than her poise and the richness of her voice. She sang "My Old Kentucky Home," not thin and sweet like the children's chorus, but with wisdom and sorrow.

May Rose and Dessie sniffed and wiped their eyes.

The parlor audience applauded until the night watchman appeared in the entry. He spoke to Mr. Townsend, who turned to Hester.

"Men from the camps have come near to listen. Tom wants to know if he should drive them off or let them stay."

The Hershman brothers peered forward and lifted their brows as if to expand their hearing. The street was quiet, unusual for a Saturday night.

Hester looked perplexed. With everyone staring at Mr. Townsend and listening for Hester's decision, May Rose had a few moments to include him in her line of sight. His stare had both unnerved her and produced a flush of pleasure. She had a secret admirer, a safe one who might never do more than watch from a distance.

Hester frowned. "If they're not wearing spikes, they may come to the porch to listen. As long as they're respectful."

Preacher Gowder swung around on the piano stool. "Then, let's have 'O! Susannah!'" His fingers made the piano sound like a plunking banjo. Hester and Mr. Cooper stood and harmonized with Wanda.

The water in May Rose's eyes made the scene as blurry as her ideas of what to do next. She wanted so much for Wanda. When the trains resumed, Hester was going to help her find work in Pittsburg or Charleston. If Wanda still refused to leave her mother, perhaps Hester and Dessie would protect her.

On the second repetition of *"O! Susannah! O don't you cry for me,"* Dessie elbowed May Rose and pointed to the window. The wood hicks were singing along.

When Wanda sang "Beautiful Dreamer," the Hershman brothers leaned forward with mouths ajar, and at the song's end, applause and stomping erupted from the porch. Wanda took her seat beside May Rose, looking nearly as confused as the night she'd walked in her sleep.

"Tonight," Hester announced, "the electric will go off at nine. Tomorrow and Monday, eight." She looked toward the hall where her brother had stood. "After that, we don't know."

LIKE PUNISHMENT for the evening's pleasure, worry roused May Rose in the middle of the night and kept her awake with one bad thought after another. With no supply trains for the past five days, Hester said staples at the store were severely reduced. Worse, the Donnelly boys were about to live in the same house with Will, Charlie, and Glory. And where was Jamie, and what would become of Wanda?

As soon as she smelled coffee, she dressed and felt her way down toward the light in the kitchen.

Dessie punched a hole in a can of Borden's milk and poured a drop into her coffee. "Wasn't that nice last night? Everybody happy and sad at the same time. Better than church."

May Rose laughed. "Shame on you. You should go to church now and then."

"I've lost the habit. I hear Mr. Herff and Mrs. Donnelly are gonna say 'I do' at the end of the service today."

"My reason for staying home. I'll help you, and Hester can go."

"Oh, she never does, except for a funeral. She tells folks she needs to help with dinner, but I think she likes Humpty-Dumpty better when she don't have to hear him preach. Mr. Townsend goes, maybe because of how it would look if he didn't. Lots of people go for something to do." She sighed. "Sure wish I needed something to do."

May Rose leaned across the table to speak confidentially. "I was almost embarrassed, watching Hester and the preacher last night, the way they sang and gazed at each other."

Dessie blew on her coffee. "They got something between them, wouldn't you say? I think he'd marry her in a minute—even if she wasn't a good catch and him a poor man. But there's more than his crazy mother stopping her. Hester don't think Mr. Townsend could get on without her. She acts like every woman's ready to take advantage and he's got no judgment a'tall. But she also thinks no woman alive is good enough." Dessie got a mischievous smile. "So? Should Hester be fretting about you?"

May Rose suppressed a smile. "Nothing I know about."

MAY Rose pushed down on Wanda's shoulder and pulled the brush through the knots in her hair, a daily ordeal.

Wanda squealed. "You don't know how that hurts!"

May Rose handed her the brush. "You do it, then, one hundred strokes at night, one hundred in the morning."

"Wanda!" Dessie knocked and called from the hall. "Suzie's sent for Wanda."

Wanda jumped from the bed.

May Rose blocked the door. "No."

"Yes, why not?"

"Suzie will take advantage. You can't be the least way in her debt."

"You don't know everything." Wanda pushed her away.

May Rose ran after her down the stairs.

"Winifred," Wanda said.

Suzie's cook stood at the kitchen door. "Suzie said fetch you. Sweetheart, I think your ma's dying."

Wanda's eyes shifted side to side.

"I'll go with you," May Rose said.

Wanda raced for the door and turned around. "Get the preacher. Please. I don't want her to burn in hell."

May Rose ran past men who leaned against the hotel and bar buildings, past campfires and card games along the river. She hurried past the Hershman brothers, Mr. Townsend, and others returning home from Sunday service. She got a stitch in her side, stopped, walked, and ran again.

She met Preacher Gowder and Ruie on the church steps. "You're needed. Someone's dying."

He looked stricken. "At the boardinghouse?"

"It's Evalena, Wanda's mother, at Suzie's."

He exhaled with extra force. "Tell the gravedigger. I'm not going there."

Ruie tugged at his arm. "Is it someone we know?"

"Not this time." He turned his mother toward their house.

May Rose hurried around him and stopped in his path.

He shook his head. "I'm not going. I'm sick of deathbed conversions. A woman like that, who's sinned all her life, made no attempt to reform, now she wants to sneak by. What does it say to the pitiful few who sacrifice the world's pleasures—*everything*—to walk the narrow way?" His voice trembled.

Humpty-Dumpty, May Rose thought. *Had a great fall.* "This sinner has a daughter, Wanda. She's the one who's asking, and she's at an impressionable age. Think what it will mean to her if her mother is saved."

"That she can live any old way and still get to heaven."

Ruie's curls bobbed. "Don't be so righteous, Humphrey. Get the woman saved."

He sighed, like he'd known all along his case was lost. "I'll go and pray with her, but I'm not taking Mother into that place." He transferred Ruie's arm to May Rose. "You can take her home with you."

Ruie staggered against her. "I'm cold. Humphrey, let's get on and build up the fire. Why, he's leaving! Where's he going?"

"To save a sinner," May Rose said.

"That's nice. Are we going too?"

"We'll stop at the boardinghouse."

"Good. I think it's dinnertime."

Preacher Gowder soon outdistanced them. May Rose supported Ruie all the way to the boardinghouse, but when she took her through the front door, Ruie broke loose and pranced along the hall toward the rich aroma coming from the kitchen. There, Hester and Dessie soared around each other like birds, pulling sausage pies from the oven and dishing up sweet potatoes.

Hester startled when she saw them. "Mrs. Gowder. What a surprise!"

"I brought her here to wait for the preacher," May Rose said.

"We'll stay for dinner," Ruie said. She dipped her fingers into a tray of bread pudding and brought a bite to her mouth. "Tough and dry. You baked it overlong."

May Rose avoided Hester's eyes and ushered Ruie to the parlor where the Hershman brothers snored lightly under sheets of newspaper. Ruie sat with a thump. "Who are these men? Is this a Christian home?" The old gentlemen peered over their papers.

"They were here with us last night," May Rose said. "And they're in church every Sunday. Mr. Wilbur Hershman and Mr. Hobart Hershman." May Rose raised her voice. "Gentlemen, Mrs. Ruie Gowder."

Ruie pursed her lips as the old gentlemen stood, looked puzzled, nodded a greeting and sat again.

Pale and frazzled, Preacher Gowder returned from Suzie's. "I've done my duty. It will be up to you to surround the girl with good examples. And if anyone talks about me going into that place, I'll count on you to set them straight. Mother, we can go now."

"I need to warm up," Ruie said. "And there's sausage pie for dinner."

Mr. Townsend appeared in the archway. "Preacher Gowder, Miss Ruie, is this your Sunday to dine with us?"

"It must be," Ruie said.

May Rose escaped to the kitchen and whispered to Dessie. "I can't let Wanda be alone with this." She hurried from the house and ran along the path to the bar.

Suzie met her at the top of the stairs. "I want you to know, if Evalena's going to make a trip of it, she needs to finish somewhere else. Be unlucky if she dies here."

"And so unlucky for her," May Rose said.

Evalena looked like her trip would not take long. Her eyelids raised briefly then fell down. Wanda held up the green dress. "This here stinks. What's she gonna wear?"

For burial, May Rose thought. She moved to the bed and held Evalena's dry bony hand. "The new blue dress. She can have it."

"I'm done here," Evalena whispered. Her face looked skeletal.

"You need rest and food. Wanda, has she eaten anything?"

Wanda kicked the green dress into a corner. "She means she's through working for Suzie. The preacher made her promise to quit."

"That's good."

"So I gotta take her somewheres else."

"Maybe not right away," May Rose said.

Wanda looked too hopeful.

"I'm better," Evalena whispered.

"Bring the dress," May Rose said. "And my clean nightgown."

Wanda left. May Rose sponged Evalena's face and hands.

"You're awful good to me," Evalena said. "And to Wanda. I think you was meant to come here."

May Rose had to ask. She sat by the bed and took Evalena's hand. "You're the only one who can tell me. Are you Jamie's wife?"

Evalena breathed in deep rasps. Finally she spoke. "No, honey, you are."

Her answer made May Rose feel no better.

She and Wanda spent the afternoon watching Evalena sleep and wake. Wanda startled at every unexpected sound and every flicker of her mother's eyes. By nightfall, Evalena's breath seemed more regular, and they returned to the boardinghouse.

In the kitchen they found Dessie laughing with Tom. "The best was when Ruie said her son was going to bring Suzie and the girls to the Lord. No one at the table said a peep. Even the preacher knows he'd be out of a job if he tried to convert Suzie's bunch."

They carried bread and butter sandwiches to their room.

"If Ma don't work for Suzie," Wanda said, "what we gonna do?"

"We'll take care of her," May Rose said. She doubted Evalena would need anything.

CHAPTER 22

...though sympathy can't alter facts,
  it can make them more bearable.

— BRAM STOKER: DRACULA

Campfires smoldered in the morning drizzle, spreading smoke over the valley. All night there'd been voices on the street and occasional pistol shots, and Wanda had again walked in her sleep. Hester had found her in the downstairs hall and brought her back to the room. Today the mill would saw its last logs.

The kitchen smelled of yeast and wet wash. Bread dough rose in a four-loaf pan on the shelf above the stove, and water steamed in big kettles.

May Rose wiped a breakfast platter, tense with uncertainty. Her promise to take care of Evalena had been easy when the woman seemed about to die.

"A perfectly good boiler in the washhouse," Dessie muttered.

Hester stirred bluing powder into a pan of water for the laundry rinse. "Your stove will be free when you need it."

The washwomen, plump matrons with sweaty foreheads,

angled their basket of wet sheets between May Rose at the sink and Dessie at the worktable.

Dessie mixed dough for noodles. "All this damp is bad for my bread," she said. "And it would be nice if my kitchen wasn't the through-way."

May Rose carried a stack of dishes to the cupboard. "Shall I clean the upstairs rooms next, or gather acorns?"

"You may take the morning off and stay over there with Wanda and her mother," Hester said.

"I think they want some time alone."

"That's natural," Dessie said. "Is Evalena any better?"

"I see no change. But you may be interested to know—Evalena was never married to Jamie."

Hester looked up from stirring. "That's good."

She'd stopped thinking of herself as Jamie's wife. Now she felt bound again.

"It's another blow for Wanda," Dessie said. "But like I said, if you and her get away from here, who's to know or care?"

May Rose found it odd, this importance of a legal connection to a faithless man.

She wiped steam from the window and peered at the slope of shacks and tents. "The rain has stopped, so I'll go for acorns now."

"With wood hicks all over the place, it might not be good for a woman to be out alone," Hester said. "Our Italians had their men walk over with them this morning."

Dessie dusted flour over the table and plopped a ball of noodle dough in the center. "I might ask Tom to round up the acorns."

"Tom, Tom, Tom," Hester said. "Do you know, May Rose, our watchman says Dessie's cooking is better than the food in Camp Four. And he's the cook."

"Cookie, not cook," Dessie said. "The cook bosses, the cookie does the work." She laughed and winked at May Rose. "Tom likes his food with a woman's touch." She rolled the noodle dough thin as shoe leather.

May Rose smiled at their playful shift in tone.

"I see what Tom likes," Hester said. "Dessie, you should go along and help Tom find those acorns."

"I might just, since you suggest it. I could use some air."

Hester smirked.

"Tell me what to do while you're gone," May Rose said.

"Noon, we feed the washwomen plus the boarders. Liver paste sandwiches in the parlor for the boarders, in the kitchen for the help. A little onion to go on the sandwiches if they want it."

Hester tapped her spoon on the edge of the pot. "Dessie, can you get the door?"

"She's all floury. I'll go," May Rose said.

A tall bony-shouldered boy stood on the step, clutching a damp felt hat. Red hair curled on his forehead. "I'm a good Christian and a hard worker and I need a job, it don't matter about pay." He blinked. "I haven't ate in a while."

Hester came to stand beside her. "I'm sorry, we don't need anyone."

He leaned against the doorframe. "I'll work every day and you can feed me every-other. Till I can get a job in a camp."

May Rose backed to the pie safe and waited to see what Hester would do.

Hester held the door midway. "Has the store cut you off?"

"No, ma'am. I'm new, walked over the mountain from Dodson. I didn't know the Winkler camps was shut down."

"Dodson? So you're not one of ours, and you come all that way. Dessie, do we have anything?"

May Rose stepped aside as Dessie opened the pie safe and brought out a half loaf of stale bread.

The boy shoved it into an inside coat pocket. "What do you want me to do?"

Hester shook her head. "There's no work today."

"Tomorrow?"

"I'll ask my brother. Don't tell anyone about this."

When he left, Hester said, "I don't know what's got into me, giving out food when we're about to run short. That boy better tell nobody." She pulled the curtain over the window. "No more handouts, Dessie, do you hear?"

Smiling, Dessie rolled up a sheet of noodle dough, cut a thin slice and uncurled it on the floury surface. "What happened to the supplies from the camps? Tom said they brought down what was left in their storerooms. Where'd all that go?"

"A few houses emptied out when people followed the horse teams," Hester said, "so Mr. Townsend put camp bosses and cooks there. I'd say that's where camp leftovers are."

Cooks and crew bosses—important people, as determined by Mr. Townsend. May Rose wondered if her value would go up or down when Hester told him she was truly Jamie's wife.

WANDA SLID a liver paste sandwich into her pocket. "Suzie says if Ma don't work she can't stay." Her voice seemed timid.

Hester had left to talk with Mr. Ramey. Dessie and Tom were gathering acorns in the woods, and the washwomen were hanging sheets in the attic.

May Rose handed Wanda the wet bread pan, anxious about what Evalena might do if she recovered, and wondering if anyone would rent a room to a converted whore.

"Suzie says there might be a way to let Ma stay. Business is off, and Ma never did eat much, so it won't hurt to keep her till the men get back to work and she needs Ma's room. But then…" Wanda kept her head down.

"Oh, I see." May Rose threw the wash cloth into the dish water. "Suzie wants you to take your mother's place. A little girl!"

"She'll give Ma a place to stay…if she can have you."

"What?"

"She don't want me no more, she wants you."

"Do Suzie's work? Never. Not you, not me."

Wanda pushed a towel into the corners of the bread pan.

"Listen to me. Your mother went to work at Suzie's for you."

"I know."

"What happens to you if I do what Suzie wants? You'll end up there too, or somewhere like it."

"What about Ma?"

"There's time yet. I'll think of something." Everything seemed beyond her power. "How is she today?"

"Got the shakes."

May Rose ladled a cup of broth from the brisket simmering on the stove. "Carry this over and be sure she drinks it. We have to get her strong."

She walked Wanda through the grass to the back gate. "If Suzie asks, tell her I'm thinking over her offer."

"You are?"

"I doubt I'll think of much else."

May Rose waited at the fence, glancing at wood hicks while she watched Wanda step carefully along the path toward Suzie's, the cup of broth held out so it would not slop. A child who'd never been safe.

When she turned toward the house, a man in a checkered shirt stood in her way. His gray beard was stiff as the hair of a pig. The swamper boss, Bright.

"Pardon me, Mr. Bright, I've work to do."

He didn't move. "I've come to speak to you about a job."

She hesitated, wondering if he was offering work.

"Word is," he said, "Mr. Townsend's looking for some o' the camp bosses to be guards and make men behave theirselves on the streets."

"I don't know anything about that. Please see Mr. Townsend." She walked around him.

He circled ahead of her again. "I spoke to him already. I'm the man for the job—them wood hicks won't give me no trouble, I guarantee."

"Good luck, then."

He blocked the kitchen steps. "It happens he's against me."

"Please see Mr. Townsend at his office." She turned toward the front of the house.

He walked beside her. "He'll hire me if you say so."

"You're mistaken."

"He's against me 'cause of you, that morning in church."

"Mr. Bright, I have no influence."

"Mrs. Long." He seized her arm. "Mrs. Long, it's up to us here on earth to carry out the Lord's judgment. That's why I'm going after Jamie Long, nothing against you. Do you know where he is?"

She wrenched her arm away. "He's dead."

"What if he's not?"

She stopped in the grass.

Bright smiled like he'd caught her. "There's talk he was seen at the Dodson camp."

"It doesn't matter."

"'Course it does. Speak to Mr. Townsend and I'll forget about Jamie Long."

"You forget the Lord's work easily, Mr. Bright. And you're wrong, I'm a servant in this house. I don't advise Mr. Townsend."

"It's on your head, then. Jamie's outlook, I mean."

"If my husband is alive, which I doubt, he'll have to look out for himself."

"On your head, you hear?" He closed the gate and walked toward the river campground.

Inside, she leaned against the door. The Hershmans sat in their parlor chairs, heads back, their snoring a rude accompaniment to the ticking of the grandfather clock and the painful beat of her heart. She would not bargain with Bright, not for Jamie. Others needed her more.

She knocked on the door to the Townsends' parlor.

"May Rose," Hester said. She had a cautious look. "Do you need something?"

"I need to know what you said to Suzie yesterday."

"It was nothing bad, just a word."

"Then you can tell me."

"Has something happened?"

Too many things. "I have concerns."

Hester opened the door wider. "Do you want to come in?"

May Rose shook her head. Hester glanced at the parlor where the Hershmans snored. "Normally Suzie and I steer clear of each other. We don't conflict, and from time to time we help each other out, like if one of my boarders has been rough with a girl."

"Was that it this time?"

"No. Maybe you think this is none of my business, but I told Suzie she'd have to deal with me if she tried putting Wanda to work."

Her knees went weak. "Thank you for that." She laughed, a high giggle. "Now she wants me."

Hester sighed. "Of course she does. She may want all she likes. We'll not let her have you."

Encouraged, May Rose said, "If Suzie puts Evalena out, may I keep her in my room?"

"Oh, my," Hester said. "I'm afraid not. The house would get an entirely different kind of reputation."

May Rose took a step back.

Hester sniffed. "I'm not as bad as you think."

THE ELECTRIC SHUT down soon after dinner. May Rose shared a circle of lamplight with Dessie and Tom at the kitchen worktable and waited for Wanda to return from Evalena's bedside.

"One hour of electric in the morning, and one hour at sunset, that's the word I got," Tom said. Even delivering bad news, Tom smiled, as though the darkest truths had a brighter side. She thought he must be the best-liked man in Camp Four.

"And days shorter and darker." Dessie didn't look sad at the prospect.

Smiling did not help May Rose dispel her sense of doom, nor

her anger that the value of women derived from men. Dead or alive, her man was gone, so to help Wanda and Evalena, she needed the influence of another. It might take months or years for Barlow Townsend to decide she was important enough to heed her plea. At present her only hope seemed to be Dr. Hennig, who'd said she could do better than Morris Herff.

"Mr. Townsend's keeping four men as mill guards and hiring two more bosses from the camps to police the town," Tom said. "Them two will room and board here starting tomorrow."

Dessie snorted. "Where are we supposed to put them? Already you got the midnight man sleeping on your cot when you're not there."

Tom squeezed her hand. "I might move myself into the house."

May Rose diverted her gaze. Tom and Dessie had known each other two days. She knew how it felt, the suddenness of desire. She tied her shawl around her shoulders. "I'm going to find Wanda."

Walking in the dark toward the back gate, she bumped against the night watchman.

He extended his arms, making a barrier stout as tree limbs. "Someone running this way."

The gate clanged and Wanda dodged by. "It's a kid," he said. "Hey, you!"

"She belongs here," May Rose said.

Inside, Dessie had her hands on Wanda's shoulders. "Is it your ma?"

"Yes." Wanda sobbed.

"She's passed?"

"Ma said 'don't come back, never.' She don't want to see me no more."

CHAPTER 23

For life be, after all, only a waitin' for somethin' else
than what we're doin';
and death be all that we can rightly depend on.

— BRAM STOKER: DRACULA

In the following days, Wanda slowed to a walk, gave yes and no replies, and faded from view.

"It don't feel right, her not being underfoot," Dessie said.

"Sorrow is a great presence in life," Mr. Cooper said to May Rose. "Therefore, we need music." To Wanda he said, "Go along to school with me. When we come home, we'll have a singing lesson."

"I don't want to sing," Wanda said. "And I'm not going to school."

Evenings, May Rose read aloud from *Evangeline* while Wanda lay on her stomach and stared at the wall.

"You know your ma wants to be with you," May Rose said. "She's keeping you away from Suzie."

"You said that already."

May Rose sorted through cloth scraps. "Shall we make a new doll?"

"Don't matter."

"I told your ma you were going back to school."

"Why'd you say that?"

"Because it made her happy, as it would me. What shall I say, that you do nothing but lie in bed?"

Wanda lifted her head. "What're you gonna tell Suzie?"

May Rose smoothed a length of black ribbon. "I'm working on a plan."

Wanda looked short of belief.

"I'll slip over and say goodnight," May Rose said.

Evalena was more welcoming than Wanda, and her company easier to bear. "I might live," she whispered.

May Rose held her hand. "I'm sure you will." She was sure only that life was as mysterious as death.

"Please let Wanda see you. I'll come with her."

"Not now. But you…" Evalena closed her eyes. "Be careful."

May Rose stayed until Evalena's lamp burned low.

Suzie stopped her in the hall. "Have you give thought to my offer?"

"I'm considering," May Rose said.

"Don't take too long."

Early the next morning, Tom called her to the yard. "Wanda's gone off. She slipped past me while I dumped acorns for the pigs." He pointed toward town.

May Rose hurried along the main street, peering through the crowd, ignoring the jostling of wood hicks and pushing away arms that tried to slip around her waist. During a normal day, she could see along the length of any street. Now too many men loafed about and cluttered the view.

Hours passed, and Wanda did not come home. Dessie sent Tom to tell the town guards to watch for her. May Rose asked for her at Suzie's and at the school.

Mr. Cooper confirmed the Donnelly boys were presently in school. "Usually I'm not glad of that," he said.

At lunch, she asked Dessie and Tom where she might take Evalena if Suzie put her out. Dessie shook her head.

"I slept a couple of nights in a lean-to by the tannery before I come here," Tom said. "The air's bad down there, but I can take that better than a frosty night with no roof."

When the night watchman woke, Tom took May Rose to see the lean-to.

Tannery buildings lined the river. Tom pointed to vats where skins soaked in the tannin mixture and to wooden beams where men pounded and scraped cow hides. "This here won't be shutting down," he said. "They got stacks of skins and a good supply of tan bark yet to chop and grind. Leather-making takes some time."

She held her breath but the odor soaked through anyway.

"The air's better today," he said. "Wind's blowing the other way."

Her eyes watered.

"It's the rotted animal fat and flesh that stinks. The workers get used to it, but see the river and the banks, mucky with the tannin and all else what's emptied out. You take upstream of the sawmill, there's trout aplenty, or was, before the wood hicks fished it dry. Downstream, nothing. Still, we got to have shoe leather, don't we? Harnesses and saddles. And glue." He smiled. "Ain't it the way? One thing gets better, another gets worse."

The lean-to was hardly more than wood slabs angled against a wall of rock. Smoke seeped through cracks at the top.

May Rose looked at Tom. "Someone's there."

He shouted a greeting. When no one answered, he peered into the open end and motioned her to follow. Inside, two wide planks of yellow lumber lay on the damp ground, and on them, the redheaded boy who'd begged at the boardinghouse. He turned glassy eyes toward them but did not sit or speak.

"Oh, my." May Rose squatted beside him and touched his

forehead. It was hot and dry. The lean-to might be no worse than wood hicks' tents and shanties, but she hated to see this boy here with only a fire pit in the ground and no proper door or chimney.

"I stole them boards and toted 'em here," Tom said, "but don't mention that to the boss. A feller can't sleep on wet ground."

"Is there no other place for Evalena? And this boy, too?"

"You might ask Mr. Townsend that question."

The people she cared about did not seem to be important to him.

They made another trip from the boardinghouse with an old rug, a blanket, and her lunch. Tom carried a can of water from a hillside spring and helped the boy sip. They gathered wood and piled it near the open end of the lean-to.

"It's a bad time to be a stranger," Tom said. Temperatures hung near freezing every night.

"I'll come tomorrow," she told the boy.

Wanda did not return for dinner. The house now fed four additional men, the two town guards along with Tom and the midnight watchman, but Hester had ordered Dessie not to increase the amounts she cooked. "Everyone gets a full plate, but there'll be no seconds, and no waste," she said.

May Rose ladled potpie, working smoothly and speaking in an ordinary tone while shaking inside for Wanda. Dessie carried plates two at a time to the dining room. Each time she returned her black eyes danced. Hester, she reported, was giving the salesman a little sermon about hard times.

Dessie passed the last plate back to her. "How about you carry Mr. Townsend's dinner to his parlor?"

Here was her opportunity. Since the wreck, he'd kept himself apart. She hadn't missed him, not like she'd miss Dessie or Tom, and not like she missed Wanda's quips and quirks. He seemed a person who did not bend to anyone else's opinion. In their brief encounters, the slowness and precision of his words made her feel inferior, yet she was drawn to him because he had the power to give and take away. For Wanda's sake, she had to ask if he knew of a place for Evalena.

"He'll cheer up, seeing you," Dessie whispered. She took the plate from May Rose and set it on a napkin-covered tray. "Go on. You'll see I'm right."

Her approach might be crucial, but she did not know what it should be. Work on his sympathy? Add sway to her skirt?

At her knock he called, "Come in."

He sat in a wing chair, his head bent over a book held close to the kerosene lamp.

She paused in the doorway and considered how she could influence this quiet, deliberate man. With Jamie, she had not needed to consider. A rush of heat had propelled them.

He looked up, dropped the book, bent, fumbled for it, and stood. "I thought you were Dessie." He lifted the book. "It's *Dracula*. Have you read it?" With the lamp behind him, she could not see his expression.

She held out the tray. "You said the story is frightening. I find everyday life frightening enough."

"Ah, but the story ends well. It produces anxiety but brings relief. Everyday life does not always resolve so nicely. You may take the book if you like."

"If you recommend it. Shall I set this somewhere?"

"There, please, by the lamp."

She set aside an ashtray with a half-smoked cigar and placed the tray on the table.

He cleared his throat. "Hester tells me she intends to help you find work elsewhere, when the trains run again."

May Rose could not see his face. "She's kind to let me stay until then."

"It's good for her. My sister likes to work, but she should not try to do everything herself."

He extended the book. "And you?" For a moment they held it between them, then he released his hand. "You're not working too hard?"

"I'm fine. The work is not too hard." This seemed the moment to begin a confidence, but he drew back and lifted the napkin from his tray.

"Let me know if you like the ending," he said.

In the hall, she slipped the book into her pocket.

"Well?" Dessie said. "That took a little time."

"He was reading."

"You need help," Dessie said.

True. But he did too. With Jamie she'd needed only to respond.

Later, Dessie sent her to Mr. Townsend's parlor to retrieve the dinner tray. He'd lit a second lamp, and he looked pleased to see her.

She took the tray from his hands, hoping he cared enough about her to help. "Do you know of a small house or available room anywhere? Not for me. I need a place for Wanda's mother. And there's a sick boy, homeless. I'd have to pay later."

He gazed at the light, as though thinking. In the silence, her hope grew.

His eyes came back to her, along with a patient smile. "The town's overrun, and there are many needs."

"So there's nothing."

"I'm afraid not."

"But what about the lumber stacked in the mill, and all those workers with nothing to do? Might they build little sheds with a board floor?"

His face lit as though she'd said something sweet and naïve. "We could never build enough, and how would we decide who gets them? Besides, I doubt the company would authorize such use of our lumber. The shutdown is nearly over. We'll make it through."

One house was all she needed.

~

WANDA RAN into the kitchen before bedtime, wearing the rabbit fur moccasins and Jamie's stiff hunting jacket with its bloody pockets, looking as wild and hardy as the day May Rose had found her. She brought in cold air and the scent of game, causing Hester to step back and shake her head. But even Hester smiled to see her.

"I'll take Ma to the cabin," Wanda said, when they were alone. "There's two hens roosting in a tree. I can get 'em back in the coop with that corn we left in the crock. I found your buried potatoes and stuff. Me and her can do the winter there. Russell won't care."

"When she's stronger," May Rose said, too relieved to say otherwise. "Right now your ma wants you to go to school." Even if they found a way to take Evalena to the cabin, they'd soon use up every resource. Then they'd be in deep winter, together but starving, and likely cut off by snow.

CHAPTER 24

Welcome once more to a home,
That is better perchance than the old one!

— HENRY WADSWORTH LONGFELLOW:
EVANGELINE

In the morning, May Rose walked Wanda through town to school. With two new guards policing the street, children ran with less abandon, and though wood hicks looked and whistled, they did not grab. Still, she cautioned Wanda to stay with others.

When she returned, she knew at once that something was wrong. Dessie stood on the back step, arms crossed under her apron. She pointed to the slope above the yard where Tom squatted by a mounded blanket. "Evalena." Dessie's voice crumbled like rust.

A few wood hicks stood by, hands in their pockets.

On the path behind the hotel, Suzie, Winifred and the girls bunched for warmth. "She's put herself out," Suzie called. "She won't let us help."

May Rose thought of dogs wandering off to die.

"She's still breathing," Tom said, "but the air and ground will freeze her."

Evalena didn't react when May Rose touched her hot face.

Tom and one of the wood hicks crouched and linked their arms under Evalena's shoulders and their free hands under her knees. May Rose followed them down Tannery Road, carrying a stack of old blankets donated by Hester. At the lean-to, the men laid Evalena beside the red-headed boy, who opened his eyes and tried to smile.

"I didn't make it too far," Evalena said.

May Rose sat on a sawed-off stump in the lean-to with her back against the rock and her feet cold on the damp ground. Without a proper chimney, smoke from the fire pit swirled back upon her. Evalena coughed. The boy coughed. May Rose could barely breathe.

"This place might be all right for someone who's not sick," Tom said.

He stayed with them while she hurried through town to the doctor's house, which sat apart from others on a knoll beyond the school. Mrs. Hennig answered the door.

"There's a sick woman," May Rose said.

Mrs. Hennig brought her husband and stood at his side while May Rose told of Evalena's decline.

"She drinks," Mrs. Hennig said.

He picked up his bag. "They all do."

"You said Annie Adams is ready for her baby."

"I won't be gone long. You check on Annie."

They walked through town, May Rose rushing to match his long stride.

"You have a house in Italian Town. If Evalena lives beyond today, I need a place for her."

"I'm particular who stays there. What can you pay?"

She stumbled. "Nothing at present. I know you once cared for her."

His shoulders slumped, and he walked slower. "Not like I care for you."

"Then let me use your house for a few days. I think she's dying—I won't need it long."

"I'm afraid not."

She touched his arm. "You said you wanted to be my friend. My husband is gone. I need a friend."

"And you want to put a sick woman in my house."

"I'll be there too."

He stopped.

She willed herself to match his gaze.

When she and Dr. Hennig reached the lean-to, Tom left them to go back to work. Inside, the doctor stooped beside Evalena and the boy. Then he stood and ran his fingers along May Rose's cheek. She smiled and tried not to flinch.

He went away and returned with two men and a large hand-cart. "I've been called to attend a birth. These men will take the boy and come back for the woman."

Evalena tossed with fever. The fire dwindled and May Rose built it up again. Three wood hicks asked if the lean-to was going to be available soon.

The doctor's men returned with the cart and laid Evalena in it. May Rose walked beside the cart toward town. Wind whipped her skirt, and she covered part of Evalena's face with the blanket. They stopped at the boardinghouse while she left a message for Wanda.

The house in Italian Town lifted her spirits, three rooms, the front one with two chairs, another with a bedstead and iron springs, a kitchen with a water pump and a stove for warmth and cooking. She spread a blanket over the bedsprings. The men laid Evalena beside the boy.

When Dr. Hennig arrived, he set a cot in the bedroom. "This is for the boy. I see no problem having them in the same room. I'll send a bed for the other room. You do intend to stay?"

"As long as they need me. We'll be fine, now." She meant he

didn't need to come back, but of course he would, now she owed him for his house.

He closed the distance between them. She did not resist as his arms crushed her to his chest, nor struggle as his breath warmed her neck. His chapped lips brushed across her mouth. Women's lot. She'd heard the words whispered since childhood.

"I have to go," he said.

She sighed in relief.

Wanda came after school, surprised at nothing but the boy on the cot.

"This is the sick room," May Rose said. "The other room is for us." All afternoon she'd opened the door to residents of Italian Town bearing what seemed gifts but might have been payments for the doctor's services. Two eggs, a few potatoes, wood for the stove, a feather tick, a pillow, another bed.

When Dr. Hennig returned in the evening, the look on his face showed he'd forgotten about Wanda, who sat in the front room with a schoolbook.

In the sickroom he put his arms around May Rose and whispered, "Send the girl home."

"Her home is with me."

He kissed her neck. "Let her go for something at the boardinghouse."

"I don't like her to be out alone at night."

"Have her sit on the doorstep, then. She'll be fine."

"She'll wonder why."

He took off his coat. "Does it matter? She's her mother's child."

"Company's come," Wanda called.

In the front room, Mr. Cooper coughed. "I'm told you have a boy here, someone I may know."

The doctor looked him up and down. "Who says this?"

"Miss Hester, at the boardinghouse. Everyone there is concerned for him. For Wanda's mother, too."

They took him to the boy's cot. "He's slept all day," May Rose said.

"It's hard to tell," Mr. Cooper said. "He might be Albert Waters, a boy in my previous school. The hair is right. He'd be grown and changed." He coughed again. "If this is Albert, I can contact his family."

"He'll improve," the doctor said, "and we'll ask him. Thank you for coming."

Mr. Cooper took a book from his coat pocket and unfolded a messy sheaf of paper. "Arithmetic. I promised to help Wanda with long division, if that's all right."

Tom arrived next, breathless from walking Nellie to Italian Town. He smiled. "She trotted along a lot better once she caught a sniff of that boar. She'll be over here a few days, see if she can start a new litter. I could use a cup of water." He sat to drink it. "I can keep you-all company a while—the midnight man's taking a turn for me."

Dr. Hennig left without a goodbye.

"Please come again," May Rose said to Tom and Mr. Cooper when they left. "Tell Hester and Dessie, everyone's welcome. Day or night."

BARLOW TOWNSEND surprised her the next morning soon after Wanda left for school.

"I told Hester I'd make sure you're all right." He glanced at the bed in the sitting room, spread with one of Hester's old quilts. Evalena had soiled her nightgown and bedding, and though May Rose had set the dirty laundry on the back step, the house held the odor.

He stood where she'd last seen the doctor. She wondered if he'd ever closed a woman in an intimate embrace. He smelled fresh. Dr. Hennig smelled of camphor and old wool.

She showed him the sickroom and kitchen.

His forehead wrinkled. "May Rose, I'd like to speak frankly."

"Please do."

"This…" He waved his hand around the room. "This isn't the sort of arrangement that will be good for you, however well it serves the moment. Should you ever think of marrying again, making a good marriage here, I mean. This is Dr. Hennig's house. Everyone knows…"

She let the silence build until her calculated reply felt true. "Mr. Townsend, I wonder if there will ever be a good arrangement for me. I'm in this house because of Wanda and her mother. Dr. Hennig provided a solution. He was the only one who did." She waited for him to suggest another way, a room for the sick in a respectable place.

He studied the floor. "True as I stand here, Dr. Hennig will take advantage."

"I have to help."

"You can leave. Let Wanda stay."

"She's too young for this."

"You nursed your aunt when you were her age."

"My aunt declined for years. I learned gradually."

"Someone will look in on these two."

Someone. "Tell Hester we're fine. When I no longer need this house, I'd like to come back to the boardinghouse, if I'm still welcome." Even when Wanda was not present, she could not bring herself to say, "When Evalena dies."

MIDDAY, May Rose opened the door and Mrs. Hennig stepped over the threshold. She offered no greeting, but spoke in an official-sounding voice. "I came to speak with the new woman making a fool of my husband."

May Rose clasped her hands at her waist. "Mrs. Hennig, I'm May Rose, the woman caring for two sick people. Would you like to see them?"

With a rustle of taffeta skirts, Mrs. Hennig looked into the sickroom. May Rose had sponge-bathed Evalena and the boy, who'd told his name. Not Albert Waters. Homer Wyatt. Both now slept.

Mrs. Hennig touched the footboard of Evalena's bed. "This is my husband's house."

May Rose opened the curtains. "You and he are generous to let us use it. These people had no place to go." The room was dim even by daylight.

In the kitchen, Mrs. Hennig looked through the back window to a yard where a woman milked a goat.

"Would you like a glass of water?" She had no coffee or tea.

"No, thank you. Mrs. Long, I appreciate what you're trying to do, but I'm sorry to see you here. You're young, but you must know by now that few men are reliable. Even as a doctor, my husband is barely adequate, else why would we be in a place God has forgotten? He's never been a good husband. You're not the first."

"I plan to nurse my patients for a few days," May Rose said. "That's all."

They walked together to the front door.

"You'll be wise not to make any lengthy plans with him," Mrs. Hennig said. "He'll lose interest, and then what will come of you?" Mrs. Hennig shifted her eyes to the sickroom, where Evalena slept with her mouth open and her face gray on the pillow.

DR. HENNIG ARRIVED SO SOON after his wife left that they might have passed on the street. He squeezed her breathless, bit her lip and scratched his beard on her face. Whispered in her ear, "Call me Theodore, Theo." She said she would, but could not.

"There's little I can do for your patients," he said. "The boy will improve with food and rest. I doubt Evalena will recover. We'll move them to the front room, and give you this one."

She stepped away from his embrace. "They'll catch the draft from outside."

"This room has a door. You'll have more privacy here."

She'd told Wanda it was wrong to accept gifts with no intention of giving back, and now here she was. If she did not give, he might take, or toss all of them out.

"I'll arrange to move them tomorrow," he said. "Mr. Townsend is not satisfied with his employees seeing me only when they're hurt or sick. Today he says I must begin examining all of them for evidence of disease. He says it will be good to do while they're not working and near to hand."

Perhaps her prayers were answered. After the doctor left, she had constant visitors. Hester's washwomen stopped to welcome her to their side of town and to take away the dirty laundry. Dessie brought salt-rising bread, clean sheets, and a corked bottle of Hester's wine for Evalena. Late in the afternoon, Mr. Tackett made himself comfortable on a front room chair and retold every news item in the old newspaper Mr. Townsend had brought from the wreck. Tom looked in at the end of his shift, and Hester and Mr. Cooper sang in the front room through the evening. Dr. Hennig arrived as Wanda sang "Beautiful Dreamer," the door to the sickroom open so Evalena could hear. After a few minutes with his patients, he left.

When finally they were alone, Wanda called her to Evalena's bedside, frantic. "She's not breathing."

May Rose put her ear to Evalena's chest. She heard no sound and felt no movement. Then Evalena startled them with a gasp. Wanda touched Evalena's arm and her eyelids flickered.

Wanda lay on the bed beside her. "I'll sleep right here."

From her bed in the front room, May Rose listened all night to Evalena breathing in spurts.

CHAPTER 25

Come freely, go safely and leave
  something of the happiness you bring.

— BRAM STOKER: DRACULA

May Rose prayed Evalena might die quickly or rise up and leave her bed. When neither event looked imminent, she prayed Mr. Townsend might yet provide a solution. In other moments, she poured contempt on his head and berated herself for not speaking directly, even to beg his help. In the sickroom, and for Wanda and the visitors, she smiled.

By Saturday afternoon, the red-headed boy, Homer, was up and around, helping May Rose with small tasks and moving his cot to the kitchen. With so many people in and out of three small rooms, she was glad Homer stepped forward only when he was needed and talked almost not at all. He and Wanda helped her set the front room bed beside the one in the sickroom. Together, she and Wanda washed, turned, and attempted to feed Evalena, who winced at every touch. Wanda's look pleaded with May Rose to make her well.

"An infection somewhere," Dr. Hennig said, appearing late in the day and frowning at the side-by-side beds.

Mr. Tackett came again. "I'm so bored." He shook the doctor's hand. "It's refreshing to be welcomed somewhere different." After he told May Rose of boardinghouse meals and card games with wood hicks, he spun stories of his youth for Homer and Wanda, then carried his chair to the sickroom and repeated everything for Evalena, whose face sometimes twitched, though her eyes stayed closed.

Saturday night, Hester and Mr. Cooper visited again. Hester handed her a pan of warm bread pudding. "I asked my brother to come, but he's going over medical records with the doctor."

May Rose beamed at Mr. Cooper and hugged Hester, grateful for everything unsaid.

Sunday morning, May Rose looked out to see Tom in a mule-drawn wagon, and beside him, Russell Long.

Russell's bulk filled the doorway.

"Look what the cat drug in," Wanda said.

Tom put a hand on Russell's shoulder. "He brung a load of cornmeal to the store and about got mobbed on the street. Was rescued by Frank. He asked after you-all, so here we are."

"We're glad to see you," May Rose said, uncertain. Russell looked humbled. Without its beard, his face was full of sags and pouches. He wore stiff canvas pants and a jacket that might have come right out of the store. He spoke toward the floor.

"Spit your teeth out," Wanda said.

He flashed her a sour look. "Stop being mouthy." His face softened when he looked at May Rose. "You was to let me know did you have need. Of anything."

She watched him, cautious. "This happened quickly."

He looked away.

Wanda motioned him to the sickroom. "Come see Ma."

He pulled the camp stool to the bed and sat beside Evalena. "Old girl," he said. Evalena's eyelids flickered.

Tom could not stay. When he left Evalena's room, Russell lowered himself to the floor, stretched out his thick legs and leaned against the wall. "I'll rest here awhile if you don't mind. Drove corn to the mill yesterday, then on to here, all night."

"Rest there, on the boy's cot," May Rose said.

Homer carried in an armload of kindling and dropped it into the woodbox.

"You there," Russell said. "Take my mules outa harness and stake them somewhere to graze."

"Homer ain't got his strength," Wanda said. "I'll do it."

"Do it right," Russell said.

Eager to get away from Russell and the sickroom, May Rose went with her.

"It's better having Russell here than that old doctor," Wanda said. "He ain't doing a thing for Ma."

"He's given her a place to get well."

"And everybody knows why. You don't have to let him do what he's thinking of. Let's keep Russell around. Let the doctor go to Suzie's."

Russell snored in the kitchen through Sunday visitors until late afternoon, then sat up and decided, since it was getting dark, he might just stay another day.

In the evening, Hester and Mr. Cooper came again. Mr. Cooper fiddled "Turkey in the Straw," and Russell took a harmonica from his pocket and blew an occasional note. Homer clogged a few steps before he tired. Wanda hopped around the room, thumping her shoes on the floor and popping her head in the sickroom to see if Evalena might be watching.

When the doctor arrived, Hester said, "Next time bring Mrs. Hennig. She'd enjoy the music."

Every hour of story or song let May Rose believe in a happy outcome. But in the night, she lay with cold hands tucked in the pits of her arms and thought how things had a way of getting worse before they got better.

Monday morning, Dr. Hennig arrived while Homer was outside watching Russell chop firewood. He pressed her against the wall of the sickroom. "They're not going to leave us alone."

"It's for the best."

"Not for me."

Caught in the web of her own making, she let him kiss her.

After the doctor left, Russell sat again with Evalena. When Wanda came from school, he said, "Your ma wants to go home."

"It burned to the ground," Wanda said. "Last spring. You know."

"Somewhere like it. Home to my place, where she can smell the trees and hear the grass grow."

"Evalena hasn't said a word," May Rose said. "Not since we took her to the lean-to."

Wanda bobbed her head. "It's what she's thinking."

Russell's place was a day's walk from the cabin, and she supposed nearly as far from town. "The trip will be too hard. She'll be better off here."

Wanda waved away her objections. "It's what she wants, and you can go back to the boardinghouse."

In grief and astonishment, May Rose leaned against the wall and listened to Wanda telling Evalena how she'd recover at Russell's house. Evalena gave no sign of hearing.

Tuesday morning they padded her in blankets and Russell and Homer laid her on the tick in the wagon bed. Wanda climbed in beside her, wearing Jamie's hunting jacket and the rabbit fur boots. Homer sat beside Russell.

"You've been good to me," Homer said. "Maybe someday I can do something for you. I'm sorry you can't go, too."

No one had asked. "He has a small house. I don't know where you'll sleep."

"Him and me's gonna add a room."

She doubted Evalena would survive the trip.

Russell shook her hand. His was broad and calloused, and

with missing fingers, it gripped awkwardly. "Kindly of you to give her the dress."

"The dress?"

"That blue one you got on Evalena."

Russell had sent it. She'd never thought.

He handed down a wad of paper. "I found a torn-up sheep-skin coat down there by the wreck. This was in the pocket."

She gripped the top of a wagon wheel. "You didn't...find anything else?"

His eyes darted side to side. "There was a pistol in the coat. I've kept that."

She unfolded greenbacks, tens and twenties, and dropped them like they were hot.

Wanda looked where they lay on the ground. "You're real careless about money."

"You're right." She picked them up. "I can lose these in a better place."

"Thanks for all you done," Wanda said. "If you don't see us, don't worry. Snow's gonna come, and we might not get out till spring."

May Rose squeezed the greenbacks. "We have a plan, don't forget."

After they left, she cried freely, stripped the beds of Hester's sheets, and bundled the trash. Men on the street stepped aside as she carried her bundles through town to the boardinghouse.

"I'm not a fallen woman," she said to Dessie. "Thanks to all of you."

Dessie wiped her eyes. "Mr. Townsend did the most, wouldn't you say, making them wood hicks line up day and night at the doctor's place?"

May Rose was sorry she'd suspected the Townsends. She took the greenbacks to Hester.

"I want to stay until Evalena has passed and Wanda returns. It shouldn't be long. When the trains run again, I'll get work in another town." Inside her stocking she'd folded enough for train fare to Pittsburg.

Hester frowned at the bills. "This isn't from Dr. Hennig?"

"From Russell, my brother-in-law. I can work again if you like, but I need a day to rest."

"Take two. Dessie and I will be glad to have you back."

Alone, she found her room unbearable. Wanda had left her schoolbooks and most of Hester's hand-me-downs. She set the dolls on the bed, opened her copy of Evangeline to a random page, and read aloud:

"In the confusion

Wives were torn from their husbands, and mothers, too late, saw their children

Left on the land, extending their arms, with wildest entreaties."

The description of families wrenched apart felt too real. She closed the book and picked up the newspaper Mr. Townsend had brought from the wreck, now limp and smeared from many handlings. She noted advertisements for house girls, waitresses, kitchen girls, a colored nurse girl, and wondered, with so many positions available, why there were an equal number of positions wanted. She read news stories of the Boer War, annexation troubles in the Philippines, the story of a woman fined for wearing trousers and one of women committing suicide in New York.

"May Rose." Dessie spoke from the hall. "Can I come in?"

"Please do."

"Dr. Hennig's in the parlor. Hester says she'll deal with him if you like."

"I'll come," May Rose said.

When Hester left them alone, the doctor scowled. "You used me. Took advantage."

May Rose sighed. "Wasn't that what you planned? To use me?"

"I did my part. You didn't do yours."

"But I did. Don't you remember what you asked? I prayed for you to be removed from temptation."

He stepped closer. "You may have high hopes, but I doubt his highness will have you. You'll need me again."

"I will always pray for you," she said, as he left. She wondered if it would suffice to pray for his wife.

Because May Rose did not go down for dinner, Hester brought her dinner on a tray and stayed while she ate. "Humphrey's going to hold a revival meeting, three nights, starting tomorrow. He's hoping to save a few more souls, given there's all these wood hicks in town too poor for anything else. Come, go with us."

May Rose smiled at the walls, hers for a while longer. "I feel better here."

Hester sat on the bed and smoothed her hand over the quilt. "Tomorrow night Dessie and Tom are getting married."

"They're getting married? Dessie didn't say a thing."

"Right before the revival. They wanted it after the service, but Humphrey said the altar call might go late, and if he married them before, folks might get too cheery to repent. He asked them to hold off till Sunday, but now they've settled on it, they can't wait to get it done. I know Dessie wants you to be there but she doesn't like to show how happy she is. She knows you're sad."

"Of course I have to go." She felt happy for Dessie. That night she braved the opening pages of *Dracula*.

THE NEXT DAY, she met Will Herff in town. She sat beside him on the cold steps outside the store, hesitant to ask why he wasn't in school. "How is everyone at your house?"

He chucked a stone into the street. "We thought you liked us."

"I do like you, Charlie and Glory too, and I'm glad to see you. Are you doing all right, living with the Donnellys?"

"She's not too bad. We thought it was going to be you."

"You thought it was going to be me...what?"

"Our new Ma. We thought, you."

"Oh, Will, I was with you only a few days."

He looked away. "Yeah, but Pa said *maybe*. Then the next day he said you didn't like us and wasn't going to come no more."

"I never said that, Will. I was sad to leave. You were there, you saw."

"Mr. Townsend told Pa different."

"Mr. Townsend? Did you hear him say I didn't care for you?"

He shook his head. "Pa said he did."

Life was hard enough without people making trouble, but lies always had a reason. She could imagine this one started by Mrs. Donnelly, or spoken by Morris Herff to justify his choice, no matter if he made his children feel bad. To believe Will's version of events, she'd have to doubt Mr. Townsend, who'd gone out of his way to help.

"I like you. I miss you. Please tell Charlie I never said I didn't want to be with you."

"We're living in their house. They got beds and all, but not much to eat. Pa carves his critters day and night. Now there's no work, she's on him all the time to make something useful to sell. He says it don't matter since no one can buy anything."

May Rose thought of her potatoes. "Are you going to school today?"

He nudged a bucket on the step below. "I'm supposed to pick up coal along the tracks, but every bit's been got."

"I saw burlap sacks in your wash house. Bring them to the footbridge by the loading docks."

When she told Dessie where she was going, Dessie wrapped two buttered biscuits in a cloth. Will ate both before they reached the start of the trail.

Laurel and spruce now created the only blots of green among trees bared for winter, and sunlight lit the forest floor. They passed the glade where she'd first seen Wanda and the Donnelly boys. For a rest, they paused and cupped their hands under water that dripped from overhanging rocks, a waterfall in rainy times.

"How do you get on with your stepbrothers?"

"They beat me up, just once. Charlie told Pa and Pa strapped them."

Will swiped his wet hands on his jacket. "They say they're gonna get back at Charlie some way so nobody will know. Charlie says he ain't afraid. He sneaks around after them, says they never see."

She caught her breath. "Did they steal your father's carvings?"

"I ain't sure." He kicked at leaves and dirt. "I don't think so, no."

"Will you tell Charlie to come and see me? You too, any time you want. I wish you could bring Glory."

"She's all right. Our new ma kinda likes her."

WHEN THEY REACHED the cabin clearing, May Rose made Will wait until she decided no one else was there. Brown chicken feathers stuck to weeds and littered the blanket of dry leaves. No smoke rose from the chimney. Two chicken heads, eyes open, lay beside the chopping stump.

Inside, chicken bones covered the table. Someone had pushed the bed back against the wall. She thought of Jamie, who would never be dead until she saw his body.

Someone had pulled weeds from the potato pit beside the springhouse. Wanda, she hoped. She probed in the grass and lifted a square of turf, not yet frozen. Will had brought four sacks. They filled each one a quarter full, nearly a bushel in all, and cleaned their hands in dry weeds. As they dragged their sacks across the clearing, she looked back at the charred scarecrow. She did not want to see this place again.

She exhausted and dirtied herself dragging the sacks down the trail. At Will's new house, she dropped them on the step.

"Please get your father," she said. "If he won't come out, tell him what we've got here."

Both Morris and his new wife came to the door.

May Rose flexed her aching neck. She looked only at Morris Herff, though the speech she'd planned was also meant for his wife. "Mr. Herff, I saw your stepsons assault a girl, a child. *With their trousers down.* If I hear they've hurt your children—hurt anyone again—I'll tell Frank."

CHAPTER 26

I sometimes think we must be all mad
And that we shall wake to sanity in strait-waistcoats.

— BRAM STOKER: DRACULA

Two by two, Dessie and Tom led the procession from the boardinghouse to the church. May Rose and Mr. Townsend walked last, separated by a proper space and perhaps also by their own concerns. Because she despised her desire for Wanda to come back, an event that depended on Evalena's death, May Rose prayed for a miracle healing. She also prayed the Donnellys might reform. As promised, she prayed for Dr. Hennig, and finally, she prayed that if the spirit fell on her during the revival, no one would notice.

As a child, she'd been frightened by the frantic preaching at revivals and the spectacle of grownups shrieking and crying as they were cleansed of guilt. Yet now she knew a wounded soul might not be healed by ordinary means, nor cruel and evil hearts turned over without the exertion of a powerful spirit. She needed relief as much as anyone, but hoped not to expose her failings. Too proud, Aunt Sweet would say.

She held her coat tight at her neck and shivered in wind that made lanterns bob and their lights dance. In strong gusts, Mr. Townsend steadied her with a hand on her back, and she leaned on the arm he offered. He seemed as distant as if they'd never met.

In the church, oil lamps made overlapping halos on the walls, and candles at the front blazed each time the doors opened. Mr. Cooper went to the piano. Hester and Mr. Townsend sat with the decorum of people aware of their importance. Trapped between them, May Rose wished she hadn't come. But when Dessie and Tom stood in front of Preacher Gower and said "I do," she wiped away happy tears. They walked up the aisle and kept going, right out the door. She longed to run out with them.

The revival began as she'd expected and feared. Preacher Gowder's prayers turned into songs and shouts, and scripture moved him to rapture. He tramped back and forth on the platform, shook his holy book and jabbed a finger at the congregation. "Never forget, every last man and woman of us needs saved from our sins. Don't think there's not evil in you. Pray it doesn't come out."

When enough were sobbing, sniffling, and shouting amens, he gave the altar call. It was time for the timid to be courageous, to confess their dark hearts and hidden deeds and claim the light.

Preacher Gowder moved along the altar rail, touching heads of women who cried into their handkerchiefs. Wood hicks and old men stumbled to the front and went down on their knees, and the church filled with mumbled prayers. May Rose hung her head until a murmur from Hester made her look up. Dr. and Mrs. Hennig knelt at the altar.

A woman near the front turned her head and found May Rose. Another followed the gaze of the first, then more turned to see what spectacle in the back might be more interesting than the one in front. May Rose flushed hot, as though they'd seen the doctor pressed against her. More heads turned. How they'd love her to go forward and confirm their beliefs. She was almost sorry to disappoint them.

Hester held her hand the way one might restrain a child, but May Rose had no intention of joining the doctor and Mrs. Hennig. No matter how she worked to prove herself virtuous, people here would never stop talking about the naked girl on the mountain.

She fixed her mind on Jamie's deal with Suzie, remembered Glory's cold, wet bottom, her brothers sleeping on the floor, their beatings. She thought of Evalena and Wanda, left on their own. The Donnelly boys. In order to find forgiveness, one needed to forgive. *Not yet.*

Everyone now stood and shuffled in baby steps toward the altar or the door. In the crush of bodies, Mr. Townsend kept her and Hester together and directed them into the night.

ASSAULTED BY WIND, May Rose hurried with the boardinghouse group toward the glowing windows of home. Hester and Mr. Townsend did not explain themselves. They might have decided together to protect her from further gossip. Perhaps no one would ever speak of it.

Not until they rushed through the door did she think of Dessie and Tom, who stood hand in hand in the parlor. They'd set out their own wedding feast, cakes and sandwiches.

"Sister, break out the wine." Mr. Townsend spoke in a hearty, cheerful tone. "We'll toast the newlyweds." He helped her and Hester off with their coats and Hester ran to the kitchen. May Rose stood amazed as he kissed the bride's cheeks, shook Tom's hand, and admired the cakes.

Dessie leaned to May Rose and whispered, "What did I miss?"

"Miss?" May Rose shook her head.

"Him." She nodded toward Mr. Townsend's back. "Did the revival turn him right side up, or was it you?"

"He's happy for you and Tom."

He circled the room with a carafe, leading toasts, cheering guests with refills, telling Tom and Dessie not to think of cleaning up—he and Hester would take care of everything.

Wine slipped down her throat. To herself, her voice sounded free of care. He passed cakes, smiled as much to her as to everyone, laughed and incited laughter. Brightening faces and silly talk lifted her as the revival had not. She emptied her glass.

He paused before her. "Have you had opportunity to read the book?"

"The book?"

"*Dracula*?"

"*Dracula*, yes," she said. "A few pages."

"More wine?"

"No, thank you." She touched a hot cheek. Dr. Hennig's beard had left no mark, yet with Mr. Townsend smiling and bending close, she felt bruised.

Mr. Tackett stepped beside her. "Which book is that?"

Mr. Townsend filled his own glass and set the carafe on the center table. "The Bram Stoker mystery, *Dracula*."

"Ah, I've read it," Mr. Tackett said.

Mr. Cooper joined them, and Mr. Townsend took the carafe to his cousins.

"I found the book stimulating," Mr. Tackett said. "And shocking, if you infer its deeper meaning." He wiggled thick eyebrows.

May Rose noted Mr. Townsend's progress around the room.

Mr. Cooper frowned. "Inference depends on what's in the reader's mind. Some always find more than the writer planted."

"Planted, no. Left open, *Herr Professor*. I'm speaking of *Dracula*. The story opens our fears, our hidden desires."

"Perhaps exploits them," Mr. Cooper said.

May Rose left the room before wine and loneliness turned her into someone else.

≈

SHE SPENT Sunday reading *Dracula* and puzzling about Mr. Townsend. Had he told Morris Herff she didn't want to take care of his children? Morris had said nothing about it when she'd made her final appeal. It was possible Mr. Townsend worried about exposing her to the man's cruelty. He had intervened at other critical times, made protective appearances either from a sense of chivalry or the need to keep his employees in line.

She could not deny her awe of him. He was well-spoken and well-groomed, and his features were not unpleasant. Since the wreck, he'd kept himself apart, yet he'd been strangely warm to everyone at Dessie's wedding supper.

She let loose her wildest fancies, as if the book had a secret message, a clue to his desires. He might liken himself to Jonathan Harker, the businessman held captive in Count Dracula's castle. Three ghostly women had frightened Harker, but also lured him, especially the fair one with *"great wavy masses of golden hair."* She flushed with the idea that to Barlow Townsend she might be this woman, that he might share Harker's *"wicked, burning desire"* that she would *"kiss me with those red lips."* She imagined his pulse increasing, like hers, when he read *"I could feel the movement of her breath upon me. Sweet it was in one sense, honey-sweet, and sent the same tingling through the nerves as her voice…"*

Jonathan Harker had a wicked desire to be captured by the golden-haired woman. If a reader responded even mildly to that passage, surely he was not unfeeling. He might only need to be captured.

GUNSHOTS AND SQUEALS WAKENED HER, and strips of dawn at the curtain's edge guided her to the window, where she saw dark movement around the hog lot. She put her coat on over her night-gown and ran to the kitchen.

Dessie stood at the door, watching bobbing lantern light. "It's all right, just Tom and a few others out there. Hester decided to butcher today. Wash day's been put off to tomorrow."

May Rose held her fist to her mouth.

"Never fear, your sow's still away getting fixed up for that next litter. They're taking two of the fattest pigs. Last night Hester got wood hicks to dig a fire pit by the river to heat water, that's where they'll scald and scrape off the hair. They'll set up tables out back for cutting. We'll be canning sausage by afternoon."

She knew the work. The men would saw off the hams and bone meat and leave the rest to the women. There'd be sausage to grind, hams and bacons to rub with salt cure, fat to render into lard. They'd prepare a feast for the helpers, and send them home with a lump of fresh sausage. They'd need extra women to fix the meal, stuff sausage into jars or casings, stir the lard, and wash up all day long.

May Rose yawned. "Will anyone come to help?"

"Nobody here keeps pigs but the Italians," Dessie said. "We've not had any since our first year, so Hester's forgot how hard it is to butcher and take care of boarders at the same time. Our wash-women and their men are coming."

Mr. Townsend entered the kitchen fully dressed and carrying his hat. May Rose's feet were bare, her nightgown showed below the hem of her coat, and her uncombed hair hung down her back. She started toward the stairs, but stopped, thinking of *Dracula*, and waited for Mr. Townsend to return her gaze.

"I've been reading the book."

"Oh. Very good." He paused as though waiting for her to say more. The dining room door swung open, and Hester passed between them with a curious look. May Rose retreated to her room.

After dressing, she came down the front stairs, a longer way to the kitchen, but an opportunity to put herself in view. She passed no one. Mr. Townsend, she learned from Dessie, had gone to his office. In the next hour she set the dining room table, washed glass jars in the tub room, and helped Dessie and Hester carry pans, crocks, and knives outside.

Soon the carcasses lay on makeshift tables, scraped, gutted, and split. The Hershman brothers and Mr. Tackett came to comment and get in the way, and wood hicks leaned over the fence, offering help in exchange for a dab of meat. Crows flopped into the yard and pecked at the blood trail. May Rose stood at a table beside Hester and trimmed scraps for sausage. In the wash house, two Italian women fed and cranked the sausage grinder.

Mr. Townsend returned, observed the work and looked at the sky. "Warm day for this time of year." He walked across the yard and said a word to Tom, who took his rifle to the pig lot and fired a single shot.

Hester spoke in the silence that followed. "Did the Winkler Company just buy one of my pigs?"

"I guess it did," he said.

"I'll present an invoice."

"Do that."

Two wood hicks dragged the dead pig toward the river, trailing blood, and Mr. Townsend shouted for those beyond the fence to hear, "Spread the word—we'll put this pig to roast in a pit tonight, and tomorrow all workers and their families may come to the river for a picnic."

He smiled at their cheers.

"You might have asked me first," Hester said. "Or told me your intent."

"I just thought of it."

Hester sliced, turned the meat and sliced again. "One pig won't go far. Don't expect this house to provide anything for your picnic—not so much as a platter or loaf of bread. You may direct your employees as you like, but mine are overly busy."

"Of course they are." He sounded amused. "Perhaps Miss May Rose will help."

Hester frowned. "She's busy here."

May Rose carried a pan of meat scraps to the women at the

grinder. If they must talk about her like she wasn't there, she'd pretend not to hear.

He left the yard. Hester hacked a cleaver through a rack of ribs. "Well? I suppose you're pleased with yourself?"

May Rose sighed. "You're unhappy with me, and I don't know why." But she did.

Shortly after noon, the washwomen and their men went home with the pigs' heads and feet. Dessie had wanted them for mincemeat and head cheese, jellied meat that May Rose called souse, but Hester said they had too much else to do. She kept popping into the kitchen while they stuffed sausage into jars, as though May Rose and Dessie could do nothing without her supervision.

"Give the boarders plenty of meat for dinner," she said, "and they won't miss potatoes or bread."

Dessie sighed. When Hester left, she said, "Tom might get us a house. He cramps my little closet of a room, and I'd relish getting away from here, time to time. Naturally Hester don't like the idea of me living somewheres else. I can see her telling Mr. Townsend not to let us have a company house, though heaven knows, Tom deserves it well as anybody."

"Hester's angry with me," May Rose said.

Dessie jabbed a table knife into a packed jar of sausage to take out air bubbles. "I told you how it'd be if she saw you noticing Mr. Townsend."

"She's been good to me. And then at the revival, she and Mr. Townsend…"

"Yes," Dessie said. "I knew there was something. She likes you, but you see, he likes you, too. Look how he bought that pig."

May Rose wiped the top of a jar, laid on a rubber gasket and glass lid and pulled the clamp shut. "That was for the company. He's afraid the workers will leave."

"Some of that, too. But he was showing off. For you."

"For the company." She hid a smile.

"And last night, that wasn't just for me and Tom. Don't let

Hester's opinion hold you back. He may not be as sweet as my Tom, but he's a good provider. Think on that."

She did think on it, because it was nice to be admired by someone like Mr. Townsend. Beyond that, there seemed no use to think of him as long as she was bound to Jamie.

The afternoon was bright with gusts that pulled down the last leaves and swirled them up from the ground. They built a fire under an iron ring, set a tin washtub over it and filled it with water. Dessie set the jars of sausage into the tub and tended the fire to keep the water bubbling. In an iron pot with legs over another fire, May Rose stirred chunks of fat with a wooden paddle. Hester came outside to remind them not to burn the lard.

"Yes, ma'am," Dessie said.

Wind whipped the fires under the kettles, but the lard paddle had a bent handle that allowed May Rose to stir safely away from sparks and splatters. The fat melted and cracklings formed.

"Perfect," Hester decided.

Late in the afternoon, she and Dessie dipped from the outside barrel of dishwater and kitchen scraps and carried buckets of swill to the hog trough. Pigs had tracked the blood. They seemed agitated.

"The old sow won't miss them," Dessie said. "If anything, she'll be glad to have them gone. Animals don't feel these things."

May Rose didn't agree. Still, she'd raised Nellie's pigs for slaughter, an ending she never liked to think about, though necessity pushed people to worse things.

"Forget acorns," Dessie said. "Tom's still over to the river, digging that fire pit, and you've worked enough today. Them pigs don't have to eat tonight."

"It's light yet," May Rose said. "I won't go far, just up here in the woods."

She made a wide detour to avoid the hillside camp of tarps and tin with their idle men and scents of boiled coffee. Boys from town hung about the camp, some small enough to be Will and

Charlie. Seeing two man-sized boys who looked like the Donnellys, she hurried past.

Once under the trees, she looked for oaks and kicked through leaves for a fresh source of nuts. Half a bag would do. She scooped with the broken-handled shovel, thinking with each thrust how she differed from men, and how it mattered. They seemed less bothered by the suffering of others, and more inclined to seize advantage. Without the guidance of a good mother, little boys like Will and Charlie might grow up to be as cruel and selfish as their father.

She'd seen no more of Bright, and had told no one of his threat. Were she like Suzie, she'd have insisted he pay for her influence, whether she had any or not. If she were like Suzie, she might have put her arms around Mr. Townsend and pushed him against his parlor wall. She laughed at the thought.

With the bag in her left hand and the shovel in her right, she bent and scooped until the bag was half full. Straightening, she startled at a loud cracking of twigs. Somewhere nearby, heavy feet tramped through brush. She turned as the tramping turned to running thumps. Two men with burlap bags over their heads rushed from a grove of spruce. She flung her bag of acorns at one and missed. The other grabbed the shovel. Both seized her arms.

She kicked a shin, and the one she kicked grunted and loosened his grip, clumsy in his hob-nail boots. She stumbled away, but the other held her left arm. Howling, she circled and flailed without striking anything, and he laughed. The other man threw down the shovel, caught her from behind and squeezed his arms around her middle until she thought she'd faint. She'd feared an attack like this so long that it seemed like a recurring nightmare. She tramped her heel down on his boot, sending a shock through her leg. He laughed again and pushed her to her knees. His legs pressed in on each side of her body, clamping her in place.

The shorter one growled, "We gonna do it right here?" His bag had twisted out of place, and he pulled it back so a portion of blue eyes showed through the holes. The burlap was wet over his mouth.

The other hissed, "Shut up and undo yourself." He squeezed his legs to her sides and pushed down on her shoulders to keep her from rising. Her knees pressed into something sharp, rocks or acorns. She bucked and tried to bite his fingers. He let up on her shoulders and twisted her arms behind her. She screamed.

The shorter one came close, pulled his suspenders off his shoulders, let his trousers fall to the ground. He had no body hair. He was a boy.

The one behind twisted her arms again. "He ain't never been licked. So do it, whore."

The boy in front of her bobbed up and down, like he was cold. She only half understood what they meant her to do.

"Get to it!" The tall one shoved her forward. She pushed herself sideways, fell over his leg and tried to twist away. He stumbled over her, but seized her skirt and caught her arms. When he jerked her upright, she gathered her breath and screamed again.

He pushed her toward the boy and forced her once more to her knees, but the boy grabbed up his trousers and pointed in the direction of noises that sounded like people thrashing the brush and striking clubs against tree trunks.

The taller one listened a moment, then punched her face and pulled her into the laurel. Blood spurted from her nose. He jerked her along while the boy pushed from behind. When she stumbled, the boy slapped her head. She cried out, spitting blood, and he slapped again. The one in front kept his head down, like he was following a path, the light dim, day turning to dusk. Under their feet, the path through the maze was no wider than a single boot. Branches snapped back and she struggled to push them aside and stay upright. She swallowed blood and breathed through her mouth. The noise stopped.

When they broke through the tangles to a place wide enough for three, the one ahead turned and stuffed a rag in her mouth.

She spit it out and tried to run, but they blocked the path and the taller caught her wrist.

He pushed the rag back in. "Tie it," he said. The boy tied twine around her head. She gagged, barely able to breathe, and pushed the rag with her tongue. It moved easily, but they didn't see, now busy untying twine from the bags on their heads. She chewed the rag back in so they wouldn't know.

Stretching her arms from her sides, they used the twine to tie each wrist to a trunk of laurel. Her arms felt ripped from her shoulders. The bags on their heads hung loose, and they kept twisting them to keep the eye holes in place. She sucked foul air through the rag.

When a whacking of brush and beating of trees erupted on the slope above, the boy started to run. The other pulled him back. They crouched, whispered and gestured, then left the way they'd come. She spit out the rag, coughed and gagged. After a while the noises in the brush stopped.

Her arms grew numb, the sky darker. Stretched between the two laurel trunks, she sniffed and spit blood and flexed her back and neck to take the strain off her shoulders. Leaning and twisting right and left, she saw how, with great effort, she might pull one of the slender trunks close enough to loosen the tension on the opposite tether, maybe enough to pull her wrist to her teeth. Again and again she leaned and pulled on the left trunk until her wrist bled. She braced her feet and leaned farther. Drenched in sweat, she finally relaxed the right tether enough to wrap her fingers around it. Now she leaned the other way and pulled. Her right arm was stronger, but she could not get her wrist close enough to chew the tie at her wrist.

Then the twine snapped, throwing her back into the laurel on the left. Scratched and shaken but still tied by one wrist, she pulled herself to a crouch and listened.

Quietly, with a snap and whip of branches, something passed through the thicket, soft and wary as a fawn. She leaped to untie the remaining tether.

One moment she saw no one, and the next Charlie Herff stood beside her. She gasped. He lifted a broad-bladed knife, one she knew before she saw the nick at the fat end of the blade. Russell's knife. Wanda's. The Donnellys'. He cut the twine, then led her out to the place where her bag and acorns lay scattered.

"They've run," he whispered.

She wiped her face on her sleeve. "You made that noise, scared them off?"

"They ain't too brave, is they?" He waved the knife. "We'll get 'em."

Her heart thumped. "Charlie, not like that. We'll tell my friends, Dessie and Tom at the boardinghouse, and Mr. Cooper."

"You know who they was, don'cha?"

"I never saw their faces, but I know. Let's go tell Frank."

"Their ma will say they was to home. She lies for them all the time."

"We'll think of something. Come back with me. You can sleep in the watchman's shed."

"I got stuff to do. Couple more days, we'll get 'em."

They scooped up a few acorns then walked downhill in the dark. He left her before they reached the alley behind the board-inghouse.

CHAPTER 27

...when echoes had ceased, like a sense of pain was the silence

— HENRY WADSWORTH LONGFELLOW:

EVANGELINE

May Rose jerked awake through the night from sensations of a punch to her nose, her arms stretched from her shoulders, and twine cutting into her wrists. Each time, she sat up, certain she'd been screaming, unable to breathe, frantic for Charlie. She should not have let him go, should have marched him directly to Frank or his father. Battered witless, she'd trusted him better than herself.

Before first light, she woke to pounding on her door and Tom's voice. "Wake up! Fire across the river!" The house shook with knocking, doors slamming, men running in the hall and thumping down the stairs. She hurried into her oldest dress, stumbled into stockings, shoes.

On the porch, the morning air seemed no more smoky than usual, but as she gripped the railing the hillside across from them blazed up, reddening the sky like the sailor's warning. The few recent rains had not ended the season's drought, and gusty winds blew fire over the slope of dead brush in every direction—upstream, downstream, and uphill toward the trail and the high stand of virgin timber.

Tom and the other guards stooped at the edge of the porch with Mr. Townsend. They tied their boots, pointed, nodded. One stood and said, "Shovels?"

"In the mill," Mr. Townsend said. "Tom, come with me."

The guards ran separate ways into the campground along the river, gathering wood hicks.

Dessie threw down her apron and hurried after Tom and Mr. Townsend.

"What does she think she can do?" Mr. Tackett asked.

Hester's voice sparked. "There'll be jobs for all that's able."

The snapping and cracking grew to a roar. Burning twigs floated upward on drafts, lighting dry grass or falling into the river. Several dozen men with shovels ran past the house toward the tannery, waded across the river and disappeared in smoke.

"I'd say it hasn't been burning long," Mr. Tackett said, "or this wind would've charred the whole mountain. We're safe this side of the river, don't you think?"

The river seemed little more than rocks and shallow pools.

The dark of dawn became the dark of day. Church and school bells rang until the town emptied to the street, men with shovels, women with brooms.

Today she and Dessie intended to salt hams and bacons. It was the day of Mr. Townsend's company picnic. The day she and Charlie needed to tell his father and Frank about the Donnelly boys.

"Hester," she said. "Do you want me to work here or join the fire line?"

Hester peered at her in the smoky light. "What happened...?"

May Rose touched her sore nose and swollen cheeks.

Hester gasped. "Italian Town."

Italian Town lay in the path of the fire. Hester turned to the teacher, who'd come late to the porch. "Mr. Cooper, go across the bridge, bring the children to the school and anyone else who's not able to stand and fight the fire. Send some to the church if you need more room. May Rose, you may make coffee. Gentlemen, there'll be no sit-down breakfast today. We'll bring coffee and something else to the parlor and you may serve yourselves. If they don't beat down the fire by noon, we all may need to carry food and water to the men on the line."

"There they go." Mr. Tackett pointed to a line of dark figures spreading along the hill between fire and standing timber.

"Mr. Tackett, please fill a barrel with drinking water for the men over there," Hester said. "You'll find our little cart in the shed. Watch the fire and see where the men are likely to go for a rest. Get Suzie and her girls to help. Suzie. I'm sure you know who I mean. May Rose, forget the coffee. Go to the mill and see if my brother needs more help there."

The fire raged over a slope of tinder—dried-out tree tops, stumps, dead brush, saplings. Running toward the mill, May Rose ignored the throbbing in her nose, more alert to the wall of heat across the river. The fire seemed like something they could control unless it reached the trees or jumped the river into the mill. She held her breath as a burning twig lifted over the water and fell on a bush at the edge. The bush blazed up, but surrounded by rock and water, burned out.

Women and girls dipped brooms in the river and scooped water into buckets.

"Miss May Rose!" Will Herff pulled her sleeve. "Have you seen Charlie?" Tears streaked his cheeks.

"Charlie! Not today, come along, tell me." She pulled him across the tracks and through the mill entrance.

Dessie stood by the longest building and peered up at Tom, who straddled the roof peak near a water barrel.

May Rose pulled Dessie's arm. "Where's Mr. Townsend?"

Dessie pointed to buildings at the river's edge. May Rose and Will ran on.

"Charlie plays over there," Will said, "where the fire is. Some nights he don't come home. He never come home last night."

"Were your stepbrothers there?"

"This morning they was."

"Stay close. We'll find him."

Mr. Townsend and the mill guards were spaced along the river, shovels ready. Upstream, what looked like the entire population of Italian Town stretched between the fire and their homes, digging a firebreak. She repeated Hester's message.

"We're all right for the moment," he said. "I telegraphed for help, but by road, it will be hours before anyone can get here. I doubt anyone comes—they'll stay where they are so they can cut a break if the fire gets close to them. It's what I'd do."

Will fidgeted beside her. She laid her hand on his shoulder. "Have you seen Charlie Herff? A little boy, he looks like this one, his brother."

Mr. Townsend frowned at her face and shook his head.

She gripped Will's hand. "What shall I tell Hester?"

"Tell her to carry on at that end and send someone to us if she needs help. You and Dessie can work here, pump and carry water. See if you can bring others to help. Boys like him, too."

The mill and town were less at risk than everything and everyone on the other side of the river. Italian Town, the camps, her cabin—all could be lost if the fire got into the trees. It might rage as far as the other side of the mountain, threaten Russell's place. Wanda.

She and Will ran back to the street. Smoke stung her eyes. "Charlie wouldn't be caught in a brush fire. If he was over there last night, he's somewhere else now. Maybe at your old house?"

Will coughed. "Wood hicks are there. I checked the wash house. We hid there sometimes."

"We have to stop the fire, then we'll search. Charlie's smart. He's safe somewhere." Surely. They separated, and she ran toward the boardinghouse, giving a second look to every dark-haired boy. Women and their older children lined the riverbank from the mill pond to the tannery.

She found Hester and Winfred, Suzie's cook, at work in the kitchen. Hester promised to send word if fire jumped the river at their end of town. May Rose hurried back to the mill with the managers of the hotel, bar, and pool room. Mr. Townsend directed the younger men to rooftops, and Will and his friends to the lumber stacks. Two old men pumped buckets of water, and others spaced them around the mill.

"Roam around with your buckets," Mr. Townsend called. "Watch the roofs."

"Thank God they used up most o' the sawdust," Dessie said.

Women's cries went up near the footbridge.

From his roof, Tom shouted to all below. "Shed's on fire by the footbridge." Minutes later he called, "Bushes afire this side near the boardinghouse. Stay put, the women's getting it." He cheered. "Looks to be out. No, there's more." Everyone in the mill froze and listened until Tom cried again. "They got it!"

Fire reached a hedge of brush directly across from the mill and burned bright and crisp. With a shift of wind, its flames shot out like they were striving to reach across the river. From the roof of the drying shed, Mr. Ramey shouted, "The docks! Sparks on the docks!" May Rose and Dessie rushed buckets of water to the stacks of planks where boys stomped their feet on smoking embers. Will lay on his stomach and reached down for Dessie's bucket.

The fire now paralleled the length of town. Upriver, the break dug between the fire and Italian Town appeared to have worked, and men from that line moved uphill to join the work near the trees.

They hadn't enough buckets in the mill and they couldn't be everywhere at once. May Rose choked in rolling smoke and strained to see. Dessie stepped out of her underskirt and tore off pieces which they dipped in water and tied over their hair and faces. They backed under the eaves of the main building and waited for new calls from the men on the roofs.

"Fire below," Tom shouted. Undetected in the smoke, wood scraps smoldering on the river side of his building had lit the thick siding. Tom upended the rooftop barrel and the water flowed over the roof and splashed on the ground. They tossed buckets of water but the fire had a stubborn hold. Will came running with an ax and began to chop near the burning edges, but he was not strong enough to chop through the thick boards, and the height of the fire was beyond his reach.

Tom took Will's ax. May Rose, Dessie, and Mr. Townsend hurried to and from the pump with water buckets while Tom and Mr. Ramey cut around burning timbers. May Rose and Dessie tossed water on the last chunk that fell to the ground, raising an odor of wet, caustic ash. Her throat and lungs burned and the inside of her nose felt raw.

Cheers went up along the river. Mr. Townsend shook hands with the men, patted their backs, and hugged Dessie. He put his hands on May Rose's shoulders and whispered something she did not hear because of new cheering. He might have kissed her hair. She flinched. His hands on her shoulders reminded her too much of being pushed to her knees.

By mid-afternoon, the big cloud of smoke drifted away and the men on rooftops declared the fire put out. Across the river, stumps smoldered on black earth surrounded on three sides by furrows of brown. The fire had burned to the river and consumed two sheds by the footbridge. Women had saved the footbridge and the wood hicks' riverside campground.

May Rose walked to the street with Will.

"I hope he's run away," Will said.

"Mr. Cooper is at the school with the little ones. Go and ask if they've seen Charlie today. But Will, if your brother wants to hide or run away, I think he'll be good at it. He won't let anyone hurt him." She prayed she was right.

She rested on the kitchen steps, where the smoke odor was not as bad and she did not have to look at the charred hillside. A woman she'd not seen before offered a tin cup of water.

"Thanks for helping Evalena," the woman said. "Tell her Mary asked after her." The woman watched her drink the water. "Did you get hurt today?"

May Rose touched her nose. "Does it look bad?"

"I thought you had soot on your face, but I guess it's bruised?"

"I fell. Yesterday."

"It'll turn green tomorrow," Mary said. "Rub liniment where it hurts and lay on lint dipped in cold water. Do you have liniment? I've got some in my room. I can get it right now."

"That would be nice. Thank you."

HESTER NOW THOUGHT the picnic necessary and insisted everyone in the house attend. May Rose went only to look for Charlie.

The picnic began as a tired affair in the foreground of the black, stinking hillside for people with sooty clothes and faces, burned hands and shoes. Yet everyone was hungry, and the odor of roasted pork drew them in. Camp cooks dished up meat, including four fresh hams baked by Hester and Winifred. The Italians brought sausage links and noodles, and from somewhere there appeared pots of beans and wash pans of corn dodgers. The bar donated two kegs of beer, not near enough, Tom said. Wood hicks, Italians, tannery and mill hands drank and laughed, shook their heads and wiped their eyes. Everyone but the littlest looked worn and damaged.

Children ran through the wood hicks' campground like yearlings in a new pasture. May Rose sat with Tom and Dessie on a board seat near the food, where she could see everyone carry their tin plates along the tables. If Charlie came to the picnic, she'd see him here.

Morris Herff shuffled in line toward the food, his new wife

behind him, carrying Glory. The Donnelly boys followed their mother.

When the Donnellys reached the serving table, May Rose got up and stood beside the men slicing meat. She leaned over the table. "Mr. Herff. Have you seen your sons today?"

His wife glared. "His sons are his business. You stay out of it."

May Rose studied the Donnelly boys' blue eyes and pudgy hands, and they stopped grabbing food and stared at her face.

She turned back to Morris Herff. "Do you know where Charlie sleeps at night?"

He looked surprised. The line pushed him along.

She had nothing but suspicion and a battered face. She returned to her seat and watched the crowd. Mr. Townsend approached with one of the mill guards and spoke quietly to Tom. "Some of the wood hicks say they've seen those boys fooling around across the river." He nodded toward the Donnelly boys, now sitting with their backs against a tree.

May Rose lowered her eyes and listened.

"The teacher named them, too. He thinks they might of let a fire get out," the guard said. "Maybe on purpose. We're looking for anyone who might of saw them with a fire."

She slid her trembling hands under her legs. Like Will, she didn't believe the Donnellys had stolen Morris Herff's carvings.

Tom got up and walked away with Mr. Townsend and the guard. They stopped here and there and spoke with wood hicks at their shanties.

When the kegs emptied, jugs appeared. Loud talk and laughter lifted over fiddle and banjo music. May Rose kept her place and watched. No Charlie, no Will.

"Hey," someone shouted. "Lookie there."

Logging horses, wagons and teamsters stopped in the street. Wood hicks cheered and pulled the men into their circles. "It's over," someone said. "Trains will come tomorrow."

Boys chased through the crowd, too many with the look and size of Charlie.

CHAPTER 28

The day goes by like a shadow o're the heart,
With sorrow where all was delight

— STEPHEN COLLINS FOSTER: MY OLD
KENTUCKY HOME

Around the picnic ground, women started their children toward home. The crowd dwindled to circles of wood hicks and teamsters, low talk, and deep, tired laughter. In the waning daylight, a blanket of haze spread over the valley.

May Rose approached a teamster pushing ham and beans from a tin plate into his mouth. "Did you see a boy on the road, black hair, about so high? He's a runaway."

The teamster chewed and shook his head.

Dessie pulled her away from a group of wood hicks. "What are you doing, going about and talking with men like that?"

"Charlie Herff is missing."

"Missing? His folks just left. They didn't look like they was missing him."

May Rose let Dessie lead her back to their bench. "Mr. Herff is barely aware of his children, and his new wife doesn't care."

Dessie leaned close. "Do you know your nose is swole up and turned color? I thought this morning you looked puffy in the face."

Her nose had a bump, and she'd been breathing through her mouth. "I was punched. I meant to tell."

"God almighty, punched? A-purpose or accidental? Was it one a'them wood hicks?"

"That's how they seemed, but I think one was a boy, maybe both. The punch was deliberate. I never saw their faces."

Dessie shook her head. "We'll get 'em, men or boys." She looked back to where Tom and other cooks lifted boards from saw horses to take down the tables. "For a start, we'll tell Tom."

"There's worse," May Rose said. "They tied me in the laurel. Charlie Herff frightened them away."

"Tied up!" Dessie seized her hand. "Precious Lord. Good for Charlie."

May Rose pulled a handkerchief from her pocket and held it to her eyes. "He didn't come home last night, and his brother can't find him. Nobody saw him during the fire, and I've not seen him here. I'm terrified he's come to harm."

"Let me get Tom." Dessie hitched her skirt above her shoe tops and hustled away.

May Rose couldn't wait. She crossed the footbridge to the smoldering sheds. Surely, if Charlie had hidden in one of them, he'd have run out when it caught fire. Unless he'd been tied. Or worse.

White ash clung to her shoes and dusted onto her dress. One shed had collapsed. Its charred timbers were too warm to touch, but she might come back with a crowbar. The other shed was half-burnt, its door hanging open, no evidence of anyone inside.

"Miss May Rose." Tom spoke behind her. "It's too soon to be over here. There's hot spots and all."

Maybe Charlie had found her cabin. She imagined him there, warming himself at her stove. If Wanda were here, she'd know where to look.

Turning back, she felt the start of cramps. Tom and Dessie walked with her to the boardinghouse.

"Everyone's too wore out to look for the boy now," Tom said, "and it's getting on toward dark. Be all right with you if we start in the morning?"

She had barely strength to nod.

～

THROUGH THE NIGHT, arriving trains shook the ground and rattled the windows. In the morning May Rose stayed in bed, sick all night with cramps, and bleeding so heavily she got up only for clean rags.

Dessie brought a rubber sheet. She perched on the bed and poured something into a spoon. "I got this from Winifred. It's tincture of cramp bark. There ain't much about female trouble she and Suzie don't know. Winifred says take it twice a day."

The remedy was bitter.

Dessie went to the window. "That Herff boy is waiting to see you. He still don't know about his brother. I told him you wasn't feeling so good today. "

She lifted herself on her elbows. "Can you bring him here for a few minutes?"

"Sure. You want me to brush your hair? You'll give the boy a fright, your hair standing up and your face so nice and green."

Dessie brushed and braided her hair. "Tom says Frank's busy trying to learn who set the fire, but as soon as you're ready, you need to tell him about being tied up. Tom has some names of men in his camp that might do a thing like that, but he don't know ones in the other camps." She lowered the window blind, darkening the room. "If you're ready, I'll fetch the boy."

When Dessie brought Will, he took a few steps into the room and hunched against the wall. "Ain't found him, looked everywhere, every shed, twice. I'm sorry you're sick."

"Let me find Tom." Dessie closed the door behind her.

"I'm not too sick, just weak and tired," May Rose said. "Is anyone else searching?"

"Pa can't, he's back to work today, getting stuff ready for the startup. Last night at home he said, 'Where's Charlie?' and I said, 'He ain't been around, couple o' days,' and he asked the old woman, that's what he calls our new ma, if that was right. She said she couldn't keep track of our comings and goings and he might look up from his carving from time to time. Pa said to her boys, 'What did you do with Charlie?' and they gave him some sass or other. They're near as big as Pa and they wouldn't stay still and bend over so he could whip their butts. He started swinging his belt and they took off. Pa said for me to find Charlie and get him home."

She lay back and stared at the ceiling. "Will, the night before the fire, Charlie found me in the woods, tied up. He scared away the ones that tied me. He had a knife." Her voice cracked.

Will widened his eyes. "You was tied? Where did Charlie get a knife?" He hugged his knees. "Them Donnellys cussed me over some knife, but I never seen it. Was it them tied you up?"

"I think so. Their faces were covered."

"Maybe they tied Charlie somewheres."

"We have to get people to look."

"Pa don't like folks knowing our business. The old woman says if Charlie's run off, good for him."

"Will, go to where your pa's working. Tell him every place you've looked. Tell him what Charlie did for me. Tell him I'm afraid he's tied somewhere now. Tell him about the Donnellys."

Will pushed his back up the wall. "I'm sorry you're sick."

"It's nothing bad. I'll be up and around soon."

After Will left, Dessie brought Tom.

"I was getting acorns," May Rose said. "They had sacks on their heads. I saw enough to make me think they were boys, but big."

Tom and Dessie looked at each other. Tom said, "How big?"

"Not so much tall as stout." Thick arms squeezing her middle. Hands pushing down on her shoulders.

"I'd say Frank might have an idea who they are," Dessie said. "Mr. Cooper, too. They know all the kids."

"Could be wood hicks," Tom said. "There's boys in some of the camps."

May Rose twisted the edge of her blanket. "I don't care what they did to me. I believe I know who they are, but I can't prove it. We need to find Charlie. He's been sleeping out across the river, I think. That's why I wanted to look in the shed."

Tom shoved his hands in his pockets. "I'll look over there, but I hope that's not where we find him."

"I'm afraid the boys who tied me know Charlie set me free. What if they tied him in the laurel?"

"Lordy," Dessie said. "Them tangles is all over. Where would you start? Back where you was tied?"

"If they caught Charlie that night, they wouldn't take him far. I don't think they'd tie him where they had me. But maybe they've got other places."

Tom frowned. "They wouldn't have to go far to hide him. But a lot of the laurel is where it's steep and hard to climb. Nobody would go in those places, night or day."

"So we won't look there," Dessie said.

Tom scratched his head. "Mr. Townsend wants me up at camp tomorrow early. Cooks and cookies first."

"I need to get dressed," May Rose said.

"I FEEL OUTNUMBERED," Mr. Townsend said. May Rose, Hester, Dessie, and Tom stood with him around the kitchen worktable. "You want me to delay getting everybody back to work, after all this time being shut down, so we can find Morris Herff's son. Is that the boy who helped us in the fire?"

"That was his brother," May Rose said. "Charlie was missing even then."

"All right. Morris can have the day to look for him."

"Two days, if he needs it," Hester said. "With pay."

"Sister." His voice pitched down.

"They've had no money in weeks," she said.

He sighed. "Two days. And I'll pay him myself. The company can't make these exceptions."

"I'd like to look for the boy," Tom said.

"Then do what you can today. Morris has older boys now, stepsons. They can help."

"No," May Rose blurted. "Not them."

All eyes turned to her. She wrapped her fingers around a chair back. "I think they did it, the Donnelly boys, hurt Charlie someway, or hid him."

Mr. Townsend looked at his pocket watch. "Do you have reason to think this?"

"I've seen them torment children. I saw what they did to Wanda, weeks ago, in the woods. So bad, Wanda didn't want me to tell. I'm sorry now that I didn't. If I had, none of this might have happened."

She heard a sympathetic click, Hester or Dessie. Mr. Townsend slid his watch into a vest pocket. "Young people play rough, and Wanda…"

May Rose slapped her hand on the table. "Don't you dare blame Wanda. I know other things, what they did to me and what they tried to do." She sat down and squeezed her fingers.

Dessie's mouth gaped. "You never said that was Donnellys. You said you didn't see their faces."

"In the woods, in the laurel, I saw the shape of them, their hands and eyes. Charlie found me. Will said Charlie had been sneaking around after the Donnellys. Charlie came right through that maze like he knew where I was. He had the knife the Donnelly boys took from Wanda."

"Wait right here." Tom let the door slam.

Hester put her arm around May Rose's waist. Mr. Townsend stared at the floor.

Tom came through the door, holding a broad discolored blade. "I found this in one of the burned sheds." The handle was charred and crumbling. He turned the blade over and held it close for her to see. It had a nick at the widest part.

May Rose covered her face with a dish towel. "That's the one."

"I didn't find anything else," Tom said.

She hung her head. "The Donnelly boys told Will they'd get even with Charlie in a way nobody would ever know."

Mr. Townsend cleared his throat. "Morris can take a few days to search. Tom, get over to Frank's and tell him to bring in Donnelly's boys. May Rose, I'm truly sorry about all of this." He patted the top of her chair. "Let's be glad you weren't hurt worse. We'll find Charlie. Now, excuse me, I'm needed at the mill."

FRANK OPENED HIS DOOR. "Well, well. Speaking of..." He backed against the wall to make room for her in the tiny space. "We was just talking of you."

The Donnelly boys sat on the broad oak desk. Frank took up most of the floor space. The boys looked away.

"I'll come back later," May Rose said.

"No, no," Frank said. "Step inside. This here's John and Harry Donnelly. I asked them in for a little talk, but it turns out they wanted to tell me something. Boys, this is Mrs. Long. Now tell her what you told me."

They hunched on the desk, eyes downcast.

"They know who I am," May Rose said. "I saw them in the woods with Wanda, weeks ago, remember? Then I saw them at the school bridge and again the other evening when I was picking up acorns. You remember that, don't you?"

The younger chewed the edge of his finger.

"Boys?" Frank asked. "Spit it out."

The older swung his legs against the desk. "Don't believe nothing she says. Our pa's dead 'cause of her."

"I don't need to hear that," Frank said, "and you should forget it. Tell her about the fire."

The younger one mumbled.

"Let's have it, boys," Frank said. "Say it to her face, or I will."

He shrugged. "She done it."

"*I* set the fire?"

"Wanda."

She laughed, a short, rude burst.

"We saw her do it."

She smiled at Frank. "Wanda left town last Tuesday with her mother and Russell Long. Lots of people saw them go."

The boys squirmed. "Maybe she snuck back."

"You sit quiet," Frank said. "I saw her go, and I know she ain't been back. I watch, you know."

May Rose motioned Frank to follow her outside.

"Them boys don't fool me for a minute," he said. "Soon as I mentioned the fire they started squirming and accusing."

"I've come about Charlie Herff. Please make them say what they've done with him."

"I'm about to get to it. Mr. Townsend said I could put off everything else for a day or two and look for that boy. But if we don't find him near town, I figger he's long gone."

CHAPTER 29

How blessed are some people, whose lives have no fears...
to whom sleep is a blessing that comes nightly,
and brings nothing but sweet dreams.

— BRAM STOKER: DRACULA

On the hillside above the boardinghouse, wood hicks packed gear and tore down shanties. Yesterday many had joined a fruitless search for Charlie. Tom had gone as far as her cabin. Frank had kept the Donnelly boys half the day, but could not get them to admit to anything.

May Rose slipped down the front stairs to the flush toilet. She came out of the little room as the kitchen door swung open and Mr. Townsend strode by. He turned back. "I've sent an alert to the camp bosses, and we'll ask all mill hands to keep an eye peeled for your boy."

Grateful, she pressed his hand between hers. He put his other hand on top and smiled. She never knew what to say to him beyond the simplest words. "Thank you."

Hester entered from the parlor. "I thought you were in a rush."

"We're having a word about the missing boy." His voice

carried a tone of correction. May Rose pulled her hands away, mumbled good morning to Hester, and hurried into the kitchen.

Tom stood by the door, his pack at his feet. Dessie leaned over the sink. "I have work, too," she said. "Some of us never got to shut down." Tom strode to the sink and leaned over her back. She shrugged him off. "Just get on. Go do your job."

"See you the weekend, then."

Dessie didn't look around.

"May Rose," he said, "We asked everyone in town."

"I know you did. Dessie, if you don't hug your husband, I will."

"I've done that already," Dessie said. "Can't I have a cry in peace?"

May Rose pecked Tom's cheek. His face turned red.

After Tom left, Hester paced in the kitchen and watched through the window. "When the wood hicks set up all around us, I felt like they were choking off my air. Now I kind of hate to see them go. They made things interesting, didn't they?"

Dessie wiped her eyes. "I suppose next time they blow in for a weekend you'll be inviting them for dinner."

Hester smirked. "Possibly."

The process of getting back to normal had been discussed and analyzed in the dining room and kitchen for some time. Coal, cattle, and hay arriving first—coal for the trains, cattle to be slaughtered for the camps, hay for the horses. Horse teams and handlers, cooks, bosses and mechanics going up to the mountain camps ahead of the others. All sidings in use, Mr. Townsend's dispatchers managing the flow of trains to the camps, the telegraph agent scheduling the main line trains. Mr. Ramey and others working all night to sort supplies for the store and camps.

All that clamor reached the boardinghouse. May Rose watered the pigs, now getting to be hog-size. She tried to scratch Nellie's ears but drew back when the hogs bumped and snapped at each other in the small lot. Maybe just warning snaps, but they could catch a finger. She shivered in the cold air. When she'd seen him last, Charlie had not been wearing a coat.

She'd retreated to her room when Dessie tapped and opened the door, her dark eyes wide. "Will's in the kitchen. Got somebody with him." May Rose hurried down the stairs, joy building with every step.

He didn't have Charlie, but his sister Glory, wrapped in a ragged quilt, a bundle half his size. He pushed her to May Rose. "There's a fight at our house."

He ran out. She and Hester and Dessie looked at each other, then at Glory.

"You and your strays," Hester said.

"I have to get Will out of that house." May Rose dropped Glory into Dessie's arms, hurried upstairs and ran back down with her coat.

Dessie shook her head. "May Rose, you don't know what you're gonna light into. Get Frank."

May Rose buttoned her coat. "Soon as I find Will."

Hester took Glory. "For heaven's sake, send Tom or one of the guards. Oh, that's right, they're gone. Never mind, Baby and I will get Frank."

May Rose and Hester parted at the boardwalk. Hester scurried on with Glory toward Frank's office, and May Rose turned toward the highest street. Walking at a trot, looking for Will and listening for sounds of a fight, she nearly collided with a big boy running toward her. A Donnelly, his brother close behind.

A blast of shot spattered grit. The boys dodged and ran, but stopped farther down the street, jumped in the air and waved their arms, taunting. "Hunky! Crazy old cocksucker!"

In the yard above, Morris Herff held the butt of a shotgun against his shoulder while his wife yelled and tugged at the gun. May Rose crouched against the bank. He fired again, and the boys, out of range, shouted back. Along the street, doors opened briefly and slammed shut.

Frank came running. "Morris, what the hell?"

May Rose stood and glanced back. The street was empty, the boys gone.

Herff lowered the shotgun. He had a bloody face.

Her heart thumped in fear that Will lay in the house, beaten bloody, like his father.

"Morris," Frank called. "You want the doctor?"

Herff dropped the shotgun and fell over.

Frank waved to May Rose. "Go and fetch Dr. Hennig. He's at church."

She rushed past him and up the steps to the yard. "Let his wife do it. I have to find Will."

Mrs. Herff picked up the gun and prodded her husband's body. "This is my house and my gun. He beat my boys and shot at them. Take him to jail afore I kill him."

Will stepped out from the side of the house, crying, but not bloody. "She gave them a board, and they whacked Pa with it."

Mrs. Herff whirled the gun toward Will and May Rose, but Frank ran forward and grabbed the barrel. She held on for a moment, then let it go, ducked into the house and slammed the door.

"Now fetch the doctor," Frank said.

May Rose hurried along the street with Will. "Did they say anything about Charlie?"

"They kept saying they didn't know nothing about him. They and Pa was knocking each other all over the house. I run Glory outside and kept going, that's when I brung her to you. When I come back, John swung a board and hit Pa in the face. Pa went down and Harry took the board and hit him again."

"You can't stay in that house."

"I gotta help Pa."

"Go back to your place. If it's locked, ask Frank to find a key."

At the church, May Rose waited on the boardwalk while Will went inside. Dr. Hennig's face tightened when he saw her, then he hurried away with Will. She turned toward home, desperate for the comfort of a child in her arms.

By the time she reached the boardinghouse, she was shaking. Hester rocked in the parlor with Glory asleep on her shoulder.

May Rose held out her arms. "I'll take her now. I hope it's all right to keep her here for a while. Mr. Herff's family is in a bad way."

Hester adjusted a strand of Glory's fine hair. "She's good where she is for the moment. Would you help Dessie with dinner, please? When Baby is sound asleep, I'll lay her on my bed."

That noon, only Mr. Tackett and the Hershman brothers ate in the dining room. Mr. Cooper was in bed with a cold, and Hester took dinner for herself and Glory to her room.

May Rose paced in the kitchen. "I should check on Will, see if things have quieted down."

"If Donnellys are running loose," Dessie said, "you should stay put."

THERE WAS no Sunday afternoon rest. May Rose and Dessie idled in the kitchen while Hester took charge of Glory.

"You'll hurt your back, carrying that child all over," Dessie said.

Hester sat beside May Rose and settled Glory on her lap. "She's clingy right now. Wouldn't you be, coming out of that family? Poor monkey. May Rose, does she talk?"

"I don't know." Seeing Morris Herff's bloody face had increased her fears for Charlie, who drifted in her mind, unanchored and alone.

Dessie brought triangles of buttered bread and a cup of milk to the table, and Hester helped Glory lift the cup so she wouldn't spill. Together they watched her like they'd never seen anything so fascinating.

"Ladies?" Mr. Townsend stopped by the hall door. He frowned at the spectacle of a child on Hester's lap.

"This is Morris' youngest," Hester said.

He blinked. "I see. Frank says there's been a family distur-bance. So...?"

Hester cut him off with a sharp look.

"Well," he said. "May Rose, Frank is waiting in my parlor to speak on a matter of interest. If you would join us there?"

She caught her breath. "Charlie?"

"Nothing new at this time. Dessie, we'll have coffee. Sand-wiches, too, if you please."

He opened doors for her and closed them softly. His parlor smelled of dead cigars. Frank stood in front of a window, looking ill-at-ease.

Mr. Townsend gestured to wing-backed chairs each side of the small table. "Please sit." He carried a leather-padded chair from its place against a wall. "Dessie is bringing refreshments, so we can take our time. It's been an odd Sunday, hasn't it? No Sunday dinner. We've all worked like Monday."

"I been doing overtime," Frank said.

Mr. Townsend nodded. "So have we all."

"But I don't get overtime pay."

"Nor I." Mr. Townsend smiled. "I hope soon we'll both have a few days' rest."

She laced her fingers, impatient for the interview to begin so it could end.

"We thought you might advise us on the Herffs' domestic situation," Mr. Townsend said. "Since you care about the children."

"I care about the Herff children, not the Donnellys."

"Nobody cares about Donnellys," Frank said, "except to get rid of 'em. They've brung it on theirselves."

"The Herffs and Donnellys are separated for the moment," Mr. Townsend said. "Morris and the boy have returned to their former house. I've told Mrs. Donnelly—Mrs. Herff—she'll have to pay rent on her house. Which she can't, because without Morris, she has no means of support. Do you think it's possible they might patch things up?" He looked at May Rose.

She spoke after a long pause. "Someone will be killed."

Frank nodded. "Morris says she gave the boys a board to beat him."

Mr. Townsend frowned.

"They bunged up Morris' face, knocked out some teeth, broke his right arm and some fingers when he tried to cover his face. I told their ma she'd be smart to get them away afore I ship them to reform school."

Mr. Townsend muttered an unclear word. "Nobody told me about broken bones. I'll have to wire for the new filer. For everybody's sake, maybe Morris should move on, too."

"For everybody's sake? What about Charlie?"

"We'll wire other towns to watch for him. If he comes back, we can send him on to Morris."

"Boys run off all the time," Frank said. "Who knows, he may be better off where he is."

"Will won't go without Charlie," May Rose said.

"Then you should encourage him. I hate to lose Morris, but the mill can't wait for him to heal. No, it's best they all go. Tell them you'll keep looking for the boy, and send him on when he's found. Morris must have family somewhere to help him out until he can work again."

Dessie entered with sandwiches.

"Excuse me." May Rose ran from the room. In the kitchen, she pulled Glory from Hester's lap.

"May Rose, what's wrong?"

"Everything." She jiggled Glory and paced. Glory squirmed to be down, and she set her on her feet.

Hester pulled the child away from the hall door as Dessie came through.

Dessie looked from one to the other. "Mr. Townsend is going back to the mill. Is something wrong here?"

May Rose kept her eyes on Glory. "A few little things. Mr. Townsend is going to replace Morris Herff at the mill. He has a broken arm and fingers, and is less able than ever to take care of his children. Frank told the Donnellys to get out of town. Mr. Townsend thinks the Herffs should find a new town, too."

Glory crawled back into Hester's lap and snuggled against her chest.

"At least Frank has solved the Donnelly problem," Dessie said.

Hester kissed Glory's hair. "Passing the Donnellys along to another town isn't exactly solving a problem."

May Rose got her coat. "I can't wait any longer—I have to help Will."

At the Herff house, Dr. Hennig stopped on the steps, blocking her way. He gazed at her a moment before speaking. "Do you ever think of me?" His breath was visible in the cold air.

She crossed her arms over her coat. "You helped Wanda's mother. I think of that."

He took her hand, but when she resisted, let it drop. "Say you love me. It doesn't matter if it's not true."

"I saw you in church. At the altar."

"Her doing. She makes me feel ashamed. I never feel ashamed when I'm with you." He looked ready to clutch her.

She stepped back. "I've come to see about Mr. Herff."

"He'll live. I don't know about myself. I've lost my job, I suppose you know. My replacement will come on tomorrow's train."

She was glad for herself and for Mrs. Hennig. "I wish you well, and safe journey."

"Your Mr. Townsend says I have a reputation. I've been here since this town was built, five years. Suddenly he does not like my reputation."

"There must be better places to work. A city. Mrs. Hennig might like that."

"I know what this is about," he said. "Why I'm fired."

She thought of Mr. Townsend's hand pressing hers, how he'd replaced her with Mrs. Donnelly.

Will opened the door.

"I have to go," she said.

The house was warm, recently occupied by men from the logging camps. They'd left cots of wood and rope.

Morris Herff sat on one of these. His nose and lips were scraped and swollen, his right arm in a sling and his fingers bandaged. He breathed in grunts. Bird wings and squirrel tails stood out in clean patches on the wall, evidence of carvings no longer there.

She stood near the door. "I wanted to make sure you're all right."

He glanced and looked away. "This started with you. And Mr. Townsend."

She felt a pang of remorse. If neither she nor Mrs. Donnelly had entered this house, Charlie might be here now.

"Pa. She only helped."

"I never beat anyone," she said. "Think of that."

"The Donnellys are leaving town," Will said. "I'm gonna bring Pa's workbench from their house soon as they're gone. We'll be better now."

"Better?" A puff of air exploded between Herff's lips. "I'm no use to Townsend now. He'll chuck us out."

She wished she could deny it. "Are there family you can go to until you're well?"

"It's none of your business if there is or ain't."

"I care about your children."

"Puhh." His word sounded like spit.

"Will," she said. "We'll keep Glory tonight. And I'll do something."

HESTER HAD PREDICTED her brother would come to the kitchen at bedtime, looking for the last piece of cobbler. May Rose and Dessie waited there with her, their hands folded on the table. Glory sat on the floor biting the limbs of May Rose's smallest doll. Dessie had brought a lamp from her room.

Mr. Townsend did not appear surprised to see them together so late in the evening. He pulled out a chair and sat beside Hester. "We'll have electric in a few days, as soon as we build up the sawdust pile."

She tapped her fingers. "We'll get along."

Dessie poured canned milk in a bowl of cobbler and set it at his place. Hester pulled Glory to her lap, and May Rose got up and stood by Dessie at the sink.

Hester spoke before he got the first spoonful to his mouth. "If Morris Herff can't support his children here, he'll likely not do it anywhere else."

"Oh." He passed a look to each of them.

"Will could go to Camp Four," Dessie said. "He could help Tom, and Tom would look after him."

"Surely you can find something in the mill for Morris to do," Hester said. "The boy, too, if he won't leave his father. Might'n there be a job in the mill a boy could do?"

"Will should go to school," May Rose said. "I'll take care of their house and mind Glory."

Brother and sister stared at each other. Mr. Townsend set his spoon beside the bowl and nudged it into alignment with his forefinger. He tilted his head toward May Rose and Dessie, then back to his cobbler softening in milk.

In the hall, the clock chimed ten times. When it stopped, he said, "No."

"No?" Hester's voice peaked.

May Rose clenched her jaws.

He put his elbows on the table and his hands, prayer fashion, against his mouth. "Yes. I'll find something for Morris to do at the mill. But no, May Rose does not have to dedicate herself to the Herff family, not when the company needs help. Not when she could earn a good wage." He lifted his eyes to May Rose, who heartened at the words "good wage."

Hester narrowed her eyes.

He leaned back in his chair, and spoke again to Hester. "We've lost wood hicks. Maybe some will return, but in the meantime I'm sending yard men to the camps, and moving a few young men from the office to the yard. You can imagine how little that pleases them."

Hester stared at May Rose. "All temporary, I assume."

"Everything will be in flux. May Rose, if you're willing, you can work with Clyde, our purchasing manager. We'll put the preacher with him too. Humphrey can get one of the Italian women to take care of his mother, since Mrs. Donnelly—Mrs. Herff—is leaving town."

She ignored Hester's small frown. The position he offered sounded like one that might disappear, but even a few days of office work could help her to a similar position in another town.

"I'll help Will's family on Saturdays."

He cleared his throat. "We'll see what Morris wants. In the meantime..." He looked at Hester and Glory. "What do you propose to do with this one?"

Hester rubbed Glory's back. "I'll let you know."

CHAPTER 30

Despair has its own calms

— BRAM STOKER: DRACULA

For two days, women and boys hacked paths through laurel near town while smaller children led May Rose and Mr. Cooper to their play places and hidey-holes. Mr. Ramey, who had many customers living in the hills, said he asked everyone about a runaway boy.

Frank said she shouldn't get her hopes up. She had recurring thoughts of the Donnellys tied and whipped until they confessed, and regretted that he'd so quickly rid the town of them.

May Rose had no one to hold for comfort. She understood why Wanda had gone away with her mother, and why Will was devoting himself to his father, but Glory had chosen Hester, like she knew Hester was the important woman in the house. Like she knew Hester would stay.

"That child," Dessie said, pumping bathwater for May Rose, "likes Hester's motherly bosom, don't you see. And Hester's better able to care for her, isn't she?" Sounds of Glory splashing, squealing, Hester laughing, came from the tub room. May Rose sat in the kitchen with her feet propped on a chair.

"Everything works for the best," Dessie said. "You have a fine job now. Maybe it will work into something permanent."

May Rose flexed her aching feet. "I can't move crates and barrels all day. I survived today, but I don't know about tomorrow."

Dessie looked over her shoulder. "None of us knows about tomorrow. But crates and barrels? I thought you was going to be in the office." She winked. "With Mr. Townsend."

"That's what he said, but he left on the train this morning. Clyde—the boss—put me outside to sort supplies for the camps. All day I unloaded, pushed carts, and reloaded everything on camp cars."

"All by yourself?"

"With Preacher Gowder and three boys Mr. Cooper said were doing themselves no good in school. Clyde kept coming outside and yelling at us. We didn't know right from wrong."

Dessie hefted the pot to the stove. "Let the preacher and the boys move the crates," Dessie said. "You do the paperwork."

"Clyde does the paperwork."

Dessie laughed. "I don't think so. Clyde's near blind."

May Rose put her feet on the floor. "Blind! He doesn't act blind."

"He sees a little out the sides of his eyes, but he can't hardly see to read and write. Walter reads for him and does his numbers."

"Walter? I think I replaced Walter. Someone said Mr. Townsend sent him to the yard."

"Uh, oh," Dessie said. "Tom said Walter was eyes for Clyde."

"Tom knows Clyde and Walter?"

"Clyde got Tom hired here. He's Tom's uncle."

"And Clyde is blind?"

"Just about. Walter's his grandson. Clyde probably put you

outside to make you quit, so Mr. Townsend would take Walter off yard work and put him back in the office."

~

"Mr. Burns?" May Rose stopped at the doorway to the purchasing office.

Everyone else called the purchasing officer "Clyde." He looked like he'd shrunk in the wash, but was clean shaved and doused with barber's stinkum.

His voice snapped like a dog. "What do you need?" Behind round glasses, black eyes guarded his territory.

"I can help with your bookwork," she said.

"You're working where I want you."

She stepped away from his door and followed him into the common room where accounting and payroll clerks bent over their books.

"I suppose it don't suit you," he said.

"I can manage." It might kill her. "But..." She lowered her voice. "I can do what Walter did, here in the office. And say nothing about it."

He did not move or speak. Pens scratched on the clerks' books. "Mr. Burns?"

He peered at her from the eye on one side of his face and then the other. He motioned, and she followed him back to the corridor where the general superintendent, a finance officer, the paymaster, and Clyde worked behind doors with their names lettered on frosted windows. Mr. Townsend, whose office was at the end of the corridor, had not returned from his meeting in Lewisburg.

That night she said to Dessie, "He's still trying to make me quit."

She'd gotten her way. She was Clyde's assistant, but he didn't want her. He didn't teach, he yelled and reprimanded, punishing her for knowing his secret. He had names and addresses of every supplier in his head, plus transportation costs and expected arrival times. He knew the quantities of fresh meat and staples each camp needed for a week, the amount one logger needed to consume in a day to work efficiently, what sold well at the store and what did not, and he told her only once. She sat at his desk with piles of open ledgers, expected to leap-frog from one to another as fast as his mind worked, to write in appropriate columns, and not splatter ink.

In her room at night, she jotted notes from memory, not just to survive the job, but to conquer it.

It was Sunday morning of a cold, hard-raining weekend, and most wood hicks, including cooks and their helpers, had stayed in camp. Dessie had the day off to clean the house in Italian Town, the doctor's house. Tom had bought it. Cheap, Dessie said.

May Rose opened the door at the top of the back stairs and started down with a bundle of clothes to wash by hand. Over the squeaking of the kitchen pump, she heard her name and stopped. Hester and Mr. Townsend were talking about her.

"It may be better to let her move on, like she planned," Hester said.

"I thought you liked her."

The pump handle stopped. "I like her very much. I'm thinking of you."

May Rose held her breath, heard the creak and clank of the firebox door falling open on its hinges. The sound of a shovel digging into coal.

"She has fine qualities," Mr. Townsend said. "Ladylike, but accustomed to hard work."

A chair scraped against the floor. Hester's heels clicked. "Barlow, you're not thinking. She's half your age."

"She's not foolish or flighty or vain, like many young women."

"She's not for you. Her husband may be alive."

"Suzie says Russell Long found the body."

"Hmmph," Hester said. "Suzie."

"She knows everything."

"And naturally you inquired. Barlow, find work for May Rose in another town, before it's too late."

Silence. Fingers tapped the table.

"Even if her husband is proved dead, you can't marry her. The talk will ruin you with the company. Innocent or not, the story of her undressing for the trainmen will never go away, people like it too much. It will always bring up gossip about her and Dr. Hennig. Your employees will question your judgment."

"They're ignorant. Why should I care?"

"You have to care."

"I want to help her to a better life."

"I see what you want," Hester said.

May Rose backed up the steps, the bundle clutched to her chest.

Barlow Townsend hadn't said marry, hadn't used that word while she stood hidden on the stairs. She'd heard Hester say it, and say he shouldn't. May Rose moved Hester to a cold corner of her heart.

In the following days, she avoided Hester and stopped trying to understand Mr. Townsend, who now spoke no more than greetings. Admirable qualities, he'd said. She could not say what those were. But used to hard work? That she was.

In Clyde's office, she endured insults, repeated instructions and trade secrets and browsed through files of invoices to help herself memorize. She paid for a long telegram to Albert Jonson, General Delivery in Fargo, read classified ads in the Pittsburg Press, paid off Jamie's store bill, and accumulated dollars in a new leather handbag.

She had no word from Wanda, no news of Charlie, just nights of tears and restless sleep. As long as she kept her job, she could stay in the boardinghouse until Wanda was free. Guilt about the meaning of Wanda's freedom led her to pray every night for Evalena to be restored to health. She prayed also for Charlie to be kindly treated, wherever he was.

If not too exhausted at the end of the day by Clyde's best efforts to prove her worthless, she allowed herself to wonder what marriage to Mr. Townsend might be like. He wasn't repulsive, and he allowed at least one woman to be heard. At Hester's suggestion, he'd reassigned Morris Herff as a lumber grader.

She missed Wanda, grieved for Charlie, and felt Will's pain. He said his father didn't miss filing saws, but was sad all the time and no longer carved.

"Carving lets him forget," Will said. "Pa don't want to forget Charlie."

Dessie said she suspected Hester and Morris Herff had come to an agreement about Glory, now sealed in Hester's heart and home, her little feet playing up the front stair, clattering along the hall and down the back. Only once did she hear Mr. Townsend say, "Hester, I hope you know what you're doing."

May Rose left letters for Wanda at the post office, in case Russell came to town without seeing her. "He'll be in," Mr. Ramey said. "He's got Sears-Roebuck packages waiting."

At Christmas, she learned that Russell had come to town, gotten his mail but left nothing for her, no word if Evalena lived, nothing from Wanda.

"They don't care that I worry," she said to Nellie. The pigs had been sold off, and Nellie was growing fat with piglets inside. Surely someone could at least write two words—"*everything's fine.*" Unless it wasn't.

After a dry start to winter, snow came, drifts as high as her shoulders, no trains going up the mountain, no logs coming down. Men and boys turned out to cut icy corridors to the mill. May Rose went to work, afraid of being displaced, but old Clyde stayed at home. An engine plowed up the track and met a stranded train of logs. The saws shrilled again.

The last day of December or the first day of January, she turned twenty-one. There'd been a dispute about her time of birth, Aunt Sweet and the midwife busy and unable to agree if the hands of the clock passed midnight before or after she arrived. More than her age, everything that had happened since September made her work quietly and put away girlish thoughts. She had nothing to do but make herself useful and wait.

Mr. Cooper now sometimes met her as she came from the mill at the end of the day. The first time was an accident, a collision of coats in snow that swirled from the ground and hid the other's approach. Discovering their identities, they laced arms and bent into the storm. At the boardinghouse porch, they stomped snow from their shoes, used the broom to brush each other off, and swept, laughing, through the front door to warm air and scents of roasting ham.

"Why, Mr. Cooper," Hester said, greeting them from the parlor. "Your cheeks are quite red."

Wind-burned and smiling, Mr. Cooper's face looked almost healthy.

Only four sat together in the dining room that evening, the Hershman brothers, Mr. Cooper, and herself, Mr. Townsend away again on business, and Hester busy as usual with Glory. Mr. Cooper began relating children's malapropisms and embarrassing things the little ones revealed about their parents. May Rose covered her mouth with a napkin and controlled the level of her laughter, but when he shouted everything again for the Hershmans, she burst out like her corset strings had snapped. Mr. Cooper, emboldened by her hilarity, fell into a pattern of offering her a first quiet telling, then a loud repeat for the old gentlemen.

His eyes betrayed him, open to hope. She did not want to hurt him.

In following weeks new boarders came and went, crowding the house and making it easier to separate herself so Mr. Cooper might not think she was avoiding him. She left work at varied times, an easy maneuver because Clyde didn't work by the clock, but on the way home she often found Mr. Cooper waiting at the mill entrance. Suddenly the quiet, reclusive teacher was full of humorous stories and, most compelling, rumors of Charlie.

She loved his wit, but his hands trembled, his breath was sour, his confidences sometimes bitter. His talk switched from amusing capers of children to the sins of bankers and wealthy industrialists. "People who have money can do things," he said. "Convince bankers to give them more. You see, they never lend to people who desperately need it. Rich people borrow money easily and pay pitiful wages so they can get richer. They think they deserve wealth because they've been clever."

She remembered her first pitiful wages. Even now, she didn't earn as much as the preacher or the other clerks. She half-agreed with Mr. Cooper. "I don't suppose anyone gets rich without a lot of help along the way."

"Ha," he said. "Show me a rich man and I'll show you a thief. Start with our lumber barons—they stole these forests."

"I would like to think it's possible to do well without hurting someone."

"Maybe in the best of worlds. Not here."

His opinions reminded her too much of Jamie.

He wanted to leave Winkler. "I used to think learning could make people better and more sensitive to each other," he said. "But people hold on to ignorance like a family heirloom. Family makes the child, and work makes the man. When a man earns little and feels trapped in his work, he's likely to drink and hurt his family." She was glad that Glory would not be brought up by her father.

Charlie had been missing for three months, and was now a legend among school children. "They say Charlie set the fire to get rid of the Donnellys," Mr. Cooper said. "They've made a pact never to tell, though they think he's dead. Lost in the woods, killed by a bear, beaten by the Donnellys, fallen from a trestle, frozen, drowned."

May Rose stopped expecting Charlie to step from behind a tree.

Every Saturday afternoon she went to the Herff house to cook and help Will wash their clothes. She bought shoes and a coat for Will and said, "It doesn't matter," when he said his father wouldn't like it. Morris Herff never spoke to her and always left the house while she was there.

"He's ashamed," Will said.

Influenza came to town with a March thaw and closed the school. May Rose, Hester, Dessie, and the new cleaning girl took turns being sick and caring for each other. Returning to work after two days of sickness, May Rose was startled to find Walter, Clyde's grandson, in the purchasing office.

"Pap's sick," Walter said.

Walter was a handsome, high-spirited young man, and having him in the office cheered everyone. He complimented her journal and ledger entries and admired all she'd memorized. Because both had done everything at Clyde's direction, neither felt competent to work alone nor to take the lead. After about ten days, the flu died out, but Clyde had pneumonia.

Clyde had made them a perfect team, but sometimes they acted like kids with the teacher out of the room. The first time Walter said, with Clyde's voice and accent, "That's an *absorbatant* price," she laid her head on the table, covered it with her arms, and laughed until her stomach hurt. "We'll echersize our right to pay in ninety days," he said. Thankfully, he did not imitate Clyde's silent, poisonous farting.

Mr. Townsend had seldom looked into the purchasing office, but now he passed the open door like a monitor.

"Too much fun in here," Walter whispered. He had a young wife and child, otherwise she might have let herself think about him.

CHAPTER 31

I suppose that we women are such cowards
That we think a man will save us from fears, and we marry him.

— BRAM STOKER: DRACULA

Together, she and Walter approved orders and payments for routine purchases, but they referred anything unusual to Mr. Townsend. Like most of the clerks, Walter turned quiet and deferential in the presence of their boss and insisted May Rose approach him when they had questions. "He likes you more'n me. You ask him."

Her awe of Mr. Townsend had long since worn off, but like Walter, she did not want him to think her incompetent. In Clyde's absence they'd had a surge of requisitions for large pieces of equipment. Walter said the camp and mill bosses were trying to sneak one by.

"I'm sorry to bother you," she said, each time she rapped on the frosted glass of Mr. Townsend's office door and approached his desk.

One late afternoon while stamping requests "denied," he looked up in his thoughtful way. "I'm told the snow on the street is glazed over with ice. If you like, we might walk home together."

These were days of thaw and freeze. On the street, they dug the edges of their heels into the frozen crust until they reached a path someone had dusted with cinders. Then their steps relaxed. He complimented her work. "Of course, Clyde has the benefit of years. Someday Walter will be ready to take over." He stopped and lit a cigar.

Though she did not intend to stay in Winkler, she felt a pang of envy, wishing he'd admit she was the better candidate for the job. Walter had longer experience, but she was smarter.

"But now," Mr. Townsend said, "I don't think Clyde will return to work. The company is sending a new man, experienced in purchasing, though not in lumber operations. I want Walter to work with him, for a couple of reasons. For one, Walter and his wife are living with Clyde and taking care of him." He didn't name the other reason.

"I understand." With Mr. Townsend so frugal, he would have no extra person in the purchasing office. A man, supporter of a family, always came first. A woman was supposed to find a man or a relative to take her in.

"Is there somewhere else I can work?"

He took her arm to help her across the street. "There may be another place, if you're interested."

Another place. *Admirable qualities*, he had said, but never to her face. *Used to hard work*. He had no idea how much she had learned in a few months about the needs of the Winkler Company. But perhaps he did.

She expressed her anger only in chilly breaths of air and careful steps on the snow. "I'd like very much to hear about it."

"You may need some time to decide, and I need to check a few things. Shall we speak of this another time? The new man will not be coming for a week or so."

"Of course." Paying room and board and saving for the future left her little choice. She had to work.

A few days later he again suggested they walk home together. At the mill entrance Mr. Cooper appeared briefly at the edge of her vision, but she forgot him, listening for the moment when Mr. Townsend might speak of her new position. The streets were slushy now, and he seemed in no hurry.

Halfway along, he said, "So. Hester has her child."

"I'm glad." Glory, the flash of color in their dull, discreet landscape.

"I've never thought of having a child, but Hester has the right idea, someone to carry on after you, someone to plan for. And someone for your old age. You like children, I see. Wanda, and the Herff youngsters."

"I do." She listened for him to describe another child care position, a difficult undertaking that might require time to consider, perhaps a child who wasn't quite normal.

He led her around mounds of dirty snow. "I've run this over in my mind so often. Sometimes it seems right, and other times I'm not certain. But here it is. I'm thinking of buying another boardinghouse, and I'd like you to manage it."

His quiet, flat tone understated the importance of his offer. She nearly whooped. Manage a boardinghouse. She'd like it and she could do it—she'd lived with Hester and been trained by Clyde. She covered her excitement with caution. "It sounds interesting." He'd said "buying," not "building." There was no other boardinghouse in Winkler.

"There's a property in Charleston, our state capitol."

Wanda, she thought. Will. Uncle Bert and the girls. "Is Charleston far from here?"

"Less than a day by train. I go there from time to time."

She imagined a parlor like Hester's, separate quarters for herself and Wanda in a real city with brick streets and sidewalks, singing lessons for Wanda. She'd leave a forwarding address, send or come back for Wanda, encourage Will and his father to come too. Maybe Dessie and Tom would visit. Hester might have devised this position to get her away from Mr. Townsend, but she didn't care.

"I want Wanda to live with me."

"That will be no problem. She'll be company for you. I might be able to visit no more than monthly." He took her gloved hand and held it between both of his. A chill wind blew across the snow. "There's something else. I hope we might have a child together."

She let her face go blank to hide her shock. The poor man had no idea how his words insulted and diminished her. She did not need to ask if his offer included marriage. But she'd have a board-inghouse. Wanda. Possibly a child.

"What name would the child have?"

"Townsend, naturally. I'd adopt him."

She pulled her hand away and gathered her coat collar to her neck. "I see."

His face reddened. "I'm leaving in the morning for Lewisburg, then Washington for a week. I hope you'll be ready to discuss my offer when I return, but if you decide against it, I'll understand."

As easy as that. He'd understand, like her answer would make no great difference in his life, like it was not a grave, heart-shaking matter, an upheaval. If she said yes, they would share responsibilities, not only in business. He expected to father her child.

She matched his cautious look. "Next week, then."

Disrespectful as it was, his offer seemed the path of greatest promise, far more than she'd had from Jamie, though she doubted her bloody womb could carry anyone's child.

Quiet now, they entered the boardinghouse together. She walked up the front stairs to her room, changed her mind, and continued down the back to the kitchen. "I'll not be here for dinner," she told Dessie.

The hallway of Suzie's place smelled of stale beer and laven-der. It was working hours, but Suzie welcomed May Rose to her parlor like she was overdue for a visit. With no ornaments, chair pads, or rugs to soften it, the room seemed temporary, as gray and plain as Suzie in her stiff, old-fashioned dress. But the air was warmed by a squat iron stove, and a ceiling light fell on bowls and platters of food—sweet potatoes, fried chicken, stewed tomatoes, deviled eggs, slaw, yellow cake.

Suzie talked around the food in her mouth. "This is nice, having company. Help yourself, there's extra plates. Grab that fork and spoon over there."

She saw no reason not to.

Suzie wiped grease from her thin lips. "We hear Evalena's still living."

"I'm glad." May Rose filled a plate and held it on her lap. The stewed tomatoes were slightly sweet. "Did you talk with Russell?"

"Not all winter. We heard from someone who saw him. Guess you know Jamie's dead."

May Rose bent her head to hide her face. "There's been no proof."

"Russell piled rocks over the body, what parts he found. Animals, you know." Suzie sighed.

May Rose laid her spoon on the plate. Russell. Wind slammed the side of the building, and the lights flickered.

Suzie looked up. "Spring's coming." She wagged a chicken leg. "So. You've got a big job in the company, but it don't pay much. Are you ready to make something of your life?"

Not by marriage to Barlow Townsend, even if someone proved that Jamie was dead. "A gentleman has made me an offer. A boardinghouse in Charleston."

"A boardinghouse? Sounds like a businessman." Suzie chewed the last bit of skin and gristle from the chicken leg. "Would the house belong to you?"

Working with Clyde had given her new respect for people with long experience, like Suzie. "He hasn't said."

Suzie cut two thick slices of yellow cake. "Tell him you want the house in your name. If he says no, tell him you've got better offers."

"But I don't."

"Say you might go into business with me. Now don't be looking down your nose when you don't know anything about it. It's a serious offer, any town you say. You don't want a boarding-house—it's all work and no money."

"And never gets the latest news."

Suzie laughed. "Do I know your gentleman?"

"I'm sure you do."

"Have you give him a sample yet? Jamie said you was hot for it from the first he saw you. Said you was the one took him to the wagon where your pa caught you."

May Rose flushed. "Not my father. My uncle." The shame of discovery flashed over her again, now with resentment that Jamie had told Suzie. And who else?

"If you've let your businessman have it already, find a way to hold him off till things is settled. Forget about pleasuring yourself, keep your head." Suzie frowned, as if remembering. "If in a year or two you find yourself let down, come to me. We won't have to stay in this hole and you can choose your customers. You'll be window dressing, saved for big money. Evalena's girl can go with us, though in a better place you'll need to class her up or keep her hid."

"I'm taking Wanda with me to Charleston."

"Sounds like you've decided. All right, then. If you have children, get lawyer papers. Money in trust." Suzie lifted a bottle and a glass. "A sip of wine?"

May Rose took the glass. "I have female trouble, Winifred may have told you. Do you think I can have children?"

"I've been surprised before. See one of them Charleston doctors."

"One thing more," May Rose said. "Do you know what happened to Charlie Herff?"

Suzie took a long drink. "That we don't. The girls has been praying for him."

~

IN THE FOLLOWING WEEK, pesky details of Hester's business took on new meaning. Broken dishes, a toilet that did not always flush properly, the lack of screening material on any windows. How men ignored the outside rug and tracked snow, mud and coal dust into the entry. A new boarder taking the place at table long claimed by Hobart Hershman. Complaints about food. Complaints about smoke from Mr. Cooper's room, the transgressions Hester had mentioned her first day—nonpayment, alcohol, women. The need to maintain a pleasant tone in all circumstances.

Hester did half the cleaning, part of the cooking, all the ordering, kept her accounts, presided as hostess, and now spent a lot of time with Glory. May Rose had no idea if Mr. Townsend would help, or if he'd understand how nearly useless she became, at least one day each month. Jamie had not.

While Mr. Townsend was away, May Rose listened for hints of how to manage, and formulated questions. Did the house come with staff? Regular boarders? Did Mr. Townsend—*Barlow*—expect the boardinghouse to earn money, a profit, above the cost of operation? Worries sprouted like weeds in corn. Would there be opportunity to seek Hester's advice? *Did Hester know?*

When the preacher and his mother came to Sunday dinner, Hester said, "May Rose, see if you can keep Mr. Cooper and Humphrey from arguing. I'll try to keep Miss Ruie from falling asleep in her plate."

Maintaining order seemed another of Hester's gifts. May Rose smiled at the men as they helped themselves and passed platters. Any argument between Mr. Cooper and the preacher would at least be gentlemanly. In her own house she'd have to manage or turn away boarders who were crude and disorderly, men who might be like Bright or the Donnellys. Mr. Townsend contributed restraint and dignity to this house, but he would not regularly be in Charleston. Most of the time, he would be here, in Hester's boardinghouse.

Today, perhaps because Mr. Townsend was absent, Mr. Cooper dared to criticize the creator and sustainer of everything in Winkler—the company and its miserable wages.

"Winkler employees have decent houses," Preacher Gowder said. "That's more than many have."

"Decent only because the town is recently built," Mr. Cooper said. "But store prices are much higher here than elsewhere. Everything a man earns goes back to the company, so families are always in debt."

"Poverty in itself is not bad," the preacher said. "Our Lord and Savior lived in poverty. A simple life, in a harsh, dry land."

"Our Lord and Savior had two parents with him all the time." Mr. Cooper raised his voice. "And his father was an independent man. Our Lord worked with his father, learned his trade. Here, children run the streets and get into devilment. How can their fathers give guidance, when they work more hours than daylight in the mill, or come home from the camps only at week's end?"

Preacher Gowder shook his fork. "It's the job of teachers to make them good citizens."

From the other end of the table, Hester frowned at May Rose. This might be a test, though if Hester knew of her brother's proposal, she had not spoken of it.

"Our responsibility is children's minds," Mr. Cooper said. "You preachers have their morals."

"Mr. Cooper," May Rose said, "will you take cream for your apple betty?"

The preacher's coffee sloshed onto the tablecloth. "A decent town has citizens who love the Lord. But there are too many here for one poor shepherd."

"Ah! Exactly so!" Mr. Cooper thrust his fork at the air. "And there's only one shepherd, poorly paid, because the price of lumber rules this town. Poverty is required, otherwise workers would have means to go somewhere else. Long hours and poor wages give men no time to reflect, no time to be happy. A healthy soul has time for leisure, high ideals, visions of a better life. And beauty."

As though suddenly remembering others at the table, Mr. Cooper lifted his water glass to May Rose and then to Hester. "Here, at least, we are blessed by rare instances of beauty."

"Amen." The preacher smiled at Hester. "Money, you'll agree, isn't everything."

Hester looked at May Rose like she had a lot to learn.

～

BY THE TIME Mr. Townsend returned, he'd become Barlow in her mind, partner-to-be. Because he'd reached out to bring them closer, even in that unorthodox way, because she'd been reviewing his every word and glance, she noted the quiver of anticipation in his voice and bearing. Her answer mattered.

The walk to work was their only opportunity to speak privately without causing notice. The ground was clear and dry, and they walked along, separated by a proper distance.

"Does Hester know of your offer?"

"Not at this time."

She'd thought Hester at least suspected. "When would you tell her, before, or after?"

"You might think about that, decide what would be better. It wouldn't do to keep it from her forever. She'll hear, some way."

"Tell me about the boardinghouse."

"It has a resident staff—a cook and her husband, the handyman. Arrangements with a laundress. It's said to be in a decent neighborhood. I haven't seen it myself."

"We would not be married."

"Not now."

Neither had mentioned knowing that Jamie was dead, but she did not want to marry Barlow Townsend. Unmarried, she'd be free to leave. "But the house would be in my name?"

"I hadn't thought about it."

"There would be provisions for children. We'd see a lawyer."

"Naturally." He cleared his throat. "Should we go and see the house together? We can stay overnight, get a better idea that way. If you like the house, we can complete the transaction."

She was not ready to share the intimacy of travel nor to complete anything. She anticipated a test of will. He might not want to put the house in her name until she proved herself by bearing a child.

"I'll trust your judgment about the suitability of the house. But I have a request. I've lost touch with my uncle and cousins. In December I sent telegrams, one to Fargo, and one to our former address in Ohio, but they came back, undeliverable. Can you help me find my family?"

He promised to do his best.

That evening she sat in the parlor until time for the electric to shut down, eyes on her knitting, ears tuned to Barlow Townsend as he countered Mr. Cooper's arguments against capitalism in a mild and amused way, and later, as he attempted to talk with Glory. She'd never seen him show anger. He'd be solicitous of her needs. If she could not confide in Hester, Suzie would advise how to handle unruly boarders. His absences would not be hard to bear, since she did not love him.

The next morning on their walk to work she said, "Barlow."

He pulled her arm through his, though the ground was even and dry and she needed no support.

"I hope the Charleston house will prove to be what we need."

He squeezed her arm to his side. His regard, along with their shared enterprise, might take her a long way toward caring for him. In the afternoon, when she carried questionable requisitions to his office, he looked as pleased as if she'd come to kiss him.

～

"I suppose I'll go back to being idiot-boy," Walter said. "With the new man, I mean." He turned red. "I'm sorry. At least I'll have a job."

Barlow Townsend had gone to Charleston to look at the house.

"It's all right," May Rose said. "I hope the new man will appreciate you."

"You seem happy," Walter said. "Will you be glad to get away from this?"

"I'll miss it, but yes, I'm happy."

"You have other prospects?"

"Possibly."

"You should marry and have a family."

"I know."

"Do you want me to file those?" He pointed to papers in her hand.

"I like filing—it's a break from thinking so hard," she said.

Everything to do with money was kept in Barlow's office—the safe, full of account books as well as cash, and the file cabinets for paid invoices. She spread the invoices on his desk and put them in alphabetical order. Then she opened the top file drawer, located the folder for the first invoice, Ace Tool and Dye, and deposited the invoice on top. She had a thick stack of paper for Jacoby Wholesalers, but the Jacoby folder was full and the drawer was packed tight. Since the Jacoby file was at the end, she moved it to the front of the next drawer.

A brown paper lay in the space left by the Jacoby file, a telegram. She lifted it to see where it belonged.

Mr. Jamie Long. She stared at the name like she didn't know who it meant. Then she saw the sender and grew faint. Margaret Jonson, her cousin, Uncle Bert's oldest daughter. She dropped into the desk chair and unfolded the paper.

FATHER DEAD STOP SISTERS ORPHANAGE STOP PLEASE COME STOP

CHAPTER 32

Let me remain with thee,
   for my soul is sad and afflicted.

— HENRY WADSWORTH LONGFELLOW: EVANGELINE

Waves of joy and distress left her light-headed. Joy to see Margaret's name, distress for their need. And slowly rising above these, anger that their grief and need had been hidden in a filing cabinet. *For how long?* Just before the wreck, Mr. Ramey had said he'd heard about a telegram for Jamie, but the date on the brown paper was nearly a year older. Uncle Bert, dead, all that time. The telegram, addressed to Jamie but meant for her, hidden in Barlow Townsend's office.

She put on her coat and left the office without speaking to anyone. At the telegraph counter she smoothed the brown paper with shaky hands, copied its address and printed the message to her cousin, Margaret Jonson, care of Mrs. Masie Armentrout, Center Street, Fargo.

MESSAGE DELAYED STOP COMING STOP LETTER
FOLLOWS STOP MAY ROSE

"My telegram." She shook the paper she'd found. "In October, right before the wreck, you lied to me."

"I don't think so."

"You said there was no telegram for Jamie Long."

"If I said I didn't have it, I didn't have it."

"I found it in Mr. Townsend's office."

He arched his brows and shrugged. "Beats me."

He took her money and tapped out her message.

She had letters to write. One to Margaret with a long explanation, and one to Wanda, with a reasonable appeal. Was Evalena dead, was Evalena well enough to travel, could they come soon and go with her?

Anger threatened to push her beyond reason. She returned to the office, sat at Mr. Townsend's desk, gripped the pen, and dripped ink and tears on company stationery. Crumpled the paper and started again. Hummed a drone as she breathed in and out and steadied herself to write sensibly. Prayed Margaret was still at the same address. Ground her teeth when she thought about confronting Barlow with the theft of her telegram.

From the doorway Walter said, "Is there something I can do?"

She had not taken off her coat. She shook her head and waved at him to leave her. She stayed long enough to finish her letters.

The clerks looked up as she carried her letters through the office toward the door. Preacher Gowder turned from counting scrip. "Do we all get to leave early?"

"Not if you want a job tomorrow." She turned around and hugged Walter. "Good luck. Tell your grandfather I'm glad I got to know him. He taught me a lot." She posted the letters at the company store.

It was early April, but spring showed only in milder temperatures. Snow had melted on slopes that got the sun, but elsewhere patches might last until June.

Dessie noticed her early return to the boardinghouse. "Here, now, are you sick?"

She told only half of it. "I've said goodbye at work. Clyde can't come back, and the company is bringing in a new purchasing manager. Walter will be his assistant."

"Mr. Townsend will find something else for you, never worry." Dessie's attempt at comfort brought May Rose close to an angry revelation.

"Yes, I'm not worrying about a job." She worried that Margaret might no longer be at the Fargo address. She worried how long she could wait for Wanda, and if Wanda would come. She might have to leave and come back for her later. That afternoon, she carried to the store a second letter for Wanda, saying if Margaret was desperate, she'd have to leave immediately.

When she came back, she paced in her room, alternately crying about her uncle and condemning herself for not sensing Mr. Townsend's deception. Uncle Bert was dead, the girls in an orphanage, and Margaret had said, "Come soon." She suspected the telegram had come to Winkler six months ago, and Barlow Townsend had hidden it. Only someone evil would do such a thing, and she'd nearly committed herself to him.

Her account at the boardinghouse was paid through Saturday. This was Tuesday, the day he expected to return from Charleston. She liked the idea of disappearing without a word, posting secret letters to her friends, letting him wonder. But she'd also like to see his face and hear his excuses when she confronted him about stealing and hiding her telegram. She wondered what she might steal from him, something that would hurt him even half as much.

Margaret might need a month to receive and respond to her letter, half that or less if she wired her reply. She regretted accusing the telegraph agent. She could not plant hope in Barlow Townsend if the agent told him she'd found her telegram. There might be only a few more hours for revenge.

Preparing for dinner, she unbraided and brushed the kinks from her hair, wet it to restore the curls, then tied them away from her face with a ribbon, like a little girl, the way Jamie had liked. She admired her hair in the mirror, the black ribbon on gold. She changed to her black dress and walked down the front stairs, sliding her hand along the polished railing in a leisurely way.

"My, you look special this evening," Hester said. "I'm delaying dinner for the arrival of the evening train. Mr. Townsend will be home."

When May Rose heard the train approach, she hurried from the house to meet him at the station. He saw her as he stepped down to the platform, and she smiled to match the pleasure in his face.

He kissed her in the shadows. "I bought it," he said. "There were others who'd made an offer. Seeing you here, I know I was not premature."

"Yes," she said. "Yes."

"We'll keep this secret a few more days. I'm hardly used to the idea, myself."

"You know best."

He kissed her again. Behind his tight thin lips, she felt the pressure of his jaw. She clung to his arm as they walked home. He told her about the Charleston house, the kitchen and parlor, the rooms that would be theirs. She clenched her teeth to keep from raging.

Dessie had cooked his favorite meal, corned beef and cabbage with carrots and dumplings. May Rose sat across from Mr. Cooper, between Mr. Townsend and the new guest, a manufacturer of steam engines, whose name she did not remember.

When everyone began to eat, she spoke in a voice brighter than she might be able to sustain. "I've had wonderful news today."

Mr. Townsend raised his brows, perhaps a look of warning. Each person at the table held a fork in midair or stopped buttering bread, looked, and waited.

"Please, everyone, eat while it's hot, don't wait for me. I'm far too excited for proper digestion. Some of you know I've been trying for two years to reach my uncle and cousins." She turned to the manufacturer. "You see, they didn't know I'd come to Winkler, and I had no proper address for them, and I think they never got my letters. All the way to Fargo, North Dakota." She smiled around the table.

The Hershman brothers leaned forward to hear, and she spoke louder. "Just last week, Mr. Townsend said he'd help me find them."

Mr. Cooper blinked. "Very kind."

Hester smiled. "And he did?"

May Rose blotted her forehead and leaned toward Hester in a confidential way. "He didn't have to find them. He's known for months where they are!" She flashed a look to the other end of the table, where Mr. Townsend straightened in his chair.

"Well, not my uncle. You see he died in an accident, I don't know when, it might have been years ago, it took so long for my cousin's telegram to find me. A telegram asking me to come to them right away! My cousins needed me, three orphaned girls, and I never knew until today. That's my news." Tears came to her eyes. She bowed her hot face and listened to the silence.

"'Please come,' my cousin Margaret said. You see, I wasn't in Jennie Town, where she thought I'd be, where she sent the telegram. Yet by the Grace of God, it came to Winkler, just before the wreck, I think. Months ago."

Dessie held a serving platter by the sideboard, spots of red on her cheeks.

"Every day I asked the store manager for mail. Soon after the wreck, Mr. Ramey said he'd heard there'd been a telegram for me, but the telegraph agent said he was mistaken."

"A missing telegram," Mr. Cooper said, "now found?"

"Exactly so!" May Rose sent her warmest smile to the head of the table. "In Mr. Townsend's office, in a filing cabinet, almost like it was meant to be hidden. Though it had been opened, and certainly read."

Mr. Townsend set his napkin by his plate. "Mrs. Long, we know you're upset by this news of your uncle's death. We'll help you investigate this matter, and help you get to your cousins. Hester, please console Mrs. Long in her room."

Hester seemed not to hear.

"I have to wonder, why hide my cousin's telegram?" She heard the hysteria in her voice.

Dessie moved to her side. The manufacturer shifted in his chair.

"Months ago, Margaret, my cousin, pleaded, 'Come soon.' Who knows what has happened since then? And I didn't know until today, by accident, just as I was about to enter an intimate partnership with Mr. Townsend. Yes, Hester, an *intimate* partnership. Never fear, he didn't offer to marry me."

"Hester, please." Mr. Townsend nodded toward the door.

"I'm finished." May Rose stood. "I'm paid up until the end of the week, but you won't have to hear me again. Now, Mr. Townsend, go ahead, explain this away. I don't care what they believe."

DISGRACING Mr. Townsend did not feel as good as she had expected. She didn't sleep, and in the morning, Hester cornered her in the kitchen. "You may leave now. I'll refund the rest of the week."

"I'm the innocent one," May Rose said. "I'll leave Saturday, when my time has expired." She felt as though she'd slashed her ties with home.

The next day she received a return telegram from Margaret, **SAME PLACE PLEASE COME**. Without assurance that her cousins were presently safe, she was afraid to delay.

"I don't like you making that trip alone," Dessie said. "Wait for Wanda."

"How long? All this time, she has sent no word about Evalena or herself. Suzie says Evalena is still living, or was, the last she heard. I don't know when Wanda might get my letter or if she'll reply. Or agree to go."

Dessie took off her apron. "Give her another chance. I'll trot over to Suzie's and tell Winifred you need to hear from Wanda. That place is better than the U.S. Mail."

At the end of a week of pacing in her room and talking with no one but Mr. Cooper and Dessie, May Rose moved into the little house in Italian Town that Tom had purchased from Dr. Hennig. Tom and Dessie used the house only on weekends when he came from camp.

"If your room here ain't got somebody in it, him and me can have it for the weekend," Dessie said.

The doctor's house looked nothing like she'd left it, but sounds and sensations from her time there echoed from the walls. Mr. Cooper, Hester, and Wanda singing; the doctor popping in and out at all hours. Homer, Evalena. The doctor's wife, Mr. Townsend. Russell sleeping on the cot.

She bought two railway tickets to Fargo, checked for mail, and inquired regularly at the telegraph office. Each day after school she met Will and helped him cook and clean.

"I'll send word from Fargo, so you'll know where to find us when you're ready to join us," she said.

"Pa needs me."

"Maybe he'll come with us, and Charlie, when he comes home."

"If Charlie's living, he don't want to come home."

Mr. Cooper stopped her on the street and asked that she send an address so he could send a copy of his book when it was printed. "It's a vampire story, like Dracula. I fashioned the heroine after you."

"I'm flattered. But with so much evil in ordinary people, why make a story about a monster?"

"Because the more grotesque and evil he is, the more satisfying the ending will be."

She bought traveling hats with veils for herself and Wanda,

and gloves and long coats, protection from smoke and cinders. An extra set for Evalena in case she had recovered. If she was careful, they'd arrive with a bit of money. After that, she'd manage.

Sunday afternoon, Dessie and Tom visited. Tom told stories of the west. She told of her life in Ohio. They spoke of everything but the boardinghouse and the Townsends. She missed Hester and Glory, Mr. Cooper, even the Hershmans.

On a pleasant evening in the middle of the following week, Barlow Townsend came to her door. "I'm sure you're surprised to see me."

"Nothing surprises me now." She invited him inside.

He carried a bottle of wine to the kitchen, came back with two glasses. She took the one he offered.

He looked contrite. "I do love you."

She sat in the rocker.

He leaned against the wall, glass in hand. "May I explain?"

"It's too late."

"We can be married."

She smiled. "It makes no difference."

"Whatever you want. I want to please you. I did everything the wrong way."

The first sip of wine warmed her throat. "I hope that knowledge guides you in the future."

"Call me names—I've called myself worse. Make demands. Ask me anything."

"How did you get my cousin's telegram?"

"I wish I'd never seen it. The telegram lay at Jennie Town for months, unclaimed. When the agent there got the warrant for Jamie Long, he remembered and sent it to Frank, as a clue, I suppose. Frank shared it with me. I knew when I read it that it was for you, not Jamie. I loved you then, but I didn't know if you'd have me, and Jamie—well, you may or may not have been married."

Jamie's recklessness had been his curse. Mr. Townsend's caution was his. Both had tried to decide for her.

"I stuck the telegram in that file, just for a day or two. It had been so long at Jennie Town, I thought another few days wouldn't hurt. Then we had the wreck. I always meant to pull it out and contact your cousin. Help you get to her."

"I would have loved you for that."

"It's not too late. Fargo is so far away. I'll bring your cousins to Charleston. Hire someone to travel with them."

His help would mean so much. She could rescue her cousins, get her name on the boardinghouse, a new life for Wanda. Follow Suzie's advice, be smart and unsentimental.

They watched each other in silence. She sipped her wine. He looked hopeful. Perhaps he did not see how in the end they would hurt and despise each other. And if there were children...

He poured more wine for himself. "When I got the telegram, winter was almost upon us. It was no time for a trip like that. I was thinking of you."

"Don't say that. You were never going to tell me. You'd have let me—no, made me—abandon my family. Barlow, this happened before. I left them once, God forgive me. The first time Jamie took my hand I knew I would give up everything to be with him."

She stood and slid her fingers into his. He pulled her close. She breathed against his cheek. "I'm glad when I touch you I don't feel anything at all."

When he pushed her away, she staggered, but did not fall.

CHAPTER 33

Thither, as leaves to the light,
  were turned her thoughts and her footsteps.

— HENRY WADSWORTH LONGFELLOW:
EVANGELINE

May Rose set a date to leave, but did not give up hope that Wanda would return and go with her. The thought of taking charge of herself and four girls in a faraway, unknown place dropped her to her knees several times a day. Good things lay ahead, she told herself, if she did not get lost in fear. She prayed for discernment, so she'd know when to trust herself and when to trust someone else, and she prayed for the confidence not to waver. Wise confidence. She'd seen enough of the other kind.

She could not remember her cousins' faces. In a dream, they all looked like Wanda as she'd first appeared, scrambling up from the ground in her brown rag of a dress.

On her second Sunday of waiting, Dessie came to see her without Tom, who she said was at Walter's, visiting Clyde. "Me and Tom's got an idea," she said. "Get those girls and bring them back here where you've got friends. If you need money for the train, Tom'll give it to you."

Where she had friends. "I'd love to do that. I'd love to be your neighbor, right here in Italian Town. But I have to work."

Dessie's silence acknowledged the problem. "Have you got no family a'tall?"

"My father might be alive. He left me with Aunt Sweet when my mother died. I was about the age of Glory."

"Never no word?"

"If he ever contacted my aunt and uncle, they did not tell me."

Dessie sighed.

"But you've given me an idea," May Rose said. "Could Tom ask Clyde to write a letter of recommendation? Saying what I learned, how well I did? I don't know if Clyde would go so far as to say I was competent, but maybe Walter would add something nice to the letter."

"Walter would be writing it for him anyway. But who knows, Clyde might admit how smart you are. He's blind and feeble, but he ain't addled."

"I'll be glad to think of you in this house," May Rose said, when Dessie stood to say goodbye.

"I'll go around to Walter's and get that letter."

"Do you suppose many know? About Mr. Townsend and me, and why I'm staying here?"

"Winifred hasn't said anything, but maybe she's being kind. I heard the preacher ask Hester, but not what she answered."

"It doesn't matter." She could not abide the pain of grudging thoughts. Daily she worked to forget, to set aside old fears and ideas that had made her weak.

Dessie brought Clyde's letter.

"You've got a good man," May Rose said. "I married a handsome fool. I'd have been better trusting myself than him."

"I suppose when you're young, you believe your man has to

be head of the house and boss of you, too. When you're older like me, you know that's a lot of tripe."

"If I'd disobeyed or spoken out, I think Jamie would have beat me."

Dessie rocked her chair. "There's a lot of that. But I doubt Mr. Townsend would be the kind to beat you."

"I think he was afraid I'd marry Morris Herff. Maybe Mr. Herff said he was going to ask me."

"So Mr. Townsend put Mrs. Donnelly in your place. Still, Mr. Herff was a poor husband. But why didn't Mr. Townsend come right out and tell you how he felt?"

"Maybe because of that gossip about me. And even I didn't know if I was married or a murderer's whore."

Dessie flinched at the word. "You always seemed a lady to me."

~

CLYDE'S LETTER of praise might have been a fabrication, but it gave her courage. *She could do what she had to do. There was no power in doubt.*

She endured a second week with no word from Wanda. Then, with her leaving date three days away, she opened the door on a hard-raining afternoon and Wanda blew in, Russell behind her.

Wanda frowned at the door. "Why you keeping it locked?" They hung their dripping oilcloths in the kitchen while May Rose hid her tears.

Wanda shied from a hug. She wore a schoolgirl skirt and shirt-waist, and her hair was cut in a short curly cap. Russell's head and face were close-shaved. Their clothes, damp around the edges, looked new.

He pulled a camp stool to the wall and sat there with his head back and his arms resting on his thighs. "We come for seed potatoes."

"You-all look good."

"We had the cooties," Wanda said.

She could not read their faces.

Russell's eyes seemed less shifty, but they did not focus on hers. "Evalena's passed."

Her heart trembled. "I'm sorry. You received my letter?"

They nodded. Wanda shifted her feet.

"I have railway tickets. I'm ready to leave."

Wanda picked up the tin cup from the window ledge, pumped water, and drank it in a gulp. "We need to stay the night. It's a long way back."

"I promised your ma we'd go away together. You can have singing lessons, a new start in a new place."

Wanda pumped water again and passed the cup to Russell. "We heard you was going away with him. Mr. Townsend."

"No," May Rose said. "Not him. I've been waiting for you, like we planned."

Wanda looked at the ceiling. "I don't believe I'll go. I like it where I am. I do the cooking."

"She'll go," Russell said.

"I'll speak for myself."

"You ain't old enough to speak for yourself."

Wanda plopped into the rocker. "I won't go. I don't know them people and them places. They won't like me."

"I won't know anybody there but you," May Rose said, "and three girls I haven't seen in so long I can't think what they look like. We'll all be strangers, but my cousins need our help." She searched for something to endear them to Wanda. "They're like me, they can't carry a tune in a bucket. They'll love how you sing."

"She's going," Russell said.

Wanda narrowed her eyes and crossed her arms.

He went outside and came back with a packet of coffee and a few potatoes to boil for supper. May Rose told them about the town's search for Charlie, about Mr. Herff's fight with the Donnelly boys, about Dessie marrying Tom, and Glory living with

Hester. They shared little of themselves. She talked about her cousins, about taking care of Aunt Sweet. In the spaces she left for them to speak, they yawned.

Finally, Wanda relented. "I have to go back and say 'goodbye.'"

"Goodbye? Goodbye to...?"

"Homer," Russell said. "Homer stayed on with us."

The red-headed boy. "Oh." May Rose looked at Wanda's sad face.

"Him and me's been ringing trees and stripping tan bark," Russell said. "Carted it to the tannery a while back. Can you wait a week to go? I'll bring her back in a week."

She agreed to wait, and he agreed to return with Wanda the following Tuesday and see them off on the Wednesday morning train.

The next Tuesday afternoon, May Rose set her baggage by the door. In the week since the appearance of Russell and Wanda, a letter had come from her cousin Margaret that sounded like tears of relief. Encouraged, May Rose returned a telegram giving an approximate time she might reach Fargo. She'd said goodbyes to Ruie and the preacher, Will, Dessie, even Mr. Ramey. She'd waited outside the school to say goodbye to Mr. Cooper and ask him to watch over Will.

By Tuesday night she knew Wanda and Russell weren't coming, yet at the station Wednesday morning she kept turning her neck and peering through fog and smoke. Wanda had a good share of Russell's stubbornness. She had never said she'd go.

May Rose listened for the last time to the whining saws and clatter of lumber. The conductor stood at the step, ready to help her into the coach. A figure in a long skirt and a bundle on each arm appeared from the mist. Hester, with Glory and a basket.

Hester set down the basket. "Dessie made some things for your trip." She put her face close to Glory's. "Sweetheart, give Aunt May Rose a hug bye-bye."

May Rose rocked Glory side to side. "Hester, I'm sorry for so much. I've admired you, and you befriended me. I made a spectacle of myself and embarrassed everyone."

Hester shook her head, her mouth clenched down. "I think I've been more angry with Barlow and his meddling. You made me right uncomfortable, but maybe I had it coming." She exchanged the basket for Glory. "Try not to think badly of him. He's so used to deciding for everyone. I tell him the company makes him do the job of three men. He says every man in the company works like three men. But now, he regrets losing you, and so do I. We all miss you."

"If you see Wanda…"

The conductor gave the all-aboard.

Hester took her hand. "I'll do what I can."

"Don't let Suzie…"

"I won't."

"Tell Wanda I'll send money if she wants to come to me, and I'll help her, wherever she is."

"Send us your address," Hester said.

The train had one passenger car, and she had it all to herself.

"Now, farther down the line," the conductor said, "the coaches have padded seats. Sometimes a train will have a dining car, but you're wise to carry a few eats. The depots where they stop for water usually has people selling apples and such, and most times you can get off and find a necessary room."

There would be layovers. She'd have to change trains. The station master had penciled an itinerary, only an approximation.

"I made the trip to St. Louis once," the conductor said, "never as far as Fargo."

May Rose set Dessie's basket beside her on the seat with her traveling coat. Her hat was dark blue with a matching veil. She let it down to hide her wet face. With a jerk, the train pulled away. She fixed her mind on Margaret, Leola, and Mary Agnes. Because of the fog, she had no last view of Winkler.

When sunlight burned through the mists, she raised her veil and put her face close to the window. On the slopes near the track, pale sprouts poked through a rusty mat of leaves. Here and there bramble bushes bore speckles of lightest green, pale dots on winter stems. Useless and troublesome to humans, these seemed always the first to come back to life, the hardy ones. Perhaps something in nature needed them. This year she would miss the bloom of mountain redbud and dogwood, unless they grew in North Dakota.

The conductor came in from the caboose. "We stop at Jennie Town to take on water. After that, next stop Elkins."

At Jennie Town, a family waited on the platform beside boxes and bundles, a man, a tall boy and girl, a smaller boy, all dressed for travel. On their journey to West Virginia, Jamie had made friends, played cards, but never introduced her to anyone. Despite her resolution to be strong, she was shy of new people. She pulled down her veil, drew black wool and knitting needles from her carpetbag and listened to the passengers entering the coach.

"Miss May Rose."

She dropped the needles and pulled up her veil. Above her stood a tall red-headed boy. His eyes were healthy blue.

"Homer?"

He bent, slid a box under a seat and picked up her needles. Behind him, Wanda waited in the aisle, her mouth in a lopsided smile.

Wanda handed Homer a faded tapestry bag and plopped down on the flat wooden bench. She pulled her hat off like she'd had enough of it. "Russell sold out. Guess where we're going?"

Russell stood in the aisle, his eyes darting side to side. He reached behind him and pulled forward a dark-eyed boy with a sharp chin, a boy who looked like Will. *Charlie.*

~

From the Author

Dear Reader,

Thank you for picking up your copy of *Girl on the Mountain*. Readers are everything to authors, and I appreciate you more than I can say.

When this book was published, I had no intention of writing a series, but I was encouraged by readers to continue the story of May Rose, Wanda, Charlie, and others. I hope you will enjoy the Mountain Women Series.

Other readers will appreciate hearing your opinion on the book before they commit to it—and of course I would also like to hear from you about my story, or my characters, or whatever other thoughts the book raised for you. Please leave a review to let me know what you think. You may contact me on www.carol ervin.com.

Warmest Regards,

Carol Ervin

AFTERWORD

In the late nineteenth century, development of geared locomotives enabled logging companies to exploit the last virgin forests on the steepest slopes of the Appalachians.

There was no town named Winkler, and no Winkler Logging Company in West Virginia, but scores of towns grew up around sawmills, and some became permanent settlements. The history of West Virginia logging, sawmills, and of locomotives like the Shay in West Virginia is well preserved at Cass State Park; in publications like *Goldenseal*, the magazine of West Virginia traditional life; and in Roy B. Clarkson's *Tumult on the Mountains: Lumbering in West Virginia—1770-1920*.

Logging and lumber operations continue to be a vital part of West Virginia's economy.

COLD COMFORT

BOOK 2 OF THE MOUNTAIN WOMEN SERIES

Fifteen years after riding away to Fargo, Wanda leaves her child with May Rose and returns to the mountains of West Virginia to visit the one person she hates–her granny, ex-moonshiner Lucie Bosell. Recently widowed, Wanda is penniless and troubled by fits of rage.

Reunited at the Bosells' mountain hideaway, Lucie and Wanda engage in a game of cat and mouse, Lucie ordering Wanda to create a dynasty of Bosells and Wanda scheming to get Lucie's money. But Lucie has even grander plans. Prohibition has come to their state, making moonshine worth more than ever, and Lucie intends to get back in the business.

Playing along, Wanda finds that being as cruel as Granny Lucie hurts her chances with a compelling man from her past. Worse, the old woman's high-stakes business attracts dangerous people.

Wanda discovers the hard way—revenge is cold comfort.

Look for *Cold Comfort* on Amazon.

ABOUT THE AUTHOR

 I've been lucky. Years ago, I wanted to live on a farm, and my husband said "Let's do it." When personal computers were introduced, I wanted to know about them and own one, and lucky me, the school where I taught offered a course in Basic. When we bought our first computer, I discovered the writer's best friend--word processing. Before that, I could not write without crossing out most of a typewritten or handwritten page, and progress seemed impossible. When I wanted to shift from teaching to writing, the first Macintosh computers came out, and I was lucky enough to have, along with technical and business writing, the first "desktop publishing" service in my area. And when finally I had the leisure to give a lot of time to a novel, my husband didn't merely tolerate my commitment, he encouraged it.

Inspiration for the Mountain Women series came first from the mountain wilderness, both beautiful and challenging for those who live there. I appreciated accounts of early 20th century life and industry, the forerunners of today's technology and culture. When I read Roy B. Clarkson's non-fiction account of lumbering in West Virginia, (Tumult on the Mountain, 1964, McClain Printing Co., Parsons, WV), with more than 250 photos of giant trees, loggers, sawmills, trains, and towns, I found the setting for the first book in the series. Finally, I was inspired by men and women of previous generations who faced difficulties unknown today. Researching and writing these novels, I have felt closer to the lives of grandparents I never knew.

Learn more about author Carol Ervin at http://www.carolervin.com

facebook.com/carolervin.author

amazon.com/stores/Carol-Ervin/author/B0094IOERY

bookbub.com/authors/carol-ervin

ALSO BY CAROL ERVIN

Other Novels

Ridgetop

Dell Zero

ACKNOWLEDGMENTS

No one writes a book alone. I'm grateful to many advisors, especially husband Chuck Ervin, sister Diane Plotts, editor Tamara Eaton, and my talented critique partners Eamon Ó Cléirigh, Megan Carney, and Gail Rennie, plus a dozen others on critiquecircle.com. You made this work a lot of fun.

Made in United States
Orlando, FL
05 March 2024

44426800R00188